QARSOON

QARSOON

SPACE UNBOUND BOOK 4

DAVID C. JEFFREY

Qarsoon

ISBN: Paperback: 978-0-9986742-8-5
        eBook: 978-0-9986742-9-2

Published by Sylvanus Books
www.davidcjeffrey.com

First printing: 2026
Printed in the United States of America

For Donald and Julie Jeffrey

CONTENTS

Where is the Life we have lost in living?
Where is the wisdom we have lost in knowledge?
Where is the knowledge we have lost in information?

— T.S. Eliot, *"Choruses from the Rock"*

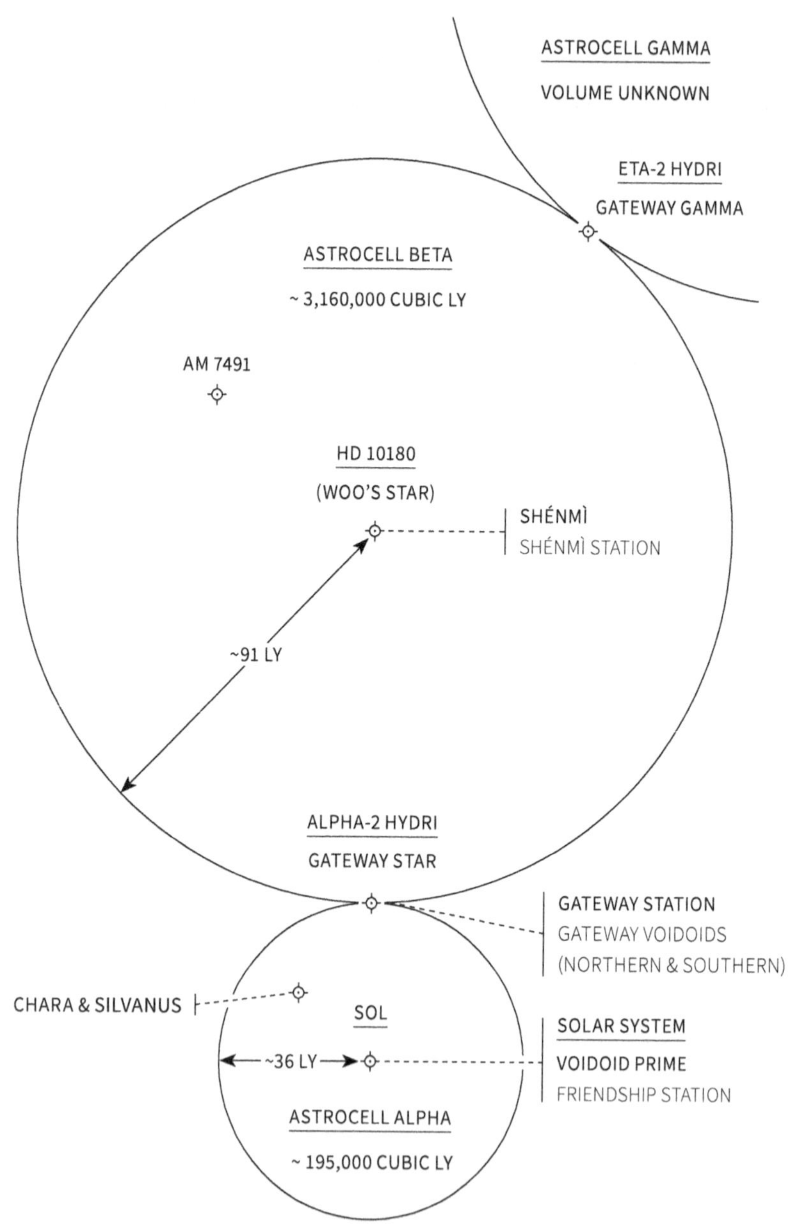

SPHERICAL REGIONS OF SPACE ACCESSIBLE BY VOIDJUMP
NOT TO SCALE – BOUNDARY LINES THEORETICAL (LY = LIGHT-YEAR)
ASTROCELL GAMMA
VOLUME UNKNOWN
ETA-2 HYDRI
GATEWAY GAMMA
ASTROCELL BETA
~ 3,160,000 CUBIC LY
AM 7491
HD 10180
(WOO'S STAR)
SHÉNMÌ
SHÉNMÌ STATION
~91 LY
ALPHA-2 HYDRI
GATEWAY STAR
GATEWAY STATION
GATEWAY VOIDOIDS
(NORTHERN & SOUTHERN)
CHARA & SILVANUS
SOL
SOLAR SYSTEM
~36 LY
VOIDOID PRIME
FRIENDSHIP STATION
ASTROCELL ALPHA
~ 195,000 CUBIC LY

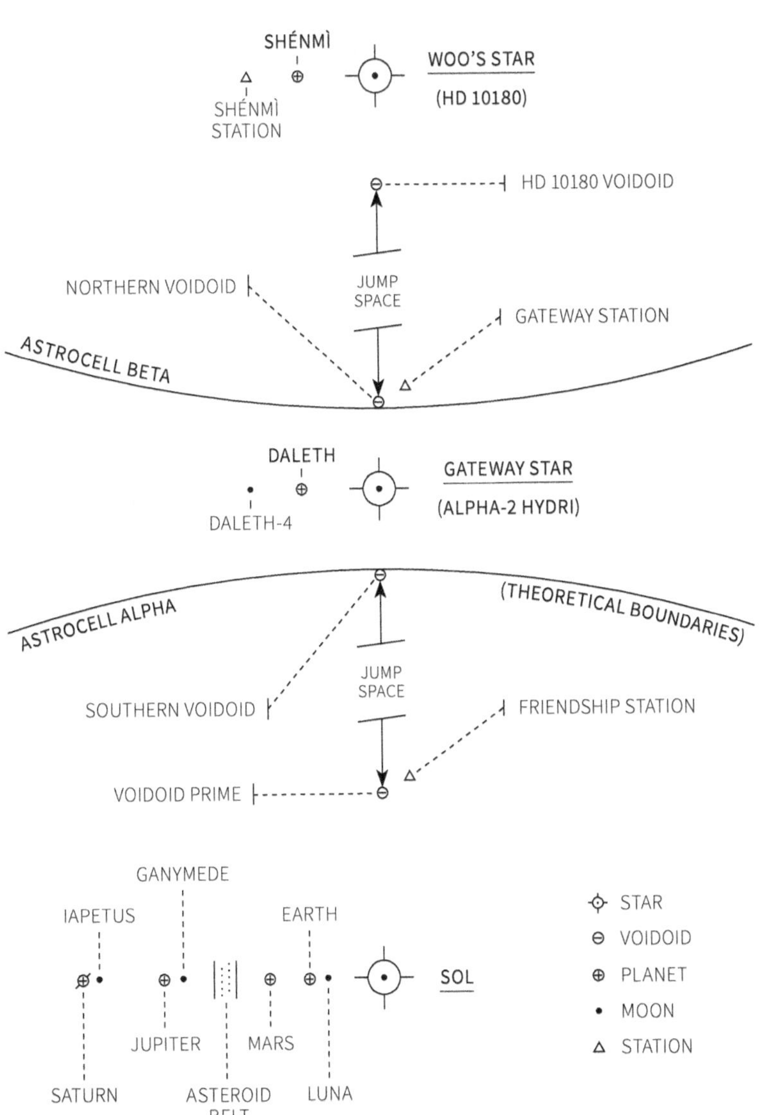

EXPANDED VIEW OF GATEWAY STAR
WITH SCHEMATIC OF KEY LOCATIONS - NOT TO SCALE.
(DISTANCE BETWEEN ALL VOIDOIDS & HOST STAR ~ 13 AU)
SHÉNMÌ
SHÉNMÌ STATION
WOO'S STAR
(HD 10180)
HD 10180 VOIDOID
NORTHERN VOIDOID
JUMP SPACE
GATEWAY STATION
ASTROCELL BETA
DALETH
DALETH-4
GATEWAY STAR
(ALPHA-2 HYDRI)
ASTROCELL ALPHA
(THEORETICAL BOUNDARIES)
SOUTHERN VOIDOID
JUMP SPACE
FRIENDSHIP STATION
VOIDOID PRIME
GANYMEDE
IAPETUS
EARTH
SATURN
JUPITER
ASTEROID BELT
MARS
LUNA
SOL
STAR
VOIDOID
PLANET
MOON
STATION

PART ONE

When one burns one's bridges,
what a very nice fire it makes.

— Dylan Thomas

1

Domain Day 67, 2223

THE corpse lying on Aiden Macallan's doorstep was well dressed, had a full beard, and wore bright red lipstick. Without question, it was the last thing Aiden expected to see as he opened the door to leave his quarters.

The man was lying on his back, face frozen in an expression of surprise mixed with indignity. His red lips were curled in angry disbelief, his eyes fixed wide open and utterly devoid of life. The small, clean hole in his forehead, obviously made by a small-caliber weapon, was a shade of blood red that perfectly matched the man's lipstick in a tragically unintended fashion statement.

Aiden stepped back. His heart pounded. Bile rose in his throat. But his shock was quickly muted by relief that his wife and child had not been present when he opened the door to this grisly scene. The apartment was, after all, his family's residence on Luna, even though they spent very little time here together. Skye and their three-year-old daughter, Bri, were light-years away in Astrocell Beta at Shénmì Station.

Aiden reached for his pocket comm and punched the emergency key for Station Security. "This is Captain Aiden Macallan. A dead person with a gunshot wound to the head is lying on my doorstep, Compartment 3-B. Get someone down here ASAP."

Not waiting for the dispatcher's inevitable demand for more details, Aiden disconnected without another word. What more needed to be said?

He looked up and down the corridor. No one was in sight. The only sound he heard came from an overhead ceiling fan badly in need of lubrication. He bent down to examine the victim more closely. The man appeared to be in his early thirties, slender, with a tawny complexion and dark hair. He was dressed in formal wear—black slacks, shiny shoes, and a black tunic over a white shirt with a black silk bowtie. His beard was thick and dark, juxtaposed jarringly against his red lipstick.

Aiden felt for a pulse at the man's neck to confirm the obvious. Then he moved the head to one side to examine its back side. No exit wound. The small slug was still inside where it would do maximum damage with minimum mess, crashing around inside the cranium, randomly pulverizing brain tissue before expending its kinetic energy. Obviously a professional hit.

Aiden knew better than to contaminate a crime scene, but something curious caught his eye. The man's mouth was partially open. Something small and shiny sat farther back on his tongue. It reflected ambient light from the corridor with a faint glint. Aiden gently pried the man's jaw open, noting the absence of rigor mortis. He reached in and removed a small round crystal, its surface cut into multiple tiny facets, regular enough to appear nearly spherical. It was about two centimeters in diameter, clear, but with a light blue tint. A tiny, darker blue symbol was embedded at its core. A *Triquetra*, a Gaian symbol with ancient Celtic origins. He recognized it immediately and drew in a sharp breath. A dark pit of fear opened in his gut. It was a message crystal, one from a unique set owned only by Skye and himself, existing nowhere else.

Message crystals, referred to as *telegems* by the spy types at DSI, were highly encrypted on a molecular level, readable only by their intended recipients. Use of the technology was restricted to the military and intelligence communities, prohibited to the public at large. He and Skye were given their set of telegems as a gift from

Dr. Elgin Woo, the illustrious, multiple–Nobel Prize winner and founder of the Cauldron, where almost everything was clandestine.

Aiden and Skye had agreed to use them only to deliver highly sensitive messages between them when far apart. Messages for their eyes only. Sadly, it was a necessary precaution now that President Michi Takema was no longer in power. The political environment within the United Earth Domain had degraded considerably since her term as president had expired. Now led by Earth First party champion, Rudolph Adler—an astonishingly small-minded and narcissistic isolationist—the UED had become dangerously polarized, rife with spies, disinformation, and xenophobia.

Aiden held the crystal in the palm of his hand and examined it more closely. No question about it. The telegem could not have come from anyone other than his wife. Skye was reaching out to him with some critical information or query in a way that was impossible to intercept before reaching him in person. But who the hell was the messenger? Aiden had never seen this man before, and he surely would have remembered it if he had. Whoever he was, he'd been killed moments before hand-delivering the telegem to Aiden.

Aiden fully understood the serious legal trouble he'd bring upon himself by removing the crystal from the scene before the security team arrived. But then, who needed to know about it? He looked around again, making sure he was still alone, then closed his hand around the crystal and pocketed it.

While waiting for security to show up, questions inside Aiden's head began to pile up. If the killer had wanted to prevent the messenger from delivering the telegem, why hadn't he just robbed it from him at gunpoint, thereby avoiding the complications of murder? Had the messenger known he was being pursued and at the last moment attempted to swallow the telegem before it could be taken from him? Swallowing a crystal that size would be difficult, if not life-threatening. But an even more disturbing question occurred to him. If the killer was so determined to prevent Aiden from receiving the message, they must have known something about its contents and about the consequences of Aiden finding it.

And how did the messenger receive the telegem from Skye in the first place? How did he get from Shénmì Station, out in Astrocell Beta, to Luna here in the Sol System?

That last question could be answered by checking the passenger and crew manifest of all the vessels that had arrived at the station over the last few days. In this time of heightened security, every person aboard every vessel was accounted for and officially registered by the DSI, the Domain Security and Intelligence service. That included passengers and crew of all commercial vessels and, nowadays, extended even to military vessels. Aiden had friends in high places. He was, after all, still captain of the now-legendary *Sun Wolf*, still the only voidship in existence with the zero-point drive. He could pull strings and get access to those records. But first things first. He needed to unlock the telegem and access its message.

And before that, he'd have to deal with the security team. They were approaching now, three of them, one woman and two men. The man in the rear pulled a hospital gurney behind him. It carried one empty body bag, and its wheels clattered noisily over the corridor floor. Leading the way was Lieutenant Seymore Sprague, a man Aiden knew only too well. Sprague was a middle-aged Caucasian gone to seed, with an expanding paunch that put an unseemly strain on the lower buttons of his gray service shirt. He wore a neatly trimmed goatee but apparently hadn't shaved the remaining parts of his face in several days. His thinning brown hair was combed back in a delusional attempt to hide the bald spot spreading across the crown of his head. The slack expression on his face was a well-practiced disguise, belied by keen blue eyes that glanced down at the dead man first before looking up to focus on Aiden's face.

"Why am I not surprised, Captain Macallan?" he said with a gravelly voice tinged with sarcasm. "Trouble seems to follow you everywhere."

Aiden made a theatrical shrug. "I'm just that kind of guy, Lieutenant." He and Sprague had a history, much of it unpleasant. The man could be a real asshole, but Aiden had to admit he was good at his job.

"Odd," Sprague said, as if genuinely mystified. "This time, it wasn't you that someone was trying to kill."

Aiden pretended to smile. "Just my lucky day."

Sprague nodded knowingly, then introduced the other two officers with a wave of his hand. They said nothing, trying to look bored, but were visibly disturbed by the sight of the corpse at Aiden's feet. Sprague instructed the woman to take detailed photos of the body and the surrounding crime scene while the other officer prepared the body bag.

Sprague looked down at the corpse again, thoughtfully stroking his goatee. He shook his head in disdain and said, "Looks like a Vor-lover to me."

He was, of course, referring to a fringe segment of Earth Domain's population who believed that not all cloneborgs were the inhuman monsters known as the Netvor. "Vor-lover" was a derogatory term for a Sympath, which is what the well-meaning idealist lying on his doorstep would call himself. Sympaths were self-proclaimed champions of social justice, supporters of the marginalized and persecuted. When in public, they chose to present themselves in ways that deliberately contradicted their otherwise obvious gender. Hence the red lipstick and full beard. But it was the Sympaths' adamant assertion that some special population of cloneborgs existed who were not Netvor at all—in fact, were more human than not—that earned them the hateful slur *Vor-lover*.

Aiden stared at Sprague blankly and said nothing.

Sprague cocked his head, looking sideways at Aiden. "So you just opened your door, and this unfortunate soul was lying right here, in this exact spot, with a hole in his head. Is that right?"

The man's voice conveyed suspicion, as it always did. It was his normal tone, an almost laughable cliché of his occupation. "That's right. And I called for security immediately."

Sprague pursed his lips and said, "When you found him here, did you see anyone else in this corridor?"

"Not a soul."

"Did you touch or move the victim?"

"I did only what anyone with an ounce of compassion would do, Lieutenant. I felt for a pulse at his neck to see if he was still alive. There wasn't one. I concluded he was dead."

"Did you move the body at all?"

Aiden figured the best strategy here would be to stick to the truth as closely as possible. Now was the time to reinforce his credibility before the lie he'd have to tell within the next minute.

"I briefly turned the man's head to one side and looked for an exit wound. That's all."

Sprague's eyes widened. "And why did you do that, Captain?"

Aiden felt his patience slipping but spoke with an even voice. "Curiosity."

"Scientists," Sprague said as if uttering an obscenity.

"Any other questions, Sprague?" Aiden said. "I've told you all I know, and I'm already late for my flight."

Aiden didn't wait for an answer and stepped past the two officers who were now lifting the corpse into the body bag.

"One more thing, Captain."

Aiden stopped and turned. "What is it?"

"Did you remove anything from the body? You know, just out of . . . curiosity?"

Aiden felt the slight bulge of the telegem crystal in his pants pocket and resisted the impulse to reach for it. He looked straight into Sprague's eyes, not letting his gaze wander to the left—an unconscious telltale sign of lying well known to savvy investigators—and said, "No, I did not."

With that, Aiden turned to continue down the corridor. Sprague made no move to impede him but said, "I *will* have more questions for you, Captain Macallan."

"I'm sure you will, Lieutenant," Aiden said without turning, already several paces down the corridor. "And I'll do my best to answer them from 127 light-years away."

Aiden's last comment was not merely a flippant dodge. He was indeed scheduled to catch a hopper to the Bullialdus Space Port, where he would take a shuttle up to the *Sun Wolf,* now in a low geo-sync orbit, 92 kilometers above the lunar surface. The ship and his crew were there waiting for him to launch their next mission into Astrocell Beta, which included Shénmì Station, 127 light-years from Sol.

He looked at his wrist chrono. It was just after 07:40. His hopper was supposed to depart in 20 minutes. They'd just have to wait. Something far more pressing had arrived at his doorstep—without knocking.

After covering some distance in the direction of the station's shuttle port, he turned around and headed back toward his apartment. He stopped at the last corner and peeked around it to confirm that Sprague and his entire team, including the gurney, had departed from his doorstep. Aiden jogged back to his apartment as quickly as he could manage. It might have been the only time he'd ever lamented the invention of gravity transducers, the revolutionary technology that mimicked normal Earth gravity at ground level in most off-world habitats. Right now, Luna's native 0.166 G would have helped to speed up his pace.

When he got to the door of his apartment, he reached into his pocket to make sure the telegem crystal was still safely concealed. Reassured by the feel of its smooth, hard surface, he unlocked the door, entered, and securely double-locked it behind him.

2

SOL SYSTEM
Tycho City, Luna

Domain Day 67, 2223

Accessing a telegem crystal of this kind was almost as ingenious as the fabrication of the crystal itself. It was all based on biometric signatures, and there was no one way of setting it up. Every set of crystals had its own unique sequence programed into its lattice structure at the time of its synthesis and committed to memory by the user. Once unlocked, the telegem needed to be paired with a separate, one-of-a-kind reader for its contents to be decrypted, usually as a holographic projection. That device was in Aiden's apartment, hidden in plain sight.

He removed his jacket and went straight to the bookshelf next to his workstation. Several unassuming nicknacks occupied one shelf, mostly memorabilia from past adventures and acquaintances. There was a preserved groundfruit from Silvanus, the planet where he'd been stranded many years ago and where he'd discovered a global sentience called the Rete, humanity's first contact with an alien intelligence. Next to it sat a silver lapel pin signifying the rank of colonel, the figure of an eagle with outstretched wings. It had belonged to Colonel Victor Aminu, the DSI agent who'd started out as an adversary and ended up sacrificing his life for the crew of the *Sun Wolf*—and for all humanity, as it turned out.

He'd removed it from his uniform and left it in his quarters before carrying out his suicide mission.

Sitting inconspicuously inside an opened bivalve seashell that came from Elgin Woo's planet Shénmì, a white diamond gleamed brightly in the desk light. It was one of many thousands that he and his crew had found in an abandoned mining hopper on the planet Sirota, the planet where the Rodina Mining Collective had been slaughtered by Cardew's cloneborgs.

Then there was a small ceremonial peace pipe carved from pure catlinite, a wedding gift from Billy Hotah, his Tactical Officer on the *Sun Wolf*, a Lakota warrior who was now one of his closest friends. Another wedding gift sat next to it, a jade figurine of a woman, Mother Earth, given to him by Skye. The woman was Gaia, and she carried a basket that held a blue and green globe, the living planet Earth. But this figurine had a hidden purpose. It was a telegem reader in disguise.

Aiden picked it up and turned it over to expose a tiny opening embedded in its base. It held a microphone and a highly sophisticated sound analyzer. To activate the reader, he held it close to his mouth and spoke the word "Cernunnos." A subtle hum awakened inside the figurine. Aiden placed it on his workstation table and removed the telegem from his pocket.

He took a deep breath and held the telegem firmly between his thumb and ring finger, the prints of both fingers in full contact with the faceted surface. He raised the crystal to within five centimeters of his right eye and stared into it without blinking. He counted off three seconds, moved the crystal to his left eye, and did the same. The telegem grew warm to touch, the signal to proceed to the last part of the sequence. He gently pressed the crystal to the center of his forehead, the optimal placement to detect his brain's beta waves. After another three seconds, the dark blue Triquetra inside the telegem began to brighten until it glowed electric blue.

The crystal was now unlocked.

Aiden removed the blue-green globe from the figurine's basket and replaced it with the unlocked telegem. It was the same size as the sphere it replaced and fitted snugly inside with a faint click. The crystal flashed once, and a 3-D holographic image materialized three feet in front of him. His wife, Dr. Skye Landen, looked out at him with a warm smile, beautiful as ever.

He recognized her surroundings, her private quarters on Shénmì Station where she served as director of the Shénmì Project. She had blonde hair tied into a ponytail and startling blue eyes that could glow with relaxed warmth one moment, then penetrate with brutal objectivity the next. Aiden had witnessed the transition many times before, as he did now, within five seconds of her initial greeting. It was a look that conveyed dire concern.

"Aiden," she said without prelude, "Jo came to see me this afternoon. She seemed both excited and afraid. She told me that a hidden colony of others like her, other *human* cloneborgs, does indeed exist. It's what she suspected all along, what she told both of us from the very beginning. She said she'd been contacted by one of them, in person, while she was down on the surface at our research camp. Don't ask me how. She didn't explain.

"Apparently the same mutation in the Netvor's cloning process that happened to her also happened to all these others. She said the mutation was probably carried by a virus that spread through some of the Netvor creches. Like with Jo, it prevented their central nervous systems from developing Netvor brains. Physically, they're still cloneborgs, with highly augmented bodies. But mentally and emotionally, they're perfectly human. Biologically, they classify themselves as *Trans sapiens*. But as a people, they call themselves the Libera. It's like we're *Homo sapiens* but call ourselves humans. Jo firmly believes that an alliance with the Libera is our only hope of stopping the Netvor from overrunning all human worlds.

"She said these Libera have special knowledge of what the Netvor are planning, how and where they're growing in numbers, plus details of their military strength and tactical deployments. They're convinced that the Netvor are just as committed to wiping them out as they are to wiping out all humans."

Skye paused here to calm her breathing. Aiden sat back, stunned. Jo was the sole survivor of the cloneborg creche on Nead, a Netvor cloning facility that he had obliterated with thermonuclear missiles from the *Sun Wolf* back in 2218. Her story was unique, or at least it was at the time. She had acquired a mutation that prevented a drastic alteration of her central nervous system during the fetal stage of development in the cloning process. The alteration was designed to turn her, and all the other cloneborgs, into Netvor agents and warriors—superhuman psychopaths, devoid of empathy, virtually immortal, and extremely dangerous. A breed of beings programed to replace the human race by wiping it out as the first step in their relentless march toward absolute supremacy over all known space.

Jo's genetic mutation prevented that alteration from happening to her. Her brain and central nervous system developed in the same way as a normal human being. The rest of her body, however, developed the super strong, agile, and indestructible qualities of a Netvor cloneborg, hyperaugmented with advanced synthetic components.

Aiden and the crew of the *Sun Wolf* had taken her in and eventually adopted her as one of their own. She, in turn, had adopted the infant boy, Rene, that the *Sun Wolf* had rescued from the wreckage of the Rodina mining colony on Sirota. After enduring xenophobic persecution during her brief stay on Earth, Jo had returned to Shénmì Station with Rene in tow. Outside the purview of science and research communities, she was still considered a cloneborg, a Netvor, a monster, the ultimate enemy of all humans. Death threats had driven her back to the only people she trusted and loved—Skye, Aiden, and his original crew of the *Sun Wolf*, along with the full-time personnel of Shénmì Station.

"That's not all, Aiden," Skye said after catching her breath. "This Libera person Jo met—she said his name was Keen—told her that his colony has mastered a ship-cloaking technology that's far superior to what the Netvor are using for their surprise attacks on Alliance ships. Not only do they have better cloaking, but they've also developed a way to defeat the Netvor's own cloaking capability. Now these Libera can actually see cloaked Netvor warships from great distances. On top of that, they have shielding technology that's way better than the Netvor's and infinitely better than the Tyson Field shielding our Alliance ships use. It's a game changer, Aiden. All of it."

Now that *was* interesting. Aiden had first encountered the cloneborg shielding technology several years back when the *Sun Wolf* confronted one of Cardew's warships. It nearly cost him his life and the lives of his crew. It was an advanced gravimetric technology that, despite the best efforts of elite Alliance scientists, could not yet be defeated. If the Libera shielding was *better* than the Netvor's, and if the Alliance could acquire it, that alone *was* a game changer.

"But there's more, Aiden," Skye continued. "Keen confided in Jo the exact location of the planet that he and the other Libera have colonized. They suspect that the Netvor know that their colony exists, but they don't know where it is yet. The Netvor are aware of the Libera's technological superiority and consider them an existential threat. Keen thinks it's only a matter of time before the Libera colony is discovered, its technology hijacked, then the colony wiped out with overwhelming force.

"Keen wanted Jo to go with him to join the colony, right then and there. But her child Rene is up here on the station, and she wouldn't go without taking him. Instead, she tried to persuade him that forming an alliance between the Libera and humans, to stand against the Netvor, would be the best way to protect both of our peoples. But apparently the Libera want nothing to do with humankind. They don't trust us. And honestly, Aiden, why should they? The way Jo was treated on her visit to Earth . . . just appalling!

"Still, Jo is convinced she can change their minds. She's the only *Trans sapien* to have lived among humans, so she's in a unique position to argue the case. But she doesn't think she can do it alone. She told Keen that she knew of only one human who could act as an effective liaison between humans and the Libera, to pave the way for a working alliance."

Here she sat back and smiled at him. Aiden swallowed hard. He knew what was coming.

"That's right, dear heart," she said. "Jo means you. Aiden Macallan, captain of the *Sun Wolf.* The only man who still has the ear of military leaders of both the Earth Domain and the Allied Republics of Mars. Jo wanted me to contact you and ask you to go to this colony with her, to help her make a convincing case for an alliance."

Aiden could hear his pulse pounding in his ears and felt a headache coming on. He sat back and rubbed his eyes with his hands as if to banish from sight the dark and turbulent visions of all the possible futures that lay ahead. Once again, he was being asked to risk his life to play a pivotal role in the survival of the human race. And this time it made him angry. Hadn't he done enough? He was 44 now, getting too old for this hero shit. *Been there, done that.* Besides, he had a child now. He was a parent and a husband. He was ready for a normal life. Wasn't he . . . ?

But Jo was right about one thing at least. Who else among the entire human population had the status and the outsized reputation—mostly unwanted by him—that he'd gained from the harrowing exploits he and his crew had been through? Sure, the Earth Firsters still hated him and even wanted him dead. But the sane segment of the population, what was left of them, seemed to recognize that Aiden's deeds had improved humanity's chances of surviving the threats it faced, including the self-inflicted ones. If anyone had the gravitas to bring together two races that would be deeply suspicious of one another into an alliance that could save them both . . . well, it was him. And, unfortunately, he knew it.

The holographic image of Skye continued with her message. "I entrusted the delivery of this telegem to a colleague of mine, William Scantz. He's an optical technician with the Allied Mapping Project here and happened to be on his way to Luna to attend a formal awards ceremony. He doesn't know the content of the telegem, only that it's urgent and that it must get to you as soon as possible. I instructed him to hand-deliver it to you in person, no other way.

"But there's another telegem he'll deliver to you, along with this one. It's from Jo, for your eyes only. She wanted to give you the co-ordinates of the Libera's colony planet so you'll know where to go in case she can't tell you in person. The coordinates weren't written down anywhere. Jo used her phenomenal photographic memory to keep them inside her head. I gave her one of my telegem crystals, one that only you can open. She brought it to her own quarters to encrypt the coordinates inside it just before taking a shuttle down to the research camp. She promised to give it to Scantz before he left the station for Luna.

"That was yesterday, and now no one can find her. The team down at the camp searched everywhere, and they're still looking. If this Keen person was still down there, maybe she left with him, like he wanted her to. I just don't know how they could do it, at least not without being noticed. Besides, Rene is still up here with us at the station. He's only five years old, Aiden. She'd never leave here without him. Not willingly.

"I'm sure you realize that you're reading these two telegems at least 21 days after we recorded them. That's how long it will take for Mr. Scantz to get from here to Luna on the fastest vessels with the quickest connections. But Jo and I decided not to trust a maser transmission through the Holtzman network, not even encrypted at military level. It would have reached you within eight hours. But the contents are just too sensitive, and we believe Netvor agents are everywhere now. I'm hoping you'll get this before you leave on your way here. And maybe Jo will have turned up by the time you arrive . . .

"At any rate, now that you have her telegem, you are the only other person who knows exactly where this planet is. It's *dangerous* information, Aiden. Be very careful, okay? I'm signing off now. Bri and I are looking forward to seeing you soon. I love you."

3

SOL SYSTEM
Tycho City, Luna

DOMAIN DAY 67, 2223

A second telegem? From Jo?

Aiden's mouth went dry. He ran the holographic message back to repeat the last part of Skye's message. Yes. He'd heard the words correctly. William Scantz had been given *two* telegem crystals to deliver to Aiden. The second one had been recorded by Jo, revealing the exact astrometric coordinates of the Libera's colony planet, information that Jo wouldn't even share with Skye, fearing the danger it carried for anyone with knowledge of it. Information that, if it fell into the wrong hands, would mean certain disaster. Not only for the Libera, but potentially for the entire human race.

So where was the crystal now?

Was it still somewhere on Scantz's body? In a hidden pocket? Inside a hollow shoe heel? Or somewhere that Sprague and his security goons would find after a thorough examination of the corpse? Or had the assassin taken it from Scantz, either before or after he'd shot the man? And if the assassin was a Netvor . . .

Aiden tried to find solace in the knowledge that Jo's telegem could only be opened by him and no one else. The message would self-destruct if anyone else tried. But it was not a comforting thought. If Jo's crystal had indeed found its way into Netvor hands, and they wanted it opened at any cost, he'd have to expect a very unpleasant visit from some very unpleasant beings who would do very unpleasant things to him to access the crystal's contents.

If that wasn't bad enough, without Jo's message, Aiden had no way to find the planet himself. Astrocell Beta, the most likely region of space to search, was huge—well over 3 million cubic light-years in volume, containing over 45,000 main sequence stars, not to mention another 5,000 or so dwarf stars, all of which might support planetary systems of at least two or more planets per star. There wasn't a chance in hell that Aiden, even with the *Sun Wolf,* could find that colony without knowing exactly where to look.

Aiden's wrist comm chirped at him. He punched Open. "Captain Macallan. This is Commander Silva. I'm here at Bullialdus, in the cargo depot. I've finished checking in all our shipments. The hopper pilot radioed me to say you haven't shown up yet. Are you still coming?"

Damn. He'd been too distracted to keep track of the time. "I apologize, Commander. I'm on my way to the terminal now. It'll be about a 30-minute hop to Bullialdus. See you soon."

Aiden closed his comm without waiting for Silva's response. He took the telegem crystal into the bathroom, tapped it once on the metal sink, then flushed it down the toilet. Once opened and read, a single tap on a hard surface triggered a transformation within the crystal's molecular lattice structure, turning it into a water-soluble crystal similar to common table salt. It would be completely dissolved well before it reached the station's treatment plant.

He fought the impulse to delay the *Sun Wolf*'s departure and search more deeply for the missing crystal, the one from Jo. But that would require bureaucratic red tape and would provoke unwanted questions. He grabbed his jacket, locked the door securely behind him, and headed off toward the hopper terminal. He glanced at his chrono again and quickened his pace. The sound of his boot heels striking the deck plates echoed down the long, dimly lit corridor. Several lighting fixtures were out, the walls needed a deep clean, and the air was too warm, stuffy with too much CO_2. This neighborhood of Tycho City, 20 meters below the lunar surface, was around 90 years old and not aging gracefully. *Just like me*, he thought, slowing his pace to catch his breath.

When Aiden reached the terminal, he gave the hopper pilot a perfunctory salute and climbed aboard. It was a military hopper, reserved for his transfer to Bullialdus Space Port. It could do about 800 kilometers per hour. Which was good, because the Bullialdus crater was nearly 400 kilometers north of Tycho City. The closest shuttle port, the one he would normally use, was at Orontius, only 80 kilometers away. But it was temporarily shut down for repairs after the latest moonquake had cracked some of its launch pads.

Aiden strapped into his flight chair. The launch hangar depressurized, and the stubby little craft catapulted upward, out of the silo, and leveled off. The main thruster ignited, and the hopper shot across the airless lunar landscape.

Aiden sat back for the ride and took a deep breath. Silva would be grumpy over Aiden's tardiness, but what's new? It didn't take much to get under the man's skin these days. Commander Miguel Silva was Aiden's new second-in-command on the *Sun Wolf*, and not by Aiden's choice. Silva had been the Executive Officer aboard the SS *Parsons*, stationed at the HD 10180 voidoid, guarding the system's most valuable planet, Shénmì, and the UED's most important research outpost, the Shénmì Project.

The *Parsons* had been attacked last year by a Netvor warship that popped out of the voidoid in the blink of an eye, laser cannons blazing. The *Parsons* was hit in the stern but didn't have enough time to target the enemy warship before it mysteriously disappeared from sight. The damage was serious, and the *Parsons* lost nearly half of its crew, including its captain, Marcel Asaju. Silva had taken over command of the ship, secured it, and miraculously brought the ship limping back to Shénmì Station, saving the lives of the remaining crew. After that, Commander Silva had acquired an aura of hero status for his actions.

But then things took a tragic turn for him. Just weeks later, Silva's wife and young son had been stationed on the ill-fated

Gamelan Station in the Emwi star system when it was blown up by a Netvor suicide bomber. All 133 lives aboard were lost, including Silva's family. The bitterness he suffered from the destruction of his ship and crew suddenly metastasized into a far deeper and all-consuming hatred of the Netvor.

That's when the Admiralty decided to reward Silva with the most coveted voidship posting in the entire Alliance—Executive Officer of the *Sun Wolf,* under the captainship of Aiden Macallan. Aiden's long-time second-in-command and close friend, Roseph Hand, had finally decided to leave the *Sun Wolf* for his own command, a post promised to him back in 2217 after the Battle of Chara. That left the XO position open right around the same time as Silva's moment in the spotlight. Aiden's personal choice for XO had been summarily overridden by the Admiralty in favor of someone with greater patriotic celebrity in the public eye—a poster boy for the Alliance's fight against the Netvor, a sympathetic figure with a tragic backstory. After six months aboard the *Sun Wolf,* Silva still hadn't fit in. And as far as Aiden could tell, the man hadn't even tried. It seemed that Silva's bitterness, not his heroism, was now who he was, to the core.

Aiden glanced out the hopper's viewport at the stark, unforgiving moonscape and watched the towering eastern flanks of Wurzelbauer Crater recede from view. Within one minute, the hopper skimmed over the gap between the enormous Pitatus Crater and the smaller Hesiodus Crater sitting 10 kilometers to its west. Past the gap, the hopper began crossing the immense, dark-gray lava plains of Mare Nubium. The bleak, featureless flatlands stretched unbroken until the distinctive König Crater appeared in the north, and not long after that, the huge Bullialdus impact crater loomed up in front of them.

As the hopper descended and slowed, Aiden spotted the Bullialdus Mass Driver, its 400-meter-long accelerator rail gleaming in the merciless lunar glare. Even from this altitude, the bulging hubs of the accelerator coils were clearly visible, evenly spaced along the driver's graceful length. It was still kicking out 12-kilogram pellets of processed, iron-rich regolith, one every five seconds at lunar-escape velocity for orbital catchment.

The Bullialdus Space Port was situated near the crater's center. Three orbital shuttle craft sat on circular launch pads like silent hawks, poised for flight. The hopper made a soft landing, and a pressurized gangway unfolded from the port's passenger entrance to make an air-tight seal with the hopper's exit hatch. The hatch opened, and Aiden leapt out, making his way quickly toward the port's cargo depot. There, he found Miguel Silva standing impatiently just outside the cargo master's office with a compad in his hand. Cargo Master Margo Meyers remained seated in her cubicle, staying as far as possible from the confrontation she knew was about to take place.

Silva was 38 years old, born on Luna but with Earthside family roots in the Brazilian Republic. He had dark hair and dark eyes, a stocky build a couple of inches shorter than Aiden, and a rectangular face that would have been uncommonly handsome were it not for the man's constant brooding. He made a show of glancing at his chrono, then handed the compad to Aiden without a greeting. "You need to sign off on this cargo manifest."

Aiden scrolled through the list and nodded. "I assume you checked through all the containers to confirm their contents."

The muscles in Silva's jaw flexed, and he spoke flatly. "I did. Sir."

Aiden understood the man's frustration. Even as the ship's Executive Officer, he still couldn't do the final sign-off on something as trivial as a cargo manifest. New security protocols assigned that responsibility to the ship's commanding officer alone. But Silva's frequent displays of annoyance over such slights were tiresome, nonproductive, and sapped valuable energy from the dynamics of crew comradery. Silva wore his resentment like a badge of martyrdom, the "hero" of the *Parsons* relegated to second-in-command rather than given his own ship. It was clear to Aiden why the Admiralty would be disinclined to give Silva his own command. In his present state of mind, the man was simply not fit for command. But it was less clear why they'd deemed Silva even fit for second-in-command, much less on a ship as vital to the Alliance as the *Sun Wolf.*

Aiden signed the manifest with his fingerprint and handed the compad back to Silva. When Cargo Master Meyers emerged, Aiden said, "Looks good, Margo. Have it all loaded up in the ship's main cargo bay. The *Sun Wolf* departs in two hours. Is that enough time for you?"

She gave him a thumbs-up. "You got it, boss."

Silva turned to him with a sour expression. "Another mail run, eh, Captain?"

Here we go again. Aiden strived to keep things positive when his XO got into these moods. "If you want to look at it that way, Silva. But we *are* performing a valuable service for our people out there in Beta. A service no one else can provide."

Admittedly, Aiden didn't like the idea of being UED's delivery boy either. But the *Sun Wolf* could get from here to any star system in Astrocell Beta within eight hours. That included two voidjumps and traversal of about 52 astronomical units of realspace. Compared to the four weeks it would take for the fastest voidship to do the same, the *Sun Wolf* was the only practical choice for delivering high-priority equipment and personnel to outpost stations in a timely manner.

"That includes reinforcing our military installations," Aiden continued. "Those service men and women are risking their lives every day to help protect the rest of us. You wouldn't want to let them down, would you?"

This tactic didn't always work for Silva, but it seemed to quell his resentment for the moment. Instead, he transitioned from resentment to contempt. "I hear you found a dead Vor-lover on your doorstep this morning."

Aiden turned to look him in the eye. "And who told you that?"

"I monitor security comms," he said smugly. It was one privilege afforded to command-level officers on any station where their ships were docked. And Silva didn't miss a single opportunity to exercise any privilege of rank he could scare up.

"Yes," Aiden said. "A dead person where I didn't expect one. That's why I was late. And they call themselves Sympaths, Silva. They're harmless and have nothing to do with the Netvor. You know that. No matter how misguided they might be, the term 'Vor-lover' is a hateful epithet, beneath a man of your rank and character."

He and Silva had locked into this kind of verbal combat on too many occasions. It was always a pointless waste of energy.

Silva looked back at him with hard-set eyes. "The only good Vor-lover is a dead one."

Aiden stared him down, not rising to the bait. Sure, the man had a legitimate grudge against the Netvor—they had killed his family and many of his crewmates and had destroyed his ship. But turning that anger on a Sympath? Silva had gone off the rails.

Aiden shook his head and said nothing. But Silva pressed on. "Oh, I've offended you. Maybe you're a Vor-lover, too."

Aiden moved forward to place his face three inches from Silva's, fists clenched at his sides. "You're out of line, Commander. Right now, I don't give a shit about what the Admiralty wants. Keep this up and I'll bounce you off the *Sun Wolf* so hard you'll feel the sting of it for the rest of your miserable life. And you know I can do that."

The two of them stared each other down, face-to-face, heat rising between them like a volcano about to erupt. Silva finally looked away, but his eyes still burned with resentment.

Aiden moved in even closer, fighting the impulse to punch the man in the face. He kept his voice even and deliberate. "Is that clear, Commander?"

Silva stepped back from Aiden's aggression but locked his eyes on a point somewhere just above Aiden's forehead. "Perfectly clear. Captain."

Aiden's shoulders relaxed. He took a deep breath in and let it out slowly. He'd gotten way too close to violence this time. *Don't let this asshole get to you. Don't stoop to his level.*

Silva turned without another word and walked toward the elevator, head held pretentiously high.

Good gods. Why me? As if he didn't have enough to worry about. The telegem message from Skye, the disappearance of Jo's telegem, and the disappearance of Jo herself . . . All of it came back to him like a punch in the gut.

But now one thing was clear. Out of all the destinations the *Sun Wolf* was scheduled to visit, Shénmì Station would move to the top of his list. He needed to talk with Skye in person, in secret. Maybe she could give him a better understanding of what Jo was asking him to do, and maybe some idea of where she might be now.

4

SOL SYSTEM
Low Lunar Orbit

Domain Day 67, 2223

THE transport shuttle launched from Bullialdus Space Port just after 10:00, about one hour later than scheduled, thanks to Aiden's unexpected delay. The cargo had been efficiently loaded and secured, and he and Silva were seated directly behind the pilot's cabin. Silva still seemed put out and didn't speak more than he needed to. Aiden gave a mental shrug and looked out the shuttle's viewport as they ascended toward the *Sun Wolf* parked in orbit. The viewport was made of ClearLum, the latest iteration of transparent aluminum. It provided a crystal-clear view of his ship as they approached.

Even after his many years aboard the *Sun Wolf*, Aiden's initial wonderment over his ship's elegantly powerful design had not diminished. It was officially registered as a UED Science and Survey vessel, not a military vessel. Like the SS *Argo*, the survey ship he'd served on earlier in his career, the *Sun Wolf* was marginally smaller than a military battle cruiser at 210 meters in length and 26 meters at its widest. It was constructed with super-light, super-strong materials, weighing in at 8.7 kilotons. Like modern battle cruisers, its slender fuselage had a slightly hexagonal cross section, tapered forward to a narrow point, offering minimal targeting profiles for enemy beam weapons. While not technically a military vessel, the *Sun Wolf* was equipped with the most updated weapons systems and had superior shielding capabilities. The ship was, in truth, a top-of-the-line warship in disguise, a wolf in sheep's clothing.

But the *Sun Wolf* had one extraordinary feature that set it apart from every other voidship: the zero-point drive. In 2218, the ship had been fitted with Elgin Woo's revolutionary drive system, the ZPD for short. It had been installed in secret at Woo's clandestine research mecca, the Cauldron, with minimal alteration of the *Sun Wolf*'s outside appearance. The zero-point drive effectively eliminated the zero-point energy field of space—the quantum equivalent of inertia—directly in front of and around the ship. That allowed an initial pulse from its conventional antimatter drive to "accelerate" the ship instantly from standstill to any fraction of light speed, up to 92 percent. Eliminating inertia also meant eliminating the forces of acceleration that would otherwise crush the crew to a bloody pulp and tear the ship apart. The reverse process was used to bring the ship to a dead stop, instantaneously, at its destination.

Woo's ingenious creation had never been duplicated, and, much to the consternation of military and commercial sectors, he had yet to grant the use of his confoundingly esoteric technology for any other voidship. The only other ZPD in existence was the original prototype that powered Woo's own space yacht, the *Starhawk*.

The shuttle pilot expertly matched airlocks with the *Sun Wolf*. Aiden thanked him, and he and Silva boarded. While they made their way to the bridge, the shuttle disengaged, moved to the *Sun Wolf*'s cargo bay, and proceeded to transfer their cargo with robotic haulers.

Aiden entered the bridge to find his crew already at their stations preparing for the first of several voidjumps ahead. He'd been fortunate to keep his original crew largely intact since the *Sun Wolf* was first commissioned, with only two exceptions, one being his new XO, Miguel Silva. Pressure on the Alliance to build more warships and train new crews kept ship personnel in constant flux.

Voidship crewpersons with the most experience were frequently transferred to new ships to help train others in their areas of expertise.

But the *Sun Wolf* had been spared that disruption. The Admiralty had wisely recognized the singular value of the *Sun Wolf* functioning at peak efficiency. That meant keeping its original crew intact, with its long record of success, under the leadership of its most competent—if annoyingly independent—captain.

Aiden nodded a silent greeting to all, then sat at the command chair, situated at the center of the cabin's circular area. Unlike the romanticized spaceships in popular sci-fi dramas, the *Sun Wolf*'s command bridge was buried deep inside the ship's body, heavily shielded against both enemy weaponry and the intense gamma radiation from its antimatter drive when engaged for in-system maneuvering. No physical windows looking out into space, everything outside seen only through sensor telemetry. The large forward screen, occupying nearly 60 degrees of the bridge's circular bulkhead, displayed virtual feeds from dozens of external sensors.

Three operational stations were situated directly in front of the command chair. To his right was Comm/Scan station, occupied by Lilly Alvarez, who was busy transmitting launch data to Luna Flight Control. Alvarez was among the rare and dwindling number of professional spacers who were Earthborn. She came from a family with old roots in Oviedo, Spain, a subtle Castilian accent still gracing her speech. Her narrow face was accented by high cheekbones and framed by long, dark hair braided loosely past her shoulders. She glanced back at Aiden briefly as he settled into the command chair. Her large, deep-brown eyes—oversized for such a small, fine-boned face—telegraphed a silent welcome.

Helm station was located directly in front of the command chair. Licensed Pilot Lista Abahem reclined in the pilot's couch, silent and serenely entranced, preparing herself mentally for the psychic dislocation of the impending voidjump. Like all graduates of the Intersystem Pilots Agency, Abahem rarely interacted socially with anyone outside the cloistered, all-female Kinship of Pilots. She was tall, fine-boned and willowy, with a gaunt appearance that could easily be mistaken for anorexia were it not so common among pilots. Her eyes were an unusual shade of green, her skin pale but aglow with a healthy tone. Like all pilots, her head was kept perfectly hairless to facilitate neurolinkage with the ship's AI through her neurolink cap.

Tactical station was on Aiden's left, the domain of Lieutenant William (Billy) Hotah, Weapons Systems Officer, whose eyes were glued to the tactical screen occupying the entire width of his console. Hotah was an intense young man, 28 years old, and of Lakota descent. Before his posting on the *Sun Wolf*, he'd served aboard the SS *Endeavor*, the Service's flagship. Hotah had seen considerable combat action in the Battle of Chara, a pre-Alliance conflict between UED and ARM forces in 2217. He was credited with several crucial kills against ARM Militia warships, a tactical feat now documented in Service Academy textbooks. A red speckled band was tattooed across his face, extending from ear to ear, passing over the bridge of his nose. It gave him a feral look that belied his razor-sharp intelligence. Aiden had lost count of the many times he'd been deeply grateful that he and Billy Hotah were on the same side.

Medical/Life Support station was situated to Aiden's right against the bulkhead directly across from him. Medical Officer Dr. Sudha Devi had just finished her safety check of the ship's life-support system. She swiveled away from her console to face Aiden with a subtle smile and warm brown eyes that conveyed humor mixed with unsettling perceptiveness. At age 58, she was the oldest member of the crew. A solidly built woman from a long line of New Delhi physicians, her dark hair fell in waves to her shoulders, a long streak of gray running through it on one side. She had graduated from Luna U Medical Center, summa cum laude, and had been a practicing physician for nearly 25 years before her posting on the *Sun Wolf*.

To Aiden's immediate left, Commander Silva sat blank-faced at Ops station, the only crew member apparently unexcited about their upcoming mission to six different star systems, scores of light-years away.

The Drive Systems station was situated just beyond Ops, against the left bulkhead. It was occupied by the newest member of the crew, Drive Systems Engineer, Lieutenant Samuel Assan. He was tall, athletic, in his mid-thirties, with dark brown skin, a smooth-shaved head, and an infectious smile. Born on Luna after his parents had relocated from Ghana, New Africa, Assan had a PhD in engineering from Luna U and had moved up quickly to a posting aboard the SS *Endeavor*. He became a member of the *Sun Wolf*'s crew after the ship's original Drive Systems Engineer, Zachary Dalton, was tapped to head up the Alliance's Propulsion Research team. Other than Dalton and Elgin Woo himself, no one knew more about the ZPD and its potential applications. Assan's openness and optimism had proven to be an excellent fit for the *Sun Wolf*'s crew.

The Data Systems station, present on all other voidships, no longer existed on the *Sun Wolf*. Hutton, the ship's AI, was now so well integrated into the ship's systems that a dedicated data officer was superfluous. In truth, Hutton could run the whole ship by himself, if needed. Unlike any other Omicron-3 AI, Hutton's personality had been created and nurtured by Aiden himself, to the point where—for better or worse—the two had become each other's alter ego.

Aiden addressed the crew. "We've got a full schedule of deliveries out in Astrocell Beta. Six different star systems and ten separate destinations in all. I've posted a detailed itinerary on your personal compads. Our cargo hold is full. Our first stop was scheduled for the HD 4308 system where we have three stops to offload the greatest bulk of our cargo. But I'm making a minor change. Our first stop will now be the Shénmì Station, at HD 10180."

He looked around, saw several knowing smiles, and raised his hand in defense. "Okay, I know. You all think that just because my wife is there and I haven't seen her in over four months, that's why I've made the switch. Well, I admit, you're partially right about that. But it's also because the station's Allied Mapping Project desperately needs the new eight-meter mirror we're bringing for their infrared telescope. You all know how important their work is, astrometric mapping of all the stars out in Beta. We can't jump to any of those stars without the precise data that they're generating.

"But yes, while we're offloading that mirror, I'll be spending a few hours with Skye. You're welcome to debark and spend that time on the station, but we will still follow protocol to leave at least two crew members aboard. That assignment will be up to you."

"Oh, good," Devi said with a straight face. "I hear the new cuisine at the station's cafeteria is exquisite."

Samuel Assan, who was still learning to decipher Devi's dry wit, said, "Really? Wow. Finally, some decent chow."

The rest of the crew looked at him, grinning for a moment before they burst out laughing. Except Silva, of course, who looked sour as ever. Alvarez said, "No, *not* really, Samuel. Shénmì Station is known for its particularly boring meals. They really need a new chef out there."

Assan shook his head but couldn't suppress a smile. "You guys are always messing with me. I'll get you back for this."

"All right, everyone," Aiden said. "Resume stations. It's a two-hour hop to V-Prime."

V-Prime, short for Voidoid Prime, was the Solar System's voidoid, the system's jump portal into the rest of Astrocell Alpha, previously known as Bound Space. V-Prime was 13 AU away, nearly two billion kilometers. At 92 percent light speed, that was a two-hour trip in realtime, but only 46 minutes of dilated shipboard time.

Aiden leaned back into the command chair, satisfied that he'd successfully explained away the switch in itinerary. What he'd said about AMP's replacement mirror was true enough, but his true agenda now was meeting with Skye before doing anything else.

"Helm," Aiden said, "move us out to five thousand kilometers."

The ZPD was best engaged when far removed from any significant gravitational fields, in this case, Luna's gravity well. The ship used its auxiliary antimatter drive to cover the distance. When it was in position, Aiden gave the command. "Helm, on to V-Prime, maximum ZPD."

Pilot Abahem gave a thumbs-up and tapped her virtual board. The ship's huge EM generators—the muscle of the zero-point drive—kicked in to cast a powerful control field in front of the *Sun Wolf*, pushing the zero-point field of space away from the bow of the ship, creating a ship-sized pathway lying directly ahead. A split second later, the ship's antimatter drive burst into action with a one-second pulse. Within nine seconds, the *Sun Wolf* had "accelerated" to 91.9 percent light speed and held steady at that velocity. The only sensation Aiden experienced was a slight sinking feeling in his gut, but no G-forces. And now they were zipping along at 275,210 kilometers per second, the physics of inertia temporarily suspended.

5

EVEN though Aiden had experienced it hundreds of times before, the visual effects of travelling at relativistic velocities never ceased to amaze him, and he'd established a tradition of running live feed from the ship's external optical sensors on the main screen during ZPD transit.

Counterintuitively, stars did not stream by on the outside like snowflakes past a moving vehicle. Instead, the star field in front of them collapsed into a condensed dome of blue-white dots dead ahead, surrounded by a periphery of black nothingness that was bent inward on all sides, giving the impression of tunnel vision. A smaller screen displayed the rearward view, where only a scattering of extremely redshifted stars appeared directly behind them. The rest of it looked like a vast empty hole.

The *Sun Wolf* pulled out of ZPD into realspace just 46 minutes later, shipboard time, and began its approach to Friendship Station from one thousand kilometers out. Friendship Station had been constructed in 2170, one year after humanity had stumbled upon that mysterious quantum phenomenon now called Voidoid Prime sitting nearly 13 AU due north of Sol. The station was positioned adjacent to the voidoid's space-time horizon and served as a traffic control center and communications relay point. It had acquired its name, Friendship Station, in the spirit of cooperation engendered by the Ganymede Pact, cosigned by the UED and ARM, which mandated free access to Voidoid Prime "for all mankind." It guaranteed freedom to voidjump anywhere within the 36-light-year radius of Astrocell Alpha. On paper at least.

As the *Sun Wolf* approached, Station Control hailed them. Control had been notified of the *Sun Wolf*'s imminent arrival, of course, but its personnel always seemed surprised by the *way* the ship arrived. From their point of view, the *Sun Wolf* had materialized out of nowhere. No sign of its approach would be detected by their considerable array of sensors, nothing to indicate the *Sun Wolf* even existed until it appeared moments ago, 1,000 kilometers out.

Aiden requested clearance for the Alpha-2 Hydri system, a mere formality at this point since the *Sun Wolf*'s transit had already been cleared at the highest levels. After checking registration information for the ship and its Licensed Pilot, the Control officer confirmed that their entrance corridor was clear and said, "Have a good trip, Captain."

Aiden watched Pilot Abahem enter the commands to bring the ship into position 500 kilometers from the voidoid and align it with the entrance coordinates. From there, a 2 G burn would boost the ship into the voidoid with an entrance velocity of around 4.5 km/sec. The *Sun Wolf* could easily manage an entry velocity over ten times higher than that. But because a ship always popped out the other side travelling at the same velocity it had upon entry, Aiden opted for an exit that would allow more practical comms with the two Alliance warships stationed there. He wanted to touch bases with both captains and to send an encrypted message across the system to Gateway Station before engaging the ZPD.

With the ship in position, Abahem donned her linkage cap, a pale translucent thing that always gave Aiden the impression of being alive. Which it was in some sense, being inhabited by a horde of nanobots, micro-AIs working in concert to establish a seamless link between the pilot's brain and the ship's Omicron AI.

It took about one minute for the link to complete, then Abahem signaled her readiness with a thumbs-up.

Aiden said, "Proceed."

The *Sun Wolf*'s antimatter drive kicked in at 2 Gs. A sudden ultralow rumble filled the bridge, accompanied by a barely perceptible sensation of lateral G-forces along the axis of thrust just before the ship's inertial compensators kicked in. Inertial compensation not only negated the G-forces the crew would normally experience, but it also allowed the ship's decks to lie parallel to the axis of thrust, while the G-transducer provided a constant "downward" force of 1 G at deck surfaces. Laymen called it "artificial gravity." Spacers called it essential to life working the Deep years on end.

All eyes focused on the forward-facing main screen. Like all voidoids, V-Prime was 18.2 kilometers in diameter, give or take a few hundred meters. And, like all voidoids, its surface shifted visible light into the X-ray range, making V-Prime virtually invisible, marked only by the absence of background stars. To the naked eye, it looked like a big black circle of nothingness seen from any angle and perfectly opaque. The ship's navigational sensors had to rely on high-energy X-ray pulses to lock on to its position to calculate precise jump parameters.

Aiden glanced around at his crew. Outwardly, they looked calm, even bored. But he knew it was mostly an act. Even the most experienced spacers never felt comfortable approaching a voidoid, and Aiden was no exception. It was such a thoroughly exotic entity, so beyond the ordinary, and too much like a spooky dream of death waiting to swallow the dreamer.

Hutton's soothing, disembodied voice filled the bridge. "Voidjump in 30 seconds."

The crew watched as the eerie emptiness of the voidoid rapidly filled the main screen, blotting out the star field. The *Sun Wolf* sped toward it, aimed directly into its gaping maw, into the abyss. At the very instant the tip of the ship's forwardmost sensor wand penetrated the voidoid's space-time horizon, the entire mass of the ship disappeared into it.

As he often did at the instant of a voidjump, Aiden sat back and closed his eyes for the perceived split second it took for the jump. Only this time, when he opened his eyes again, it seemed the voidjump was still in progress. And standing before him in a gauzy, shimmering light was none other than Elgin Woo. He was smiling at him from ear to ear.

Woo looked the same as the last time Aiden had seen him, over five years ago. An unusually tall and thin Asian man in his mid-sixties, his head was shaved bald as a cue ball. His long gray mustache was braided meticulously at each end and dangled below his chin on either side of his perpetually smiling mouth. He seemed to be wearing a 19th-century British military coat, red with two parallel rows of buttons running down the front.

Typical Elgin. Ever the trickster.

Woo appeared to be speaking to him, emphasizing his words with animated hand gestures, but Aiden heard no sound coming from his lips. A moment later, Elgin Woo was gone. The sight of the ship's bridge reemerged into Aiden's field of vision. The *Sun Wolf* had just popped out of the voidoid into the Alpha-2 Hydri system, 36 light-years from Sol.

Aiden sat for a moment, attempting to center himself. He looked around the bridge. No one else seemed to have experienced anything unusual about the jump. Was he going mad? Hallucinating? He wasn't taking Continuum anymore—he'd beaten that drug habit years ago—so it couldn't be that. But then, ever since his otherworldly encounter with the Rete on Silvanus, he'd developed a disturbingly intimate relationship with dreamtime, an alluring siren knocking on the door of his consciousness at unexpected times. There was another world, but it was in this one, and he often found himself standing astride both with one foot planted in each.

He noticed Pilot Abahem had turned around to look at him, something she rarely did right after a voidjump. The look on her face was both bemused and bewildered, along with a subtle smile that showed more in her eyes than on her face. The moment passed quickly, and she turned back to her post as if nothing out of the ordinary had happened. That she may have shared some aspect of his experience came as no surprise to Aiden. The connection Licensed Pilots had with the voidoids was a gift they cultivated from an early age, a kind of transphysical telepathy. It was one of the reasons they were so good at what they did.

But Aiden's musings were quickly jolted by what he and his crew saw on the forward screen as the ship moved away from the voidoid. The shattered wreckage of one Alliance battle cruiser tumbled slowly in space, jagged fragments of its fuselage scattered randomly.

"Level One alert engaged," Hotah said. These days, Aiden had the ship automatically assume a Level Two defensive status immediately after any voidjump. Hotah had just activated Level One. That meant shields at maximum strength, weapons systems primed and ready.

Aiden turned to him. "Tactical?"

Hotah had already initiated near-range tactical scans of the surrounding space. "No other vessels within a one-light-second radius. I'm running a long-range scan now."

Aiden's stomach began to knot up. The last posting update had listed two Alliance battle cruisers stationed at this voidoid—the RMV *Essex*, an ARM ship, and the UED's SS *Takema*. The RMV prefix stood for Republics of Mars Vessel, whereas SS was for UED's Service Ship. He knew the *Takema*'s captain personally. Captain Alain DuBois.

"Alvarez, zero in on the wreckage. Try to ID the ship and look for any escape pods in the vicinity."

After one tense minute, Alvarez said, "I'm receiving a distress signal from somewhere near the debris field. Locating it now . . . There!"

She displayed on the forward screen an enhanced view of what appeared to be a standard escape pod about one kilometer removed from the bulk of the wreckage. The name RMV *Essex* was clearly stenciled on its surface, along with its ARM registration number

C-1382. Every Alliance warship was equipped with two escape pods in case the crew had to abandon ship in an emergency. Most Alliance warships had crews of 10 to 12 members. Each escape pod could accommodate up to six people with life-support systems good for up to five days.

Aiden leaned over Alvarez's console for a closer look. "Just one escape pod?"

"Yes, I'm seeing just one. It's broadcasting an automated Mayday signal."

"Hail the pod, Lilly. Use all standard frequencies."

Alvarez switched on the main RF transceiver and said, "RMV *Essex*, this is the SS *Sun Wolf*. We're receiving your Mayday and are within 10 kilometers of your position. Do you copy?"

She repeated the hail two more times before a woman's voice responded. "SS *Sun Wolf*, this is Lieutenant Sula Bondar of the RMV *Essex*. Our ship was attacked by an unknown vessel three days ago. I have six other crew members here with me. Some are injured. We need immediate assistance."

Aiden linked the comm to his command chair and spoke. "Lieutenant Bondar, this is Captain Aiden Macallan. We're coming to you now. Are you aware of any other survivors? Including your captain?"

Bondar's voice sounded hoarse and exhausted. "No other survivors that we know of. It happened so fast. The ship's bridge sustained the most damage. I believe most of the bridge crew, including Captain Kovalenko, have perished."

"I'm sorry to hear that, Lieutenant," Aiden said, feeling his anger rising. This was another surprise attack by the Netvor. No question about it. "Do you have a functional A-9 airlock?"

One of the fine-print requirements written into the Alliance pact was that the airlocks on all military ships and their transport craft would be standardized to accommodate all physical transfers between the UED and ARM forces. And that included escape pods, for obvious reasons. But the transition had been slow on the ARM side. Aiden hoped that Bondar's pod had been properly updated. Otherwise, a rescue would be impossible unless ARM's bare bones escape pods were equipped with enough suits for an EVA transfer, which he doubted.

"Yes, Captain," she responded, clearly relieved. "We have the A-9 airlock, and I believe it's fully functional."

"Good. We will approach within 500 meters, then send out our landing shuttle to mate with your airlock. The lander operator will be Commander Silva, and he will maintain contact throughout the operation. We will ready our medical bay to receive your injured."

"Thank you, Captain." The emotion in Bondar's was clear and unguarded. "*Thank* you."

Aiden signed out and turned to his XO with a questioning look. He'd just assigned Silva to head up the rescue mission and was curious to see how he'd respond. To his credit, Silva seemed energized by the prospect. He nodded back to Aiden and said, "I'm on it, sir. I suggest bringing along Dr. Devi in case we encounter injuries that require immediate attention."

"Good idea." Aiden was going to say the same thing but was glad Silva had said it first.

"Pilot, move us in. Let's get those people aboard."

6

ALPHA-2 HYDRI SYSTEM
Southern Voidoid

Domain Day 67, 2223

"An incursion this far into human space," Lieutenant Bondar was saying, "is unprecedented, Captain. I don't understand how a Netvor ship could've gotten through the Gateway voidoid, past all the warships we've got stationed there. Not without being detected."

Sula Bondar sat in a chair across from Aiden in the *Sun Wolf*'s ready room nursing a cup of hot tea, both hands clutching the mug as if it were a gift from the gods. After she'd finished transferring her remaining crew aboard, Aiden had summoned her to get a firsthand account of the attack.

Bondar was a short, muscular woman in her early forties with dark blonde hair and brown eyes. She spoke with an accent that sounded Eastern European but softened by years of living among international Alliance crews. She had a nasty-looking bruise on her right forearm and a two-inch-long laceration on her forehead that had been expertly nanostitched by Dr. Devi. Unfortunately, many of the other survivors were in worse shape. Burns, broken bones, and barotrauma from sudden depressurization were responsible for most of the injuries. One crew member was in critical condition with a life-threatening pneumothorax, the result of explosive decompression from a hull breach. All of them were in the medical bay, being tended to by Dr. Devi with assistance from Lieutenant Assan, who had training in emergency medical treatment.

"I sent out a distress call," Bondar went on, "just after we made it safely to the escape pod. But the pod's radio transmitter doesn't have the power to reach Gateway Station, all the way across the system, and the ship's Holtzman transmitter was destroyed in the attack. Otherwise, we could have reached Friendship Station on the other side of the voidoid."

Aiden nodded. He never understood why the Alliance didn't equip their escape pods with basic Holtzman transmitters. If one had been aboard Bondar's pod, she could have sent a Holtzman signal back through the voidoid, and it would have reached Friendship Station in the same amount of time it took a ship to voidjump—no time at all. Then the station could have sent a ship through the voidoid to rescue her and her crew within hours.

"Did you get a good look at the hostile ship?" Aiden asked. "Could you positively ID it as a Netvor vessel?"

Aiden realized it was a dumb question the moment he uttered it. Current intelligence confirmed that Netvor warships had been built on specs stolen from the Alliance. Cardew's forces had even hijacked an advanced UED shipbuilder platform, which had never been recovered after his demise. It was probably still in use by the Netvor somewhere out in Astrocell Beta, manufacturing Netvor warships with designs nearly identical to Alliance ships. It would be impossible to tell the difference in the chaos of combat.

To Bondar's credit, she didn't point that out to Aiden. She only shook her head and said, "Not really. The attack was a total surprise. No indication that a ship had emerged from the voidoid. No sensor readings. No time to power our shields. Nothing until that ship just popped out of nowhere and hit us with a couple missiles. I caught only a split-second glimpse of it after its missiles launched. Then it disappeared again just as quickly."

"In that glimpse, did you notice anything unusual about it? Any ID markings?"

She thought about that for a few seconds, shaking her head slowly, then said, "No, only that it looked a little like one of ARM's older warships . . . wait. Yes, there was something else. A symbol and a number on its hull . . ."

Aiden perked up. "Can you describe it?"

Bondar's eyes went blank for a moment before refocusing. "It was like parentheses surrounding an empty circle, but connected to the circle by a straight line from the inside of each parenthesis. And next to it was the number 17. Our ship's sensors would have caught more if we hadn't been hit so quickly . . ."

She covered her face, fell silent, and shook her head. Aiden decided not to push any further. What she had described was more than enough to confirm his suspicion that the attacker had been a Netvor vessel using its new cloaking tech. Even down to its sudden disappearance after firing missiles. That jibed with the intel reports suggesting that Netvor warships might have to temporarily decloak before firing any of their weapons.

But what disturbed Aiden as much as the attack itself was Bondar's first question. How could a Netvor vessel get through Gateway Voidoid into the Alpha-2 Hydri system without being detected by the massive military operation stationed there to guard it? Gateway had the most sophisticated sensor network anywhere outside Earth space. The most obvious and troubling answer would be that Netvor warships could execute voidjumps while remaining fully cloaked. That they could freely jump in and out of star systems completely unnoticed, sneaking past the defenses stationed at all the strategic voidoids. And if that were true, the Netvor would be only one stealthy voidjump away from the Solar System and humanity's home world.

Aiden filed that dark thought away for another time and said, "One more thing, Lieutenant. What happened to the SS *Takema*? I was under the impression that two Alliance ships were stationed here, and one was the *Takema*."

She nodded. "The SS *Takema* was ordered away this morning to cover another posting that had been left unguarded. Captain

DuBois said it was the HD 20003 system. We're stretched pretty thin out here these days."

Aiden understood. The Alliance was tasked with guarding the voidoid of every star system in Astrocell Beta that hosted a human presence. To date, there were a total of nine star systems in Beta where either mining operations or research stations were located. Each of those systems needed at least one Alliance warship stationed at its voidoid. Plus, any operation working on a planetary surface should, ideally, have an additional guard in orbit. With the heaviest military presence already positioned at Gateway Station, the Alliance had damned few assets left to cover all those bases.

"Thank you, Lieutenant," Aiden said, softening his voice. "You've been very helpful. And your courageous actions in saving the lives of your surviving crew members are to be commended. It was well done. You can be proud of that."

Bondar smiled weakly and nodded. "*You're* the one who saved our lives, Captain. We're damn lucky you found us when you did. We wouldn't have lasted another day in that pod. And I'm afraid at least one of my crew won't make it at all unless he gets state-of-the-art medical attention soon. The only medical facility out here that can save him is at Gateway Station. And it's way across the system, 26 AU away. That's 11 days away at best."

"Well, Lieutenant. You're in luck. This is the SS *Sun Wolf.* I can get you there in about four hours—one and a half hours shipboard time—and we're headed there ourselves."

Bondar's eyes widened as if she'd just woken from a bad dream. "The *Sun Wolf*? That *Sun Wolf*? Sorry, in all the confusion, I just didn't . . . and you're *the* Captain Macallan?"

Aiden tilted his head and smiled. This kind of recognition always made him uneasy. "For better or worse, yes. I'll send a transmission ahead and ask that Gateway Medical have its trauma room prepped. In the meantime, get some rest, Lieutenant. Some food, if you wish. The galley is yours, and your crew's. Whatever you need."

Aiden and Bondar stood. She reached out to shake hands. "Thank you again, Captain." A new light shone in her eyes, the kind that can help banish dark visions of violence and terror. Aiden wondered how long that light would last.

After Bondar left, he sat and composed two messages for Gateway Station. The first was to Gateway Medical. The second was a deep-encrypted message for Admiral Stegman reporting the attack on the RMV *Essex* and asking for an emergency meeting with him upon their arrival.

Admiral Benjamin Stegman oversaw the Alliance forces operating out of Gateway Station. Aiden would press him to authorize a drastic change in the *Sun Wolf*'s current mission. He couldn't stop thinking about Jo's quest, about her claim of the Libera technology that could defeat Netvor cloaking, and how critical it would be to acquire that technology. That would require finding the Libera first, then convincing them to help. Before it was too late. The Alliance had to make that a top priority now, and he and his ship were the only agents capable of pursuing it realistically. But with growing rumors of Netvor spies afoot, it had to be done with utmost secrecy.

Aiden was confident that Admiral Stegman would listen to what he had to say, given their long history together. But Stegman ultimately answered to the UED's current administration. Given President Adler's extreme isolationist ideology and xenophobia—and appalling ignorance—that could be a problem. If it came down to it, Aiden would need to take matters into his own hands. It wouldn't be the first time.

He sent the messages on their way via maser transmission, even though they would reach Gateway Station only 20 minutes ahead of the *Sun Wolf*. He returned to the bridge and directed Pilot Abahem to take the ship to Gateway Station, maximum ZPD. Before resuming the command chair, Lieutenant Billy Hotah intercepted him and asked for a word. In private.

Back in the ready room, Aiden said, "Have a seat, Hotah. What's on your mind?"

After four years together aboard the *Sun Wolf*, Aiden had almost gotten used to the young man's exotic appearance but was still taken aback every time they spoke face-to-face. Hotah's smooth, copper-toned complexion and high cheekbones accentuated his gaunt face and framed intense dark brown eyes. His black hair, considerably longer than Aiden's, was parted in the middle and fell shoulder length at either side. But his most striking feature, of course, had always been that band of red dots tattooed across his face from ear to ear. Aiden had never asked him about it, or his Lakota ancestry, and Hotah never volunteered any account of it.

Hotah was silent for a long moment, watching Aiden's eyes with the serene intensity that defined his natural state. Then he said, "A dead Sympath at your doorstep?"

Aiden drew in a long breath and leaned back. "Bad news spreads fast, eh?"

Hotah said nothing, but Aiden thought he saw a shade of concern darken his eyes.

When the man remained silent, Aiden said, "What about it?"

Hotah said, "Not a coincidence."

"No. I'm aware of that."

Hotah nodded calmly. "You're still in danger. Personally."

And that was it. Billy Hotah could always sense when threat levels escalated, whether it was for the ship or for its captain. That kind of second sight used to give Aiden the creeps, but now, after it had saved his life on several occasions, he was just fine with it.

"That may be the case, Hotah," Aiden said, stroking his beard. "Maybe I need you to keep your eyes especially wide open these days."

Aiden had sensed it, too, a darkness creeping closer like a malevolent storm front on the horizon.

Hotah's face expressed nothing more than keen awareness of the present. "Yes. I agree."

More silence. Finally, Aiden said, "Good."

At that, Hotah stood, made a barely perceptible nod, and left the room.

~ ~ ~

A voidship could not jump from just any voidoid inside Astrocell Alpha directly into Astrocell Beta. The only way a ship could get from Astrocell Alpha, where the Solar System was, to Astrocell Beta was to jump to the star called Alpha-2 Hydri first, emerging from its southern voidoid, then cover the 26 AU of deep space to reach the northern voidoid where the voidoid into Astrocell Beta existed. That voidoid was called Gateway Voidoid, or simply the Gateway. One AU was about 150 million kilometers. So 26 of them was a very long way. Even the fastest voidships took over ten days to cross it, including a turnaround at midpoint. For the *Sun Wolf*, at 92 percent light speed, it took only four hours of realtime—an hour and a half of shipboard time—to reach Gateway.

Upon arrival, the *Sun Wolf* pulled out of ZPD to a standstill 100 kilometers from Gateway Station. From there, the ship moved in on conventional drive, slowing into a docking maneuver. Like Friendship Station, Gateway Station had been built in stationary position about 32 kilometers from the voidoid's space-time horizon. Construction was in its fourth year, and already it was nearly twice the size of Friendship Station. Its eight docking arms were large enough to accommodate standard voidships. Six were currently occupied by Alliance battle cruisers. Another eight warships were stationed in space at various positions around the spherical voidoid, covering all quadrants.

The *Sun Wolf* was guided into one of the two unoccupied docks and secured. Aiden put Silva in command and directed him to oversee the transfer of the injured *Essex* crew to the station's medial facility. Meanwhile, Aiden tagged Billy Hotah to accompany him to Gateway's command center. They were met in the receiving area by two officers from Admiralty Security and ushered through a standing XRF scan machine.

The X-ray fluorescence scans were now standard procedure at all Alliance checkpoints to screen people entering or leaving any human-occupied base of operation. It was the quickest way to identify bones made of carbon nanotubes. Netvor agents would be unable to pass an XRF scan without setting off alarms. To date, however, no such agents had been nabbed by it. So, while its efficacy remained unproven, the presence of scans at all entrances was considered an effective deterrent to covert infiltration by the Netvor. Aiden didn't share that confidence.

After the scans, he and Hotah were accompanied on a long walk into the station's core. After passing through two more checkpoints, manned by armed guards, they were ushered into Admiral Stegman's waiting room. Just as Aiden prepared to sit, the door opened and Ben Stegman emerged, a beaming smile on his face. "Aiden! Good to see you. It's been too long."

7

ALPHA-2 HYDRI SYSTEM
Northern Voidoid, Gateway Station

DOMAIN DAY 67, 2223

ADMIRAL Benjamin Stegman had been Aiden's captain on the Survey Vessel *Argo*. After the Chara Conflict, he had moved up the chain to Vice Admiral of the Science and Survey Division, a branch of the UED's Space Service. Then one year after that, he'd been promoted to Admiral and was awarded the top spot as chief of the entire Space Service. Now he oversaw all branches of the Service, including its largest one, the Military Division.

But to Aiden, first and foremost, Stegman was a longtime friend and mentor, and, if truth be told, was the father Aiden never really had. Stegman had personally brought Aiden aboard the *Argo* back in 2209 as a troubled young man who'd spent three horrific years at Hades, the Domain's most notorious federal prison, on charges reeking of profoundly corrupt politics. After an early release and exoneration, Aiden had proved his worth by earning his PhD in planetary geophysics with top honors at Luna University. Aiden had come a long way since then on his own merit, but he owed many of the opportunities he'd been given to Ben Stegman.

Stegman was 62 years old with thinning gray hair on top, a thick, walrus-style mustache, and a pair of bushy, gray eyebrows that hovered above his alert, brown eyes. He was trim and fit for his age and stood with an upright posture that put him at eye level with Aiden. The two men stood for a moment just grinning at each other. They'd been through enough shit together over the years that no words were necessary for the moment.

After a warm handshake that would have led to a hearty bear hug under other circumstances, Aiden introduced Hotah. "This is my Tactical Officer, Lieutenant Willam Hotah. I wanted him in this meeting for reasons that'll become clear after telling you why I've come. There's no one I trust more."

Stegman shook Hotah's hand. "Yes, I know who Lieutenant Hotah is, by reputation and from his impressive military commendations. It's a pleasure to meet you in person, Lieutenant."

Hotah made a brief nod. "It's an honor, sir."

Stegman motioned to several padded chairs facing his desk. "Please, sit."

Instead of returning to his desk, the admiral pulled up one of the chairs to face them. "I received your report about the attack on the SS *Essex* just before you docked. But that's not all you wanted to discuss, is it?"

"No. There's much more."

Stegman sat back, folded his hands on his lap, and said, "Tell me."

Aiden proceeded to recount the incident of the dead man on his doorstep that morning, the telegem message Skye had sent to him, its revelational content, and the crucial telegem message from Jo that he'd never received and was now presumed missing. This part of it was news to Hotah, too, and prompted him to sit up with renewed focus.

Aiden stopped there to let the implications sink in before continuing. "The attack on the *Essex* sets a disturbing precedent. As far as I know, none of Cardew's original forces—including their current iteration as the Netvor—have ever been detected here in the Alpha-2 Hydri system. Not since they disappeared into Astrocell Beta seven years ago. If one of them is here now, on this side of the Gateway, how did it get here? If it got through Gateway's beefed-up defenses without being noticed, their cloaking tech is a lot better than we thought. And it would explain a lot of the surprise attacks we're seeing, like the one against the *Essex*."

Stegman leaned forward, focused on Aiden's account, and said, "I was afraid of this. It confirms recent reports from our intelligence sources. Gathered from accounts of ship crews surviving these attacks. And believe me, survivors are rare. The *Essex* was lucky to have lost only half of its crew. Most other ships? Sitting ducks. You heard about the SS *Wilmington*, right? Out at Woo's Star? Just two weeks ago. Vaporized."

Aiden had heard about it, of course, and had been especially nervous about it occurring in the system where Shénmì Station was located. Where Skye and Bri lived. He'd also heard about the unexplained ship-sized explosion witnessed by the SS *Jakarta* just minutes after it jumped into the system to replace the *Wilmington*.

"It doesn't help," Aiden added, "that the Alliance hasn't come up with better shielding technology for its warships. The Tyson Field is outdated. Good against beam weapons but lousy at stopping missiles. And the Netvor know it. Their attacks now are mostly missile strikes."

Stegman had heard the shielding complaint a million times, and he didn't want to hear it again. He moved on. "This story about a hidden colony of so-called *Trans sapiens* with key knowledge about the Netvor's cloaking tech . . . It sounds too good to be true. Do you believe it?"

"They call themselves the Libera, Ben. And your question is a good one. Under the circumstances, I think it's worth every effort we can make to find an answer. You know Skye. She believes it's true. And Jo. You've met her. I personally trust her without reservation. Whether or not this Libera person told Jo the whole truth—that's the only real question. But can we afford to ignore it? Especially now, when we're losing so many of our ships to these surprise attacks?"

Stegman sat in thought for a moment before saying, "I think I know where you're going with this, Aiden. You want to take the *Sun Wolf* on a wild goose chase to find this hidden colony of

Libera. But without the coordinates, you don't have the faintest idea of where it is, do you? Somewhere out there in Astrocell Beta in over 3 million cubic light-years of space. And even if this colony does exist and you found it, it sounds to me like they won't be welcoming you with open arms, much less considering any kind of alliance to share their tech with us."

Aiden nodded patiently with each probable obstacle. "I understand all of that, Ben. It's a long shot, I know. But after leaving here, I'm taking the *Sun Wolf* to Shénmì Station—it's on our list of deliveries—and I'll talk with Skye. She's the only one on the station that Jo confides in, and probably the last person she spoke with before disappearing. I'm hoping to get a better take on what's going on, maybe even find a way to recover the content of Jo's message, along with the missing coordinates."

Stegman looked doubtful, and in truth, Aiden was grasping at straws. But he firmly believed that if anyone had a chance of doing any part of this, it was him and his crew, and he said as much to Stegman.

"You realize, of course," Stegman said, "that the *Sun Wolf* is the single most valuable asset in the Service. Hell, in the entire Alliance. Even though you're technically registered as a Science and Survey vessel, we all know how important you are to the military. I'd be obliged to run this by Drew, and I don't think he'd be crazy about allowing the *Sun Wolf* to go off chasing windmills, especially now when you're needed here more than ever."

Admiral Drew Prescott was chief of the UED Military Space Service. Aiden knew him personally. He was a tough nut to crack, but his intelligence had never been in doubt.

"But, as you said, the *Sun Wolf* isn't technically a military vessel," Aiden protested. "I'm not a military captain, and this mission could easily be categorized as nonmilitary. Purely exploratory. Besides, Ben, you're the boss of the entire Service. You don't really *need* to consult Prescott about it."

Stegman shook his head slowly but couldn't suppress a smile. "There's the Aiden Macallan I've always known. Always pushing the boundaries."

Aiden shrugged. "What can I say? No risk, no gain."

Stegman unfolded his hands from his lap and ran a hand through his thinning hair. "Okay. Let's start with this. Meet with Skye. Search for any clues you can scare up. If you get lucky and hit on a solid lead, send me an encrypted Holtzman transmission, and I'll authorize a preliminary search for this hidden colony. But just that, a search only. If you actually find this planet and confirm the presence of a Libera colony, you're not authorized to make contact without further instructions."

"No contact? But—"

Stegman held up his hand. "No 'buts,' Aiden. You know that even I can't authorize you to negotiate an alliance between us and a virtually unknown league of individuals, especially one populated by a race of beings so closely related to our enemy. I mean, what if you struck a deal with them that the Alliance couldn't—or wouldn't—uphold? Then we'd have these Libera folks against us, too."

Stegman had a point. And even if Mars was agreeable to such an alliance, the Earth Domain, under its current administration, would surely veto it. Unless, of course, the threat level to Earth from the Netvor rose to a tipping point . . .

"All right," Aiden said. "I can live with that. For now. I'll keep you posted on what I learn from Skye, or anything else I can dig up on Shénmì Station."

Stegman nodded and made a move to stand. Aiden stopped him. "One more thing, Ben. If I do get a lead and end up leaving Shénmì Station to follow it, I can't deliver the cargo that I've got on board to their destinations. I'll need to offload it here at Gateway and ask that it be delivered by other Service ships."

Stegman was not smiling when he asked, "How many deliveries are you scheduled for?"

Instead of answering, Aiden handed over his compad displaying the complete itinerary and itemized cargo listing. Stegman looked at it with a sour expression. "Seriously?"

"Except you can scratch off Shénmì Station. I'll deliver the telescope mirror to the Mapping Project, since I'm going there anyway."

Stegman had that look on his face that said, *Oh, well, thank you for small favors.* But he said, "We can't spare what ships we have left to run these kinds of lengthy deliveries, Aiden. Especially now when we're losing them faster than we can build and crew them."

"All the more reason for me to find the Libera and work something out as soon as possible."

Stegman remained silent, and his face hardened. Aiden feared that he might backpedal and renege on the whole idea. Then he said, "I'll sanction your proposal because I think it's worth the gamble. But only with a few conditions."

Time for compromise, Aiden thought. "And what would those be?"

"You keep your cargo deliveries aboard. If you *do* find a solid lead, you come back here to Gateway Station and report to me in person. No Holtzman or maser transmissions, no matter how well encrypted. If your lead is convincing, I'll authorize your search mission. With top-secret designation. Then you can offload your deliveries here and be on your way. But if you hit a dead end on Shénmì Station, you'll still have your cargo aboard, and you'll go on from there and finish your deliveries."

Aiden nodded. "All right. If I come up empty and there's nothing more I can do, we'll resume the deliveries."

Stegman squinted at him. He hadn't missed the part about "if there's nothing more I can do." He knew Aiden too well. But he just harrumphed and handed the compad back to Aiden. "Okay then. Off you go."

As Aiden opened the door for Hotah and himself to leave, he turned to face Stegman. He truly loved and respected his grumpy old friend. "Thanks, Ben."

Stegman's eyes softened, just a little. Aiden could see a hint of concern in his eyes. "Good luck, Aiden."

As he and Hotah made their way back toward the docking port, Hotah said, "Will you be telling the rest of the crew the real reason for changing our mission?"

Aiden knew Hotah wouldn't have asked the question if "the rest of the crew" hadn't included Miguel Silva. "Not until the mission actually changes. If I get any clue to where this Libera colony is, then game on. I'll tell the crew about it then. For now, it's just you and me."

Hotah was silent for another 20 steps, then said, "Superman won't like it."

It was Hotah's private nickname for Silva. Aiden thought it was amusing and apropos but never let on that he did. "You don't care much for Commander Silva, do you?"

Hotah gave him a look that said, *and you do?* But he replied, "Commander Silva thinks he's better than everyone else. He looks down on anyone who doesn't look like him. Or anyone who doesn't believe the bullshit that he does."

It was an admirably succinct assessment, Aiden thought. And Silva himself had never attempted to prove otherwise. His openly political support for the UED's new president—for his ideology of racial exclusion and lust for personal power—ran counter to the temperament of most spacers, people who lived and worked in deep space beyond Earth's reach. Miguel Silva was apparently one of the few exceptions.

By the time he and Hotah boarded the *Sun Wolf*, it was nearly 23:00. After a long day, Aiden wanted to give his crew some shut-eye before jumping to Woo's Star. He was scheduling sleep rotations when the station's alarms went off. It was a Level Three alert, notifying station personnel to be prepared for a potential emergency. Within one minute, Admiral Stegman's face appeared on Aiden's command screen. He looked angry.

"Captain Macallan. We've just received a distress transmission from the colony out at Daleth-4. They're under attack from orbit by an unknown vessel. The transmission went dead after 30 seconds. It's only an automated Mayday signal now. I'm directing you to take the *Sun Wolf* out there without delay to investigate. You can get there within two hours. You are authorized to engage and kill any hostile vessel you encounter and to commence rescue operations for the colonists, if needed. You're cleared by Control for immediate departure."

Oh shit. Aiden took a deep breath. "We're on it, Admiral. I'll keep you posted."

Daleth, a gas giant similar to Jupiter, was the third planet in this star system. Daleth-4 was its fourth moon. Aiden turned to his crew and said, "Sleep? Who needs sleep? Pilot, take us out and set course for Daleth, maximum velocity."

8

Domain Day 68, 2223

THE *Sun Wolf* pulled away from the station to a safe distance, then engaged its zero-point drive. It would be around 46 minutes, shipboard time, back to the star's planetary system. During that time, the crew seemed uncharacteristically quiet, and Aiden knew why.

Except for Assan and Silva, they had all been to Daleth-4 on one previous occasion. It had been an unforgettable experience. Back when the moon was designated simply d-4, it was the location of Cardew's infamous Dark Fort, a hidden outpost run by Cardew's henchman, Black Dog, where kidnapped scientists had been brutally brain tapped for their knowledge. The brain-tapping project, augmented by a corrupted Omicron-3 AI, had been Cardew's quick and ruthless way to acquire the technological foundation on which to build his nascent "Posthuman Realm."

On Domain Day 104, 2218—a date etched in Aiden's memory—the *Sun Wolf* was tasked with rescuing the survivors imprisoned there and left to die after Cardew's forces departed for Astrocell Beta. Aiden and his crew had found only seven scientists still alive. Their condition was appalling. Their minds had been virtually wiped, with great skill and not gently. Physically, they were still alive but just barely. Mentally and emotionally, they were empty. Most of them died within months. It had been a dark epiphany for Aiden, when the true depth of Cardew's evil had become shockingly clear to him. An evil that was still afoot, advanced by the descendants of Cardew's cloneborgs, the Netvor.

Lieutenant Assan finally broke the silence. "Who would want to build a colony at the same place where the Dark Fort was? That place has got to be swarming with bad vibes."

"It's a company mining colony," Aiden said. "They're from SignaCorp Metals. There's a metal-rich asteroid belt about 2 AU from Daleth, and SignaCorp started a lucrative operation there about two years ago. When the DSI was done investigating the remains of the Dark Fort on moon 4, they declared its underground structure safe and available for occupation. SignaCorp grabbed it up for pennies and began housing equipment and employees there. It was a good deal, too. A huge, pre-built habitat, complete with functional life-support systems and a shuttle launch facility. Workers established a permanent colony there and called it Bayit. As it grew, they started to bring their families along. Including their children . . ."

Aiden stopped there. He didn't want to think about what they might find when they got there. Assan picked up on the collective mood, looked around at the somber crew, and fell silent himself. Silva looked vacant and said nothing.

Two hours after departing Gateway Station, the *Sun Wolf* popped out of ZPD about 10,000 kilometers from Daleth. That was as close as the drive could bring them to the planet's massive gravity well. Hotah already had the ship at Level One alert in case the hostile ship they were looking for was still in position above the colony. If the *Sun Wolf* could surprise it, they might catch it uncloaked—or even unshielded—and could attack before it reacted.

The *Sun Wolf* began a slow approach with micro pulses from its antimatter drive. The planet Daleth was a Class-I gas giant similar to Jupiter in size, mass, and atmosphere. Among its collection of moons, Daleth-4 was one of the largest. Nearly 3,800 kilometers in diameter, it was slightly bigger than Jupiter's moon Io. It orbited Daleth once every three days at a mean distance of about 460,000 kilometers above the planet's roiling cloud tops, and it was tidally locked so that one side always faced inward toward Daleth. That's where the Dark Fort had been built, hidden from view.

When the *Sun Wolf* approached the outward-facing surface, it leveled off at an altitude of 80 kilometers and began moving laterally over the moon's airless, crater-pocked surface. The only notable feature here was a communication relay station the Bayit colony had installed on this side of the moon to maintain radio contact with the rest of the system.

As the *Sun Wolf* passed over the moon's limb to the back side, the bloated face of Daleth came into full view dead ahead, its turbulent, multicolored cloudscape filling the main screen.

"There!" Hotah said, eyes glued to his tactical screen.

"Main screen. Magnify," Aiden said.

A warship appeared on the forward screen. It was about 2,800 kilometers away and positioned in low orbit not far from the coordinates of the Bayit colony. At first glance, it looked like an ARM Victory-class battle cruiser. Except the propulsion housing at its stern looked larger and more elongated than the standard beamed core antimatter engine. A symbol was stenciled on its hull marked in black lines, along with the number 19. It was the same symbol Lieutenant Bondar had described seeing on the ship that attacked hers, but a different number. The one she saw had been numbered 17.

So, there were at least two Netvor warships in this star system—

"Incoming missile," Hotah said calmly. "Looks like a nuke. At about 300 Gs. Impact 42 seconds."

The *Sun Wolf* had three ways to defend itself against missile attacks—its zero-point-bubble shielding, a ZPD evasive maneuver at 92 percent light speed, or intercepting it by laser cannon. The first option was a passive defense and considered risky against high-accel missiles. The second option was energy expensive and, in this case, would require initiating the zero-point drive uncomfortably close to the Daleth's gravity well. That left the third option, Billy Hotah's favorite. Gunning it down with laser fire before it hit them.

These were the moments that Hotah lived for and, to Aiden's never-ending annoyance, that he'd become infamous for. After launching his own missile toward the enemy ship, Hotah paused for a moment—just long enough for the whole crew to get a good look at the lethal missile screaming toward them—before firing the ship's laser cannon. Aiden gritted his teeth. *Showboating again.* But Hotah never failed. He always hit his mark with time to spare, and Aiden continued to cut him slack. If the adrenaline rush that Hotah got from cutting it close made him a better shot, then so be it.

The *Sun Wolf*'s laser cannon sent a two-gigawatt laser pulse from its business end to pack 50 megajoules of destructive energy into a pinpoint on the nose of the missile's warhead. The resulting blossom of star-hot plasma expanding in empty space was almost as beautiful as it was deadly.

Hotah turned the laser cannon toward the Netvor ship and began targeting it, just in case the missile he'd launched at it didn't do the job. But it was too late.

"Look!" Alvarez said, pointing to the screen.

The Netvor warship made no attempt to intercept the *Sun Wolf*'s incoming missile. Instead, its image became fuzzy and indistinct for a few seconds, then it vanished from sight. The missile behaved as if its targeting computer had suddenly lost contact with the target, and it continued on toward the point of its last known contact. It passed right through the exact spot where the Netvor ship had been and kept going until its autodestruct detonated 30 seconds later.

Aiden exchanged glances with Hotah. "We'll talk about what just happened later. Right now, we need to check on the Bayit colony."

He had a bad feeling about what they would find. It had been over four hours since someone down there had sent a distress call out to Gateway Station, counting the time the transmission took to reach the station and the time it took the *Sun Wolf* to saddle up and get here.

When the *Sun Wolf* pulled into position above the colony, his worst fears were confirmed. The entrance to the original structure had been built at the base of a one-kilometer-high crater wall. The underground habitat occupied a single level with a floor area of over 5,000 square meters and divided into a labyrinth of rooms and halls of all sizes.

There was absolutely nothing left of it now. Except an enormous crater still glowing with molten regolith.

"A nuke," Hotah said with an emotional catch in his voice. "A big one, too."

Alvarez glanced at her sensor readouts. "It's hot down there. Radiation levels off the chart."

Aiden glanced at Dr. Devi. The look on her face was a dark mixture of anger and grief. "There won't be anything, or anyone, left down there to save."

"Silva," Aiden said. "What're the latest census numbers for the Bayit colony?"

Silva stood frozen, his face drained of color, no doubt reliving the loss of his own wife and child to a Netvor bomb in the Gamelan explosion. Aiden had to repeat his question.

Silva looked around, dazed, then snapped out of it and consulted his compad. "As of four months ago, a total of 148 people. Almost a third of them children."

Devi shook her head. "Why . . . ? *Why* would the Netvor do this?"

A dark silence filled the bridge. Devi's question echoed like a death knell. Aiden tried not to think about his own child, three-year-old Bri. How precious she was to him. How horrible the loss of *any* child was. How inhuman it was to deliberately and so violently take the life of a child. Of so many children at once . . .

Inhuman. Nothing could have convinced Aiden more that the Netvor were truly not human. They did not belong in the same universe that he and the rest of humanity inhabited. He vowed that he would do everything in his power to make sure they never did.

Aiden felt his face flush with anger. "Hotah. Any sign of that ship?"

"Nothing. All scans are empty."

"Alvarez?" At Comm/Scan, she had better long-range sensors than Tactical, but slower.

She shook her head. "Not a trace."

"Their cloaking is damn good," Assan said, clearly struggling to recover from his own rage. "And they're obviously able to stay cloaked while under propulsion."

Just one more tactical advantage the Alliance had to deal with.

Hotah turned to look at Aiden. He said nothing, but the message in his eyes was as clear as if spoken out loud. *We need to find the Libera, find them fast, and we need their help.*

~ ~ ~

Two hours later, the *Sun Wolf* pulled out of ZPD back at Gateway Station. It was after 04:30. Aiden and his crew had been awake for nearly 24 hours. He was itching to get to Shénmì Station sooner than later but knew they all needed to catch up on sleep if they were to stay sharp. He radioed Admiral Stegman with a brief account of the Bayit colony massacre, including his conclusions about Netvor advances in combat technology. Stegman was still awake himself. The admiral took both reports with grim resignation.

When Abahem moved the *Sun Wolf* within the station's protective defense perimeter, Aiden had her move the ship farther in, past the station and closer to the voidoid's space-time horizon. She halted just 50 meters from its thrumming electrostatic surface. It was an unorthodox move. Most spacers felt profoundly uncomfortable lingering so close to a voidoid's gaping maw. But it was becoming more common now with the growing possibility that a Netvor warship could approach unseen, pop out of nowhere, and get off a few well-placed shots before disappearing just as quickly.

Aiden ordered a six-hour sleep cycle for the whole crew while Hutton would stand watch, as he always did anyway. He retired to his own quarters. Even though he was bone tired, he couldn't sleep. The biochemicals of rage still coursed through his veins. Visions of the glowing crater that had once been the Bayit colony smoldered in his brain, its raw heat preventing the cool vapors of sleep from closing in around him.

Aiden turned over, fluffed his pillow, and closed his eyes again. He could sense the immense power of the voidoid as it consumed dark energy just 50 meters from where his head lay. It was like a humming inside his head as he drifted off. A musical tone. His musician's knack for perfect pitch told him it was E flat. According to Woo's theory of the living universe, it was the unique song of the nearby voidoid. In Aiden's half-awake state, he was playing that E flat on his old Upton double bass. A long tone held steady with his bow. Soothing him to sleep . . .

Then, for the second time in as many days, he opened his eyes to find Elgin Woo standing next to him, smiling broadly. This time, instead of the red British military coat, he was dressed head to toe like Aladdin of the old Arabian folklore. He donned bright blue balloon pants, a blousy white shirt under a gold-edged purple vest, a red sash around his waist, and a red chiffon turban sitting atop his head at a rakish angle. *How the hell did he do that? And why?*

Woo stepped forward in his gold babouche slippers with their curled-up toes and spoke. This time, Aiden could hear his words very clearly.

"Hello, Aiden! I apologize for contacting you this way, but as you remember, I left Astrocell Beta to explore Astrocell Gamma as a guest of the Luminous Ones. They are intimately related to the voidoids, and that's how I can reach you like this, only when you're very close to a voidoid, as you are now, or actually inside one during a voidjump. But never mind all that. I need to tell you something important right now while I can.

"I'm sure you've recognized the danger you're facing now, that all of humanity is facing. It is *real*, believe me, and it will get worse.

The Luminous Ones have seen it because of their sensitivity to gravitational fields everywhere, and so I see it as well. These offspring of Cardew's, the Netvor, have mastered the manipulation of G-fields. They're using it to cloak their warships in a way that will guarantee their goal of eradicating humanity and dominating the entire galaxy.

"On the bright side, I believe that you are headed in the right direction, Aiden. These '*Trans sapiens*' I'm hearing about have deep knowledge and new solutions for defeating the Netvor by using their own G-fields against them. And of equal, if not greater significance, there is one among them who may hold the most significant key to finding all the gateways in our galaxy, the same quest that I myself am pursuing with the Luminous Ones. She is a brilliant mathematician, and the Netvor are actively seeking her out to brain tap her. If you find these *Trans sapien* people, you must absolutely *not* let her fall into the Netvor's hands. If they acquire her knowledge, it will be the end of human history."

Then Elgin Woo vanished. Leaving only the deep E-flat humming of the voidoid serenading Aiden's growing anxiety.

9

AFTER a less than satisfying period of sleep, visited by memorable dreams that he nonetheless could not remember when he woke, Aiden returned to the bridge and assumed command. When the crew settled in, he directed Pilot Abahem to move the *Sun Wolf* out from its protective cover near the voidoid and into position for voidjump. She guided the ship to align it with the exact point on the voidoid's "surface" corresponding to the astrometric coordinates of their destination, HD 10180, aka Woo's Star. She gave Aiden her thumbs-up, and he signaled her to proceed. The *Sun Wolf*'s antimatter drive kicked in at 3 Gs. In less than one minute, it plunged into the voidoid, a place where time and space did not exist.

Aiden sat back, closed his eyes, and felt the usual tingling sensation of a microsecond voidjump. No bizarre apparitions this time. Only the echoing of Elgin Woo's puzzling words during his bizarre visitation the night before.

When he opened his eyes again, the *Sun Wolf* was well past the voidoid at Woo's Star, cruising at just over five kilometers per second. Silva logged in with the SS *Jakarta*, the UED battle cruiser standing guard at the voidoid's exit point. The *Jakarta* had replaced the ill-fated SS *Wilmington*, the ship destroyed by a cloaked Netvor warship a couple weeks earlier. The *Jakarta* was now on high alert, 24/7.

Hotah confirmed a clean tactical board out to a half million kilometers, and the pilot set course for the star's planetary system. They had about 40 minutes, shipboard time, before reaching Shénmì, and Aiden wanted to pick Hotah's brain about a subject his Tactical Officer knew better than most. "Lieutenant, can you tell me everything you know about this new cloaking tech the Netvor are using?"

Hotah turned from his console. "I can tell you what I've picked up from the intelligence reports. That stuff is mostly harvested from eyewitness accounts in the field, including from survivors of destroyed ships. But I can tell you my own conclusions, and conjectures, based on everything that's been documented, if that's what you want."

"That's exactly what I want."

Hotah swiveled his chair around 180 degrees to face Aiden directly. "I think the Netvor's cloaking tech is derived straight from their shielding tech. It's all about gravity fields."

Hotah said nothing more. By nature, he was a man of few words. Not because he had nothing to say. On the contrary, Billy Hotah was one of the smartest people Aiden had ever met. Real-world smart. If encouraged, he could expound at great length, and with great acumen, on any topic that interested him. But only if the encouragement came from the right person.

"Go on," Aiden said, always hoping he was the right person but never sure.

Hotah nodded. "Remember the shielding capabilities Cardew had on those two warships he stole, the RMV *Markos* and the SS *Conquest*? The *Markos* used it five years ago at Friendship Station to defeat the simultaneous fire it took from two UED battle cruisers. It emerged without a scratch before blasting those two ships and going on to wipe out the rest of the battle group. Single-handedly."

"Remember it?" Aiden said. "How could I forget?"

It was one of the worst defeats in UED history, thanks in large part to the *Markos*'s unbeatable shielding and to the UED's inadequate shielding on their own ships.

"Then later," Hotah continued, "when we encountered the *Markos* out here at Woo's Star, we couldn't touch it. We tried laser cannons, missiles, and rail guns. Everything just bounced off, deflected away from the target."

"Right," Aiden said. "The way Dr. Ebadi explained it at the time was that Cardew's scientists had figured out how to use the Füzfa Effect in the real world. By stacking superconducting electromagnets, they could generate powerful EM fields to bend space-time in the same way a mass does in space. Bending space-time *inward* to simulate a gravity well. Cardew used it to create his synthetic gravity bombs and tried to shut down the voidoids with them."

"That's right," Hotah said. "And from there, they moved on to shielding. His scientists figured out how to manipulate the EM fields to bend space-time in the *opposite* direction, outward, to simulate 'negative' gravity. A force that repels instead of attracts. Using the same stacked EM generators, they could amplify a negative gravity field and distribute it around the ship as a protective envelope. It shielded the ship from particle beams and lasers as well as kinetic weapons like missiles and rail guns."

When Hotah fell silent again, Aiden said, "And . . .?"

Hotah folded his hands in his lap and sat back. "So now I think they've gone one step further by going back to the original design of bending space-time inward to simulate a gravity well, but with the ship at the bottom of the well. And they've done it in such a way that bends light, or any kind of electromagnetic radiation, *around* the ship, preventing it from reflecting back to be picked up by sensor scans. Presto: a fully functional cloaking field that makes the ship virtually invisible to both active scans and passive sensors. It's essentially the same principle as microlensing but with a twist."

It was ingenious, Aiden had to admit. When a beam of light enters a strong gravitational field, it will bend its path due to the warping of space-time caused by gravity. Instead of hitting the object that's creating the gravitational field, it follows a curved trajectory around it. But the last time Aiden checked, that only applied to supermassive gravitational fields, like the gargantuan black holes at the heart of galaxies.

When Aiden pointed that out, Hotah said, "That's right. In a natural setting. But with enough energy and a properly tuned EM field, the Füzfa Effect can be manipulated to *simulate* a high-intensity G-field within a limited radius, just big enough to surround the ship."

"Right," Aiden said. "But it's not intense enough to act as a shield against weapons. It can't repel high-energy beam weapons or high-G missiles. Their cloaking can't double as a shield in combat."

"Correct. It's only effective against the kinds of radiation an enemy would use to detect its presence. But that includes every kind of scan we've got—radar, side-looking radar, stereoptic lasers, thermographic mapping sensors, photometers, UV and neutrino detectors, quark resonance scanners, and magnetometers. The works. Hence, the cloaking effect."

"Impressive. But can their ships be cloaked and shielded at the same time?"

"No," Hotah said. "That's the thing. It's either one or the other. The EM field cannot be shaped in two different ways at the same time. The cloak won't act as a shield against weapons, but it *will* prevent our targeting computers from 'seeing' it, and that means we can't calculate accurate firing solutions. You can't hit a target you can't see."

"Clever," Aiden said. "What about using their weapons when they're cloaked?"

"No," Hotah said. "They can't use their weapons when their cloaking is engaged. The space-time warpage around the ship prevents it. The warpage won't allow them to even target their prey. They'll always need to uncloak before firing."

"What about firing their weapons when shielded? We've seen that they can do that."

"Yes, but that's only because they're able to leave small sections of the ship unshielded, like weapons ports, while the rest of the ship is protected. The *Sun Wolf* can do that, too."

"But they're not doing that now, are they?" Aiden had read the recent tactical reports.

"Not as much as they were, at least. That's because Alliance warships figured it out and started targeting those exposed ports to blow up Netvor ships. So now they shield the entire ship and only drop the shield just before firing their weapons. The problem with that is it takes time to power the shields back up, and they're vulnerable during that time window. So now I think they're starting to use cloaking more in combat situations, rather than relying on shielding. They can uncloak, fire, and recloak within seconds, then disappear before we can target them. That way, they don't even need shielding because no one can see where they went."

Aiden nodded. "That's why they prefer attacking single, isolated ships. Their best strategy is to stay cloaked, sneak up on their target, uncloak, and fire. The perfect way to destroy an enemy ship before it has a chance to see them and fire back. And if there's no other enemy ship in the vicinity, they're not vulnerable to attack by a second ship while they're trying to power up their shielding. They just recloak and go on their merry way."

"Correct again," Hotah said. "Hit-and-run is their best strategy, picking off single poorly shielded ships, one at a time. Like our warships guarding the exit points of the voidoids. Like the *Wilmington* a couple weeks ago. Then it becomes a war of attrition. The more single ships they destroy, the fewer we have left to guard all our assets, and the more we resort to assigning single ships for the job. Vicious circle."

"Last question," Aiden said. "Do we know yet if they can voidjump while cloaked?"

"No and yes," Hotah said. "No, because they can't *enter* a voidoid while cloaked. For the same reason they can't do it while their shielding is up. Both capabilities depend on creating synthetic gravity fields. And ever since Cardew tried to shut down the voidoids with his gravity drones, the voidoids don't tolerate gravitational anomalies like that anymore. The voidoid will either shut down before the ship enters, or it'll swallow the ship whole and make it disappear forever. The Netvor must know that, too."

"And the 'yes' part?"

Hotah paused for a moment before answering. "This is conjecture only," he said, "but I believe that a Netvor ship, equipped with a really good AI like the Omicron series, can make low velocity voidjumps virtually undetected. If the ship shuts down its cloak a couple seconds before it enters a voidoid, then powers it back up a couple seconds after it emerges at its destination, it could avoid detection at either end of the jump. Surveillance sensors are always positioned kilometers away from the exit point to catch the usual high-velocity voidjumps. By the time a slower Netvor ship is within detection range, it's already cloaked."

"That must be how those two Netvor warships got into the Alpha-2 Hydri system without being detected," Aiden said. "The one that attacked the *Essex* and the one that nuked the Bayit colony. Right under Gateway's nose."

"That'd be my guess," Hotah said. "Theoretically, any number of Netvor vessels could have slipped past the Gateway and already be operating inside the Apha-2 Hydri system."

"And if they can get past Northern Gateway into Alpha-2 Hydri," Aiden said, "they can just as easily leave the system through Southern Gateway, right into the Solar System." A shiver went up his spine at the thought.

Both men fell silent for a moment before Hotah turned back to his tactical board. Several minutes later, just after 12:30 local time, the *Sun Wolf* pulled out of ZPD in the vicinity of Shénmì Station and began moving in slowly.

Like most research outposts, Shénmì Station was spartan compared to the major strategic stations like Gateway and Friendship Stations. Yet it was the first one established in Astrocell Beta, the largest and most important. Its purpose was to study the remarkable planet it orbited, Shénmì, first discovered by Elgin Woo in

2217. The research operation was called the Shénmì Project, and its chief director from its inception was Aiden's wife, Dr. Skye Landen.

When the *Sun Wolf* pulled within five kilometers, Aiden adjourned to the ready room, linked into the station's comms network, and initiated a call to Skye's personal comm. No answer. Which was unusual. Skye always kept her personal comm with her, strapped to her wrist, everywhere she went. Especially when she knew Aiden was soon to arrive.

He called Skye's office. The assistant director answered, said Skye hadn't come in yet and suggested calling her lab. When he called the exomycology lab, where Skye spent most of her working hours, the tech there said the same thing: Skye hadn't been to the lab this morning. No one seemed particularly concerned. Except Aiden. It was beyond unusual. He'd never had trouble reaching Skye the moment the *Sun Wolf* pulled in. Something was wrong. He knew it.

His mouth went dry. A cold sweat dampened his forehead. That all-too-familiar black ocean of fear began seeping in through the cracks, threatening to burst through the walls. Fear for himself was bad enough. But fear for his wife and child was infinitely worse. He began a cyclic breathing exercise to suppress his impulse to panic.

It didn't work.

10

Domain Day 68, 2223

Pilot Abahem moved the ship in slowly and brought it to a halt at a half kilometer out. Despite its preeminence in Astrocell Beta, Shénmì Station's docking hangar could accommodate only smaller transport and utility vessels. Larger voidships like the *Sun Wolf* had to use their own transport shuttles to ferry personnel to and from the station.

Dr. Devi, Commander Silva, and Pilot Abahem agreed to stay on board while the others prepared to take the shuttle over to the station. Silva contacted the station's docking crew and began overseeing the transfer of AMP's new telescopic mirror. While Alvarez and Assan were leaving the bridge for the shuttle bay, Aiden told Hotah to wait up while Aiden made one last call, this time to the station's security chief, Colonel Marcus Crestfield. He asked Crestfield if there had been any recent security alarms or otherwise unusual activity.

"No," Crestfield said. "Nothing I know of. Why? What's up?"

Aiden didn't want to cause undue alarm, but he could tell that the colonel's invisible trouble antenna was already humming. "Nothing's up, Colonel. Just a routine check. Can't be too careful these days. Thank you."

Aiden signed out before Crestfield could respond and turned to Hotah, who'd overheard the exchange. "Follow me, Lieutenant."

When the two were alone in the elevator, Hotah glanced at him and said, "The armory?"

"Correct. I'm getting a bad feeling about this."

Hotah gave him that *I-told-you-so* look but said nothing.

The *Sun Wolf*'s armory packed a variety of handheld weapons locked under tight security, accessible only by the captain and the XO. They were all projectile weapons, mostly "smart guns" designed for use in a variety of extreme environments, both pressurized and hard vacuum, and in zero gravity. If the weapons were to be used inside a spaceborne habitat like a ship or orbital station, only frangible bullets were allowed, rounds that fragmented on impact. It reduced the risk of a stray round puncturing a pressurized hull in deep space.

Hotah looked lovingly at the array of weapons before him, like a wolf licking his chops.

"Down, boy," Aiden said. "I want us both to pack handguns only, no carbines, nothing to alarm the station's personnel. We can do open-carry in thigh holsters. That's not an unusual sight over there, with military and security people coming and going."

Hotah nodded with a resigned sigh, tearing his gaze away from his favorite weapon, the SR-13 Spacer Carbine. It was a hefty assault-style weapon with three barrels intended for use on a planetary surface. "Too bad. My SR-13 can fire shock rounds. Those are piezo-electric projectiles that generate an electrical charge on impact. Most effective against a Netvor."

"Why is that?"

"Why? Do you realize how electrically conductive carbon nanotube is? Twice as conductive as copper. A Netvor skeleton made of carbon nanotubes would light up if I hit one of those freaks with a shock round. Massive nerve disruption. Might not kill it, but it would immobilize it long enough for you to walk up and put a bullet through its eye socket. And that *would* kill it. Are you sure you don't want me to bring my SR along?"

Aiden thought about it but decided to stay with a low-profile presence on board the station. Hotah shrugged. "Okay, boss."

But when Aiden grabbed his usual midweight .40-caliber pistol, Hotah stopped him. "That's a nice piece, Captain. But if you anticipate bumping into one of these Netvor psychos, I suggest something more powerful."

Aiden raised his eyebrows at him. There was only one handgun in their armory with more punch than the .40 caliber. It was the .45-caliber Titan, and it was a beast. The eight-shot semiautomatic pistol could push a 325-grain slug out of a six-inch barrel with 60,000 psi barrel pressure. Something you didn't want to fire inside low-G environments without your back up against a wall. They were issued only to the military, and only for ground-based operations. By law, they weren't allowed aboard *any* spaceborne vessels—frangible rounds or not. Two of them were here, in the *Sun Wolf*'s armory, only because Lieutenant William Hotah had special dispensations from the highest levels.

Aiden shook his head. "I can't use one of those."

"Why not?"

"I've never fired one before, but I know they kick like a mule. I probably couldn't hit an asteroid from 10 meters with one."

Hotah nodded patiently. "Okay. But consider this. The Netvor have skeletal systems made of multiwalled carbon nanotubes. That includes their skulls. You said it yourself, a hundred times stronger than steel. A head shot with a solid full-metal-jacket round is the most reliable way to stop one of these bastards before they get to you and rip your head off. One of the barrels of my SR-13 can fire a high-powered armor-piercing round. That would do the job. But, since you don't want me to bring that, the .45-caliber Titan is one of the few handguns with any chance of doing the job in close quarters."

Aiden's weapon of choice suddenly felt smaller in his hand.

"Your midweight .40 caliber," Hotah continued, "might be able to knock a Netvor down with three or four fast taps to the head, but it's not going to drop one before it gets to you. Unless, of course, you're lucky enough to hit an eye socket. That'd be an unobstructed shot to the brain, an instant stopper. But would you bet your life on one lucky shot in an attack scenario?"

"I get your point, Hotah. But if I can't shoot straight with that thing, it's worse than useless. With my .40 caliber, at least I'd stand a chance. Besides, we're wasting time. We need to get over there now and make sure Skye is okay."

Hotah shrugged again. "Have it your way, Captain. But at least load up with these." He handed Aiden a box of 200-grain full-metal-jacket cartridges. "Frangible bullets are useless against skulls made of carbon nanotubes."

"Right," Aiden said, pressing the new cartridges into his clip, growing more tense with the sound of each one clicking in place. "And anyway, you'll have my back with your Titan, right?"

"Roger that."

Hotah grabbed his tactical backpack and stuffed it with a few essentials. They strapped on thigh holsters and secured their weapons. Hotah's Titan looked comically oversized sitting inside his standard thigh holster. But to Aiden, it was a reassuring look. "Let's go."

Assan and Alvarez were waiting for them in the ship's shuttle bay. They eyed the holstered handguns, and Alvarez said, "Are we expecting trouble?"

"Not really," Aiden said casually. "But the Service recommends heightened precautions these days and has authorized handgun carry for its ranking officers."

A slight lie. But a believable one.

Lieutenant Assan looked concerned. "Should I be armed, too?"

Aiden made himself look relaxed and amiable. "No, no. It's just routine. You and Alvarez are free to wander around the station all you want, but stick together. Hotah and I will be visiting Skye. Then I want us all back aboard the ship in three hours."

Assan piloted the shuttle across to the station's docking hangar. Even after four years of construction, the Shénmì Station's cavernous hangar area was still open to the cold vacuum of space. Along with several utility vessels docked there, a small cargo carrier sat forward on the launch ramp, preparing to meet *Sun Wolf* to off-load the telescope mirror.

The shuttle docked with a dull clunk and was secured in place by powerful magnetic clamps. Since the hangar was unpressurized, the station relied on pressurized boarding bridges to transfer personnel between docked vessels and the station's interior. The four of them waited inside the shuttle's airlock until they heard the muffled thunk of the boarding bridge mating with the outer hatch to make an airtight seal. The hatch opened, and they walked the 20-meter length to another hatch that opened into the station's interior. Once inside, they were greeted by security personnel who checked IDs and ushered them through the XRF scanner.

Aiden stopped there, looked at his chrono, and spoke to Assan and Avarez. "Be back here no later than 15:30. Got it?"

They nodded and headed off down Corridor D, which Aiden knew was the quickest way to the station's commissary. While he and Hotah headed off in the opposite direction, he filled the lieutenant in on Skye's failure to answer her comms and her apparent absence from her usual workplaces. Before boarding the lift down to the personnel quarters, Aiden made one more call to Skye's comm. Still no answer.

Inside the elevator car, Aiden's stomach began to churn. He sensed Hotah's subtle shift into hunter mode. As the car came to a stop, they both unsnapped the safety straps on their holsters. The elevator door opened to a wide, empty corridor. It seemed usually quiet. But then it was the middle of a workday. Most of the residents were probably away at their jobs. Still . . .

As they neared Skye's quarters, Aiden assigned Hotah to patrol the corridors on either side while he checked Skye's apartment.

"Is that wise?" Hotah said. "Shouldn't I back you up, at least past the front door into the apartment?"

Hotah had a point, but if trouble was afoot, Aiden didn't want them both cornered in the same enclosed space at once. Plus, Hotha could watch for any trouble approaching from the outside. Hotah didn't like it but agreed.

Now by himself, Aiden turned a corner and walked down the corridor past several other apartments. He came to Skye's door and knocked, calling her name. Nothing. He reached for the locking latch. It was unlocked.

Aiden removed his weapon and held it out in front of him with one hand. With the other hand, he opened the door swiftly and stepped inside the short entryway. The door closed automatically behind him, locked to the outside. He called Skye's name. No response. He turned the corner from the entryway into the living area. What he saw made his heart stop.

Skye stood facing him, her eyes wide with terror. A tall, pale-skinned man stood directly behind her. He had one very large hand clasped tightly around her neck, just loose enough for her to breathe. In his other hand, he held a cruel-looking black pistol aimed directly at Aiden's head. It was a flechette gun, capable of firing a high-velocity stream of tiny flechettes at 220 per second, more than enough to transform Aiden's head into a bloody pulp in about the same amount of time.

The man spoke with a low, resonant voice, utterly devoid of inflection. "Drop the gun now. Do not speak."

Skye looked terrified but not panicked, her eyes filled with rage. The man's hand around her neck had completely immobilized her in front of him, using her body as a shield. Only his head was visible above Skye's.

Aiden was too stunned to respond. The man tightened his long, articulated fingers around Skye's neck until she could no longer breathe. Her face paled, desperation in her eyes.

"I said drop the gun. Now. Or your wife dies."

"Okay, okay!" Aiden lowered his pistol, bent at the waist, and laid it on the floor at his feet. The man loosened his grip on Skye's neck. She coughed, struggled to catch her breath, then started to breathe heavily.

"Good," the man said, his voice sounding neither pleased nor displeased. The pupils of his dark brown eyes widened suddenly, alarmingly. The entire circle of the iris in both eyes were now unfathomable black pits. Deliberately revealing his identity. *A Netvor.*

"You know what I am now, Captain Macallan. And you know what I can do. I could easily decapitate your wife with one quick squeeze of my hand. So do exactly what I say."

Aiden swallowed and nodded. "Where is my daughter? Where's Bri?"

The smile on the Netvor's face looked almost real, but his eyes held no empathy. "She is safe. For now. Do as I say, and she will remain safe. Do you understand?"

Aiden glanced at Skye, questioning. She spoke, her voice sounding hoarse. "Bri is safe. She's with the Campbells."

He could breathe now, just a little. The Campbells were a married couple who ran a combination preschool and playroom for children on the station. It would be the normal place for Bri to be at this time of day, while Skye was at work.

Aiden glanced impulsively at his gun lying on the floor at his feet. The Netvor saw it and said, "Kick the gun away from you. Far away."

Aiden complied, sending the pistol skidding across the floor three meters away. Now he regretted his decision to enter Skye's apartment alone, without Hotah. But considering the utter control the Netvor had over the situation, he doubted it would have made a difference.

"What do you want?"

Again, the synthetic smile. His face was pale, unusually smooth and without wrinkles. He had no facial hair, but the hair on his head was thick and black, cut short. His eyes were wide set, and his nose was long and aquiline, reminiscent of Jo's. His mouth looked small with thin lips. His rectangular head was perched elegantly atop a long, swanlike neck. He wore a nondescript beige work suit with a LifeLine insignia embroidered on one side of his chest. He stood spine straight and preternaturally still, no shifting of weight from foot to foot. Aiden detected no physical signs of breathing, no rise and fall of the thorax.

The Netvor finally said, "You must know what I want."

With one hand still clasped around Skye's neck, the Netvor used his other hand to place his weapon into a thigh holster and reach into a pocket. He pulled out a telegem crystal and showed it to Aiden. *Jo's telegem crystal.* "I believe you've been looking for this, correct?"

Aiden swallowed hard. Now he understood.

The Netvor's eyes, black pupils wide and deep, burned into Aiden's. "I want you to open this for me."

11

WOO'S STAR SYSTEM
(HD 10180)
Shénmì Station

Domain Day 68, 2223

"You can call me Frank," the Netvor said, blank faced.

Frank. Really? The statement seemed terrifyingly absurd for about a half second. Then it was just plain terrifying. Aiden tried to keep himself from trembling and pretended to relax. "Looks like a telegem crystal. So what?"

"Very good," Frank said, playing along with Aiden's feigned cluelessness. "It happens to be the telegem that your friend Jo intended for you. It never got to you because the messenger never had it in the first place. In a fortunate turn of events, I intercepted it."

Aiden suddenly felt sick. "You 'intercepted' it? What did you do to Jo?"

"I did nothing to her," Frank said, pretending innocence. "I tried to, of course. I thought her telegem massage was already on its way to you, so I had no recourse but to find her and force the information out of her. But after a brief chase—she is surprisingly fast for a mutant—she escaped on the shuttle down to the planet. What I didn't know at the time was that she'd left the crystal in the messenger's mailbox when she couldn't find him in person. She assumed that he'd pick it up on his way out to catch his flight. She didn't know that he'd already left for Luna and that her telegem would end up just sitting in his office unattended. I didn't know it either. But once I figured it out, it was easy to break in and retrieve it. Then all I had to do was wait about three weeks for you to get here so you could open the telegem for me . . . And here we are."

Frank smiled again, his grasp on Skye's neck just loose enough for her to breathe. She was doing her best to hold up, but stark panic was clearly just beneath the surface. Noting her distress without sympathy, Frank said to Aiden, "And now you will open the telegem for me."

"I doubt there's anything in that message that would be of any use to you," Aiden said, stalling for time. "Probably just a greeting and mundane updates of daily life up here."

Frank's eyes narrowed. His grip on Skye's neck tightened a fraction more. "Don't play games with me, Aiden Macallan. We both know what's in Jo's message. I have listening devices everywhere on this station, including personnel quarters. If Jo had spoken the coordinates out loud to your wife, the exact numerical sequences that she encrypted into the telegem, we wouldn't be having this little encounter. That did not happen. But now I have the telegem. You are the only one who can unlock it. And you will do it now."

Skye gasped for breath, her eyes wide with fear, both hands clawing at Frank's iron grip.

"Okay! Stop hurting her. I'll do it."

"Wise choice," Frank said, loosening his grip again. He extended his other hand out toward Aiden, the crystal resting in his palm. "Here. Take it from my hand. Your wife and I will stay just like this until it's done. No more talk. No more games."

Aiden's hand shook as he took the crystal. "I can unlock it, but I don't have a reader."

With his free hand, Frank retrieved his pistol from his holster. He held it casually but ready. Then he smiled with a hint of sneer. "Not a problem. We will use your wife's reader. The crystal Jo used belonged to your wife and can be deciphered by her personal reader."

Aiden knew Skye kept her telegem reader somewhere in her apartment, but he didn't know where. And he'd forgotten what it looked like. He glanced at Skye. She nodded back reassuringly.

"And remember," Frank said menacingly, "I know how these telegems work. I know that when it is successfully unlocked, the embedded indicator changes color. Anything short of that, and your wife dies. Understood?"

Aiden nodded. He had no choice. He would not sacrifice Skye's life, or Bri's, for the secret location of the Libera's colony. Call it cowardly, call it a shameless retreat from the greater good. Aiden would freely admit to all of it. But right now, the lives of his wife and child meant more to him than anything else in the universe. More than his own life.

The unlocking sequence was different for every set of crystals. It was secretly programmed by each user. As he had done back on Luna, he held the telegem between his thumb and ring finger, the prints of both fingers in full contact with the faceted surface. He raised the crystal to his right eye and stared into it without blinking, counted off three seconds, then held the crystal to his left eye and did the same.

The telegem grew warm to touch, the signal to proceed to the last step. He brought the crystal to his mouth and spoke the word, "Cernunnos." The dark-blue Triquetra inside brightened until it glowed electric blue. Aiden held the crystal out for Frank to show him it was now unlocked.

"Good," the Netvor said. "Now your wife's reader."

Aiden shrugged. "I don't know where it is."

Frank's grip tightened again. "More games?"

"No, no. Honestly. I don't know where she keeps it."

Maybe it was the desperate sound of truth in Aiden's voice, along with the plausibility of what he'd said, that caused Frank to loosen his grip. He spoke over Skye's head. "Where is your reader, Skye?"

As an added layer of security, every telegem reader was usually disguised as some unassuming object. Like Aiden's figurine of Gaia back at his Luna residence. But Aiden couldn't remember how Skye had disguised her reader. Only she could identify it.

Skye coughed once, drew in a deep breath, and said, "It's on the kitchen shelf, over there next to the sink. It's the orange flashlight. The MiniStar."

Frank nodded to Aiden and said, "Get it."

MiniStar flashlights were common on the station where frequent power outages made them indispensable. Everyone had one in their quarters or carried one on their person. They were often made in whimsical colors with cheerful patterns, probably to counter the frustration people felt when forced to use them.

While Aiden couldn't remember exactly what Skye's reader looked like, he was sure that it was *not* a MiniStar flashlight. He glanced again at Skye, questioning. She gave him a look that only he could read. A deception was afoot.

He held his hands up in surrender. "Okay. I'm going to walk over there right now and get the reader. Please do not hurt her anymore."

MiniStars came in various sizes. This one was about eight inches long, nearly two inches in diameter, and flared out at the lens. He picked it up and was surprised by how heavy it felt. Even if it had been converted to a telegem reader, it would not be that heavy. It occurred to him that this MiniStar might conceal something altogether different.

He brought it back and spoke to Frank. "You do know that a personal reader can be actuated only by its owner, right? No one else can do it."

Frank eyed the flashlight with suspicion. "That's her telegem reader? A flashlight?"

Aiden shrugged. "All personal telegem readers are disguised as something else. You must know that, too."

Frank nodded, still skeptical. "Yes, I know that. And I know that readers are voice-activated. But where is the crystal receptacle?"

"The lens cowling unscrews," Skye said, "and the reader receptacle is underneath."

Aiden held the flashlight out, but Frank said to him, "Show me."

Aiden swallowed hard. This was not going well. He had no idea how much of what Skye had said was deception.

She shook her head and said, "The cowling is locked until I voice-activate the entire reader. The voice analyzer is in the flashlight's tail end."

Frank raised his pistol with his free hand. He aimed it at Aiden. "Give it to her now."

Aiden handed the flashlight to Skye, butt end first. Still immobilized by Frank's grip, she grasped it in her right hand.

"Activate the reader," Frank said, tightening his grip on Skye's neck as a reminder of how easily he could kill her.

The moment of truth. Aiden's heart pounded.

Skye held the flashlight upside down in a tight grip and brought the butt end of it to her mouth. But instead of speaking the code word, she snapped her arm downward and back to jab the flared end of the flashlight into Frank's thigh. A bright blue electrical discharge flashed from the point of contact. Smoke rose from it.

Frank's eyes went wide. His mouth opened but no sound came from it. His whole body went rigid, then convulsed. His grip on Skye's neck went slack. He dropped his pistol. Skye held the stunner in place until she could free herself. Frank fell to the floor. Skye stumbled to one side and landed on her knees, just one meter from where Aiden's pistol lay.

Aiden made a dash for the pistol. But Frank had already recovered. He swiped at Aiden's ankle as he passed by. Aiden tripped and landed on his back. Lightning bolts of pain exploded from his ankle. The telegem crystal slipped out of his hand and rolled across the floor.

Frank rose up on his knees and reached out to recover his own pistol.

"Aiden!" Skye shouted. She had picked up his gun but was in no position to shoot. She tossed the weapon toward him. He caught it, still lying on his back. He fumbled with the pistol until he had it firmly in hand. His finger found the inside of the trigger guard. He rolled over just in time to see Frank grab hold of his own gun and aim it at him.

Aiden took aim at Frank's head and squeezed the trigger. The semiautomatic was set for a three-shot pull. All three slugs hit Frank in the face. Unfortunately, none of them found an eye socket. Instead, the metal-jacketed bullets ricocheted off the Netvor's skull, leaving craters ripped free of skin and tendon. The impacts knocked the Netvor to the floor again.

Aiden tried to stand, but pain shot up his ankle. He collapsed and fell to the floor. He lost his grip on his pistol. Again, Frank recovered quickly. He grabbed his pistol and aimed it at Aiden's head. *Uh-oh. Game over—*

At that instant, the front door exploded open, its locking mechanism shattered by one shot from Hotah's .45-caliber Titan. Stunned, Frank turned to face the opened door. Just in time for Billy Hotah to blast another round straight through Frank's left eye socket. The Netvor's head exploded. Purple blood, brain tissue, and fragments of carbon-black skull sprayed the wall behind him. The body slumped and collapsed to the floor. A motionless, inert object.

Hotah moved in and stood over the corpse, a grim smile on his face. He looked over at Aiden and said, "Like that."

Emergency alarms blared throughout Shénmì Station, punctuated every 30 seconds by an automated voice directing all personnel to "shelter in place."

Aiden ignored the pain in his ankle and got to his feet. Skye rushed over to him. They embraced. She pulled back and looked at him. "Not the greeting I had in mind for us."

"You're alive and in my arms," Aiden said. "That's the best greeting possible."

Then he glanced at the "flashlight" still in her hand. "A stun gun? Disguised as a flashlight? Seriously?"

"Seriously illegal," Skye said. "It packs about three million volts with an electrical charge of nearly three microcoulombs."

"Holy shit. How did you . . .?"

"Jo helped me build it. She knows a lot about Netvor anatomy."

Aiden remembered Hotah's comment about the extreme electro-conductivity of carbon nanotubes. He beamed at her. "You are amazing."

Hotah made a polite cough just loud enough to be heard over the alarm klaxons and said, "Hate to break this up, you two, but Station Security will be swarming this place in a minute. They're going to be jacked up. I suggest placing our weapons on the floor and standing calmly with our hands visible in front of us until they show up."

Hotah gathered up the fallen handguns and placed them on the floor next to his own.

They didn't have to wait long.

12

Domain Day 68, 2223

A contingent of five armed and hyper-alert security types arrived at Skye's apartment. Three of them burst through the open door, weapons raised. The other two remained on guard just outside the door. The lead officer, a tall woman with a shock of red hair and pale blue eyes, took in the scene quickly and professionally. She saw that none of the room's three living occupants had weapons in their hands and saw three guns lying on the floor. She relaxed a fraction but still barked out, "Don't move! Hands on your head."

Her two companions split off and quickly searched the rest of the apartment, weapons held up and ready, while she kept an eye on her three captives. Her stance relaxed even more when she recognized Skye. "Dr. Landen? What the hell? Are you okay?"

"Yes, Sergeant Flynn. I'm fine. We've had a bit of an incident here."

Flynn glanced around, saw the Netvor on the floor with only half of a head, and said, "Uh-huh. I can see that."

Then she motioned toward Aiden and Hotah. "And who are these two?"

"This is my husband, Captain Aiden Macallan, and his Tactical Officer, Lieutenant William Hotah. They're here from the *Sun Wolf*."

Flynn's eyes widened in recognition. Her gaze lingered on Hotah's face longer than would be considered respectful. Hotah had that effect on people upon first meeting. She lowered her weapon and nodded a greeting to Aiden and Hotah.

Her two team members emerged from their search. One called out, "All clear."

Flynn directed one of them, a man she called Kurt, to stay with her while the other one joined the rest of the team standing guard outside the door. She spoke into her wrist comm. "HQ. Douse the alarms but maintain the shelter-in-place order until further notice."

The screeching alarms suddenly stopped, leaving Aiden's ears still ringing.

Flynn said, "You guys can relax. And you can reclaim your weapons."

But she did a double take, then frowned when she saw Hotah's Titan .45 lying on the floor. "Is that what I think it is?"

Hotah nodded. "Yes, it is."

"You know how illegal that thing is? Especially here on this station. Do you have papers for it?"

"Yes, ma'am, I do," Hotah said, smiling pleasantly. "Signed by Admiral Stegman. Want to see it?"

Flynn let out a sigh, declining to call Hotah's bluff. "No need. But can anyone tell me what the hell happened here?"

"Long story," Aiden said, still undecided on how much to reveal. "But to start with, that dead man over there is a Netvor agent. He broke into Skye's apartment and threatened her life, demanding information he thought she had. I got worried when Skye failed to answer her comms, so Lieutenant Hotah and I came here to investigate. We found the Netvor holding Skye hostage. There was a standoff. Shots were fired. The Netvor was killed."

"A Netvor agent? Here on the station? How is that possible? Everyone who comes here is meticulously vetted beforehand, and everyone is scanned by the XRF when they come aboard."

"That's a very good question," Aiden said. He didn't want to imply any undue lapses in station security, so he offered another possibility. "We think the Netvor are making extraordinary advances in concealment technologies. That might include tricking the XRF scans."

Flynn shook her head. "Great. Just great."

She put on latex gloves, walked over to the corpse, and picked up the fallen flechette pistol, holding it up by the trigger guard with two fingers as if it were a scorpion about to strike. Scowling at the obscene weapon, she dropped it into an evidence bag that Kurt held open for her, then began rummaging through the corpse's pockets. She pulled out an ID badge and showed it to Aiden. "Says his name is Franklin Simmons, and he's a Life Support tech. Kurt, check our census database for this guy."

Flynn turned back to the corpse, lifting its left arm to get a better look at the Netvor's wrist comm. It looked like any other standard-issue wrist comm, except for the tiny indicator light on its underside. It was blinking red. Flynn reached for it.

"Don't touch that!" Hotah barked.

Flynn froze, then looked back at Hotah, obviously annoyed. "And why not?"

"It's a detonator. And it's primed."

"What?" Flynn stood and stepped back from the corpse. Aiden and Skye followed suit.

Hotah turned to Skye. "Give me your tricked-out flashlight, Skye. The one with the three-million-volt surprise."

The cold focus in Hotah's voice silenced everyone in the room. Skye retrieved her flashlight, aka stun gun, activated it, and handed it to Hotah. He knelt next to the corpse, placed the business end of the device on the outer edge of the wrist comm, and triggered it. Brilliant white light flashed with a jarring staccato crackle, leaving the wrist comm in smoking ruin.

Hotah stood and casually handed the flashlight back to Skye. "All clear."

Flynn looked at Hotah. "What the . . . ?"

"Suicide contingency," Hotah said. "What else would you expect from a Netvor agent?"

Flynn shook her head. "But there're no explosives anywhere on his body."

"It's a remote detonator," Hotah said. "Have your team search all the nooks and crannies of the station, start with locations at key structural points."

Flynn's eyes widened in sudden realization. "Like Gamelon Station . . ."

Aiden swallowed hard and glanced at Skye. But she was already busy calling the Campbells to check on Bri and Rene. She listened, breathed a sigh of relief, and said to Aiden, "The Campbells were a little rattled by all the alarms, but the kids are all okay."

Aiden let out a long-held breath, then limped to a chair and sat, rubbing his ankle. It hurt like hell but didn't feel broken. Flynn left the room with Kurt to talk with the rest of her team outside the door. Skye leaned into Aiden and whispered, "Where is the telegem crystal?"

"Oh shit!" Aiden scanned the floor around him. He'd last seen the crystal rolling out of his hand across the floor just after he'd gone down.

He was about to start crawling around in search for it, when Hotah said, "Looking for this?"

The spherical, blue-tinted crystal sat in the palm of Hotah's outstretched hand. The room's ambient light sparkled off its multifaceted surface. Who'd have thought that such a small, insignificant bobble could hold the key to humanity's survival? "Well, you're just full of surprises today, aren't you, Mr. Hotah?"

Hotah smiled with simulated humility and handed Aiden the crystal. When they heard Flynn make a move to reenter the apartment, Aiden deftly dropped the crystal into his pocket.

Flynn entered frowning. "I just got the lowdown on this Franklin Simmons character. He arrived here at the station just two months ago. He was an employee of LifeLine, a private contractor that the Service uses to maintain its off-world life-support systems.

Simmons passed all the vetting and security checks, including XRF scans. Our medical examiner is on his way now to remove the body and clean up. I suspect he'll confirm that Simmons is one of these Netvor creatures."

Skye shook her head. "That's troubling."

"You bet it is!" Flynn said. "If the Netvor are churning out new models this good, there's no way to screen them in a crowd. They could be everywhere now. Even more here on the station."

On that disturbing note, Flynn and her team departed. Minutes later, the ME and his assistant came in, collected the corpse, and cleaned up the mess. Neither of them said a word. The shelter-in-place order was lifted, and Assan and Alvarez showed up at Skye's door looking concerned. The sight of the door's shattered locking mechanism didn't help. Aiden reassured them and said that he'd explain later. He ordered them back to the ship and said that he and Hotah would follow shortly.

When the three of them were alone again, Aiden held a finger up to his mouth and made a deliberate glance at the ceiling. Frank had mentioned having listening devices planted everywhere, for sure in this room, Jo's room, and in Skye's office. If Frank had accomplices, they could still be listening. Aiden couldn't open the telegem and discuss its contents here.

Hotah held up his hand. He dug into his tactical pack and pulled out a small, odd-looking device with antennae and LED readouts. *An electronic bug detector.*

"More surprises, Lieutenant?"

Hotah proceeded to scan every inch of Skye's apartment. Bingo. He found and destroyed three cleverly hidden listening devices. Skye was appalled. And angry.

"They're probably in Jo's apartment, too," Aiden said. "The Netvor obviously know that Jo exists and knew right where to find her. That's common knowledge, not a secret. And like Jo said, they also know that a hidden colony of others like her exists somewhere in Astrocell Beta, and they're desperate to find it. Frank guessed that Jo would eventually be contacted by someone from that colony, so he wired her room for sound and waited. He bugged Skye's room, too, because she's the only one Jo visits to confide in."

Skye shook her head. "That explains how Frank knew Jo and I recorded telegem messages and that Jo's message revealed the whereabouts of the Libera colony."

"And he guessed right," Aiden said. "Jo came here the day after meeting Keen and told you everything. Except she didn't tell you the coordinates of the Libera planet—not explicitly, at least—only that she knew what they were and would give them to me in an encrypted telegem. Frank heard that and tried to intercept Jo to force the coordinates out of her. She's lucky to have gotten away from him."

"Frank must have an accomplice back on Luna," Skye said. "Someone he instructed to intercept Scantz and take the crystals from him before he could deliver them to you."

"Right. But that accomplice failed. He *did* intercept Scantz, but he didn't find either one of the crystals on Scantz's body. Yours or Jo's."

"His *body*?" Skye said, eyes wide. "They killed William Scantz?"

Aiden grimaced. "Sorry, Skye. I didn't have the chance to tell you before now. I found his body on my doorstep. He'd hidden your crystal inside his mouth. Probably did it when he realized he was being tailed. That's how I found it. His assassin must have fled the scene before looking there himself. When Frank learned the crystals hadn't been recovered from Scantz, he started poking around here on the station and found Jo's telegem still sitting inside Scantz's mailbox."

Skye lowered her head, pain in her eyes. "I got Scantz killed. That poor man—"

"Don't go there, Skye. You didn't kill him. A Netvor agent did."

The three of them fell silent. Skye finally said, "So where is Jo now?"

"Good question. And what's in her message?"

"I'll get my telegem reader," Skye said. "The real one this time."

She pointed to a small ceramic sculpture, about eight inches tall, on the same shelf where her "flashlight" sat. "It's a model of a cup fungus," she said. "A scarlet cup, to be precise, aka *Sarcoscypha coccinea*, from the family Pezizaceae of the Ascomycota fungi."

Aiden laughed. "Only a mycologist would disguise her telegem reader as a mushroom."

"Yes, and this one works quite well for that purpose. See the scarlet-colored cup? It's the perfect size for a telegem crystal to fit snugly inside."

Aiden took the crystal out of his pocket. It had locked down again, as it was programed to do after 30 seconds of inactivity. He went through his decrypting sequence until the dark-blue Triquetra inside glowed electric blue, indicating that it was unlocked and ready to read.

Skye turned her sculpture upside down and spoke into the base. "Blessed be." Then she set it on the table, right side up. A subtle hum vibrated from inside. Aiden placed the crystal inside the cup. It settled in with a faint click. The crystal flashed once, and a 3-D holographic image materialized three feet in front of them. It was Jo.

13

WOO'S STAR SYSTEM
(HD 10180)
Shénmì Station

DOMAIN DAY 68, 2223

To describe Jo's appearance as striking would be shamefully inadequate. Exotic was more fitting. She looked to be in her early thirties—but then she had been born that way, a clone emerging from her uteropod as a fully grown woman. She was tall, well over six feet, thin, and wiry. Her skin was a deep ebony of African lineage, but her hair was natural blonde, straight, and cut short. Her facial features were distinctly Asian, closer to Chinese than any other, but with a narrow aquiline nose. Her almond-shaped eyes were a startling green. She looked healthy and strong. And even when smiling warmly, she looked dangerous.

"Hello, Aiden," the holographic image of Jo said. She had one of the most beautiful smiles Aiden had ever seen. Genuinely human in every way.

"I hope you are well. I'll make this short. I don't have much time, and I want this message to reach you as soon as possible. While I was at the research camp on Shénmì, I was contacted by another . . . person . . . like me. A *Trans sapien*, not a Netvor. His name is Keen. He told me that there are many more like him and me. They think there was a virus that spread through a lot of the

Netvor creches on several different planets. It carried the mutation that prevented us from becoming Netvor and instead turned us into *Trans sapiens*. Now they have a colony on a planet somewhere in Astrocell Beta. They call themselves the Libera and call their planet Qarsoon. Its location is extremely secret and must never fall into the hands of the Netvor. The Netvor want to wipe them out even more than they do humans. Right now, the Libera are more of a threat to the Netvor because of their superior technology.

"Keen has a cloaked ship waiting for him right now, orbiting the far side of Shénmì. He wants me to go with him to the colony, to join their ranks. He thinks I should disassociate myself from humans and leave humanity to its own fate. But I believe an alliance between humans and the Libera is the only way to save *both* of our races from assured genocide at the hands of the Netvor. I tried to convince him of this, but he thinks the Libera wouldn't even consider it. They don't trust humans and doubt that they could ever coexist with a race that's so self-destructive.

"But I honestly believe that if they could trust any human, it would be you, Aiden. You are in the best position of anyone I know to persuade the Libera, *and* your people, to join hands in a common fight for survival. The Libera have made incredible technological advances, but only humans have the military resources to turn them into effective weapons against the Netvor.

"I am about to take the shuttle back down to the research camp on Shénmì. I'll meet with Keen again and tell him I can't go with him now, especially not without my son. It's more important to remain here among humans as the only Libera they know right now, as an emissary in our pursuit of an alliance. To show them how much more they have in common with us *Trans sapiens* than they think.

"After meeting with Keen, I'll come back here to Shénmì Station and await your arrival. I'm hoping that you will take me to their colony in the *Sun Wolf* and help me negotiate with them. In case I'm unable to tell you the colony's location in person, I am including in this message the exact coordinates of the Libera's planet for your eyes only. Guard it with your life. Goodbye, Aiden. I look forward to seeing you soon."

Jo's image vanished. Aiden and Skye glanced at each other, invisible question marks bouncing back and forth between them.

"I wouldn't trust humans either," Lieutenant Willian Hotah said without humor, speaking for ancestors who had a long and tragic familiarity with broken promises and dishonorable lies. Impossible to forget or forgive.

After Jo's image disappeared, another one materialized inside the hologram. It was a long string of numbers and symbols. The precise astrometric coordinates of the planet the Libera had named Qarsoon. It identified three values, pinpointing an exact location in three-dimensional space. Aiden transferred the figures to his wrist comm, double-encrypted and biometrically locked. He told Hotah to do the same but knew the coordinates had already been secured in Hotah's photographic memory. Then he tapped the crystal briskly on the kitchen sink and ran water over it until it dissolved.

He turned to Skye. "I have to ask you this. How would Jo know for sure that Keen was really a human cloneborg like herself—a *Trans sapien*—and not a Netvor agent setting up an elaborate trap? I mean, he just pops out of the forest on Shénmì near Jo's research camp and introduces himself . . . ?"

"I asked her that myself," Skye said. "Remember how your pilot, Lista Abahem, could spot a Netvor? She has this uncanny gift of seeing auras around people, a kind of bioelectric emanation. The art of seeing and interpreting auras has been practiced in the Gaian tradition for centuries. All living creatures have auras, not just humans. But the Netvor do not. Elgin, in his offbeat way, said it was because the Netvor don't have souls. Lista could spot a Netvor right away by their total *absence* of an aura."

Aiden did remember. "It's how we confirmed that Jo was not a Netvor when we picked her up at Nead after she escaped the creches. We wouldn't let her aboard until Lista used her gift and gave us the go-ahead."

"Exactly. It turns out that Jo has the same gift, and Lista taught her how to use it. She said Keen's aura was clear as day. He's not a Netvor."

"What about Frank?" Aiden asked. "He's been on the station for two months. Wouldn't Jo have spotted him at some point?"

"Not if Frank didn't want her to," Skye said. "If he knew she could ID him in that way, it would have been easy to avoid contact. Jo spent a lot of her time downside at the research camp, and the Life Support techs generally keep to themselves on the station's lower level. They even have their own mess area down there. It's likely their paths never crossed, especially if Frank didn't want them to."

Aiden nodded. "Okay, so when Jo escaped Frank's attack, her plans had to change. Do you think she left the planet with Keen?"

"I think it's likely. After her close encounter with Frank, she wouldn't be inclined to come back here for more. Too dangerous. I don't think she had a choice, even if it meant leaving without Rene. She couldn't just stay on the planet forever, hiding out, and Keen might have offered her the only way out. He probably had a landing shuttle stashed somewhere nearby."

"Then where? Off to the Libera colony Keen told her about?"

Skye shrugged. "Where else?"

Aiden opened his wrist comm again and decrypted the coordinates. "Skye, do you have access to AMP's current astrometric database?"

"Sure do," she said, sitting down at her deskcomp.

AMP, the Allied Mapping Project, was based here at Shénmì Station. It was charged with the monumental task of calculating the exact astrometric coordinates of all the main sequence stars in Astrocell Beta. For voidships to execute successful jumps to any of those star systems, their precise location in three-dimensional space had to be known. It was simply impossible to jump without them.

Astrocell Alpha, Earth's home turf, had been well mapped over the 50-plus years since the voidoids were discovered. But astrometric mapping of the newly discovered Astrocell Beta was still in its infancy. Of the 50,000 stars in Beta, the Allied Mapping Project had wisely chosen to start with the 7,000 main sequence stars most likely to harbor habitable zones. Most of those had been mapped by now, and the project was currently into mapping thousands of less likely star systems, including binary systems that harbored at least one sunlike star. But it was not a given that Jo's coordinates would match anything AMP had logged in so far.

As the director of the Shénmì Project, Skye had direct access to AMP's most updated database. She dialed it in and initiated a search for Jo's coordinates.

"Just so you understand," she said, "searching the data for a planet by its coordinates is virtually impossible. The project catalogs the coordinates of stars only, not specific planets, because that's the data voidships need to execute jumps, and stars are where the voidoids are. If you're heading for a particular planet, you jump to the star system it occupies, then locate the planet's position from there. And besides, the coordinates of a planet are effectively the same as the star it orbits. Most planets are within 50 AU of their star, not far enough for the main coordinate numbers to look much different."

"Got it," Aiden said. "So even though Jo's coordinates are for a planet, entering those coordinates into the search algorithm should default to the star system it occupies."

"Correct. And I broadened the search program's margin of error a smidgen to make sure it captures the star. Then you'll have the jump coordinates you'll need to get there."

Aiden and Hotah leaned over Skye's shoulders in anticipation. But after repeated inputs, she frowned and sat back. "There's nothing at those coordinates and no star near enough to the coordinates to be the planet's host star."

"What?" Aiden said. "Are you sure?"

"Positive. The nearest star is a binary system. It's one that AMP just added to their database last month. It's in the Reticulum constellation, over 104 light-years from Sol. But it's not near enough the point in space described by Jo's coordinates to be the star system this mystery planet occupies."

Curious. "What system is it?"

"It's called AM 7491, classified as a wide binary system. Two stars, A and B, circling one another but separated by 1458 AU. That's over 200 *trillion* kilometers. Definitely a wide binary."

The AM designation threw him off at first before remembering it applied to stars newly cataloged by the Allied Mapping Project, replacing the old HD designations. "How far is it from Jo's coordinates?"

"Nearly 500 AU from the binary's primary star. Too far away to be a planet in orbit, even the crazy kinds of elliptical orbits you sometimes find in binary systems. But if it *was* a planet, the project's high-power multiband scopes would have picked it up, and according to the most recent data, there are no planets at all in this system."

"Well, shit. *Something's* got to be there. Maybe there's an error somewhere in the coordinate numbers."

"Possible," Skye said. "But considering the source, I doubt it."

Hotah shrugged. "Why don't we just take this over to the people at AMP? They've got the equipment to zero in on that spot. Maybe they'll see something they missed during their general sweep of the system."

"I don't think that's a good idea," Aiden said. "Bringing it up would raise too many questions. You know how scientists are. I'm one, and I'd sure as hell ask a few. And if there are any more Netvor agents on board, we have no idea what areas they might have infiltrated. It's too risky to share these coordinates anywhere beyond us."

"Then what's the plan, boss?"

"The plan, Lieutenant, is to saddle up, head out to this binary star, and look around."

"Sounds like fun," Hotah said, meaning it.

"But first, we'll head back to Gateway Station, unload our cargo deliveries, and get Admiral Stegman's formal approval. Then we'll jump from there to the binary system. If the Libera's planet is anywhere near that system, they've got to be using the system's voidoid to get there. There's no other way. And if they can do it, so can we."

He turned to Skye. "I need to see our daughter before I leave. Just to . . . hold her in my arms. I miss her so much."

Skye smiled at him, took hold of his hand, and said, "Come with me."

<u>14</u>

DOMAIN DAY 68, 2223

"ARE you serious, Captain?" Miguel Silva said, his face florid and contorted. "You're proposing that we seek out and deliver ourselves on the doorstep of a Netvor hotbed? Following directions given to you by this Netvor friend of yours?"

Here we go again.

After a painfully quick farewell to Skye and Bri, the *Sun Wolf* was on its way to the system's voidoid, and Aiden had just finished informing the crew about their new mission. They had listened intently as he recounted Jo's message. He was careful not to reveal the exact coordinates of the Libera's hidden colony, even to the rest of his crew, until the *Sun Wolf* had made its jump to AM 7491. He emphasized how an alliance with the Libera would be pivotal in humanity's fight against the Netvor—including the acquisition of technology to defeat Netvor cloaking—and assured them that Admiral Stegman had agreed with his assessment.

And now, as expected, Silva had begun his protests. It surprised Aiden only that Silva chose to rant so openly in the presence of the crew, as if he meant to sway them.

"First of all, Commander," Aiden said, vowing to keep his cool. "Jo is *not* a Netvor, and that's been proven in more ways than one. You should know that and refrain from clouding your judgment with ill-informed prejudices. Secondly, if these Libera folks are like her—and I have every reason to believe it—they're not Netvor either. They are *not* our enemies. They fear the Netvor at least as much as we do. We share a common enemy, and we can help each other to defeat them."

Silva shook his head with a sneer. "Now whose judgment is clouded? This Jo person was cloned in a Netvor creche! She was built like a Netvor. She looks like a Netvor. She *is* a Netvor. And this so-called mutation of hers that supposedly makes her more like us? That could be utter bullshit, another clever ploy to insinuate Netvor agents deep into our ranks. Frankly, Captain, I'm surprised that you trust her at all, and even more surprised that you let this dangerous imposter anywhere near your wife and child."

Okay. Now this asshole had crossed the line. "I advise you, Mister Silva, to keep my wife and child out of this. Furthermore, as an officer in the Service, you have a sworn duty to carry out all orders given to you by your superiors 'without prejudice.' Look it up."

Silva glowered at him and said, "When we meet with Admiral Stegman, I will formally request to transfer off the *Sun Wolf* and be reposted elsewhere."

Aiden shook his head but said nothing. He had to admit it would be a great relief if Silva's request to transfer off the *Sun Wolf* was accepted. He didn't need this kind of distraction. No executive officer was better than an angry and divisive one. Admiral Stegman might even approve of it if he were fully apprised of Silva's unfitness for this mission. Aiden decided it would be the first thing he'd bring up with the admiral when they pulled into Gateway Station.

But it was not to be.

~ ~ ~

The *Sun Wolf* pulled out of ZPD at the AM 7491 system voidoid just after 17:00 and began positioning for its voidjump. Immediately after comms came back online, Aiden received a hail from the SS *Jakarta* stationed at the voidoid they were about to enter, informing him of two high-priority Holtzman transmissions waiting for him. One was a widecast straight from the Alliance Central Military Command on Ganymede to all military assets throughout both astrocells, and the other was addressed only to Captain Macallan of the *Sun Wolf*.

The widecast news from Alliance Central was shocking. Earlier that day, around 12:00 noon Galactic Standard Time, the entire outward facing hemisphere of Saturn's moon Iapetus—the inhabited side—had been hit by an extremely powerful and intensely focused gamma-ray burst originating from an unknown artificial source assumed to be a hostile force located out near Jupiter. It wiped out all five of the human habitats on Iapetus. That included three mining operations, one research facility, and one military outpost. An estimated total of 3,750 people died within 30 minutes, a figure that was bound to grow as rescue crews arrived from the moon Rhea, the next nearest human colony.

Iapetus, like most of Saturn's moons, was in a tidally locked orbit around Saturn, with one hemisphere perpetually facing away from the planet. All of Iapetus's habitats had been built on that side primarily for better observation and communication with the rest of the system. The gamma-ray burst was triggered from a point in space near Jupiter directly facing the inhabited hemisphere of Iapetus from about 5.3 AU away, an astonishing distance that underscored the extreme power and focus of the emission. The source was assumed to be a robotic device called a *graser*, a gamma-ray laser weapon developed by the Netvor. Aiden and his crew had encountered two of those horrifying weapons, in two different star systems. And they had discovered planets that had once been alive with diverse biospheres but were now dead, deliberately killed by Netvor grasers.

Furthermore, within one hour of the Iapetus attack, a widecast Holtzman transmission was picked up at multiple locations within the Solar System claiming to be from the "Posthuman Empire," known to humans as the Netvor. It warned that the same device was recharging and moving into position to attack Earth with even greater devastation. The device would be impossible to detect or destroy, a reference to the Netvor's invincible cloaking and shielding technology.

But Earth could be spared such a tragedy if the Alliance revealed the location of a certain colony of renegade mutant Netvors calling themselves the Libera. The message claimed that high-level elements of Alliance intelligence services were now in possession of the colony's coordinates. Unless those coordinates were revealed within three Earth days from that moment, all life on Earth would be annihilated. That would happen at 12:00 GST, Domain Day 71.

The second transmission was from Admiral Drew Prescott, chief of the UED Military Space Service, stationed at Gateway Station, second in command under Admiral Stegman. It was addressed to Captain Macallan of the *Sun Wolf* and had been recorded over an hour earlier. Aiden told Alvarez to run the message on the main screen.

Admiral Prescott's troubled face appeared on the screen. The fact that Prescott was reaching out to the *Sun Wolf*, rather than Ben Stegman, gave Aiden a sinking feeling.

"Captain Macallan, this is Admiral Prescott. I realize you're still out there at Woo's Star, but I'm sure by now you've heard the news of the horrific attack on Iapetus by these Netvor bastards. And I have more bad news. Gateway Station was attacked by a Netvor vessel attempting to voidjump out of the system. The station sustained considerable damage along with some fatalities and many injuries. Admiral Stegman was among the injured. After suffering head trauma, he's in a medically induced coma to reduce the risk of fatal brain swelling. But he's stable, and the doctors here are confident he'll make a full recovery.

"We didn't detect the Netvor ship until it suddenly uncloaked within 10 kilometers. It fired four missiles at the station, then started a high-velocity run at the voidoid in an apparent attempt to jump out of the system back into Astrocell Beta. Our point-defense system at the station stopped all four missiles, but the last one got too close before it detonated. The explosion damaged a section of the station where Admiral Stegman happened to be at the time.

"But here's the crazy thing. The attacking Netvor ship was powering up its cloak again as it came in, probably attempting to foil our targeting computers, but when it reached the voidoid's horizon, it just exploded. Completely disintegrated. In short, we didn't kill it. The voidoid did. Our science people are all over this with their theories on how the Netvor's synthetic gravity tech interacts with the voidoids. But my priority is what comes next.

"I was not privy to Admiral Stegman's mission plans for you and the *Sun Wolf*. But since he's out of commission, I'm assuming command. Whatever that mission was, Captain, I'm suspending it and reassigning you to a higher-priority one. Because your ship is the only one that can move around in a blink of the eye, we need you back in the Solar System as soon as possible to spearhead the search for this goddamn graser device before the Netvor trigger it.

"I've talked briefly with the heads of our intelligence agencies. They claim to know nothing about this so-called hidden colony of mutant Netvor, and for once, I believe them. I doubt anyone else will figure it out before the Netvor ultimatum expires three days from now. So our only option right now is to locate this weapon and destroy it. We have to assume that it's still cloaked, so it'll be hard as hell to find before it's too late. But it's the only shot we've got. Billions of lives on Earth are at stake.

"As you know, the only way you can get back to the Solar System from where you are now is to pass through the Gateway here. But there's a problem with that. Tons of debris from the Netvor attack are floating around directly in line with the voidoid's exit point. Any ship trying to jump into this system right now will collide with it and likely sustain catastrophic damage. It may take up to a day to clear it for incoming voidjumps. I've sent Holtzman notices to everyone working out there in Beta, warning them not to use the Gateway until further notice. That means you'll have to wait awhile before you can get back to the Solar System and join the search. You'll be notified the moment the Gateway is cleared. That's it for now, Captain. Out."

The screen went blank.

Aiden glanced around. The crew looked stunned. The Netvor had penetrated the Solar System. Earth was in mortal danger. Not next year or next month. But right now.

All eyes turned to him. He faced a decision that might be the most difficult one he'd ever had to make. More risky and fraught with disaster than any he could imagine.

It took him about 15 seconds to make up his mind.

"Alvarez, reply with 'message received.' Hutton, please lock down all communication transmissions from this ship, starting now, to be accessible only with my biometric permission. That's full Code Black protocol."

"Yes, Captain," the AI's voice said in a calm, lyrical voice. "It is done."

Silva bolted upright, his eyes on Aiden like lasers. "What are you doing, Captain?"

"I have chosen to disregard Admiral Prescott's orders," Aiden said, addressing the entire crew, "based on his incomplete knowledge of the situation compared to my own. We will now continue the mission that Admiral Stegman would have authorized."

"You can't do that," Silva snarled. "Regardless of what you *think* you should do, you have direct orders from the admiralty, and you're bound to follow them."

"I *can* do it," Aiden said. "And I will. Let me remind you once again, Commander, that the *Sun Wolf* is a survey vessel under the jurisdiction of the Science and Survey Division. This is not a military vessel, and I am not an officer in the Military Space Service. I am not bound to take orders from the Military Division if those orders have been superseded by ones from higher up the command chain. That would be Admiral Stegman, head of the entire Space Service."

Aiden knew he was stretching things here. And so did Silva.

"Orders from Admiral Stegman," Silva said with a smirk, "that have not yet been formally issued. Besides, Admiral Stegman is out of commission, and Admiral Prescott has replaced him as head of the Space Service."

"Admiral Stegman is not dead," Aiden said. "He's in a medically induced coma, which I'm confident will soon be un-induced. The intent of his orders was clear enough for me. Formally issued or not, they still take precedence."

Silva paused for a moment and contrived a posture of concession to Aiden's last point. He cocked his head to one side and said, "Captain, you've overlooked the most obvious solution. No one in the Alliance knows the coordinates of the Libera colony, no one except us. Let's comply with the Netvor's demand. Give them the coordinates and save Earth. So what if the Netvor find this so-called Libera colony and wipe them out? Better them than us."

Aiden couldn't believe his ears. He stared at Silva, unblinking, fists clenched. "Aside from being downright heartless and cowardly, Silva, that's just plain stupid. Do you seriously think that, even if we did give them the coordinates, the Netvor would just say 'thank you' and leave Earth alone? No. Their primary goal is to eliminate the human race, remember? They're going to burn Earth whether they get the coordinates or not.

"The only reason they didn't send the graser straight toward Earth the moment it entered the Solar System is that they genuinely believed someone in the Alliance knows where the Libera colony is. They just decided to use Iapetus as a demonstration of what they can do with their weapon, to show us they're not bluffing and to tighten the screws on the Alliance into giving up the goods. But make no mistake, they *are* going to burn Earth, regardless.

"This three-day grace period they're granting the Alliance to cough up the coordinates is pure bullshit. In reality, that's only how long it'll take the graser to move into a better position to incinerate Earth. The Netvor are just threatening to do what they've been planning to do all along, and they're using the threat as a ploy to get what they desperately want—the whereabouts of the Libera. We should be thankful the Netvor actually believed that rumor about the Alliance knowing the coordinates. If nothing else, it gives Earth a brief reprieve and gives us more time to stop the attack. Time that we're wasting right now with me having to explain this shit to you."

Before Silva could respond, Aiden turned to address the crew at large. "I am happy to entertain any rational arguments for or against my decision. But before you do, let me explain why I believe pursuing the Libera colony is a better option than going on a needle-in-a-haystack search for an invisible object roaming somewhere in the Solar System."

15

DOMAIN DAY 68, 2223

STILL in shock from the news of the attack on Iapetus, the crew gave Aiden their full attention.

"Granted," he began, "the *Sun Wolf* can navigate around the Solar System more quickly than any other ship. Even so, what is the probability of finding a cloaked Netvor graser somewhere near the orbital path of Jupiter before this three-day deadline expires, given that (a) the *Sun Wolf* can't even jump into the Solar System for at least another day; (b) the graser will have moved on from its last known position to acquire a better one for attacking Earth, many millions of kilometers away by the time we showed up out there; and (c), most importantly, it'll be cloaked. We couldn't detect it even if we were sitting right on top of it."

Aiden paused and tilted his head up. "Hutton, I know you're following this. Please give me the probability of the *Sun Wolf*, with its zero-point drive, finding and destroying the Netvor graser within three days from now, given all the parameters I just laid out."

"Correction," Hutton said, his voice tinged with the professorial tone he often reserved for such moments. "It is less than three days' time. It is now just past 18:00, 6 hours after the attack on

Iapetus and the Netvor ultimatum. We now have approximately 66 hours."

Aiden gritted his teeth. "Hutton, cut the crap."

"I apologize," the AI said unconvincingly before continuing. "Coincidently, Earth and Jupiter are very near opposition right now, a point in the recurring 13-month cycle where they come closest to each other. Currently they are separated by just over 4 AU. That's roughly 600 million kilometers. I predict the graser will want to move much closer to Earth than it was for its attack on Iapetus, for optimal destruction. Considering the applicable orbital mechanics, no more than 2.5 AU from Earth would be my estimate. If the graser can manage up to 2 G constant acceleration, it could easily position itself somewhere within that distance from Earth by the stated deadline. But all of that is irrelevant if we are attempting to locate an object that is cloaked and impossible for us to detect."

"The probability, Hutton, if you please." Aiden sometimes wondered if the AI just enjoyed hearing himself talk.

"Yes. The probability. Under the circumstances you have laid out, it is approximately 0.01 percent."

"Thank you, Hutton," Aiden said, turning back to the crew. "The key to all this is the Netvor's cloaking and shielding technology. They have it. We don't. Without it, we don't stand a chance of finding the graser before it wipes out Earth, much less winning any war against them we could possibly fight after that. That's why I believe the best option now is for us to find the Libera and persuade them to let us use their tech to defeat Netvor cloaking. Then we can return to the Solar System with the means to locate the graser and destroy it."

Aiden had just laid out a classic low-probability/high-consequence risk equation. He glanced at each crew member in succession. Alvarez looked thoughtful but amenable. Hotah looked eager. Assan looked like he was still processing the whole thing. Pilot Abahem looked serene while nodding slowly. Devi looked like someone solving math problems that led only to more questions.

Silva was seething but had the good sense to keep his mouth shut. At least for now. The man was undoubtedly saving his coup de grace for later.

Sudha Devi still looked unconvinced. Aiden said to her, "Doctor, you have questions?"

"Yes, I do," she said. "Let's ask Hutton to do the same probability analysis on your proposal and compare it with the alternative."

Aiden nodded. "Okay, fair enough. Fire away."

"Thank you," she said, not smiling, dead serious. Devi was not playing games. "Hutton, what is the probability that (a) we'll find the Libera colony at a set of coordinates where the AMP data says nothing exists; (b) after finding the colony, the Libera don't shoot first and ask questions later, reacting to an unknown intruder who's just discovered their secret location; (c) the Libera will agree to even interact with us; (d) that, if they do, we can convince them to share their technology with us; (e) the tech is compatible with our systems and can be installed on the *Sun Wolf* quickly enough; (f) the *Sun Wolf* can return to the Solar System in time to locate the graser with the new tech, and (g) we can move into position to target the graser without it seeing us first? All before the deadline expires?"

Aiden had already considered most of those factors himself, and Devi had succinctly covered it all, plus a few extras of her own.

After the briefest of pauses, Hutton said, "I have insufficient data to predict the probability of what you ask with a high degree of accuracy, Dr. Devi, primarily because the psycho-social disposition of the Libera is unknown. We know nothing about their colony and how it is structured, and we cannot assume that all Libera are like Jo in wanting to help humans."

"I understand," Aiden interjected. "But we're asking you to go out on a limb here for your best estimate."

"Applied to an Omicron-3 AI like me, *going out on a limb* refers to a mode of operation where the best possible solution can be surmised based on an extremely limited amount of information. A fully mature connectionist network like mine excels in making sense of incomplete or contradictory information. Is this the mode you wish me to employ?"

Aiden suppressed his impatience. Had he given his old friend Hutton *too* much personality? "Yes, Hutton, that is the mode I wish you to enter."

"Given the factors Dr. Devi mentioned, I estimate a 19.3 percent likelihood of success."

It wasn't much. Aiden had wished for more. Still, it was a lot better than 0.01 percent. But for Aiden, it didn't matter anyway. His gut told him it was the right thing to do. The stakes were too high, nothing short of humanity's survival. It was a risk that simply had to be taken. No other choice made sense.

Aiden did another round of glances at his crew. Except for Miguel Silva, he saw only affirmation in their faces. "All right then. Off we go."

Before Aiden could resume the command chair, Silva approached him, chin raised defiantly. "Since you have locked down the comms, Captain, I am unable to report this insubordination to the admiralty or to file an official protest. So I will file my protest now, with the crew as my witness. I hereby refuse to be part of this treasonous venture. I request that, before you proceed, you return to Shénmì Station where I will disembark and self-terminate my post on this ship."

Ah, so tempting. "Your protest has been duly noted, and your request to disembark at Shénmì is denied. We can't waste another second of time. But more to the point, Silva, I don't trust you. What's to keep you from broadcasting your grievances and uninformed opinions far and wide, including the nature of this mission? With Netvor ears everywhere, that would endanger the mission and lives of my crew. And your life too, I might add. So, tough shit. You're along for the ride whether you like it or not."

Silva opened his mouth to protest, but Aiden cut him off. "And I'm warning you here and now, Commander, if you make any move to sabotage this mission, or to disrupt it in any way, you will be confined to your quarters for the duration. Under lock and key. Understood?"

Silva was literally shaking with anger. He looked like a red-faced time bomb about to explode. "This is treason. I intend to relieve you of command. *Sir.*"

This bullshit had gone far enough, and the bridge was not the place to continue it. The rest of the crew looked as if they agreed. "Commander Silva. A word. Now. In my ready room."

"Why?" Silva said, his face flushed. "You don't want your crew to hear any more about the danger you're putting them in? Not to mention the repercussions they'll suffer when this fool's errand of yours goes sideways, and the rest of humanity pays the price?"

"In my ready room. Now."

Aiden moved closer to Silva. They stood face-to-face, inches apart, eye to eye, unblinking. The electricity of violence crackled in the air between them. When Silva made no move to comply, Lieutenant Hotah stood from his station and moved smoothly to Aiden's side. Like a jaguar on the prowl. Now two pairs of eyes bore into Silva's face. Hotah's gaze, Aiden guessed, had a far more visceral impact. Silva seemed to shrink in size. He turned and marched off to the ready room. Aiden followed him in.

Aiden closed the door behind him and sat, not behind his desk but in one of the two padded chairs arranged facing each other. He motioned for Silva to sit. The XO refused and remained standing, his posture rigid. He spoke through gritted teeth.

"I have nothing more to say, Captain."

Aiden closed his eyes for a moment and slowed his breathing. He remembered a technique Skye had taught him and envisioned his anger as a dark red thundercloud roiling in his stomach. He had choices. He could control the energies that hurt him, the primal forces inside all of us, the ones that made us less and not more. He chose to raise that anger up into a higher place. Not to diminish its fundamental energy, but to change its color. A transmutation from passion to compassion. With invisible hands, he lifted the dark knot of turmoil from his stomach and raised it up through his chest, past the checkpoint of his throat, and into his forehead where vision had no boundaries. Then he opened his eyes.

"Miguel," he said quietly. "I cannot truly know what you've been through, losing your wife and child to a Netvor suicide bomb. I'm frightened to even imagine it. It's my greatest fear, to lose that part of my life, to have it ripped away by such cruelty. To the extent that I *can* imagine it, I do understand your hatred for those responsible. Your thirst for revenge. I'd be right there with you if it had happened to my family. I honestly don't see how you can even function as well as you do. I don't think I could do it myself."

Silva's stiffness seemed to ease up, but only to bend downward, the way a tree does in winter under the uncaring weight of last night's snow. His lips tightened together until they were bloodless, and his eyes welled with the fluid of unbearable sorrow.

"But we have a job to do," Aiden continued. "You and me and this crew. A job that's bigger than all of us. To save billions of other families back on Earth. I believe I know the best way of doing that. Not perfect, not without tremendous risk, but it's the best shot we have. I know you can see it too, but anger and hatred are potent blinders. It's within your power to take those blinders off. Not to forget, but to rise above. For the sake of all the other fathers and mothers, sons and daughters whose lives are in our hands. Work with us. Please. Here and now."

Silva's shoulders trembled. He wiped a tear from his cheek, a quick and bitter gesture. Without meeting Aiden's eyes, he said, "I can't."

Aiden glanced away. If this horror had happened to him, could he honestly say he would have the strength to rise above it in the way he'd asked Silva to do?

Aiden sat back, feeling his resolve to stay in that higher place slip away. "If that's your choice, Commander, so be it. But while you remain on this vessel, you will comport yourself in a professional and respectful manner. Is that clear?"

"Perfectly clear, sir," Silva said like a man cast adrift in an ocean of despair where profound bitterness was his only life raft.

Feeling betrayed by the angel of compassion, Aiden stood and moved to face Silva, eye to eye. "You're dismissed, XO. Return to your post."

Silva said nothing, made a defiant about-face, and marched out the door.

Aiden sat back, closed his eyes, and rubbed his forehead. *Dear Lord of the Wood. Why me? Why this ship?*

He missed his old XO and closest friend now more than ever. He was happy for Roseph Hand that he'd gotten his own command, but right now Aiden needed Ro's calm, understated wisdom, his incisive intelligence, vast knowledge, and the stabilizing effect he'd always had on the crew. The difference between him and Miguel Silva was night and day.

Aiden took another moment to compose himself, then followed Silva out the door to the bridge. He sat in the command chair and spoke to the helm. "Pilot, I've entered our new jump coordinates into the nav computer. Please move us into position for voidjump and proceed."

At exactly 18:56, Galactic Standard Time, Domain Day 68, the *Sun Wolf* plunged into the voidoid, on its way to a desolate binary star system lost in some godforsaken corner of Astrocell Beta, in search of something that was, by all accounts, not there.

PART TWO

— 22 Days Earlier —

Think you're escaping and run into yourself.
Longest way round is the shortest way home.

— James Joyce

16

WOO'S STAR SYSTEM
(HD 10180)
Shénmì Station

Domain Day 46, 2223

THE man following Jo down the corridor, on her way to the shuttle bay, was tall and lean. His shoulders were broad and powerful. His face was blank, except for eyes that burned with apathetic cruelty. He moved swiftly and smoothly like a leopard locked on its prey. She quickened her pace and adjusted her eyesight to second sight, the way Pilot Abahem had taught her. She looked back at him again. The space around the man was blank. *No aura.* He was not human. He was a Netvor. An agent in disguise. And she knew what he wanted.

He was 10 meters behind and closing. She was 20 meters from the right-hand turn ahead that would bring her into the shuttle bay's receiving lobby. Two security officers were always stationed there with multiple security cameras covering the entire area. Adrenaline surged through her body. *Fight or flight?* Her brain calculated a hundred variables within one second. Physically, she and the Netvor were built the same. It would be a close fight. But not a smart one. Conclusion: *flight.*

The Netvor could easily overpower the two security officers, but he would end up blowing his cover if he did. If she could just turn the corner in time and enter the security area, the Netvor would probably not follow. He would back off and live to fight another day.

But he was almost on her now. His huge hands flexed mechanically, fingers opening and closing with murderous intent. She broke into a run, her backpack bouncing wildly off her shoulders. She heard him running after her, closing in. She felt his hand grasp at her backpack, pulling her back. She jerked forward with all her strength. The Netvor's hand slipped off just as she reached the corner. She didn't slow down to make the turn. Startled by her sudden appearance, the two security officers bolted upright and reached for their weapons. Jo glanced behind her. The Netvor hadn't followed.

She slowed down to a jog and held up her hands to the officers. "Sorry! I'm late for the shuttle. I didn't want them to leave without me."

Both officers recognized her and eased off. The male officer looked annoyed but said nothing. The female officer smiled at her. "It's okay, Jo. You just gave us a start. Can never be too careful these days."

"Sorry about that, Dor," Jo said, making a show of being out of breath from the run, even though she wasn't.

Security Officer Doreen Hall tilted her head toward the boarding bridge. "Better get going, then. They've been waiting for you."

Jo nodded a thanks. Security never made her go through the XRF scans. It was pointless. Her enhanced bone density would set off the alarms every time. But most of the station's regular personnel knew Jo. Knew who she was and who she was not. The station had become the only place now where she felt at home.

Before entering the boarding bridge, she made one last glance back toward the corridor entrance. No Netvor. The realization that a Netvor undercover agent was here on Shénmì Station started to sink in. How long had he been here? She didn't recall ever seeing him before. How had he passed the XRF scans to even get aboard in the first place? She decided it was not the time or place to make such an astonishing claim to station authorities. She had to get off the station now.

It wasn't until she was inside the shuttle and the hatch door closed behind her that Jo finally began to breathe normally, and the tension inside her began to uncoil. She joined a group of six other research scientists in the passenger compartment and was met with polite nods. Four were women, and two were men. As usual, she sensed that the female humans were more comfortable in her presence than were the males.

Skye, her closest friend here on the station, had once suggested that Jo's imposing appearance—her size and athletic musculature—was more threatening to men, who instinctively compared themselves to others in terms of physical prowess. And while some women seemed threatened by her exotic good looks, they were generally more likely to see in her a supportive, self-empowering light, more worthy of admiration than intimidation. Jo had been skeptical of Skye's theory, but after nearly five years living among humans, she was inclined to agree with it.

As she sat and strapped herself in, Jo tried to make sense of what had just happened. The most immediate question was why had the Netvor agent been trying to accost her? It must have something to do with Jo's recently acquired knowledge of the Libera colony and its exact location. Keen had warned her how desperate the Netvor were to find the Libera and how dangerous it might be for her to have their planet's coordinates in her possession.

But an equally disturbing question was how had the Netvor agent known she even *had* the coordinates? She would have to tell Keen about the incident when she met with him planetside. She knew he wouldn't be happy about it and knew it would change things for her. Jo's original plan to return to the station after meeting with Keen was now in doubt. But what about her son, Rene? She would have a lot to think about on her shuttle ride to the surface.

As the shuttle approached Shénmì for a landing, Jo's attention turned entirely to the viewport and to the amazing planet below. Shénmì had been discovered by Elgin Woo in 2217, and he'd been stranded there alone for 10 months. Back then, it was only the second living world discovered beyond Earth, the first being Silvanus in the Chara system. Shénmì was an Earthlike world in almost every way—position in the system's habitable zone, size, atmosphere, rotational period, surface gravity, pressure, and temperature. Its biosphere, however, was at a stage analogous to Earth's early Jurassic period, minus the huge carnivorous reptiles. The life-forms here had evolved in a different direction and were stunningly diverse, even outlandish.

But Shénmì's most remarkable feature was its recurring "beanstalk events." Dubbed beanstalks by Dr. Woo, these impossibly strong and motile structures rose up from the planet's equator, periodically and unpredictably, into the vacuum of space nearly 36,000 kilometers above the surface where their terminal pods opened to dispersed panspermia seeds. Jo's research team was engaged in DNA-mapping the seeds for comparison to life-forms found on other habitable planets in Astrocell Beta. The research was the cornerstone of Dr. Skye Landen's Shénmì Project.

After debarking the landing shuttle, Jo hurried to her quarters, removed her backpack, and sat on her cot. The encounter with the Netvor agent had left her shaken, and she needed a moment to pull herself together. The air wafting through the open window over her cot was warm and humid, heavy with the floral scent of alien plant life. The research camp had been built on the equator near the cave where Woo had lived before being rescued, and not far from where the beanstalk he'd ridden down to the surface had emerged. The camp was a series of eight dome-like habitats, some designed as living quarters and others as laboratories.

Jo rummaged through her pack looking for the small signal transmitter Keen had given her. It was disguised as a common writing pen. She clicked it three times. The high-frequency signal would be picked up by Keen in his hidden camp 20 kilometers away. He'd been waiting for her return to meet again and discuss her decision. The three clicks was a signal that she would arrive at his camp within an hour.

She put on her backpack again and walked over the damp mossy ground to the next dome. The research team leader, Ariana Philips, looked up as Jo entered. Philips was better than most at suppressing the split-second startle response that Jo's appearance elicited from people when she showed up somewhere unexpectedly. Even from those she'd known for years, it hurt every time. Like a tiny wound that never had a chance to heal.

Jo kept her voice calm and casual as she informed Philips that she would be away for the afternoon collecting fungal specimens associated with the pendulum trees growing in the hills nearby. Once out of sight from the camp, she launched into a fast, steady run. With her physical augmentations, she could cover 20 kilometers of forested terrain in about 40 minutes without breaking a sweat.

On her way, she startled a small group of hexalemurs that had been grazing on the abundant mosses and ferns. Like all the animal life she'd seen here, their morphology was bilaterally symmetrical, but they bore six legs, three on each side. Otherwise, they looked so much like lemurs that Elgin Woo had named them hexalemurs. No larger than an average Earth dog, they were covered with short, glossy brown fur. As herbivores, they were docile and always moved in family groups. Their large eyes conveyed intelligence and curiosity as they watched Jo pass by before continuing to graze.

Ten minutes later, she entered a grove of pendulum trees and stopped to marvel at their exotic three-branch structure and the steady clocklike cadence of their wooden pendulums. Each pendulum was nearly four meters long, tipped with a bulbous seed pod, and they swayed back and forth in perfect synchrony with all the other trees in sight. She loved the soft, rhythmic murmur that throbbed inside these remarkable groves.

Several times in the past, Jo had hiked out to this spot just before dawn to sit and wait for the show. Every morning, just as the first lance of sunlight touched the tree's uppermost branches, the pendulous seed pods began their mysterious synchronized dance.

When all the trees were synchronized—hundreds of them—with all their pendulums swinging back and forth in perfect unison, the sheer volume of air in movement was more than enough to set up a deep ambient heartbeat. It pulsed throughout the grove at 36 beats a minute, exactly one half the tempo of the average human heartbeat at rest. A human heartbeat like her own. It always filled her with both happiness and sadness. Happiness knowing that she was indeed more human than Netvor. Sadness knowing that she would never fit into the human world, never be accepted as a real member of the human family.

But Keen had given her hope. Maybe now she would find her real family. The Libera.

Jo placed her hand on the trunk of the nearest pendulum tree, just to feel that organic pulse one more time before continuing her run.

She finally came into a clearing ringed on all sides by a species of coniferous trees that grew abundantly here in the highlands. Keen stood at the far end of the clearing and waved to her. She waved back and skirted the edges of the tree line until she reached where he stood. He smiled at her—a real smile, warm, but tinged with irony—and said, "Jo."

Like all of Cardew's "infiltration" clones from the early days, Jo and Keen had been designed with the appearance of average human beings to facilitate their seamless integration into the human population at large. The developmental mutation that had left Jo more human than Netvor had affected that process in un-predictable ways, including her unusual appearance. But for Keen, the same mutation had not noticeably altered the physical appear-ance intended for him. He looked the part in every way.

He was several inches shorter than Jo, mesomorphic but not fat. He looked Caucasian with a rounded face, a cleft in his chin, and warm brown eyes. His hair was cut short, auburn in color, and he sported a short beard of the same color. Wearing wire-rimmed glasses, the current retro fashion among Earthers, gave him a bookish look common to office workers everywhere. He smiled with perfectly straight white teeth.

And he had an aura. He was not a Netvor.

"It's good to see you again," Keen said with a polite nod. His voice was soft but clear. He wore a very humanlike ensemble of khaki cargo pants, light-blue work shirt, and hiking boots. His stance was loose and relaxed. "Have you given more thought to coming with me to our colony?"

17

WOO'S STAR SYSTEM
(HD 10180)
Shénmì

Domain Day 46, 2223

Jo had, of course, given that question a great deal of thought and had arrived at the same conclusion she had reached during their first meeting. She had decided to remain on Shénmì Station with her son, Rene, and wait for the arrival of Captain Aiden Macallan.

Her primary goal was to convince the Libera that an alliance with humans was the only way to defeat the Netvor. But she knew her chances of accomplishing that goal by herself were slim. She could succeed only with the help of one special person. Aiden Macallan of the *Sun Wolf.* Working together, she believed they could establish a viable liaison between humans and the Libera, paving the way for a functional alliance.

But her frightening encounter with the Netvor just hours ago had forced her to reconsider her next move. When she told Keen about it, his agreeable demeanor turned to anger and deep concern.

"You realize why he attacked you, don't you?" he asked, crossing his arms over his chest.

Jo was startled by the accusation in his tone. "Yes, of course. He must have found out that I had the coordinates to the Libera colony, and he wanted to get them from me, one way or another. I just don't understand how he knew."

Keen shook his head. "I shouldn't have given you those coordinates in the first place. It was stupid of me, and it put you in grave danger. I hadn't considered the possibility of a Netvor spy planted aboard the station. At least the coordinates exist only inside your head, not written down anywhere. But how did he know you had them? You didn't tell anyone, did you?"

Jo closed her eyes and felt her face flush. "I told my closest friend, Dr. Skye Landen. But I only told her that I knew the coordinates. I didn't tell what they were."

Keen's eyes went wide. "Could this 'friend' of yours be secretly working with the Netvor agent? How well do you know her?"

Jo's embarrassment quickly turned to anger. "Absolutely not! I'd trust Skye Landen with my life, more than any other human I know. Both her and her husband, Captain Macallan."

"Okay, okay," Keen said, holding his hands up. "Then how else did this agent know you had the coordinates?"

Jo shook her head. "I don't know. Maybe he had listening devices hidden in our quarters, and he heard my conversation with Skye. I don't know!"

But Keen seemed more interested in Jo's previous comment. "Captain Macallan is Skye's husband? He's the one you believe can help you achieve this dream of yours to bring humans and Libera together in alliance?"

"I don't just 'believe' it," Jo responded, taking a step closer to him, looking him hard in the eye. "I *know* it."

Keen stepped back, again on the defensive. He took a deep breath and straightened his glasses back onto the bridge of his nose. "You might be surprised that I actually agree with you. Such an alliance would be the ideal solution, if it was at all possible. I just don't think it *is* possible. Too many obstacles. Too much distrust. On both sides."

With hands on hips, she said, "We'll see about that soon enough."

Keen looked at her sideways. "What do you mean?"

"What I mean is that Captain Macallan could be showing up at the Libera colony in just over three weeks from now. I gave him the coordinates."

"You *what?*"

Jo had been prepared for Keen's reaction, but not for the vehemence of it. His face transformed into a look of genuine human fury.

"What have you done, Jo?"

"I encrypted a telegem crystal and had it delivered to Captain Macallan on Luna. I explained my plan to negotiate an alliance between humans and the Libera. He'll understand how critical it is for both sides to unite against the Netvor. Then I gave him the coordinates of the Libera colony as insurance, just in case something happened to me before I could give them to him in person. Something like what just happened up on Shénmì Station."

Before Keen could muster another outburst, Jo explained exactly how an encrypted telegem crystal worked, how it didn't rely on radio transmissions of any kind, how it could only be read physically by its intended recipient.

Keen looked skeptical. "And the messenger? How reliable is he?"

"The messenger is a trusted colleague of Dr. Landen's. It will take him about 21 days to make the trip from here to Luna. I delivered the crystal to him earlier today, just before I caught the shuttle to come here. Besides, even if the crystal falls into the wrong hands, it can't be read by anyone other than Captain Macallan. It will self-destruct if anyone else tries."

A sudden dark thought began to twist and turn in the back of Jo's mind. She hadn't actually delivered the crystal to William Scantz in person but had left it in his mailbox when she couldn't find him. She just assumed that he would pick it up before he left for Luna, but . . .

She pushed that troubling thought aside and continued. "Once Captain Macallan gets my message, he can take the *Sun Wolf* anywhere in Astrocell Beta in less than a day. Including your colony, wherever it is."

Keen nodded, but not in a happy way. "And if he ever makes it that far, you'll be there to greet him. Because you can't go back up to the station now. Not after what happened with the Netvor agent. You do realize that, don't you?"

Yes, unfortunately, she did realize it but was trying not to think about it. If she tried to return to the station now, the moment she stepped off the shuttle, the Netvor agent would be on her in a flash. Either him or one of his accomplices, if there were any more like him on the station. They'd get to her one way or the other, including threats to harm Rene.

As if reading her thoughts, Keen said, "Your son Rene will be safer where he is with you *off* the station. As long as the Netvor agent doesn't know where you are, or how to reach you, he can't use Rene to threaten you. It would be pointless, and kidnapping Rene would only blow his cover. You simply cannot go back there, Jo. For his sake and yours."

Jo felt a hollowness opening in her chest, an abyss of sadness. She knew Rene would be well taken care of by Skye and the Campbells and by everyone else on the station that her son had so easily charmed. She would miss him terribly and knew that he'd miss her in return.

It made no difference that Rene was adopted and not her biological son. He was *her* child. Jo, in fact, could never give birth to a child of her own. Consistent with Cardew's Posthuman ideology, the early generation clones like her and Keen were created without the anatomy and physiology required to reproduce as humans did. By design, they were virtually asexual. While she had learned to accept that brutal fact, the pain of it never went away. But adopting Rene and caring for him as his mother, loving him, had eased it to a tolerable level. Now even that modicum of solace would be taken from her.

She fought back her emotions just enough to voice the next logical question. "So, where do I go now?"

"You come with me," Keen said. "Back to the Libera colony. That choice has just been made for you."

Keen emphasized his answer by pointing to a spot back in the trees about 30 meters away where a small clearing in the forest could be seen. A discreet area of space at the center of the clearing had a peculiar visual quality when looked at directly, as if some optical aberrancy prevented the eye from focusing on it. It was the spot where Keen's landing shuttle sat, he told her, hidden by some new cloaking technology the Libera had developed. Something different and better than what the Netvor used on their warships.

Keen stepped closer to her and touched her elbow gently. "Jo, the Libera are where you're meant to be. Among people of your own kind. Of *our* kind. We're not only more human than the Netvor, we're better than human."

Jo didn't care for the sound of that assessment—nor did she completely agree with it—but dismissed it for the moment. She had a more immediate concern. "We need to warn the station that a Netvor agent is up there. Maybe more than one."

Keen shook his head. "How? We can't send them an encrypted transmission. My lander isn't equipped to do that, not without access to Alliance decryption codes. And the Libera voidship waiting for us in low orbit can't do it either. We would have to send a publicly accessible transmission, one that a Netvor agent would pick up along with everyone else. That scenario would not end well, believe me."

"What do you mean?"

Keen nodded grimly. "You apparently don't know about the new 'scorched earth' tactics that Netvor agents are now sworn into."

Jo shook her head. Keen continued. "It's an ancient strategy, really, but it's always effective. If a Netvor agent is discovered and knows they are about to be captured, they will not only self-destruct but will also sabotage whatever venue they've infiltrated. In the case of an orbital station, it would most likely be with explosives. A lot of them. Everyone on the station would perish, including your son and your friend Skye."

Jo recalled an incident two years ago and the rumors surrounding it. "Is that what happened to the research station out at Gamelan?"

"Yes, it is. In the Emwi star system. The orbital station studying the ocean planet Gamelan was blown to pieces. Over 133 innocent lives were lost. The post-mortem intelligence reports proved the rumors to be true. A Netvor mole on the station had been discovered and trapped. She pushed the button to set off charges she'd hidden throughout the station. She's probably revered as a hero now among the Netvor."

Jo felt sick. She couldn't speak.

Keen saw her reaction and said, "The Netvor are committed to all-out war, Jo. Against humans and Libera alike. Individual agents are expendable for the cause. If one of these devils is found in your midst, it's better to just be aware of it without them knowing that you're on to them. Then you can make systemic adjustments without having to corner them."

"Okay, I get that," Jo said reluctantly. "But I need to at least contact Skye to let her know that I'll be away from the station for a while. And to reassure Rene that I'll be back soon."

But the moment she spoke the words, she realized how unwise even that would be. And Keen was quick to remind her why. "Without a way to encrypt a transmission for her eyes only, the message would surely be picked up by the Netvor, especially if they have listening devices planted in her quarters. Knowing who you are and the information you have, they could easily deduce where you're going and how you're getting there. We absolutely *cannot* let the Netvor know that a Libera ship is here at Shénmì, ready to take you to our colony."

Jo's brain knew he was right, but her heart wouldn't let go. Being separated from her son was bad enough, but the thought of Rene feeling abandoned by his mother and not knowing why was unbearable. Her sadness was so deep that for a moment she didn't know how to express it.

But Shénmì, the planet of synchrony, seemed to know how. A beautiful, melancholy music cascaded down from the sky above her like soft, silver rain. She looked up, and Keen followed her gaze. The haunting fragments of melody that filled the air around Jo and Keen came from a flock of *line birds* soaring gracefully overhead.

Technically, they weren't really birds at all. About the same size as an eagle but without feathers and more bat-like in appearance, they were lightly furred and red in color. When Elgin Woo had first seen them, he called them line birds for their incredibly precise formations in flight. The positioning of each one was so perfectly synchronized with all the others that they seemed to merge into a single dark line in the sky, as if it were one very long and sinuous flying creature. The line looped and curved overhead. It spiraled and danced. The sound that each one made was synchronized with the voices of all the others so that only a single articulate melody, flutelike in tone, emerged as they passed by, filling the air with sweet and sad music in a minor key.

The music was like a dam bursting inside Jo's chest, letting loose all the pain and sorrow of her fractured life—the unremitting loneliness of being so different than everyone else. She fell to her knees on the mossy ground and sobbed.

Keen knelt beside her and again placed his hand gently on her shoulder. She felt the genuine empathy in his touch, a fundamental human faculty that had been deliberately excised from the Netvor at inception but remained fully intact in her and Keen. In that moment, she saw more clearly than ever how different they were from the Netvor. They were not exactly human either. Just different. They were *Trans sapiens*. They were Libera. And she was one of them.

Keen spoke softly. "Jo, we have to go now. It's not safe for either of us to stay much longer, now that the Netvor know you're down here on Shénmì."

Jo stood, wiped her eyes, and hoisted her backpack. She was glad she'd brought it along, because it carried her compad and some essential personal effects, things she would need for a trip of indefinite length. She straightened her shoulders under the padded straps, turned to Keen, and said, "All right. I'm ready as I'll ever be. Let's go."

<u>18</u>

WOO'S STAR SYSTEM
(HD 10180)
Shénmì

DOMAIN DAY 46, 2223

Jo followed Keen through the trees into the grassy clearing. She couldn't see his cloaked landing shuttle, but up close, it wasn't exactly invisible either. She perceived where it stood by the way things looked that lay behind it, trees and rocks with an eerie shimmering quality, lacking the visual detail of adjacent objects.

Keen took a step closer to it and spoke loudly. "Baylor. Uncloak."

A small, four-person landing shuttle materialized in front of them, just five meters away. Keen looked back at her and smiled. "Baylor is the ship's AI. He's a neural net like all the Omicron-3s that humans use. With a few differences."

The crew hatch was situated about two meters up. It opened, and a boarding ramp descended to touch the ground near where they stood. Keen led her up to a crew cabin occupied by four cushioned flight chairs. He motioned to two chairs in front, side-by-side, facing a minimalist control board. They sat and strapped in.

"Where's your voidship?" Jo asked.

"It's in a low orbit that keeps the planet between it and Shénmì Station. It's cloaked, but we don't take any chances. It's got a four-person crew, including myself, and an antimatter drive that can do 3 Gs continuous acceleration. It's one of several voidships we stole from the Netvor. We named it the *Ark*."

Keen instructed Baylor to secure the cabin and launch the shuttle. The G-transducers kicked in, and the shuttle shot upward through Shénmì's thick atmosphere. Once in orbit, it took nearly two hours for the shuttle to travel halfway around the globe and intercept the *Ark*.

"We're here," Keen said as he brought the shuttle to a halt. But to Jo, it looked as if they had come to a place in empty space where nothing was in sight except more empty space.

"How do you know?" she asked.

"We use an instrument that detects disturbances in the zero-point field of space," Keen said, pointing to a small screen embedded in the control panel. "The ship will stay cloaked until the last moment, just before our docking maneuver begins. Here we go."

Then, like some impossible magic trick, a huge voidship materialized from the empty void in front of them. To Jo, the *Ark* looked exactly like an early model ARM warship. Its shuttle bay door was gaping wide open to receive them. Keen maneuvered the small craft into the bay, and the hangar door closed quickly behind them. The deep thud of the shuttle abutting against the *Ark*'s docking port was followed by the mechanical sound of the ship's pressurized passenger tunnel making contact and securing itself on the outside of the shuttle's airlock.

Keen turned to her, smiling widely like a parent about to give a birthday gift to his eager child. "Are you ready?"

Jo was unable to match his enthusiasm and felt a tinge of resentment that Keen had even expected it of her. Granted, she had chosen to come here, but in truth, it had been the only real choice available. *No, I'm not ready,* she thought but nodded with a weak smile and said, "Yes."

Keen opened the hatch to the interior of the *Ark*.

"Willkommen, Jo!"

The words were spoken by a man standing on the other side of the hatch door. He had sandy-blond hair, blue eyes, a square jaw, and a warm smile.

"English please, Hans," Keen said to him.

"Yes, of course," the man said, making an abbreviated bow. "Welcome aboard the *Ark*."

Keen introduced him. "This is Hans Vedderman, the *Ark*'s captain. Like you and I, Hans received extensive knowledge-base uploads at his birth creche and is fluent in all the major languages of Earth. But for now, we'll keep it in English, if you don't mind."

"Fine by me," Jo said. "Good to meet you, Captain Vedderman."

Vedderman smiled again with hands held out. He was a thick-set man with an upright posture, but nearly a head shorter than Jo. "Call me Hans, please. The 'captain' part is merely a functional honorific. It is a pleasure to meet you, Jo. We have all heard so much about you."

Jo didn't know if that was a good thing or a bad thing and wondered how much of what the Libera had heard about her was true. Keen took her by the elbow and led her into the ship's control bridge. "Let me introduce you to the rest of the crew. Like Hans, they've kept the names they were given in the creches. But, like you, I have chosen a completely different name for myself."

The bridge looked smaller than the *Sun Wolf*'s, the only other voidship bridge she'd ever been allowed on, and it had fewer control stations. Seated at one station, surrounded by a semicircular bank of monitors, was a young woman, slender with long dark hair and large brown eyes. She turned toward Keen and Jo and smiled.

"This is Ananya Kumar," Keen said, "our Comm/Scan officer."

"Svaagat," Kumar said, tilting her head to one side. "But I understand we're doing English for this trip. So, welcome aboard. Pleased to meet you, Jo."

"Likewise," Jo said, returning Kumar's smile with a nod. There was something about her that Jo liked instantly.

Keen turned toward the other crewperson, a diminutive Asian woman with a round face, short black hair, and distinctly unfriendly, dark brown eyes. She turned to face them. Her expression was blank, but resentment for obligatory introductions was clear enough in her eyes.

"And this," Keen said, "is Emi Tanaka, our Tactical Officer. She's responsible for the ship's weaponry, shielding, and cloaking."

Tanaka nodded her head in Jo's direction with a quick, perfunctory bow, said nothing, and returned her attention to the monitors in front of her without a smile.

Jo continued to smile at the back of Tanaka's head for a moment longer until it became clear that she'd been snubbed. Jo glanced at Keen, who seemed unsurprised by Tanaka's brusque greeting. As if to say, *What do you expect?* Jo realized it was a sample of what Keen had warned her about, that some segments of the Libera colony would welcome her arrival while others would not. Another reminder of the obstacles she would face in winning support for her quest.

And yet, she felt instinctively that she had more in common with these people than with humans. They were *Trans sapiens* like her. Not Netvor. And when Jo used her second sight, she could easily see telltale auras around them.

"And I," Keen said, finishing his crew introductions, "am the ship's Propulsion Engineer. The *Ark*'s native beamed core antimatter drive was the Netvor's latest design, but it has been significantly upgraded, primarily under my supervision."

The note of pride in Keen's voice was clear but not off-putting. Charming, even.

Jo looked around the austere bridge and said, "Where's your pilot?"

"Ah," Keen said. "That would be Baylor, the ship's AI. He serves as pilot and navigator. Like I said, he's an Omicron-3 AI but with a twist. Now, let me show you to your quarters."

They left the bridge and took a lift down one floor. While walking the narrow corridor to crew quarters, Jo asked Keen about the rude cold shoulder she'd gotten from Emi Tanaka.

Keen sighed heavily. After a long pause, he said, "Not all Libera share a favorable view of humans. As you'll see when you join our colony, we are not all of the same mind. Far from it. There are at least two widely divergent factions among us. We've come to call them Humanists and Posthumanists. Emi Tanaka is staunchly in the latter camp. And it's not just political differences, but also opposing visions of what the Libera should become, biologically and culturally.

"The Humanists are mostly human friendly. But the Posthumanists like Emi want nothing to do with humans and have no sympathy for those who do, even among their fellow *Trans sapiens*. While they have no desire to conquer human space like the Netvor do, they are more than content to let the chips fall as they may in a conflict between humans and Netvor."

Jo shook her head in disbelief. "But the Libera *must* understand what would happen to them if they stood by idly while the Netvor destroyed humanity. The Libera would become even more vulnerable. They'd be next in line for an overwhelming Netvor invasion, leading ultimately genocide of the Libera. Your colony can't remain hidden from them forever. You must know that and plan for it. And clearly the best plan is to ally with humans."

"I understand your logic," Keen said, hands up in surrender. "I'm just saying that you and your Captain Macallan—if he ever manages to find his way to our colony and survive the initial encounter—will have a very difficult time convincing enough of us to go along with your plan."

When they came to a door that Jo assumed would open to her quarters, she stopped and turned to Keen. "I have so many questions. About your colony, how it came about, how it was populated and equipped, and so on."

"We'll have plenty of downtime to talk before reaching Qarsoon, that's the name of our colony planet. Lots of time for us to learn about each other. At 3 Gs continuous, it will take us 6 days just to reach this system's voidoid and make a jump. Then it's another 10 days after that to reach Qarsoon. That's 16 days total. So it's a long ride. Now, here are your quarters."

Jo dismissed Keen's attempt to evade her questioning and persisted. "The first question I want answered, right now, is: Why me? Why have you, along with enough of the Libera, gone to such lengths and taken such risks to find me and bring me to Qarsoon?

If what you've told me is true, I'm just one out of many *Trans sapiens* who escaped Netvor creches throughout Astrocell Beta. Why me?"

"That's an easy one," Keen said. "It's because you are the only *Trans sapien* who has lived exclusively among humans. For how long? Over five years? You are our most reliable source of deep information about humanity and their current situation. We need that information—real details, unvarnished assessments—to make important decisions about what relationships we might want with humans, if any. Plus, you are the only *Trans sapien* to have experienced motherhood. Not biological motherhood, of course, but just as real in every other aspect. You have no idea how significant that is to some of us."

Jo *did* have an idea. If the Libera colony on Qarsoon was populated by *Trans sapiens* like her, there would be no children there—no infants, no teenagers—only fully formed adults. Because that's how they all emerged from the uteropods in the creches, most of them to be trained either for infiltration into the human population as covert agents or as soldiers for the Netvor military. They could not reproduce biologically and could increase their numbers only through more cloning. Would some among the Libera wish for that very human experience of motherhood and view Jo with reverence and wonderment, a divine harbinger of the possible? Or would others view her with disgust, a traitor to the Posthuman ideal, and cast her out?

Either way, Jo realized she was in for interesting times ahead.

19

WOO'S STAR SYSTEM
(HD 10180)
En Route to System Voidoid

Domain Day 52, 2223

After six days aboard the *Ark*, it was finally time for Jo to tell her story.

The *Ark* was only eight hours away from the system's voidoid, and the crew had remained in the galley after their evening meal. It seemed to be a shipboard tradition to reserve this postprandial time as an opportunity for open-ended discussion of anything on anyone's mind while Baylor, the ship's AI, managed routine functions. But it was only the second time Jo had stayed around after their meal, having avoided all previous occasions.

After the crew had learned that Jo had given her trusted friend, Captain Aiden Macallan, the coordinates to their colony planet, she had become persona non grata. None of the crew had been happy about what they saw as Jo's dangerous carelessness. But Emi Tanaka had been particularly vigorous in her attack on Jo's judgment. And even though Keen, to his credit, had openly accepted blame for his part in giving the coordinates to her in the first place, Jo felt unwelcome to join any of the crew's more informal gatherings. She ate her meals in the galley with the rest of them at the designated serving times, but she sat apart from them and spent the rest of the time in her quarters, missing her son and her friends back on Shénmì Station.

Jo's withdrawal had not gone unnoticed, and eventually the crew—all except Tanaka—banded together to bring Jo back into the fold. After insisting that she sit among them and including her more openly in mealtime small talk, Hans asked Jo to stay and tell them her story—how and where she'd been "born" and when she had realized how different she was from the other clones in her creche. How she had escaped and what her life had been like after that.

Jo assumed that every one of the Libera had a story similar to her own and soon realized that sharing one's story was an important way of bonding with this unique community of exiled renegades. And of gaining their trust. The five of them moved from the communal dining table to what they called the "den," an open space at the far end of the galley where several comfortable couches and chairs were arranged for conversation. Jo began telling her story.

By her reckoning, she had been born in one of three creches on Nead, a planet in the HD 13808 system on Domain Day 186, 2218. Like all clones, she had emerged from her uteropod as a fully formed, mature being who looked like a human female in every respect. Outwardly, at least. Internally, she had no uterus or ovaries.

She had been given the name Mary Smith and had received the knowledge-base uploads, KBUs for short, every day just like everyone else. These were done with cranial neurolink caps and external brain-to-computer devices. Her awareness and understanding of the universe expanded exponentially as she learned physics, chemistry, mathematics, astronomy, physiology, medicine, mechanics and engineering, languages, and a version of human history—which she later discovered had been radically skewed to demonstrate the need for a Posthuman revolution.

She was taught physical skills, athletics, and hand-to-hand combat, as well as fine motor skills in manipulating research instruments and the construction of microelectronics. She learned the intricacies of genetics and the processes by which she and her fellow Netvor clones were created, along with the grand purpose behind it all—the creation of the Posthuman Realm.

While her unusual looks made her painfully self-conscious, they set off no alarms with the creche guardians and cloning technicians. The cloning process, after all, had been designed to produce a broad range of human appearances, including more exotic specimens.

But as time passed, she became increasingly aware of how different she was from the rest. Subtle things like behavioral patterns, reactions to unexpected events, gaps in emotional intelligence and capacity for empathy or compassion. And the lack of curiosity. The more she learned about where she was and why she was there, the more she realized how dangerous it was to be different in the way she was. She became more adept at concealing those differences and learning by observation how to blend in with the others.

The more she learned about humans, who were presumed to be vastly inferior to her and her Posthuman cohorts, the more it became obvious that she was more human than Netvor, both mentally and emotionally. It prompted her to delve deeper into the details of the cloning process to understand what may have happened to her.

She learned that the process started with human DNA—originally from Cardew himself, but later from other captive human sources—injected into a human egg cell that lacked its own nucleus and genetic material. These specialized egg cells had themselves been cloned into existence for this one purpose. The newly "fertilized" egg, called a zygote, began to divide and develop into an embryo, now containing the exact genetic material of the original source. The embryos were then transferred to artificial uteruses, called uteropods, where they developed into fully formed beings. But early in the process, just as the single-celled zygote began to grow into a multicellular embryo, sophisticated nanobots were introduced.

These tiny robots, not much larger than one micron in size, were programed to direct all aspects of cell building from that point on.

That included replacing bone with carbon nanotubule materials to grow into extremely durable skeletal systems. They altered organ development to replace lungs, kidneys, hearts, and circulatory systems with synthetic analogs that outperformed the originals many times over. Other nanobots directed the development of neuro-muscular systems to produce synthetic muscle tissue that gave clones superhuman physical abilities.

But the nanobots also deleted crucial genetic information that normally determines gender differences. While the clones retained the external anatomy of genitalia—a penis and testicles in males and a vagina in females—the reproductive gonads normally associated with those external anatomies were absent. No testes to produce sperm and no ovaries to produce egg cells. They *looked* identical to humans and could even function for coitus, but they could not reproduce sexually.

Furthermore, without gonads, no sex hormones were produced in the early stages of fetal development—hormones like testosterone and estrogen that, in humans, lead to the development of gender differences in the brain at later stages of development. As a result, no psychosexual gender identity or gender-related behavioral traits ever developed. All clones were created equal, virtually asexual and without gender identity of any kind. Only after "birth" were they trained to mimic male or female behavioral patterns, depending on which gender they were cloned to resemble physically.

But for Jo, and apparently for all the Libera on Qarsoon, that's where the meddling of the nanobots stopped. Were it not for a mutation in her genome, the last stage of the Netvor cloning process would have proceeded as intended. Normally, in that final stage, a breed of highly specialized nanobots was injected into the fetus designed to direct the development of the brain in specific ways at critical times. They inhibited the formation of structures in the brain responsible for a whole range of emotional responses, including empathy and the ability to love others. In worker and warrior class clones, the nanobots inhibited other areas of the brain that controlled curiosity, independent behavior, and decision making, while boosting brain centers that affected loyalty to authority.

When this last breed of nanobots was injected into the embryo that eventually produced Mary Smith, aka Jo, they failed to function as intended. During her training in the creche, she secretly began researching her knowledge-base uploads in depth and correctly surmised that an accidental mutation within her native genome must have caused the total rejection of these brain-altering nanobots after they were injected. That's when she finally knew for sure that her brain was virtually the same as that of a normal human being, in structure and function, and radically different from the other clones she lived among. She'd never felt more alone, a feeling that her fellow clones were entirely incapable of. The realization was at once exhilarating and terrifying.

She'd been able to keep her secret safe until the technicians finally discovered it when she was subjected to various bio-scans. Her brain was found to be defective. She was classified as a mutant and slated for "recycling." That same day, all hell broke loose on Nead. All the cloning facilities on the planet were being attacked and destroyed by thermonuclear missiles from an unknown assailant, and her creche was next in line. The ship attacking the creches turned out to be the *Sun Wolf*, captained by Aiden Macallan. She took advantage of the ensuing chaos, escaped her confinement, and fled to the nearest shuttle pad. Using the knowledge she'd gained illicitly through the KBUs, she managed to launch the shuttle into orbit just before her own creche was annihilated by a nuclear fireball.

Once in orbit, her shuttle was spotted by the *Sun Wolf* and was hailed by Captain Macallan. After convincing him that she was not a Netvor clone but a mutant more human than not, she was rescued and taken in by the *Sun Wolf*'s crew. The crew treated her humanely, with empathy and tolerance. She rejected the name she'd been given and chose a new one, calling herself Jo, inspired by a character named Jo March in an old Earth novel that she'd discovered hidden deep in the recesses of her KBUs. While on board, she was introduced to an orphaned infant who'd been rescued by the *Sun Wolf* as the sole survivor of a mining colony ruthlessly destroyed by the Netvor. She bonded with the baby, named him Rene, and later was allowed to adopt him as her son.

"The rest is history," Jo said in conclusion. "Nearly five years of living among humans. It's been an up-and-down journey and well documented by journalists and government hearings. I'm sure you already know most of it by now."

"We do know of it," Emi Tanaka said. "What we don't know is how much of it is true."

"Yes," Keen said. "And it's exactly those five years of living among humans—the real story—that the Libera Forum will be most interested in hearing about."

"Then perhaps I'll save it for the Forum," Jo said defensively. She had grown weary of talking about herself and wanted something in return. "I've told you my origin story. Now it's your turn. I want to hear the origin story of the Libera colony."

"Fair enough," Keen said, glancing at Hans Vedderman. "Hans is our resident historian. He's one of the colony's founders."

The captain picked up the cue and said, "Yes, of course. What would you like to know?"

Jo was grateful for the change of focus—away from her. Anywhere *other* than her.

"First off," she said, "How many of you . . . of us . . . *Trans sapiens* are there in your colony?"

"There are 732 of us on Qarsoon," Vedderman said. "With you, that will make 733."

Jo cocked her head to one side and said, "See, that's just it. How can there be so many of us? What happened to me was a freakish, random mutation. It couldn't possibly have happened to so many others over such a short period of time. Even if it was spread by a virus, how could it have gotten into other creches, on other planets? It's far too improbable to be a coincidence."

Vedderman's mood seemed to darken. He glanced silently at his crewmates before responding. "We've wondered the same thing.

I personally believe that it was not a coincidence. But I have no proof to say otherwise."

When Vedderman fell silent, Jo looked him in the eye. "That's it? You can't say any more? Or you won't?"

Vedderman held his hands out and shrugged. "I simply don't know."

Jo sensed an evasion but decided not to push it. For now, at least. "Then how about stuff you do know? Like how old is the colony? Where did the current population come from, and how did they get there? Is your population increasing, and if so, how? What kind of infrastructure do you have? Ships? Military assets. Manufacturing. Raw material sources. Energy sources. Food sources. Type of governance—"

"Whoa, whoa!" Vedderman said. "Hold up there. That's a lot of ground to cover."

"Okay," she said, starting to enjoy herself. "Let's start with right here, the ship that we're on. The *Ark*. It looks exactly like an ARM warship. Why is that?"

"Ah, yes," Vedderman said. "The *Ark* is one of five Netvor warships the colony managed to appropriate after Libera rebellions at several Netvor creches. All Netvor warships were originally built on the same specs as the voidships they hijacked from ARM and UED. The *Ark* was built on specs of the RMV *Markos*, an ARM battle cruiser. We have, of course, improved on all our ships by integrating better technology, including cloaking and shielding capabilities, navigation, and weaponry. The Netvor learned about our improvements the hard way from recent confrontations where they've ended up on the losing side. Now they know what a serious threat we are to them. That's why they're hell-bent on finding our colony and wiping us out, but not before they can steal our advanced technology for themselves."

"And if they were able to do that," Jo said, "there'd be nothing to stop them from entering Astrocell Alpha unseen, swiftly conquering the Alliance, and ultimately eradicating humans from the Solar System."

Vedderman nodded, conceding her point.

Jo nodded back at him and said, "And that's exactly why humans and Libera need to become allies to beat the Netvor. You have the advanced technology for five ships, but humans have whole *fleets* of ships that desperately need your technology. With it, the Alliance has the materials and infrastructure to turn their fleets into an unbeatable force."

"A force they could easily turn around and use against us," Emi Tanaka said. "I'm sure you believe humans would never do that, but even a cursory review of human history would prove you wrong."

Vedderman quickly intervened to avoid further escalation of tensions that had been brewing between Jo and Tanaka from the start. He moved between them and said, "So. Let's get back to the brief history of our colony on Qarsoon."

But before Vedderman could say another word, Baylor interrupted him. "Captain, the long-range CEI scanner just detected a cloaked vessel parked near the voidoid. The cloaking signature confirms that it is a Netvor warship."

20

WOO'S STAR SYSTEM
(HD 10180)
En Route to the System Voidoid

Domain Day 52, 2223

Captain Vedderman stood up so abruptly he knocked over the chair he'd been sitting in. "A Netvor warship? At the voidoid? How far away are we now?"

"Yes," Baylor said, "the mass signature is undoubtedly that of a Netvor cloaking device. It is currently 9.7 million kilometers away, stationed at the voidoid. It appears to be making a slow search pattern around the voidoid, but otherwise it is not moving away from it. At our current rate of 3 Gs deceleration, we should arrive at the voidoid in about 7.25 hours."

All five of them exchanged questioning glances. The relaxed mood in the den had made an abrupt about-face. Vedderman ran his hand through his sand-colored hair, then asked Baylor, "Is the SS *Wilmington* still in position at the voidoid?"

The *Wilmington* was the Alliance warship currently assigned to stand guard at the star system's voidoid.

"I've completed a near-infrared scan of all guard quadrants the *Wilmington* normally occupies at the voidoid," Baylor said dispassionately, "and I have detected only a slowly spreading debris field. Assuming that it is the remains of the *Wilmington* and calculating its rate of expansion, I estimate that the ship's destruction occurred approximately 22 hours ago."

Jo gritted her teeth and balled her fists. Yet another Alliance ship taken out by a cloaked Netvor attacker. And how many lives were lost this time? She glanced around at the others. "Do they know we're here? Wouldn't Baylor's near-infrared scan tip them off?"

"No, it wouldn't," Emi Tanaka said sharply.

Not satisfied with Tanaka's curt answer, Jo was about to press her for more when Ananya Kumar intervened. "The Netvor ship is cloaked. Baylor confirmed that without a doubt. Their method of cloaking prevents them from detecting active scans aimed at them from other ships, which is why they wouldn't have picked up Baylor's near-infrared scan of the area. And they can't send or receive comms while cloaked, for the same reason. It's one of their many vulnerabilities we don't have. As long as we stay cloaked, the Netvor won't know we're here."

Jo knew her physics but was confused. "Can't they pick up our thermal signature? Our exhaust plume? I thought that's the one thing that no cloaking device can hide. The laws of thermodynamics and all . . ."

"Our cloaking device *can* hide thermal radiation," Kumar said, "and can do it without violating the second law. The Netvor can do it, too, but not as efficiently as we can. It's a feat once thought impossible, one that remains impossible for the human Alliance. I can explain later, if you're interested."

"I am interested," Jo said. "And I'm also curious about how you can detect a cloaked Netvor ship at 9.7 *million* kilometers. If their cloaking is so good, how is that possible?"

"There is one property of a ship that cannot be hidden by any known form of cloaking," Kumar said. "Its mass. Or more precisely, the gravity field produced by its mass. We've developed a long-range scan that can detect a ship-sized mass at extreme distances, up to 10 million kilometers away, by detecting its gravitational field. That includes natural gravity fields created by masses in space, as well as the synthetic gravity fields the Netvor use for their cloaking and shielding tech."

"That's impossible," Jo said flatly. She had learned enough from her KBUs that gravity was the weakest of the four fundamental forces in nature, a force that weakened significantly with increasing distance according to the inverse square law. Even the most advanced quantum gravity sensors needed to be close to a ship-sized mass to register its G-field. Close, as in meters, not kilometers.

And gravitational *waves*—ripples in space-time caused by massive objects accelerating through space—were even harder to detect, being even weaker. They required highly sensitive interferometers to pick up even the largest fluctuations, like those created by massive black holes. The mass of an average voidship, even accelerating at 10 Gs, couldn't generate G waves remotely detectable by any known technology.

When Jo pointed that out, Kumar smiled and said, "But it *is* possible if you're not trying to detect gravity fields directly, if instead you're detecting the G-field's *effect* on the zero-point energy field of space itself. I can explain that one later, too—"

"Enough of the physics lessons," Tanaka growled. "We've got a Netvor warship out there sitting in our way. We need to deal with that. Now."

"For starters," Keen said, "what's it even doing here? Is it on a raid just to destroy the system's guard ship at the voidoid, or does it plan to proceed on to Shénmì and attack the station? Shénmì Station wouldn't stand a chance against a cloaked Netvor warship. They wouldn't see it coming until it was too late."

Jo felt her heart race, assaulted by visions of the only home and the only family she'd ever known bursting into white-hot plasma.

Vedderman shook his head. "That may be one of the things on their to-do list, but I don't think it's the first. If it was, why are they still hanging around the voidoid instead of immediately heading out toward Shénmì? Like Baylor said, they've been there for nearly a full day. It looks like they're in no hurry to leave."

"That's because they're waiting for *us*," Tanaka said scornfully, casting an accusing look toward Jo. "That ship's search pattern makes it even more obvious. They suspect a Libera voidship like ours is somewhere inside this system. They're predicting that we'll jump back out of the system sooner or later, with or without Jo on board. So they're waiting at the voidoid to intercept us."

"But how could they know that?" Kumar asked.

"The Netvor agent on Shénmì Station," Keen answered, averting his eyes from the rest of the crew. "The one who attacked Jo before she escaped to the planet. He found out that she was meeting with me and must have figured it out from there. I mean, how else would I get into and out of the system, if not by voidship? So now there's a Netvor warship parked at the voidoid, waiting—"

"Waiting for us to show up at the voidoid," Tanaka interrupted with a sneer, "to make our jump back to Qarsoon. They'll use the transient neutrino markers we leave behind on the voidoid's surface after our jump to calculate where we've gone. Then they'll follow us right on through to find our colony. This never would have happened if Keen hadn't gone on his wild-ass mission to find Jo. That was beyond stupid!"

"Hold on now," Vedderman said, hands raised to halt any escalation.

"*She*," Tanaka spat out, pointing an incriminating finger at Jo, "will be our downfall. You'll see. If we live long enough."

"Just a second, Emi," Kumar said. "You're our Tactical Officer. You know better than anyone else that as long as we stay cloaked, they'll never see us coming. And we *can* voidjump while cloaked. Something the Netvor still can't do. There's no way they can calculate our jump parameters if they can't detect us. They won't know when or where to look for any neutrino markers we leave behind."

Tanaka took a deep breath, nodded, and said, "Okay, I can live with that. We stay cloaked, we slip past them, and we're gone."

Jo felt her face flush. She was the underdog here and was in the doghouse to boot. But that didn't stop her. "No," she said. "We can't just slip by that Netvor ship and let them go on their merry way to destroy Shénmì Station. Because you know that's exactly what they'll do once they give up waiting for us to show up. We have to take them out now, before we jump."

Tanaka stood and brought her face next to Jo's. "Why? Because your precious human child and human friend on that station will be killed if we don't? Why should we care? Why should the Libera give a shit about humans? I sure don't. And half of our colony doesn't either."

Jo's anger rose like a volcanic eruption. She brought her face even closer to Tanaka's. "That's right. I *do* have a human child. And a very dear human friend. That's really what's eating you, isn't it, Emi? I have people I love, and who love me. Human or not, it makes no difference. Love is love. And that's something you don't have, do you? That's why you hate me. If all the rest of the Libera are like you, I don't want any part of your fucking close-minded colony!"

"You bitch!" Tanaka yelled and launched herself at Jo, fists clenched.

Like all post-Cardew clones, Netvor and Libera alike, both Jo and Tanaka had hyperaugmented musculature along with carbon nanotubule skelature. But Jo was taller, stronger, and trained in hand-to-hand combat. She was, however, not homicidal. After deflecting Tanaka's flailing attack, she deftly slipped the smaller woman into a perfectly executed choke hold while she let her own anger drain. Tanaka got the message and stopped struggling. Jo allowed both Hans and Keen to pry them apart.

"Sit!" Vedderman said like a father breaking up a fight between siblings. "Both of you."

They sat. Tanaka rubbed her neck where Jo had wrapped her up and looked at the floor. Jo slowed her breathing and rolled her neck to loosen her clenched muscles. After a few moments of silence, the temperature in the room cooled down.

Hans Vedderman was the first to speak. "Jo is right. We should take out that Netvor ship while we've got the chance. And not just to save Shénmì Station from destruction. Let's not forget who our real enemy is."

He said this last part looking Tanaka directly in the eye. "Humans and Libera have a common enemy, a very dangerous one. But right now, the Netvor are more bent on wiping us out first. We're top priority on their hit list. They fear us more because they believe we can destroy their ships at will, with minimum risk to our own. So why not prove that point when the opportunity arises? Like right now, with a Netvor ship waiting for us out there like a sitting duck."

Vedderman paused for a moment, then turned toward his Tactical Officer. "Emi, can you devise a surefire attack strategy for this encounter?"

Jo noted that Vedderman asked "can you" as opposed to "will you." Jo's opinion of his captainship rose another notch. He'd focused the question on her ability, not her inclination.

Tanaka raised her head. Pride had replaced scorn in her eyes. "Of course I can."

Vedderman nodded respectfully. "How?"

"We can see them, but they can't see us," Tanaka said. "The Netvor still don't know exactly what our ships can and cannot do. That warship *thinks* we have to uncloak before jumping, just like they do. They'll stay cloaked themselves, waiting for us to arrive and uncloak to make our jump, showing them exactly where to look for the neutrino markers. But that won't happen. So, all we have to do is sneak up on them to within optimal attack range, uncloak our missile ports, and send one down their throat."

"What about their shielding?" Kumar asked. "Their shields are impenetrable."

Tanaka smiled. "Remember, as long as they remain cloaked, their ship is unshielded, totally vulnerable. Unlike us, they can't do both at the same time. So while they're cloaked, there's no shield to stop our missile from blowing up their shit."

Tanaka paused and looked at each of the others in turn, challenging them to question her. Then she continued. "And even if they do drop their cloak to power their shields for whatever reason, that transition takes time, up to one minute to bring the shields to full power. If we're anywhere nearby during that time, we can easily target and fire within that time frame."

"And if we're not nearby?" Vedderman said, playing devil's advocate. "And their shields are fully powered?"

Tanaka shrugged. "We can beat their shields in other ways."

Kumar made an eye roll and shook her head. "Right. The *shield buster*. Don't forget, Emi, it's still an experimental device. Completely untested."

Tanaka shrugged again. "We've got a couple on board. Who knows? Maybe we'll get the chance to test one."

"A shield buster?" Jo said. "What is that?"

"It's a missile," Kumar said. "When it's launched, it's designed to send out a specially tuned EM beam in front of it. When the missile is close enough to the Netvor's shield, the beam punches a hole through the maintenance field by scrambling its resonance frequency just long enough to let the missile through. It's never been tested against a real Netvor ship."

"No time like the present," Vedderman said as he stood. "We've got a plan. Let's get to it."

<u>21</u>

WOO'S STAR SYSTEM
(HD 10180)
Near the System Voidoid

Domain Day 52, 2223

"THERE it is," Ananya Kumar said, eyes fixed on her monitor. "Clear as day."

Six hours had elapsed, and the *Ark* had approached to within 1,500 kilometers of the Netvor ship. The enemy warship was still engaged in its slow-trolling search pattern around the circumference of the voidoid. Jo hovered over Kumar's shoulder, staring at the monitor that interfaced with the ship's cloak-detection device. The screen had been a boringly uniform sea of tiny pixelated green dots until the Netvor ship crept around the far limb of the voidoid to be picked up by the *Ark*'s sensor array. The image of the Netvor ship materialized on the screen clearly outlined by dark lines of concentrated green dots. The clarity of the ship's physical details steadily increased with the closing distance.

"Amazing," Jo said. "And they still don't have a clue that we're here?"

"Not a clue," Kumar said. "It'll be like shooting fish in a barrel, as humans say. I almost feel sorry for them."

"Feel *sorry* for those fucking monsters?" Emi Tanaka said, clearly disgusted. Her hand sat alarmingly close to the missile launch button and seemed to twitch with anticipation. "You're getting soft, Kumar. All Netvor should be so lucky to meet such a quick end."

"Okay, let's do this," Vedderman said. "Emi, how close do you want to get for an optimal missile shot?"

"Hell, we could launch from here, and even if they saw our missile coming, they couldn't transition from cloak to shield fast enough to stop it from hitting them. But it wouldn't hurt to move in closer just to be safe. Maybe 300 klicks."

Vedderman nodded. "Baylor, move us to within 300 kilometers of the Netvor ship."

"Yes, Captain. It will take about eight minutes."

Jo felt an immediate vibrational shift from the antimatter drive. But she couldn't take her eyes off the screen. Baylor had called it a CEI scanner. Now she finally recognized it. "You have a Casimir-Ebadi Interferometer here? On this ship?"

"Yes," Kumar said, looking back at Jo, obviously impressed. "But it's not one of Dr. Ebadi's original prototypes. It's one of our own design. As you'll soon learn, many of our technological advances are inspired by the recent works of Dr. Elgin Woo and, in this case, his colleague Dr. Maryam Ebadi. I can see that you're familiar with her invention."

Jo nodded. Maryam Ebadi had developed a kind of quantum interferometer that could visualize the zero-point energy field of space. The device was called the Casimir-Ebadi Interferometer, a CEI. The Casimir part was for the Dutch physicist Hendrik Casimir, who came up with the original idea back in the 20th century. Dr. Ebadi had come along and developed the idea into a practical way of measuring zero-point energy.

"I've seen one before," Jo said. "They used it on the *Sun Wolf* to discover the Gateway voidoid at Alpha-2 Hydri while I was aboard. But you've modified a CEI to use as a sensor to detect the effect of a gravity field on the zero-point energy of space, not the gravity field itself."

"That's right," Kumar said. "Our CEI measures the density of the zero-point energy of space, which is effectively uniform throughout vast areas of empty space. It shows up on the CEI screen as a homogenous sea of tiny green dots. But our device can detect the slightest anomalies in the ZPE field, even from vast distances. Any object with mass creates a distortion in the field that manifests itself as gravitational attraction, which shows up as a density disturbance in the ZPE field. That's what our CEI picks up. Not the G-field itself. Used in a sensor array, it can pinpoint the position of a voidship up to 10 million kilometers out."

Tanaka interrupted them. "Uh-oh. We've got a problem."

Vedderman sat up. "What is it?"

"An Alliance warship just popped out of the voidoid's exit point. It's executing a braking maneuver, decelerating at about 6,000 kilometers per hour."

All voidships jumping into a star system, regardless of where they came from, emerged from the system's voidoid from one point alone, the exit point located at the voidoid's south pole. Course adjustments were always made soon after that, depending on the ship's destination. In this case, it appeared that the Alliance ship planned to stop at the voidoid.

"It's a replacement for the *Wilmington*," Vedderman said, "coming directly from Gateway Station. They were probably notified about the attack on the *Wilmington* through the Holtzman network out here. I'm surprised it took this long to send a replacement to guard this system, considering how important Shénmì is."

Tanaka magnified the optical image of the Alliance ship enough to make out the vessel name stenciled on its fuselage. "It's the SS *Jakarta*. It's a UED battle cruiser."

"Has the Netvor ship spotted them yet?" Kumar asked.

"Yep, looks like it," Tanaka said. "The Netvor can still use passive sensors when they're cloaked. They probably picked up the *Jakarta*'s heat signature first, then optical imagery. They've just moved back behind the voidoid, out of sight from the *Jakarta*, and . . . oh shit! They uncloaked, and they're powering up their shields."

Vedderman grimaced. "Damn! Can we still hit them with a missile before they're fully shielded?"

"Not a chance. We're still over 1000 klicks out. Even if we launch right now, they'll be protected by the time the missile gets there."

"What about our laser cannon?"

Tanaka shook her head sadly. "No. Our beam projector isn't powered up yet, and it'll take too long to do it now."

Vedderman gritted his teeth and looked at the ceiling. "My fault. We should have gone into this on Level One alert, with the laser cannon already charged."

"My fault, too," Tanaka said, "for wanting to get closer in and not taking the shot when we had the chance."

"Drop it," Kumar said. "What's done is done. We need to come up with a new plan."

"Right," Vedderman said. "A new plan. That'll depend on what the Netvor ship is up to."

"It plans on attacking the *Jakarta*," Tanaka said. "That's why it shielded up. If the *Jakarta* had just gone on its merry way toward the planetary system after its jump, the Netvor ship would probably have let it go. Their objective is to stay put and wait for us to show up. But the *Jakarta* is obviously planning to stick around and set up guard duty around the voidoid. That's going to screw up the Netvor's plans to intercept us. They'll have to take out the *Jakarta* to keep their scheme viable."

"Agreed," Vedderman said. "They'll wait just out of sight behind the voidoid. When the *Jakarta* approaches to set up its guard position, the Netvor will slip out from behind the voidoid, drop their shield, and snap off a missile shot at close range."

"It's exactly what I'd do," Tanaka said. "The *Jakarta*'s shields are shit. The Alliance is stuck in the Dark Ages with their crappy Tyson Field. It works passably well against laser weapons but can't stop modern, high-G missiles."

Jo's mouth went dry. She couldn't stop thinking about the Shénmì Station and the danger it would face if this Netvor warship remained in the system. *Rene and Skye.* "But we can still take it out, right?"

"We can," Vedderman said. "But we'd have to wait until it drops its shield to fire on the *Jakarta* first. Once their shield is down, they're totally vulnerable until it's powered up again. That's when we can easily blow them up. But by then, the *Jakarta* will be dead."

Kumar looked up from her monitor. "The *Jakarta* is slowing to a position 20 kilometers from the voidoid. That's where Alliance warships usually post guard. Looks like they're planning to set up shop there."

"What's the Netvor ship doing?" Vedderman asked.

"It's still out of sight to the *Jakarta*, behind the voidoid, but it's starting to move into attack position. They'll be about 30 kilometers from the *Jakarta* when they slip into the open. From there, it'll take 5 seconds for the missile to strike, too fast for the *Jakarta* to react."

"And that will happen in about 90 seconds from now," Tanaka said, consulting her tactical computer.

"What do we do?" Kumar asked.

"What do we do?" Tanaka said, eyebrows raised in surprise that the issue was still in question. "We do what the captain just said. We just wait for the Netvor ship to drop its shield to blast the *Jakarta*. Then we take them out while they're powering it back up. Hell, they might not even bother shielding up again if they think they're all alone out here."

"Or . . ." Vedderman said, looking hard at Tanaka.

Tanaka nodded, then smiled slyly. "*Or.* We can try out our 'secret weapon,' the shield-buster missile. We've got two, and one of them is preloaded in Silo 3."

"Good," Vedderman said. "How far away are we now?"

"We're at 380 kilometers and closing. That's about a 16-second impact time. They'll be too focused on the *Jakarta* to notice. And even if they do pick up our shield buster in flight, they'll just laugh it off, thinking they're invulnerable."

Vedderman smiled wickedly. "Arm the shield-buster missile, target the Netvor ship, uncloak our missile port, and launch on my mark."

"Target is locked in," Tanaka said a moment later. "Missile port is open on Silo 3. We've got about 30 seconds before they fire on the *Jakarta*."

Vedderman nodded. "Fire."

The *Ark*'s T-3 attack missile launched at 300 Gs and covered the distance in less than 16 seconds. The Netvor ship bloomed like a white-hot flower from hell. Within seconds, it was replaced by an expanding nebula of high-energy subatomic particles, its infernal heat rapidly dissipating in the deep freeze of space.

Tanaka grinned. "It worked."

"And the *Jakarta* had front row seats for the fireworks," Keen said. "They've got to be wondering what the hell just happened."

"They are," Kumar said, looking at her sensor readouts. "They're frantically pinging the immediate vicinity with active scans, probably terrified that they'll be next."

Jo closed her eyes and slowed her breathing. Rene and Skye were safe. For now, at least. She opened her eyes and said, "What's next?"

"Next," Vedderman said, "we do what we came here to do. Execute a jump through that voidoid out there and make our way back home. We'll stay cloaked for the jump. The *Jakarta* will never know we just slipped through the voidoid they're supposed to be guarding."

While Vedderman issued commands to Baylor in preparation for the jump, Jo turned to Keen. "Okay, maybe *now* you can tell me where this planet of yours is. Where is Qarsoon?"

"It's where no one would ever find it," he said.

Another vague deflection of the question she'd been asking them for days now. Frustrated, she decided to stop asking *where*, because obviously that wasn't working. "Okay," she said. "So *why* would no one ever find it there?"

"Because," Keen said, "nothing is there."

PART THREE

— The Present —

There is another world, but it is in this one.

— Paul Éluard

22

Domain Day 68, 2223

"Nothing is there."

Alvarez spoke the words moments after the *Sun Wolf* had jumped into the AM 7491 binary star system, emerging from one of the oddest voidoids the crew had ever encountered. All her long-range sensors were online and zeroed in on the coordinates Jo had given them.

The ship's chrono read 19:05, Galactic Standard.

Hotah had just finished his tactical scans out to five million kilometers. He echoed Alvarez's conclusion. "Nothing is there."

But for Aiden, the words didn't need repeating. Their meaning was made clear enough by the dramatically stark nature of where the *Sun Wolf* found itself. In the middle of nothing. They might as well be utterly lost in the vast infinity of interstellar space. Which in some senses they were.

Over the last 50-plus years since the discovery of the voidoids, very few binary star systems had been visited by manned vessels. Exploration priorities were always focused on seeking habitable planets in stable orbits, and binary systems were poor hunting grounds for such things. To date, almost all of the 121 star systems visited by manned voidships were single-star systems. And when ships emerged from the voidoids in those systems, they always found themselves about 13 AU directly above the star system's center of mass. Which was, of course, the single star itself. From that distance, the host star didn't exactly dominate the view, but it was clearly the brightest object on a ship's forward screen, similar to how the sun might look as viewed from Saturn. Dominant enough to give the crew a sense of place. A beacon of light and matter calling out to them from the vast emptiness of space, welcoming them into a planetary neighborhood.

But out here . . . ?

In binary systems, the voidoids were not found above one of the stars but rather above the system's common center of mass—its COM, in spacer-speak—which was always determined by the stars' individual masses and their distance apart. No matter how erratically the two stars circled each other, or how long they took to do it, their center of mass always remained fixed at some invisible point in space between them. A binary system's voidoid was always situated directly above that invisible point, about 13 AU away from it. And that's exactly where a voidship would emerge after a jump into a binary.

Here in the AM 7491 system, where the two stars were separated by 1,458 AU, the center of mass was roughly 532 AU from the largest star, designated AM 7491A, and that's where the *Sun Wolf* found itself after its jump. Like Earth's sun, AM 7491A was a G-type star, just slightly larger and brighter. But from this distance, it was nothing more than a bright star in the night sky, barely distinguishable from all the rest scattered across the deep black. Alvarez had placed the star at the center of the forward screen so everyone on the bridge could orient themselves to it.

The crew stared in silence, undoubtedly feeling the same uneasy creepiness Aiden felt. Like sailors cast adrift in an eternal ocean of night.

Hutton's voice broke the silence, sounding slightly concerned. "Captain, one of our Holtzman buoys has been deployed."

"What?" Aiden said through gritted teeth. "Who deployed a Holtzman buoy?"

"I did," Miguel Silva replied defensively. "It's standard procedure after a voidjump."

"Where the hell is your brain, Commander?" Aiden growled, feeling his face flush. "Do you realize what you've just done? This was *not* a routine voidjump. I ordered a full Code Black protocol. That includes no Holtzman buoys. You should know that. The very *last* thing we need is for the Netvor to get any hint of where we've jumped to."

Granted, it was standard procedure. Whenever a voidship jumped into a new star system, it deployed a Holtzman comm buoy near the voidoid to allow instantaneous communication between star systems throughout the astrocell, and more specifically to register its location with Alliance Command back on Ganymede. Aiden wasn't worried so much about Netvor listening devices hidden in the network intercepting their locator data. The comm buoy's sophisticated encryption had proven to be virtually impenetrable. He was more worried about possible Netvor moles planted among the Alliance personnel whose job was to decrypt and report such data.

Silva looked chastened. But not as much as Aiden would have liked. The man recovered quickly and said, "You're overreacting, Captain. It's—"

"Shut up!" Aiden roared. He turned to Alvarez. "Has the buoy actuated yet?"

A Holtzman buoy usually turned itself on the moment it left a voidship's delivery bay, but it took a few seconds to establish a connection back through the voidoid to link up with the other Holtzman devices in the network.

Alvarez grimaced. "Yes. Its link-up routine is almost complete."

"Shit." He turned to his Tactical Officer. "Hotah, target the buoy and kill it. Now."

"On it," Hotah said.

Within seconds of Aiden's last word, the ship's stern-mounted rail gun let loose three rounds of solid-tungsten projectiles. With a muzzle velocity of 10 kilometers per second, each one-kilogram projectile carried an explosive energy equivalent to 12 kilograms of TNT. With the Holtzman buoy barely one kilometer away, it was overkill. And Hotah knew it. A feral grin spread across his face as he watched the diminutive buoy explode into an expanding cloud of scintillating metallic fragments.

Aiden glared at Silva. "You'd better hope that shit doesn't hit the fan because of this. What is it with you, Silva? Do you actually *want* the Netvor to find the Libera colony?"

As he spoke it, Aiden realized it was the question that had been nagging him all along. If Lista Abahem hadn't reported seeing Silva's aura upon their very first meeting, Aiden would suspect the man was a Netvor agent in disguise. But, like all Alliance service personnel, Silva had passed all the in-depth medical tests with flying colors. Plus, Aiden would swear that his new XO's hatred for the Netvor was so visceral that it could not possibly be an act.

Aiden calmed himself and returned his attention to the forward screen displaying the sector of empty space in the general vicinity of the distant primary star. It was a realtime feed from the ship's main optical telescope. "Lilly, point out where the coordinates would be in relation to what we're seeing here."

"It's a point in space just above our line of sight to the primary star," she said, indicating the spot with a remote pointer. "It's roughly 30 to 40 AU away from our position."

"And you're still not seeing anything there? Even with the hi-res optical scope and infrared sensors?"

Alvarez shook her head, clearly disappointed. "Nothing."

Aiden took a deep breath. Had there been an error somewhere along the line in transcribing the coordinates? Had they all been duped?

"Keep looking, Lilly."

Alvarez could only use the ship's passive sensors, instruments that detect any kind of emission from the target. Using the active scanners was out of the question. It would take too long for results to come in. Detecting a target 30 to 40 AU away would take nearly half a day for emissions to reach it and then reflect back to the ship's sensor dishes to pick it up.

After nearly an hour of focused searching, Alvarez threw up her hands in frustration. "I give up. I'm not picking up a damn thing."

Aiden had an idea. "Do we have microlensing capabilities for the optical scopes?"

Alvarez made a dismissive sound and said, "Sure, but we're not looking for a black hole, so why—"

She stopped in midsentence. "Of course! Why didn't I think of that?"

"Just a hunch," Aiden said. "Try running your microlensing program through our main scope and scan the area around the coordinates. Use the highest sensitivity setting."

She did, and within 30 seconds she said, "Holy shit. There it is."

The microlensing algorithm filled in the blanks, and a black sphere appeared on the screen, highly magnified and outlined by distorted starlight coming from behind the object, wrapping around its gravity well.

"It's a rogue planet." Aiden smiled. *Bless you, Jo. You did not fail us.*

More stunned silence followed. Even Silva's eyes widened with wonder.

"How far away is it?" Aiden asked. "How big is it, and how fast is it moving?"

Alvarez's hands flew over her virtual keypad, eyes on her monitor. "It's about 34 AU from our position. The refraction dynamics suggest a rocky, terrestrial planet, slightly larger than Earth and slightly more massive. It appears to be travelling just over 10,000 kilometers per hour on a trajectory that suggests a hyperbolic flyby around the star AM 7491A. Right now, it's about as close as it'll ever get to the star, if you can call 498 AU 'close.' After that, the planet's trajectory bends around the star's gravity well and flies off in the opposite direction, back into interstellar space."

"A hyperbolic flyby," Aiden said, more to himself than anyone else. That term described a trajectory in space where, in this case, a planet passes near enough to a star for its path to be bent inward by the star's gravity but passes by with enough velocity to escape the star's gravitational pull without being captured into orbit. The resulting trajectory resembles the shape of a hyperbola, and the planet just "flies by" the star, continuing in a new direction that's been altered by the gravitational interaction.

"Here, I'll show you," Alvarez said as her hands moved across her keypad again. A basic line diagram appeared on the forward screen.

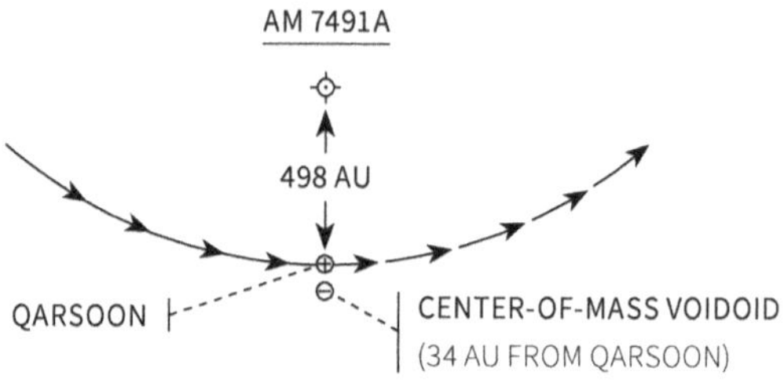

"That's why the planet is so close to the system's voidoid right now," Aiden said. "Its flyby trajectory just happens to bring it near this system's center of mass, which is where the voidoid also just happens to be."

"And where we happen to be right now," Alvarez said.

Assan looked skeptical. "Still, that's 34 AU between the voidoid and the planet. If it *is* the Libera's colony planet, that's a long trip after voidjumping into the system. Assuming they've got stolen Netvor ships that max out at 3 Gs constant accel, we're talking about a 10-day trip. One way. And even if they started out with a full tank of antimatter fuel, they'd need to refuel to get back out. It'd have to be a one-way trip unless there's a ready source of anti-matter out there somewhere, and I don't see how that's remotely possible. There's no gas giant anywhere in this system, or anywhere within light-years from here."

Aiden nodded. "Good point. But it does make a damn good hiding place. Who would ever think of looking for a rogue planet in the first place? The probability of rogue planets being habitable, even marginally, has proven to be negligible. Plus, they don't orbit stars, so there's no voidoid in the neighborhood. Which means there's no way for anyone to reach them. They just wander through empty space, isolated for eternity."

"So it's just a freak coincidence," Assan said, still skeptical, "that this one just happens to be on a flyby trajectory that brings it within reach of this system's voidoid? At this particular point in time? That's one chance in billions."

Aiden said nothing, trying to dispel his uneasy feelings about such odds.

Sudha Devi, who'd been silent up to this point, said, "Yet somehow the Libera found it years ago, and now they're using it as the perfect hiding place?"

Hotah looked at Aiden and said, "So what's the plan, boss?"

That one was easy. "We go there and check it out. It may be a 10-day trip for conventional ships, but for us at 92 percent light speed, it'll be a little over 5 hours realtime—2.5 hours of shipboard time. We can't afford to debate the issue. We've got less than 64 hours now to pull this off. So, hell yeah. Let's go."

"Roger that." Hotah beamed like a kid in a candy shop.

Silva stood and faced Aiden. "And what happens if these paranoid 'Libera' bastards greet us with nukes? They'll be cloaked, remember? Just like their Netvor cousins. We won't see them coming before it's too late. You're willing to take that kind of risk, Captain?"

"And you're not?" Aiden snapped back. "You're not willing to take *any* risk to save billions of lives on Earth? To save the very planet itself?"

The question hung in the air like an angry ghost hovering over Silva's head. He just shook his head in disgust, slumped back to the XO's chair, and said nothing more.

Aiden glared at him for a moment before sitting down at Command. Sudha Devi, who had been Aiden's psych therapist during a rough patch many years ago, approached and said, "Rogue planets? I've heard of them but don't know much about them."

Bless you, Sudha. She'd always had a knack for deflecting external tensions and fostering internal calm. He took a deep breath and let it out slowly.

"You're not alone in that, Sudha. Not many people do know about rogue planets. You'd think there'd be more interest in them since they're estimated to outnumber the stars in our galaxy twenty to one. Given at least 200 billion stars in the Milky Way, that's a whopping 4 trillion rogue planets wandering aimlessly throughout our galaxy.

"The problem is, for starters, no one knows where to look for them. And even if they did, no one could see them. They don't have a sun nearby to light them up. They're not accessible by voidoids, so no one can get to them. They're dark, cold, and dead. Most of the ones we know about were detected years ago by the UED Microlensing Project. And that project didn't last long because no one really cares about rogue planets anymore. Now they're just another peculiar item shelved inside astronomy's cabinet of curiosities."

"But these are dead planets, right?" Devi said. "I mean *very* dead. They can't be much warmer than the absolute zero of interstellar space. If they had any kind of habitable atmosphere before leaving their star system, it would have frozen and collapsed within years. Water would freeze so hard it would crystallize. No life-form could survive. How could anyone, even the physically augmented Libera, survive in such a place, much less colonize it?"

"Good question. Let's go find out."

He was about to order Pilot Abahem to proceed when Alvarez called out, "Wait. Something weird just happened to the voidoid."

23

AM 7491 SYSTEM
System Voidoid

DOMAIN DAY 69, 2223

THE *Sun Wolf* had been parked within 5 kilometers of the voidoid while they were searching for the mystery planet. The voidoid of a binary system looked just like any other they'd seen—an enigmatic sphere of deep, black nothingness slightly over 18 kilometers in apparent diameter. But when Alvarez played back a recording from the ship's rear-facing cameras, something weird had indeed just happened.

A sphere of pale white light suddenly appeared inside the voidoid at its center. Its diameter was roughly one quarter of the voidoid's. It shimmered with ghostly luminescence. Aiden had seen this phenomenon before. And part of his crew had seen it, too. Pilot Abahem turned to face Aiden with a glow of recognition in her eyes.

Then, about 5 seconds later, a brilliant, incandescent flash burst from the center of the glowing white sphere. It seemed to pull some of its ephemeral substance with it into a narrow lance of light streaming outward, disappearing quickly into the emptiness of space. Then the pale white sphere collapsed into itself and blinked out. The entire phenomenon took less than 10 seconds.

Sudha Devi and Billy Hotah spoke almost in unison. "What the . . . ?"

Alvarez looked at Aiden, wide-eyed. "Was that what I think it was?"

One of Elgin Woo's Luminous Ones? Aiden didn't say it out loud, but he sure as hell thought it. The two newest crew members, Assan and Silva, looked utterly baffled. That was because they hadn't been aboard the *Sun Wolf* to witness the ship's first encounter with one of those mysterious cosmic apparitions Elgin Woo had whimsically christened Luminous Ones.

Aiden shrugged his shoulders, attempting to appear indifferent. "I don't know, Lilly."

But he had a sneaking suspicion they would be finding out soon enough. He turned to Pilot Abahem again and said, "Proceed. Off to see the Wizard."

Five hours and eight minutes later, at 02:32 GST, the *Sun Wolf* pulled out of ZPD to halt a half million klicks from the rogue planet. Centered on the ship's main screen and telescopically magnified, it was one of the strangest sights Aiden had ever seen.

The planet was slightly larger than Earth, with a radius of 6,410 kilometers. From this distance, it would have looked similar to Earth as viewed from the moon—that is, if there had been a sun anywhere around. But there was no sun out here. No star for this planet to orbit around and to light it up. The closest star, AM 7491A, was nearly 500 times farther away than Earth was from its sun. The amount of light it shed on the planet's surface was roughly equivalent to a full moon on Earth, meaning it was barely noticeable.

Now that Aiden knew where to look for it, the rogue planet revealed itself as a circular area of almost-black space defined by an absence of stars in the middle of an otherwise seamless, star-studded backdrop. When Alvarez increased the magnification, a faint crescent of pale starlight highlighted the side of the planet facing the distant star.

Hotah broke the spell. "Tactical board is clear. No other vessels nearby. None that we can see, at least. If any Libera ships *are* around, they'll be cloaked. We won't see them unless they want us to. I've got our shields up, fully powered."

"Right," Aiden said, feeling a cold sweat coming on. "I'm guessing they've got remote sensors out by the voidoid that would pick us up the moment we jumped into the system. If so, they would know we were here in less than five hours after we popped out of the voidoid. And we did that over seven hours ago."

Assan's eyes widened. "So they could be here already. And we wouldn't know it."

The silence following Assan's observation crackled with uneasy tension. Would a searing beam of star-hot collimated energy flash out of nowhere from some cloaked laser cannon and fry them on the spot? The *Sun Wolf*'s shielding was good enough for short bursts, but not against prolonged or repeated fire from high-energy laser cannons. Aiden could only hope that Jo had actually made it to the Libera colony and had told them to expect a peaceful, non-aggressive visit from the *Sun Wolf*. That was a lot of "ifs."

"Pilot. Match the velocity of the planet and stay even with its trajectory at our current distance."

Alvarez had reported the rogue planet's velocity to be around 10,000 kilometers an hour. That was slow by rogue-planet standards. It was, in fact, 10 times slower than Earth's orbital velocity around the sun. It would be an easy maneuver for the *Sun Wolf*.

Then he asked Alvarez to broadcast a hail on all known comm frequencies requesting radio contact with any Libera vessel in the vicinity.

Then the crew waited.

And waited . . .

Sudha Devi again chose to displace anxiety on the bridge with curiosity, an easy maneuver when used on a group of scientists. She resumed questioning about rogue planets. "So how do rogue planets become . . . rogue?"

"Just for the record," Aiden said, "the International Astronomical Union officially calls them 'free-floating planets.' But I like the sound of *rogue* planets better. More rakish."

That brought a smile to Devi's face and an eye roll from Hotah.

"A planet goes rogue," Aiden said, "when it's been ejected from the planetary system in which it was originally born. Most of them are ejected during the early stages of formation when planetary systems are more chaotic with lots of disruptive gravitational interactions going on. That can lead to an unlucky world being hurled out of its orbit into the abyss. But it can also happen at any time in the lifetime of a planetary system, especially in multiple-star systems. Like binaries. Once a rogue planet is cast adrift, it's free to get pulled toward whatever large, gravitationally attractive body it happens to pass by. Which is exactly what's happening to this one."

Alvarez turned from Comm/Scan to join the conversation. "I've been studying this planet's trajectory, and I can trace it back to the star system it most likely came from. It was ejected from Beta Reticuli, another binary system just 6 light-years away. Given its velocity, that means it happened approximately 640,800 years ago. Not a long time by geological standards. And just an eye-blink by cosmological standards."

That made sense, Aiden thought, given what he'd just said about planetary ejections being more common in binary systems. Beta Reticuli was a well-known binary. It was about 97 light-years from Sol and over 5 billion years old. If this planet had been in a stable orbit around Beta Reticuli A, that was a K0 type star, one of the most likely types to harbor habitable planets.

"Whoa!" Alavarez said as more data on the planet poured in from her scans. "It's got a moon. A little larger than Earth's moon, similar in mass and composition. I can't see it clearly. It's just as dark as the planet, but I can pick it up on the IR scan."

"The moon must have stayed bound to the planet when it got kicked out of Beta Reticuli," Aiden said. "Not entirely unusual. The Microlensing Project catalogued quite a few rogue planets that held on to their moons after ejection—"

"I can't believe it!" Alvarez said, interrupting him again.

"What now?"

"I just got the spectrographic analysis results. This planet has a viable atmosphere! A relatively dense one, too. It's got to be its original atmosphere."

"That's impossible," Sudha Devi chimed in. "It has no sun. Any atmosphere like that would freeze solid and collapse without a source of thermal energy to keep it intact."

Aiden stood over Alvarez's shoulder, scanning her readouts. "Where are the readings from your mid-infrared sensor?"

Alvarez gave him a guilty look. "I didn't bother to activate that sensor. I just assumed this planet would be deep-frozen to the core."

She switched on the infrared sensor. "Holy shit . . ."

Aiden looked at the readout. It reported an average temperature of about 3 degrees Centigrade—just over 37 degrees Fahrenheit—at the surface. Cold but certainly habitable.

"It's probably due to internal heat from the planet's core," Aiden said. "And a lot of it."

"Bingo," Alvarez said, getting even more excited. "Looks like it's volcanically active. I've already spotted at least five active lava flows. In fact, the entire planet registers unusually warm on the IR scans. Not at all what you'd expect to see from a rogue planet."

Aiden, who held a PhD from Luna U in planetary geology, was familiar with the speculations about how a rogue planet could retain its native atmosphere if blessed with enough heat from radioactive decay at its core, along with heat from the molten core itself. Theoretically, that could provide sufficient thermal energy to keep its atmosphere from freezing and even to keep water in a liquid state on the planet's surface. Having a single large moon would help, too, adding heat from tidal forces it exerted on the planet. And if the atmosphere had plenty of greenhouse gases, that would be even better.

Alvarez said, "I just ran spectrometry on the atmosphere: nitrogen, 66 percent; argon, 11 percent; oxygen, 22 percent; CO_2, 0.10 percent. And a *lot* of water vapor."

"Wow," was all Aiden could say. Water vapor was the most effective greenhouse gas of them all. Along with the higher CO_2 levels and emissions from active volcanoes, it would all add up to keeping the heat in, close to the surface, preventing thermal energy from escaping into space.

"If there's *that* much water vapor," Alvarez said, "then . . ."

Aiden nodded enthusiastically. "Then there's got to be liquid water on the surface."

Caught up in the excitement, Assan said, "So we could walk around on the surface without p-suits and supplemental O_2?"

Aiden thought about that, then asked Alvarez, "Lilly, what's the estimated atmospheric pressure at surface level, given the content of the atmosphere and the planet's mass?"

Alvarez checked her board and said, "It should be just under 1,200 millibars, slightly higher than Earth's."

"Then yes, Lieutenant," Aiden said. "It'll be cold, dark as night, foggy, and the air pressure will feel like being under two meters of water. But other than that, we could walk around down there just fine without p-suits and O_2 packs."

"And so could the Libera," Devi said.

As if on cue, Alvarez said, "I'm receiving a response to our hail. It's from a source nearby. But our sensors aren't seeing any ships in the vicinity."

Aiden turned to Hotah. "Anything on tactical?"

"Nothing. They're obviously cloaked."

"Lilly, open the hail."

She did. The screen remained blank, but a man's voice came through.

"Captain Macallan. This is Captain Hans Vedderman of the Libera ship *Ark*. Please remain in position and stand down all your weapons systems."

Aiden looked at Hotah. "Do it, Lieutenant. And hands off the trigger."

Silva bolted up from the XO chair, eyes wide with protest. "Captain—"

"Shut up, Silva," Aiden growled. "Sit down and keep your mouth shut."

Aiden glared at the man until he sat back down, then told Alvarez to open comms.

"Captain Vedderman. This is Captain Aiden Macallan. We will comply. Our purpose here is peaceful, and we come at the request of one of your own. Her name is Jo."

"We know who you are, Captain," Vedderman said. Aiden detected a slight German accent in the man's voice. His tone was not hostile but wary. "And we know why you've come. Jo has explained that in detail and has made her case for an alliance very persuasively. Just be thankful that she alerted us of your arrival and for the trust she has in you. And for the trust we have in her. Otherwise, we would not be having this conversation. You and your crew would be dead by now."

Aiden's heart pounded in his chest. His shoulders tensed. *Be very careful here.* "We are indeed thankful to Jo. I personally regard her as a close friend and trust her without reservation. Our weapons systems are stood down, as you requested. I wish to discuss a matter of great urgency for my people and, I believe, for yours as well."

Aiden waited for the longest 15 seconds he had ever endured. Then the forward screen blinked to life with an auto-pan view of the space immediately surrounding the ship. Three warships had suddenly materialized around the *Sun Wolf*, each less than a half kilometer away. One faced them head-on, another sat directly astern, and the third hovered above them.

They looked exactly like Netvor warships.

24

AM 7491 SYSTEM
Qarsoon Space

Domain Day 69, 2223

Hotah took a sharp inbreath. His hands darted back to weapons control.

"Easy, Lieutenant," Aiden said in the calmest tone he could muster. "Remember what Jo told us. All the Libera's ships are former Netvor warships that they hijacked."

After a brief moment—Aiden guessed it was a deliberate pause to test the *Sun Wolf*'s reaction—the image of a middle-aged man with sandy-blond hair and piercing blue eyes materialized on the comm screen. He was board-shouldered, had a clean-shaved rectangular face, and he wore a plain gray jumpsuit with an open collar. He was not exactly smiling, but his expression seemed relaxed. *As he should be,* Aiden thought. Vedderman clearly had the upper hand here.

"In case Jo hasn't already told you," Vedderman began, "there are many among us who want nothing to do with your people and who vehemently oppose any interaction with you. They don't consider you an enemy, as such. Not like the Netvor. Nevertheless, they would have me vaporize you on sight just for being here, no questions asked. But there are others, me included, who believe we share common goals, as well as a common enemy, and we are interested in hearing what you have to say. That said, we have a problem—"

"I understand, Captain," Aiden said, interrupting Vedderman before the man could steamroll their interaction with whatever "problem" he had before Aiden could make his case. "My people are also sharply divided in similar ways. Many are uninformed, prejudiced, blinded by fear and selfishness, to the extent that they've allowed themselves to be led by a man who deliberately inflames their fears and promotes more ignorance to increase his own personal power. We are not perfect, by any means. But all of us, your people and mine, are in grave danger from a very powerful enemy. And I mean right now. Not just 'sometime soon.' None of us can afford to ignore that fact or to waste time debating it."

Vedderman paused for a moment in thought. Then he said, "There are now 733 of us Libera on Qarsoon. That's the name we've given to our planet. I'm sure most of us will agree with you about the seriousness of the threat we both face from the Netvor. But it will be difficult for you to prove *how* urgent it is for us. We're fully aware that the Netvor are actively seeking our colony. But despite the regrettable blunder that brought *you* here, we believe we're well hidden, and will remain so for many years to come. Long enough for us to increase our military strength, build our own fleet, and equip it with superior technology that can defeat the Netvor when and if they ever show up."

Aiden shook his head. "I'm sorry, Captain, but I believe that's a naïve assessment. It's a blindness that will prove fatal if you persist in it. You may have some time before they find you, but less than you think. And for us, for the people of the Solar System, and Earth in particular, we have far less time. In fact, less than 56 hours."

Vedderman's face fell. A reflexive response. A genuine one. "What do you mean?"

"At noon, Domain Day 71, Earth will be incinerated by a Netvor graser. I'm sure you know what a graser is by now, and how Cardew used one to sterilize several habitable planets in Astrocell

Beta. *Living* worlds. It's a very powerful, gamma-ray-burst weapon. And the one aimed at Earth is cloaked. We can't do a damn thing about it with our present technology. *That* is the definition of urgency. And it's the most immediate reason why we've come here for your help. Talk of alliance is crucial, yes, but irrelevant if Earth is destroyed just days from now."

The expression of shock on Vedderman's face transformed into rage as Aiden went on to describe the details of the Iapetus massacre by the Netvor graser, the ultimatum given to Earth, and its timeline. When Aiden told Vedderman the terms of the ultimatum—to reveal the location of the Libera colony or else Earth dies—the Libera captain's face turned stone cold. "Your governments know the coordinates of our colony?"

"No." Aiden held up his hand. "Absolutely not. But the Netvor apparently think they do. The truth is, no one else knows about this place except me and my crew, here aboard the *Sun Wolf*. It's just a test by the Netvor to see if anyone in the Alliance actually *does* know the coordinates and will come forward with them under the threat of global annihilation. But you and I both know that even if someone did know and revealed it, the Netvor will go right ahead and torch Earth anyway. It's been part of their game plan all along. Now they've got the weapon to do it lurking inside the Solar System, and in just over two days from now, they'll be in position to pull the trigger."

Aiden let that sink in before pressing on. "But wiping out Earth is only part of the Netvor's grand plan, and you know it as well as I do. Earth isn't even a priority. What they really want is to find *your* colony. To steal from it and ultimately wipe it out. Not later, but now. You're a greater threat to them because of your superior tactical technology. You can bet they're committing all their considerable resources to finding you. So I repeat: You don't have as much time as you think. And the humans on Earth have even less. A matter of hours.

"That's why we need to help each other and do it now. It starts with allowing us to use your tech aboard the *Sun Wolf* so we can return to the Solar System in time to hunt and kill the graser. Call it a loan, if you want, no strings attached. But if you refuse, Earth is doomed, and there's no way in hell the Alliance could ever help you in return, even if it wanted to."

Aiden paused and waited to gauge Vedderman's response. How truly human were these *Trans sapiens* who called themselves Libera?

He didn't have to wait long to find out. The mixture of outrage and sadness on Vedderman's face was undeniably human. But there was a steel blade hidden beneath it, hard and cold. And it was about to cut through.

"I'm truly sorry to hear about all this," the Libera captain began. "But I'm afraid we still cannot help you."

"Cannot, or will not?" Aiden struggled to keep his anger under control.

"Both," Vedderman said, his eyes hardening. "In fact, as I started to tell you from the very beginning, the Libera Forum has instructed me to prevent you from leaving here at all. Indefinitely."

"What?" Aiden leaned forward, impelled by an irresistible urge to reach through the screen and grab Vedderman by the neck. From the corner of his eye, he saw Hotah reach for the weapons control. Aiden shot him a warning glance. Hotah backed off.

Vedderman held up both hands. "You must understand, Captain Macallan, that the absolute secrecy of our location is, for now, our only real defense against a Netvor invasion. Keeping ourselves hidden is literally a matter of life and death. Jo has been condemned for revealing our location to you, along with Keen, the one of us who revealed it to her. They have been forgiven. They're our people. But we absolutely cannot afford any further risk of being discovered. And your return to the human worlds from here would increase that risk exponentially. We simply cannot allow it."

Aiden couldn't believe what he'd just heard. But at the same time, he couldn't dismiss the kernel of logic in it. Vedderman had a valid point, and Aiden kicked himself for not foreseeing it. Every member of his crew, seven people including himself, knew exactly where Qarsoon was. Not to mention the ship's AI, Hutton, and the ship's navigational computers.

Vedderman went on. "I don't doubt that your crew members would solemnly swear to never reveal Qarsoon's coordinates in return for the means to save Earth from destruction, or that your AI would obey your command to self-delete that information from its data banks. But let's face it, Captain, the Netvor are everywhere you live and work, including agents implanted throughout your information technologies. From the moment you return to your worlds, every minute that passes will increase the risk of discovery to the point of certainty, more rapidly than either of us can imagine. So, as much as I personally want to help prevent Earth's destruction, I—along with most of us—believe that allowing you to return would inevitably doom our own world."

Aiden slowed his breathing, tried to calm himself, and pulled himself away from his internal panic button. The *Sun Wolf* could, in fact, escape right now in the blink of an eye if he ordered it. Even surrounded by Libera warships, the *Sun Wolf* could disappear from this point in space at 92 percent light speed well before the warships could react. The ship's zero-point bubble was already fully powered. All it would take now was a nod to Pilot Abahem, who at this very moment was focused on him, waiting for just such a signal. They'd be a million kilometers from here in three seconds.

But, aside from saving their own skins, what good would that do? Their mission to save Earth from incineration would fail, without question. And fleeing the scene at this particular moment could only diminish any hopes of establishing a trusting alliance with the Libera. No. It was not time to give up. Not quite yet.

Aiden opened with the most obvious bid. "Captain Vedderman, I assure you that none of my crew members would divulge the location of Qarsoon. Under any circumstances. They know what's at stake here. And all the navigational data in the ship's AI related to where we've been will be deleted permanently long before we return, before our AI reconnects with the OverNet. You have my word."

"I don't doubt your word, Captain," Vedderman said. "Aside from Jo's unshakable trust in you, we know of your reputation. The Libera are aware of your accomplishments. We know that if you hadn't stopped Cardew's disruptions of the voidoids back in 2218, none of us would be here at all. Our corner of the galaxy would have been torn apart, atom by atom. And we know of your part in destroying Cardew himself. Even among those of us who disfavor humanity, you hold a place of honor. But it is not enough. The Netvor have ways. I'm sure that you, of all people, are familiar with what they call brain tapping. You or any of your crew would be prime targets from the moment you set foot back in your worlds. It's regrettable, but it's final. The risk to us is far too great to allow you to return."

Aiden knew Vedderman was right—and knew that he himself would have made the same decision in Vedderman's place—but it had been worth a shot.

Aiden tamped down his frustration and feigned resignation with a simple nod. "You realize, of course, what will happen to you if Earth is destroyed and the Alliance crumbles under a Netvor invasion. You not only lose a powerful ally, one with vast military and industrial resources that, with your technical help, could defeat the Netvor. Decisively. But with the threat from Earth removed, the Netvor will intensify its focus on finding you and wiping you out. Squashing you like a bug. Whether you like it or not, we're in this fight together. You need us as much as we need you."

Vedderman closed his eyes for a moment, almost as if praying. *Who, or what, would a* Trans sapien *pray to?* When he opened them again, the blue of his eyes looked deeper. Colder.

"This discussion is over, Captain Macallan. You will now accompany us back to Qarsoon. It will be up to the Forum to decide what to do with you. Please do not attempt to resist. You are surrounded by three warships. All of them have you targeted."

Aiden shook his head in dismay. It had been worth one last appeal. But now it was time to disappear. He turned to Pilot

Abahem and was about to give her the nod when Alvarez said, "Wait!"

"What is it, Lilly?"

"A voidship just came through the voidoid."

Which meant that a voidship had emerged just under five hours ago from the voidoid, 34 AU away, and Alvarez's sensors were just now "seeing" that event.

Simultaneously, Aiden saw Captain Vedderman on the forward screen jerk his head to the side, listening to something urgent that one of his crew had just said. *They had picked it up too.*

Vedderman looked back at Aiden, eyes wide. "We have company."

Alvarez said, "The exhaust plume signature is a positive hit for a Netvor warship."

The Libera had surveillance monitors stationed on site around the voidoid. They had a much better look at what was going on out there than the *Sun Wolf* had. Vedderman appeared to be listening again to someone off-screen. Then he turned back to Aiden. "It's confirmed. A Netvor warship just entered the system. With an antimatter tanker right behind it. So they're in for the long haul. And they've deployed an array of Holtzman buoys."

Not good. Those Holtzman devices would already be beaming location information back to the very last place the Libera would want it to go. The Netvor military command.

Vedderman scowled at Aiden. "Now the Netvor empire knows where to look."

Aiden controlled his breathing and faced Vedderman. "This changes things."

Vedderman gave Aiden a look that was impossible to misread. A hot blend of fear and anger. "Yes. This changes *everything.*"

25

Domain Day 69, 2223

"You led them here!" Vedderman snarled, his anger raw and immediate.

The Libera captain glared at Aiden from the *Sun Wolf*'s forward screen. A half kilometer of frozen vacuum separated their ships, but Aiden could easily feel the heat from the man's scowl. Aiden clenched his jaw. Vedderman was probably right. *But how?*

"Qarsoon has been perfectly hidden for over five years," Vedderman said before Aiden could respond. "Not a single unwanted intrusion into this system. And now, just hours after you came barging through the voidoid, a Netvor warship follows you in, heading straight toward us. Don't you find that peculiar?"

Vedderman had just sent Aiden a recorded feed from one of the Libera's surveillance platforms stationed at the voidoid. Aiden watched it as the other man spoke. It clearly showed a Netvor battleship emerging slowly from the system's voidoid. A big one. It looked like a Martian M-class battle cruiser, ARM's top-of-the-line warship, except the propulsion housing at its stern looked larger and more elongated than typical beamed core antimatter engines. And its fuel tanks were bigger. It came to a halt at about 30 kilometers from the voidoid.

A moment later, an antimatter tanker followed the warship out of the voidoid. It was a standard Type-2 tanker with updated Penning tanks, designed to be manned by a crew of no less than three. Antimatter tankers were large vessels, but it was the antimatter Penning containment hardware that accounted for most of the bulk. The actual amount of antimatter itself was usually less than 1,000 kilograms. But to keep that much antimatter safely stored required constantly maintaining a delicate balance between magnetic and electrical fields, and the machinery to do that was massive.

As Aiden watched, a small transport shuttle dropped out of the belly of the antimatter tanker, moved up to the warship, and entered its open shuttle bay. Transferring the tanker crew to the warship, Aiden guessed. After the bay doors closed, the Netvor ship moved forward another 20 kilometers, leaving the tanker behind. Then it realigned its position and ignited its beamed core antimatter drive. Full throttle, all 500 terawatts of thrust power.

The surveillance sensors calculated its trajectory based on the first 90 seconds of flight, confirming that it had set course directly for Qarsoon. Estimated time of arrival with flip-and-decel at midpoint was nine and a half days.

Then the Netvor battle cruiser did something that its ARM prototype could never do. It vanished from sight. Fully cloaked.

"Can you explain that, Captain Macallan?"

Shit! No, he couldn't. Aiden matched Vedderman's anger and said, "If you really think that we deliberately revealed to our arch enemy the location of the only ally that could save our butts, then you might as well blow us up right here and now."

"Believe me," Vedderman said without humor, "I'm contemplating doing exactly that, as we speak."

Both Lieutenant Hotah and Pilot Abahem turned to Aiden, waiting for any signal he might give. Aiden returned a subtle headshake, hoping he looked calmer than he felt.

"Listen," Aiden began. "I know it looks bad, but—"

"Bad?" Vedderman interrupted, "As in deceit? Treachery?" He was looking more and more like a man about to pull the trigger.

"So, when were you planning to tell me about the Holtzman buoy you deployed the moment you jumped into this system?"

Uh-oh. Aiden swallowed hard. He should have known the Libera's monitors at the voidoid would have caught the whole thing—the *Sun Wolf* deploying a Holtzman buoy, then destroying it with a burst of rail gun fire almost immediately after.

"It was an error," Aiden admitted, fighting the impulse to throw Silva under the bus. As the ship's captain, he took responsibility for the actions of his officers. He just didn't like doing it for an officer he'd never have chosen in the first place. "A mistake that was quickly addressed."

"Not quickly enough, it seems," Vedderman said.

Aiden seized the moment to inject reason. "Even so, the Holtzman buoy sends only a routine positional report to Alliance Command upon deployment. It includes only the coordinates of the voidoid we used to get here, not of the planet itself. And we didn't enter the coordinates of your planet into our nav computer. If we had, the jump would have failed because those coordinates don't match any known stars. So even if Alliance Command did receive our positional report before the buoy was destroyed, it would point them only to the binary's voidoid. And if anyone wanted to follow us here on those coordinates, that's just where they'd find themselves. From there, it'd be virtually impossible to detect an isolated rogue planet in the dark that just happens to be passing through, nearly 500 AU from the primary star. Not without knowing the exact coordinates of the planet itself."

Vedderman nodded, but with clenched jaw. "And yet, here we are. A Netvor battleship making a beeline for our planet. By your own logic, they must have known Qarsoon's exact coordinates beforehand. The ones you say no one else knew but yourselves."

The Libera captain was right again, and it did not look good for the *Sun Wolf.* How the hell could the Netvor have known where to go, right out of the voidoid? Aiden had a sudden sinking feeling. He glanced at Silva. The man's face was blank, an unreadable mask.

Aiden put the matter aside. "I honestly don't know how the Netvor could have gotten Qarsoon's coordinates. But now that they seem to know where you're hiding, you can't possibly object to the *Sun Wolf* returning home. No more risk of us leaking your coordinates. The cat's out of the bag, Captain. Now you're going to need our help more than ever. Just as we need yours."

Vedderman said nothing. His eyes remained hard. But logic had cooled him down a fraction. Aiden said, "So, can we talk now?"

Vedderman straightened his shoulders. "Yes, we can talk. It's best if you come to Qarsoon and meet with the chairperson of the Forum, Litha Berne. She's been following all of this very closely. You'll need to speak with her."

Aiden took a deep breath. "Agreed. But I must remind you. We don't have a lot of time for debate. Earth has little more than two days to live unless I can get back in time to save it."

"I understand. Please make ready to accompany the *Ark* back to Qarsoon. Our other two ships will remain here on patrol. We do not have zero-point drives like the *Sun Wolf* does, so it will take us about two hours. I ask that you not proceed ahead of us."

"Agreed. And I'll need to talk with Jo before meeting with the Forum's chairperson. Will that be possible?"

"Yes. She is currently at Forgeron Station. That's our orbital utility station. We'll dock there before taking a landing shuttle down to the surface. Jo is anxious for any word of her son, Rene. She wanted to come out here with us to meet you, but I thought it was best if she did not. It would have been traumatic for her to watch us vaporize you and your ship, if we'd needed to."

"Very thoughtful of you," Aiden said, still unsure of how he felt about Vedderman as a person. After a moment, a hint of a smile found its way to one corner of Vedderman's mouth. Aiden decided that he liked the man.

~ ~ ~

Two hours later, the Libera's orbital station came into view. The *Sun Wolf* and the *Ark*, travelling in tandem, slowed for their final approach. According to Vedderman, Forgeron served a similar purpose for Qarsoon as Hawking Station did for Earth. It was a shipbuilder platform, ore processing and manufacturing center, as well as a repair and equipment-fitting station. But unlike Earth's Hawking Station, which was located at Moon-Lagrange point L5, Forgeron had established a stable low orbit over Qarsoon at about 1,100 kilometers above its surface. And unlike Hawking Station, which was always bathed in sunlight, Forgeron would have been nearly impossible to see if it hadn't been lit up like a Christmas tree. In the absence of light from a nearby sun, the station was illuminated on all sides by an extensive network of powerful LED spacelights.

The station had originally belonged to the Netvor, built on specs stolen from the Alliance. Like all the rest of Libera's infra-structures, it had been "liberated" from a Netvor creche after a brutal *Trans sapien* rebellion. Bringing it to Qarsoon covertly had been a heroic challenge, Vedderman told him, an operation that had galvanized the Libera's quest for independence.

Given Forgeron's lineage, Aiden was not surprised to see how similar it looked to Hawking Station. Four massive U-shaped structures were joined at their apexes, their dual arms facing outward to provide external docking sites. Perpendicular to the docking arms, the station's central hub supported a huge cylin-drical assembly that housed smelters, fabrication factories, a hydroponic farm, personnel habitats, and a fledgling research fa-cility. An armored control/command pod occupied the remaining uppermost segment of the station. And, like Hawking Station, Forgeron's powerful gravity transducers conferred a steady 1 G to all habitable sections.

The *Sun Wolf* slowed to a stop, just a half kilometer off. Two of the station's docking arms were occupied by voidships under construction. One looked more finished than the other. A medium-sized cargo vessel hovered off to the side, accompanied by a single patrol frigate. The optical scope picked up an antimatter tanker anchored about 50 kilometers out.

Aiden hailed Vedderman again. When the Libera captain's image appeared on the comm screen, Aiden asked if the *Sun Wolf* could dock at the station so that he could board directly. "I'm on a tight timeline. When we leave here to head home, we'll need to do it quickly. No time wasted on shuttle transfers between ship and station. Can we do that?"

Vedderman didn't respond immediately—Aiden guessed he was considering security issues—then he said, "I'll allow that. Use Dock 3. Station Control will guide you in. There's a pressurized passenger ramp from there into the station. I'll take the *Ark* into Dock 4 and meet you in the passenger vestibule."

As the *Sun Wolf* began its docking maneuver, Aiden tried to keep Vedderman engaged by asking him about the ships he'd seen at and around the station.

"We have a total of eight military vessels," Vedderman said. "Five battle cruisers and three armored patrol frigates—all hijacked from the Netvor and updated with our technologies. As you can see, we're in the process of building two more battle cruisers of our own design."

Impressive. "Where are you getting your raw materials? Metal ores? Chemicals?"

Vedderman pointed upward, in a direction away from the planet below. "From our moon, Sestra. We've got two mining operations up there, churning out everything we need, although not as quickly as we'd like."

Aiden nodded. "What about that antimatter tanker? There aren't any gas giants in this system to harvest. Where are you getting antimatter to power the station and fuel your ships?"

"That's a challenge for us," Vedderman admitted. "We have to send tankers into another star system to harvest antimatter from gas giants there. That's 34 AU out to our voidoid for the jump, then another 13 AU on the other side to reach the star's planetary system. They get there almost on empty, load up the reserve tanks, then come back the same way. It takes at least six weeks in all, if everything goes smoothly. We have only two tankers. They're on a rotating schedule. The one you see parked out there just finished fueling our ships and topping up the station's power reactors, so it's only about a quarter full now. The other tanker is on its way back from the HD 3158 system, out in the Phoenix sector, still a couple weeks away."

Alvarez cut in, speaking to Aiden. "Docking in five seconds."

The ship shuddered with a low-frequency thud that rumbled through the deck plates as the huge magnetic docking arm made contact with the *Sun Wolf*'s ventral mooring plate.

Aiden decided to bring Dr. Sudha Devi and Lieutenant Hotah along with him, leaving Alvarez, Silva, Assan, and Pilot Abahem aboard the *Sun Wolf*. When he informed Vedderman of his boarding party, the Libera captain initially objected to Hotah's presence. Lieutenant William Hotah's reputation, it seemed, had preceded him, even out here among the Libera. But Aiden insisted, and further insisted that Hotah remained armed, albeit with a single, securely holstered handgun. Hotah, of course, would choose to carry his Titan .45. It was a signal Aiden wanted to send, more than anything else, as he would be walking into a colony of physically augmented *Trans sapiens*, many of whom were not happy with his visit. But Aiden wanted Hotah along not just as a bodyguard but also for his keen eyes and alertness.

The choice of Sudha Devi was met with less resistance. She was not only a medical doctor but a trained psychiatrist with genuine people skills and superlative emotional intelligence. While Aiden focused on his main mission, she could observe things he might miss on a psychosocial level, just as Hotah could do on a tactical level.

As Devi and Hotah headed for the passenger lock, Aiden lingered on the bridge and turned to his XO. "Commander Silva, you have command of the bridge. Beyond routine duties of a second-in-command, you will do nothing without consulting me first. Understood?"

Silva nodded once, his demeanor outwardly calm, and said, "Understood, sir."

As Aiden left the bridge, he asked Alvarez to walk with him. When they were far enough down the corridor and out of earshot, he stopped and said, "Lilly, I want you to keep an eye on Silva for me. You know I have reservations about him. I didn't want to leave him in command, but I can't afford to take him with me. His hatred for the Libera is palpable. His presence would sabotage what I'm trying to do down there. So he stays aboard. Watch him for me. Use my private channel to notify me of anything I need to worry about. Are you good with that?"

"Yes, absolutely," Alvarez said. "I have the same reservations about him."

She placed a hand on his arm and said, "Good luck, Aiden."

He smiled back with more confidence than he felt. *Luck. I'm going to need all I can get.*

26

AM 7491 SYSTEM
Forgeron Station, Qarsoon

Domain Day 69, 2223

"Aiden! I am so happy to see you!"

Jo ran up to greet him, dashing effortlessly over the deck plates of the station's passenger vestibule, covering the distance between them like an Olympic sprinter. Aiden feared that she would bowl him over until she stopped on a dime just in front of him. She threw her long sinewy arms around him and gave him a hug perfectly tempered for the human rib cage, a skeletal structure she could easily crush if not mindful in her enthusiasm.

She released him, stood back, and smiled broadly. "You made it. I knew you would."

Every time Aiden encountered Jo in person, her appearance jolted him in the same way it had the very first time he'd laid eyes on her. Her deep ebony skin, short blonde hair, Asian facial features, and startling green eyes all conspired to evoke a unique kind of beauty that was both pleasing and disturbing at the same time.

It took him a moment to recover from the effect before responding. "Yes, I made it. But not without considerable drama."

Her smile disappeared. "You mean the Netvor ship on its way here?"

It was not exactly what he meant, but this wasn't the time to tell her what had happened to her undelivered telegem crystal and the nearly fatal attack by the Netvor agent it had triggered. But before he could come up with a suitably evasive response, Jo's expression had already changed to one that Aiden recognized all too well, having seen it so often on Skye's face. Which is why Jo's next question was no surprise.

"Rene. Is he okay? And Skye?"

"Yes, they're both fine. I saw them just yesterday on Shénmì Station. Rene and Bri were happily playing together at the Campbells'. He misses his mom quite a lot, though."

Aiden mentally kicked himself for adding that last sentence. Upon hearing it, Jo's lower lip quivered for a second, and her eyes moistened. Aiden guessed that her emotions might have escalated from there if she hadn't finally noticed they were not alone in the spacious passenger vestibule. Sudha Devi and William Hotah stood quietly nearby. Devi stood relaxed and smiled warmly at Jo. Hotah was looking at his feet as if finding them of immense interest. Jo straightened up, went over, and greeted them both.

Aiden looked around. No one else had accompanied Jo. No guards or soldiers. The four of them were alone in the vestibule. He glanced at his chrono impatiently. "Where is Vedderman and his crew?"

"They docked farther up on the station," Jo said. "They should be here shortly."

"Before they get here," Aiden said, "I need to fill you in on what's happening back on Earth and how that's changed my priorities for this mission."

"You're talking about the Netvor's cloaked graser," she said. "It sneaked into the Solar System, and now it's setting up to torch planet Earth. Yes, I overheard the comms between you and Captain Vedderman. The Netvor think that someone in the Alliance knows the location of Qarsoon. It's horrible, and I feel partially responsible. There's a Netvor agent on Shénmì Station, Aiden. Somehow, he found out that I knew Qarsoon's coordinates and tried to get them from me. I barely escaped him, but he must have told his handlers that the coordinates were obtainable somewhere outside the Libera's safekeeping."

"We know about that agent, Jo. He's dead now." Aiden glanced pointedly at Hotah, who smiled sinfully, made a hand gesture resembling a pistol, and blew imaginary smoke from its barrel. Back to Jo, he said, "I'll fill you in on that later, but for now, don't beat yourself up. The Netvor are going to fry Earth no matter what, as soon as their graser moves into optimal targeting position. They're just using the occasion to extort any information they can get before pulling the trigger. Rumors that the coordinates might be floating around somewhere in the Alliance just gave the Netvor the bright idea to use it as a ransom demand. They'll wait to see if anything useful rises to the surface, but only for as long as it takes to move the graser into position. After that—coordinates or not—they'll kill Earth.

"The most important thing now, Jo, is for the *Sun Wolf* to get back to the Solar System, find the graser, and destroy it before it's too late. Getting back in time isn't a problem for the *Sun Wolf*. It's getting back with the *means* to find and destroy the graser. That can only be done by defeating its cloaking and shielding. You said in your telegem message that Libera have the technology to do it. I'm hoping you're right. Because that's really why we're here."

Jo nodded. "Yes, they *do* have the technology. It's real. I've seen it in action."

Aiden let out a breath he'd been holding in too long. "Good." He stepped closer to her and said, "Jo, I know your original goal in coming here was to promote a long-term alliance between humans and Libera. I want that, too. But that won't happen if Earth is destroyed first. So, for now, I'm shelving any talk of formal alliances. It'll only lead to time-consuming distractions. Time that we can't spare right now."

"I understand," she said, but with a hint of reservation. Aiden couldn't criticize any ambivalence she might feel about the fate of Earth-born humans. During her short stay among them, the ignorant, xenophobic isolationists had made it dangerously clear that she was not welcome there. But Jo was smart enough to understand the consequences of Earth's destruction, for her as well as for all *Trans sapiens*.

"I'll help you in any way I can," she said. "I'll tell you what I know of the Libera technology and how much of it could be transferred to the *Sun Wolf*. But I also need to fill you in on what kind of resistance you'll be facing here."

Before Jo could say anything more, Captain Vedderman entered the vestibule accompanied by three other Libera. One appeared to be male and the other two female. They all moved with the same powerful grace and efficiency that Jo did. None of them were smiling, and one of them looked openly resentful.

Vedderman approached and gave Aiden the kind of nod that passed for a formal handshake between two individuals from vastly different worlds meeting for the first time, wary but respectful. His blue eyes were more direct and piercing in person, his short-cut, sand-colored hair and square jaw more arresting. He stood at about the same height as Aiden but was stockier in build.

Aiden introduced his two crew members. Vedderman nodded to each, his eyes lingering for a moment on Hotah's holstered Titan .45. Then he motioned to the three people standing behind him and introduced them individually.

"This is my crew. Ananya Kumar, Comm/Scan officer; Emi Tanaka, Tactical Officer; and Keen, Propulsion Engineer."

It was the first time Aiden had met anyone else like Jo. Other *Trans sapiens*. Not Netvor, but not human-born either. Like Jo, they all appeared perfectly human in every way. But Aiden sensed something different about them, something subliminal he couldn't put his finger on. An aural quality, just beyond his perception.

Aiden smiled at each one in turn. Kumar, a tall, slender woman who looked to be in her late twenties, smiled back at him briefly. She had long dark hair and large brown eyes that sparkled with intelligence. Keen was short and round but looked fit. He wore a pair of old-fashioned wire-rimmed glasses over his wide-set, brown eyes and sported a trim beard the same color as his tawny brown hair. He also responded with a brief smile that quickly changed back to a neutral expression.

The vibe from Emi Tanaka was far less ambiguous. Aiden noticed that Hotah had focused his attention on her the moment Vedderman's crew entered the room. Hotah's relaxed, alert stance became noticeably less relaxed and more alert.

She was a compact Asian woman with short, spikey, black hair shaved to stubble at the temples. Her eyes were so dark brown they might have been jet black. She glared at Aiden, unblinking, her mouth frozen in a barely concealed sneer. And like Lieutenant Hotah, her Tactical-Officer counterpart, she also wore a holstered weapon. Her hands were held at her side, steady but ready, one of them uncomfortably close to the butt end of her pistol.

When Tanaka shifted her eyes from Aiden to meet Hotah's penetrating gaze, her posture stiffened, not a muscle moved. Like two predators meeting in a jungle where only one can reign and all others are prey.

Vedderman must have seen it, too. He moved casually to stand between the two Tactical Officers and said, "Our landing shuttle is ready to depart. Shall we?"

Following Vedderman's outstretched hand, they all moved toward a hatch at the opposite end of the vestibule. The group passed through it into a long, tubular corridor leading to the station's shuttle bay. It was cold inside. The air felt thin and smelled of aging plastics. He and Jo walked side by side while Devi and Hotah did the same a couple meters ahead of them.

"Captain Vedderman mentioned that the current population on Qarsoon was 733," Aiden said to her, leading with a safe topic. "Is that about right?"

"It stands at 732," Jo said pointedly, "not including me. But that number is not growing. Remember, *Trans sapiens* cannot reproduce the way humans do. The only way to increase their numbers is by cloning, and the Forum has, for now, decided to cease all cloning activity. At least until they can develop better ways to support a larger population. It's a matter of limited resources."

"Resources? Like energy sources to power the colony's infrastructures? Or basic stuff like food and water?" Aiden knew that

Trans sapiens were physiologically augmented far beyond human standards, but they still had to eat and drink.

"Energy sources aren't a problem here," Jo said. "This planet is still very volcanically active. Geothermal energy is readily available at many nearby sites."

"Generating electricity the old-fashioned way," Aiden said. "Steam-powered turbines."

"Old-fashioned, yes. But reliable. And water isn't a problem here either, as you'll see. It's everywhere on Qarsoon. But ingestible nutrients? That's more challenging. Right now, all food sources for the Libera come from the abundant fungi covering the planet's surface. It's processed into various forms that provide necessary nutrients for *Trans sapien* physiology."

"Fungi? Here? On a rogue planet?"

"Yes. It's incredible, Aiden. Vast forests of bizarre fungal structures, adapted to the cold and darkness over hundreds of thousands of years. You'll see when we land. Skye would love it."

No doubt about it, Aiden thought as the group passed into the shuttle bay. Skye, his exomycologist wife, would be thrilled to visit such an extraordinary planet. As for Aiden? He'd be thrilled just to leave the planet alive.

<u>27</u>

AM 7491 SYSTEM
In Transit to Qarsoon

Domain Day 69, 2223

THE landing shuttle was a big one, modeled after a G-class VTOL Planetary Lander, capable of carrying 14 passengers—seven rows of two side-by-side seats—along with two pilots seated up front. Vedderman and Keen occupied the pilot seats, while Aiden and Jo sat together in the seats farthest aft. The other four occupants were scattered in between. Sudha Devi and Ananya Kumar sat together, midway up, already engaged in animated conversation. Hotah and Tanaka sat conspicuously far apart, casting wary glances at each other.

They were informed that the flight to the surface of Qarsoon would take just over three hours, the time needed to decelerate from orbital velocity, reenter the atmosphere at a controlled rate, and perform a landing approach. The shuttle detached from the docking arm, cleared the station, and began its initial burn toward the planet. Satisfied that he could not be easily overheard, Aiden leaned closer to Jo and asked her for more details of the extraordinary technology he hoped the Libera would let him use aboard the *Sun Wolf*.

"The two most significant advantages the Libera have over anyone else," she began, "are—one—they can detect fully cloaked

Netvor vessels, even at vast distances, and—two—they can cloak their own ships in a way that's impossible for the Netvor to detect. They can even maintain their cloak while executing a voidjump, something the Netvor can't do. So I guess that's number three on the list."

"Have you actually witnessed this capability?"

"Yes," she said enthusiastically. "On my way here from Shénmì aboard the *Ark*, we detected a cloaked Netvor warship nearly 10 million kilometers away. And we were able to approach it without them knowing we were right there on top of them."

Aiden realized his jaw had dropped. He closed it and asked, "How?"

"To detect the cloaked Netvor ship, they use a CEI, a Casimir-Ebadi Interferometer. Ananya Kumar has modified it to amplify sensitivity to the slightest disturbances in the zero-point field. Disturbances caused by gravitational effects. Didn't you have a CEI aboard your ship at one time, back when Dr. Ebadi was with you at Alpha-2 Hydri? Is it still there?"

"Yes, we did," Aiden said, his excitement growing. "And yes, it's still aboard the *Sun Wolf*, right where Ebadi left it."

Maryam Ebadi was now the director of the Cauldron in Elgin Woo's absence. She had invented the CEI and brought it aboard the *Sun Wolf* back in 2218 on their mission to locate the gateway voidoid at Alpha-2 Hydri. It was still integrated into the ship's sensor array but rarely used since then.

"That's good, Aiden," Jo said, sharing his excitement. "Because your CEI can be modified in the same way to spot the cloaked graser from afar. Ananya showed me how to do it. She gave me the code sequences."

"Excellent." Aiden was pleased but didn't want to get ahead of himself. "So what about the Libera's cloaking tech? We'll need that to approach the graser without being detected. Otherwise, if it sees us coming, it will drop its cloak and power up its shield. We can't defeat Netvor shields yet. We wouldn't be able to destroy it."

Jo made a face as if to doubt Aiden's assumption about the absolute invincibility of Netvor shielding. But when she said nothing more, he continued. "How difficult would it be to install and operate this Libera cloaking tech in the *Sun Wolf*?"

"That's a little more complicated than the CEI modification, but not impossible. The Libera cloaking uses the same technology the *Sun Wolf* uses for its shielding—by manipulating EM fields to create a zero-point bubble around the ship. But the zero-point bubble they create for cloaking is significantly different than what the *Sun Wolf* uses for shielding. Their EM fields are tuned to a highly complex matrix of resonant frequencies derived from diffraction patterns of light shone through painite crystals. It's an amazing discovery, something that would impress even Dr. Woo."

Aiden didn't doubt it. Woo, after all, was the inventor of the zero-point drive that powered the *Sun Wolf*. The first phase of powering up the drive was inducing the ship's EM generators to create a zero-point bubble—Woo called it a hypospace bubble—in front of and around the ship, a region in which the zero-point field of space had been virtually eliminated. Aside from eliminating the forces of inertia—a miraculous feat that allowed the ship to reach 92 percent light speed in a matter of seconds—it also isolated the ship from the normal space-time continuum, effectively creating a discontinuity barrier that weapons fire could not breach. But manipulating the same EM fields to act as both a shield *and* a cloak? That was a Herculean achievement that Elgin Woo himself would applaud.

But with painite crystals? Aiden was an accomplished planetary geologist, both academically and in field work, so he actually knew about painite crystals when almost no one else did. What he remembered most about painite was that it was perhaps the rarest mineral in the known universe, not just on Earth.

When he pointed that out to Jo, she said, "Apparently there's an unusual abundance of painite crystals here on Qarsoon. Its peculiar combination of calcium, zirconium, boron, aluminum, vanadium, and oxygen gives it an orange-red color that diffracts light into unique patterns. The Libera have translated those patterns into algorithms, then programed them into the EM-field generators to create a kind of oscillating zero-point bubble that acts as a cloak."

Aiden could only shake his head in amazement. How the hell did they figure that one out? How could they have known? What these *Trans sapiens* had accomplished in such a short period of time was nothing short of miraculous. Almost mystical . . .

"Then it's conceivable," he said, "that this device using painite crystals could be brought aboard the *Sun Wolf* and integrated into our drive system to produce the Libera's cloaking effect?"

"I believe so. It would take more time, but it could be done in transit. I'm sure Emi Tanaka, the *Ark*'s Tactical Officer, could do it. That's her specialty."

Emi Tanaka. The surly one . . .

Aiden and Jo fell silent for a moment. He looked out the viewport, down toward where the dark planet should be, but there wasn't much to see. He had to block out the reflections of light coming from inside the shuttle before he could finally detect the boundary of the planet's atmosphere by how starlight reflected off its dense upper layer. As he looked on, an opening in the clouds revealed a pinpoint of bright orange light glimmering on the surface. Jo noticed, too, and said, "An active volcano. Lots of them on Qarsoon. Ground quakes, too. The Libera call them Qarquakes."

Interesting. Aiden suppressed his overactive science-brain to refocus on the matter at hand. "Okay, give me a quick rundown on the politics down there."

Jo responded with a heavy sigh. It was a topic that clearly troubled her.

"I've only been here for 3 days, Aiden," she said apologetically. "It took all of 16 days to get here from Shénmì. So I don't have a lot of deep insights. I can tell you what I've observed so far, but I think a short history of how the colony got started would give you a quicker insight into who these people are and how they got that way."

She was right, of course. Aiden nodded for her to continue.

The rogue planet, she said, was discovered about five years ago by one of the first groups of *Trans sapien* rebels to overthrow an entire creche. By all accounts, it was a heroic rebellion led by none other than Hans Vedderman. The rebels managed to hijack the Netvor warship stationed at the creche and fled into another star system, looking for a place to hide. The ship—which they rechristened the *Ark*—had been one of Cardew's original "seeker" ships designed to find habitable worlds and was equipped with advanced astrometric instrumentation. One of the escaped *Trans sapiens* aboard, an astronomer and mathematician named Astur Ali, used the equipment's microlensing module to spot the rogue planet and pinpoint its fortuitous proximity to the voidoid of a binary star system. She recognized that the planet was on a flyby trajectory around the binary's primary star that brought it to within 34 AU from the system's voidoid.

Meanwhile, the virus mediating the mutation that had turned the developing clones into *Trans sapiens* instead of Netvor had mysteriously spread to other creches, even to those on other planets, spawning more rebellions and more exiles. Through clandestine Holtzman communications, the *Ark* found two other groups of escaped *Trans sapiens* and was able to rendezvous with them in a star system called HD 9896. Both of them had fled there in hijacked Netvor voidships, bringing along other critical infrastructures and technologies stolen from the Netvor.

The *Ark* was chosen to make the journey to the rogue planet to assess its potential as a colony site for the exiled *Trans sapiens*. It arrived to find the planet remarkably habitable. They summoned the other two groups, and together they established a primitive foothold there. The astronomer, Astur Ali, christened the planet Qarsoon—a Somali word meaning "hidden." The fledgling colony established a tribal form of democracy and agreed to call themselves the Libera, a word from the Esperanto language meaning "the free."

Aiden was spellbound throughout Jo's narrative, his impatience forgotten. It was an amazing story, a tale of courage and indomitable thirst for freedom—like all stories of resistance against oppression throughout human history.

"What I don't get," he finally said, "is how did the genetic mutation that saved you from becoming a Netvor get into a virus in the first place, not to mention how that virus could spread to so many other creches so quickly, even to different planets. It just doesn't make sense."

"I asked the same thing. No one seems to know. But I think there's something they're not telling me."

Aiden shrugged and looked at his chrono. "Okay, I'll file that one for later. Tell me about the culture and the politics."

"There are two factions among the Libera," Jo said, "the Humanists and the Posthumanists. They differ on many important issues. The latter embrace much of Cardew's original Posthuman ideology and wish to dissociate themselves entirely from 'normal' humans. They're not like the Netvor, not programed from inception to identify humans as vermin to be exterminated at all costs. But they do view the random, chaotic nature of human evolution as infinitely inferior to self-directed evolution."

"Self-directed evolution?"

"Yes. That's where the evolutionary direction of a species is deliberately determined by individuals of that species and rigorously managed by themselves. It can only be achieved through advanced cloning technologies. The Posthumanists view sexual reproduction as haphazard, wasteful, and ultimately dangerous. They point to the vast disparity between humanity's potential and the endless loop of self-destruction it can't seem to pull itself free from. They understand the biological upsides of sexual reproduction, like how species diversity is crucial for robust and healthy populations, but they believe those benefits can be managed through intelligent cloning without all the messy trial-and-error of sexual reproduction.

"The Humanists, on the other hand, feel a certain organic connection with 'normal' humans and view sexual reproduction as more natural and in tune with what it means to be human. In fact, they're advocating for cloning new Libera with the ability to sexually reproduce, beings of two distinct genders with distinctly different genotypes. One carrying the ova and the other carrying the sperm. They also believe that the physical process of sexual reproduction consummated between two individuals would present a unique opportunity to experience beauty and transcendence.

"It's not that the Humanists aspire to *be* human, per se, only to be *more* human. They're strongly sympathetic to the plight of humanity and disagree with the Posthumanists' view that humanity is a failed evolutionary experiment. They see it more as a work in progress that still holds promise of transcendence."

Aiden could clearly see both sides of that argument. But where he stood between them, personally, was less clear. "So it's the Posthumanists I'm going to have the most trouble with."

"That's exactly right. And they're the majority right now. They won't be inclined to ally with humans, much less to help you save Earth from destruction. Not unless they get something in return. Something of great value to them."

And that was the million-dollar question. What could he offer to the Libera, on behalf of all humans, that would be valuable enough for them to reach out across the stars and lend a helping hand? He wished like hell that it wasn't up to him to come up with an answer.

Aiden was still stewing over that question when Vedderman's voice came over the comm. "We'll be landing in 20 minutes. Strap in."

The sudden sinking feeling in Aiden's gut wasn't just from the shuttle's rapid descent into the murky vapors of Qarsoon's upper atmosphere. Glancing out the viewport, his mood had turned as dark as the planet's opaque and unforgiving surface rushing up to meet him.

28

Domain Day 69, 2223

AIDEN Macallan had stood on the surface of many kinds of planets and moons over the last 14 years. As a planetary geologist who began working for Terra Corp's Survey Branch in 2209, he'd been on rocky planets—with or without atmospheres—super-Earths, ice planets, ocean planets, desert worlds, and an impressive variety of moons circling an assortment of ice giants, gas giants, and mini-Neptunes. He'd seen his share of strange things during that time, but nothing quite as strange as the place he'd just set foot on after stepping off the shuttle's passenger ramp.

Without the need for a p-suit and helmet, several things assaulted Aiden's senses at once. The most overwhelming, of course, was the darkness. It was not just dark as night. It was *darker* than night, even in the faint starlight. All planets inside star systems had "daylight" on one side or another. Even when Aiden had been on the night side of any of those planets, he'd always had a subconscious awareness that sunlight bathed the opposite side of the world on which he stood. As if the rays of the sun could echo through the massive bulk of the planet to tickle the back side of his brain with warm reassurances that the fundamental energy of life was not far away, that it had not abandoned the realm of his immediate experience.

That was not the case here. Not on the orphaned planet called Qarsoon.

Aiden could feel it. Could sense the howling absence of a mother sun. The orphaned planet had long ago surrendered to the loneliness of eternal night, wholly consumed by the black emptiness of interstellar space.

His second step from the ramp brought the next blow to his senses. His footstep was that of a man slightly heavier than he should be. And as he took that step, his ears popped with the change in atmospheric pressure. Qarsoon's slightly higher surface gravity, 1.03 G, made his 185-pound body feel more like 190 pounds, and its higher air pressure had caused his middle ear to make the noisy adjustment.

Then there was the cold. The kind of cold that inhabits an entire planet all at once and never goes away. Vedderman had provided Aiden and his crew with heavy synthetic overcoats to ease the hundred-meter walk from the shuttle's landing pad to the colony's bunker-like entrance. Granted, it was not freezing—"only 37 degrees Fahrenheit," Vedderman had said—but the dense, low-lying fog made it feel immeasurably colder. Aiden shivered and pulled the coat's insulated hood down lower over his head.

Vedderman was the last one out of the shuttle. As the ramp folded back up into the shuttle, he said to no one in particular, "Lights."

A series of pole-mounted lights came to life, illuminating a hard-packed pathway leading away from the landing pad. The path disappeared into the ground fog beyond the clearing where residual heat from the shuttle's vertical-landing engines had burned away the vapors. Vedderman led the way, and the others followed. As Aiden walked with Jo at his side, he was pleasantly surprised by how easily he could breathe the air of Qarsoon without feeling any ill effects.

When he mentioned it to Jo, she said, "The oxygen content here is actually higher than on Earth, just over 22 percent, and the rest of it is mostly nitrogen and argon. Argon is an inert gas just like nitrogen, so it displaces oxygen in the same way. Overall, it's not that much different than on Earth."

"Okay. But where the hell did all the oxygen come from? On Earth, most of it came from a couple billion years of plant life, a byproduct of photosynthesis. But here . . . ?"

Jo shook her head. "From what I understand, some of the oxygen is residual from the planet's original atmosphere, but now most of it comes from so-called 'dark oxygen.' From polymetallic nodules in the shallow oceans producing oxygen by electrolysis of seawater, completely without sunlight. It happens on Earth, too, on the ocean floors. But here, it's far more extensive. The oceans are shallower, the seabed nodules are more widespread, and their surfaces have higher voltage potentials. So production of oxygen from electrolysis is far greater here than on Earth, making up for the lack of photosynthetic plant life."

Amazing. "But O_2 production can't go on unchecked, right? Atmospheric oxygen levels greater than 24 percent would be toxic for us. And for *Trans sapiens*, too. It's got to be recycled somehow, like it is on Earth, consumed by animal life—"

"Fungus," Jo said, interrupting him with a smile.

And that's when the overpowering aroma of Qarsoon's dominant life-form hit him like a freight train. To describe it as "earthy" was not only inadequate but also an ironic misnomer, considering that Earth was over 100 light-years away. But it was the only descriptor that came to mind, at least until he began to detect faint overtones of anise, and something else . . . coffee?

"Fungi consume oxygen," Jo reminded him. "And there's a lot of fungi here. As far as they can tell, fungal life covers all land masses on Qarsoon, along with bacteria. Fungi and bacteria are the only two life-forms known to exist here now. I'm guessing that those two have adapted to the absence of a sun by evolving some complex symbiotic relationships between them."

No doubt. Aiden was not an exobiologist. But he knew enough about it that if someone had told him extensive fungal life could thrive on a rogue planet for hundreds of thousands of years without a sun, he'd shake his head and walk away from that crazy person. But now?

As the group followed Vedderman deeper into the inky fog, Aiden began to mentally tick off items that he knew fungi needed to live and grow.

Fungi needed water in a liquid state, free and unbound to other compounds. They thrived in damp environments. No problem here. Liquid water was plentiful, not only in oceans and lakes, but also as water vapor in the all-pervasive ground fog. Fungi needed oxygen for its metabolic functions. Plenty of that here, too, as Jo had explained. It could tolerate a wide range of temperatures as long as it didn't go much over 100 degrees Fahrenheit or too close to freezing, although certain psychrophilic fungi were just fine with temperatures below freezing. Here, thanks to the planet's internal core heat and potent greenhouse gases, it was a steady 37 degrees, everywhere and all the time.

And fungi *loved* to grow in the dark. Light, in fact, could even inhibit mycelial growth. No shortage of darkness here on Qarsoon. And while most species of fungi on Earth required light to trigger the formation of fruiting bodies, others could grow and reproduce perfectly well without light. So even by Earth standards, adaptation to total darkness was not impossible.

But that left one question Aiden couldn't easily answer. Nutrient sources. Fungi were heterotrophic, meaning they had to consume other organisms to obtain food, usually in the form of dead remains—organic matter referred to as necromass. They weren't like plants that derived nutrients through photosynthesis. So if no other life-forms existed here for nearly 650,000 years, where did the necromass come from to feed the fungi?

While pondering that question, the pole lamps illuminating the pathway had become less distinct as the fog grew thicker. They were now just blurs of fuzzy light in the oppressive gloom above their heads. But still bright enough to give him brief glimpses of what lay beyond in the darkness where random gaps in the fog opened up. He saw what looked like stands of tall, slender stalks, maybe two to three meters high and barely a quarter meter thick, terminating in small button-shaped heads. They looked pale gray, but no further detail could be seen in what little light reached them. Fine networks of multibranched extensions spread out from the bases of these macabre stalks, stretching upward like skeletal fingers hungrily grasping at the dank fog.

Suddenly, two flashes of blue light darted out from behind the willowy stems, twirling around in plain view before disappearing again into the thicket. They looked exactly like miniature whirl-winds, swirling vortices of blue light, about two meters tall and nearly one meter wide at the top, narrowing down to nothing where they touched the ground. They reminded him of the dust devils he'd once seen on Mars while visiting a research station at Jezero Crater. But instead of red dust, these were made of spinning lines of glowing, sapphire blue. Their movements were animated. They looked alive.

"What the . . . ?"

Jo had obviously seen them, too, but none of the others in the group had been facing that direction or had seemed to notice. She stopped and looked at him, surprised. "You can see them?"

"Yes. What the hell are they?"

"I'm not sure yet. I saw one the first day I was here. But . . ." She looked at him again, now as if seeing him for the first time.

"What?" They had stopped walking while the rest of the group carried on into the fog without them.

"It's just that . . . you actually *saw* them. After I first saw one, I started asking around to find out what they were, but mostly people just looked at me like I was crazy. So I shut up about it. Then last night, Ananya Kumar took me aside and said that she'd seen them, too, and that quite a few others here have seen them as well. But no one seems to talk about it anymore because the rest of the population thinks they're either joking around or delusional."

"But what are they? Does Kumar have any ideas?"

"Not really. But there's speculation among those who can see them that these things are spirits of the beings who used to inhabit this planet. Long ago, before it went rogue."

"Like ghosts?" Aiden said, in jest. "Seriously?"

Jo stopped, said nothing, and looked away.

"Come on, Jo. Tell me. What are you thinking?"

She turned to face him with an expression that quickly shamed his dismissive smile.

"Aiden," she said. "They have auras."

Aiden had always been skeptical of the whole concept of auras—hypothetical bioelectric emanations surrounding all living beings, including humans, that could be seen only by certain people—clairvoyants, Wiccans, and now the Gaians. But his skepticism changed five years ago when Pilot Abahem's ability to see auras had saved his wife's life. Abahem had identified the Netvor agent who'd kidnapped Skye by recognizing the absence of an aura around him. That had led to the location of where Skye was held captive and to her eventual rescue. Abahem's gift to distinguish between Netvor and humans had been useful on other occasions, too, like when she'd vouched for Jo's true identity after Jo escaped her creche and was taken aboard the *Sun Wolf.* And now it appeared that what Skye had told him yesterday about Jo acquiring the same gift was true.

"Yes," Jo said, answering his unspoken question. "I can see auras, too. Your pilot, Lista, taught me how. The Gaians call it second sight. Without it, I wouldn't have been able to assure myself beyond doubt that all the Libera I've met here are genuine. They all have auras. And so do these blue *swirls.*"

"Blue swirls?"

"That's what they're called by the people who can see them."

At that moment, Hans Vedderman emerged from the fog with a handheld luminator turned on bright and aimed at Jo and Aiden. "There you are," he said. "I thought you'd gotten lost. It's not safe to stray from the lighted trails around here. Please follow me. The entrance to the Main Hall is just up ahead, and the others are waiting."

Aiden and Jo joined the others to find themselves standing in front of a huge, rocky berm with a massive metallic disc set in its face. It was easily four meters in diameter. Its surface looked dull and scarred. Vedderman took a small circular object from his pocket and tapped it once at the right edge of the disc. The point of contact glowed green for a second before the disc began to roll back into the far side of the berm. It made a heavy grinding sound as it opened, a deep growl that only tons of solid steel on the move can make. As it rolled out of sight into a dark recess on the left, Aiden noticed it was nearly a half meter thick.

The group followed Vedderman past the hatch into a broad, gradually sloping tunnel, lit with ceiling lamps and long enough that Aiden could not see where it ended. He was relieved to find a wheeled transport carrier waiting for them near the entrance. It had more than enough seats for all eight of them, was covered on top, but open on the sides. The air inside the tunnel was considerably warmer than outside, less humid, and smelled fresh. He and Jo removed their heavy coats as they climbed aboard the carrier.

By Aiden's estimate, they traveled nearly one kilometer before the tunnel opened into a large, brightly lit living area where their carrier came to a halt in the Main Hall. It was a circular space, maybe 50 meters in diameter with a ceiling nearly 5 meters high. Scores of doorways lined the outer walls all the way around. Portions of the area near the walls appeared to be separated by low partitions, dividing it into numerous workstations and living spaces where people could be seen moving about purposefully. The center of the Main Hall was open and uncluttered. A small group of Libera stood there, watching the visitor's arrival.

Vedderman ushered the group off the carrier and spoke to Aiden. "Captain Macallan, please follow me. Jo, too."

Aiden said, "I request that Dr. Devi accompany me as well."

Vedderman paused for a moment and looked hard at Devi. If anyone could win over the sternest judge of character with a simple smile, it was Sudha Devi. Aiden himself had fallen victim to it many times, and Vedderman was no exception. He nodded politely. "Very well."

Aiden approached the small group of Libera waiting for them, and the woman standing in front came into sharp focus. She was tall, square shouldered, and stood with a regal bearing that gave even the simple tunic she wore the aspect of a majestic mantle. She had smooth pale skin, high cheekbones, thick black hair braided down her back, and fierce blue eyes that fixed Aiden with unsentimental scrutiny. She was not smiling, but her gaze was not unkind.

"I am Litha Berne," she said. "Chairperson of the Libera Forum. We need to talk."

29

Domain Day 69, 2223

"You are fortunate, Captain Macallan," Litha Berne said, "that you are no longer the most unwelcome visitors to Qarsoon. That dubious distinction now passes to the ones you led here. They are, by far, the most unwelcome. But to be honest, you are a close second."

Aiden had feared that the incoming Netvor warship would be Chairperson Berne's first point of discussion, but he honestly couldn't blame her for it. He and Berne faced each other across a finely crafted tabletop made of pure black obsidian. Jo and Devi sat next to him, on either side, while Vedderman and Keen sat in a similar arrangement next to Berne. They had retired to one of the partitioned spaces near the far wall. It was a private place but by no means completely secluded from the hustle and bustle of nearby Libera activity.

Aiden made a brief but genuine bow of contrition and said, "If our arrival here was in any way responsible for the Netvor warship entering the system, I am truly sorry for it. Please believe me that it was not our intention to lead them here. I have done everything in my power to keep your location an absolute secret, known only by me and my crew."

"And yet, here they are," Berne said, leaning her head ever so slightly to one side. "A Netvor battle cruiser heading directly toward our planet, little more than nine days away, but not before leaving Holtzman buoys behind to inform the rest of the Netvor of their discovery. The measures you claim to have taken to protect a secret that you were unwisely entrusted with were obviously not enough. Now you come to us asking for our help."

"Chairperson Berne," Aiden said, "in less than 45 hours from now, over 9 billion humans on Earth—and *all* life on the planet—will perish, killed by lethal gamma-ray bursts from a cloaked Netvor weapon. And now I'm the only one with any chance in hell of stopping it from happening. But that chance is virtually zero without the benefit of your technology to defeat Netvor cloaking. So yes, I *am* asking for your help. But not without offering something in return."

Berne raised her eyebrows, a look of mocking more than curiosity. "And what would that something be, Captain? Please don't waste your time with the arguments I've already heard many times over, not only from Jo but from your own words with Captain Vedderman. You and I both know that there's no way your Alliance could equip enough ships with our technology—and learn how to use it—in time to help defend Qarsoon against an overwhelming Netvor invasion. An invasion that will come much sooner than we expected, now that the Netvor know where to look for us. How many Netvor warships do you think will be following the one that's already here, and how soon do you think they'll be coming?"

Too many and too soon, Aiden admitted to himself. But he said, "I agree. The time it would take to even *negotiate* proposals to equip Alliance ships with your tech—given the UED's isolationist politics combined with Qarsoon's distrust of the Alliance—is out of the question now that the Netvor have you in their sights."

"So," Berne said, "I ask again, what are you offering us in return for our help?"

"Improved chances of survival."

Berne almost smiled. She knew he was scrambling for leverage but asked, "How so?"

"Even if Earth is destroyed, the Alliance will persist. Granted, Earth has always been the de facto center of the Alliance, but not all of its military and industrial strength resides there. In fact, much of it is off-Earth now, stationed throughout the Sol System and elsewhere. Nor does the entire human population live on Earth. Now that the UED's current leadership is senselessly alienating itself from its former allies, the Allied Republics of Mars is in ascendence these days. And most of the independent mining colonies throughout the Solar System will stand with them.

"What's left of the Alliance if Earth is destroyed will likely grow stronger, a more robust decentralized union without a fractious Earth sapping its energy. They'll be tougher, harder to kill, and more pissed off. If they learn that the Libera deliberately refused to help save the lives of billions of innocent humans, you'll have *two* enemies coming after you. Or at least one that will be perfectly happy if the other one wipes you out. Helping us now to save Earth from destruction will favor your chances of survival far more than if you refuse."

When Berne finally did smile, it was without humor, and Aiden knew he'd lost this line of argument. "Be that as it may," she said, "the consequences of which you speak reside too far in the future to be relevant now that the Netvor will be coming for us sooner than later. I'm sure you can see that yourself. It's not an argument the Forum will even consider."

Aiden shrugged his shoulders. He had only one card left to play. "Then I can only conclude, Chairperson, that *Trans sapiens* are not as human as they claim to be. Humans are capable of compassion. When one of us is threatened, others come to their aid. By instinct. Not all, of course. There are cruel and evil humans, to be sure. But that is not the norm among us. We *care* for each other. Most of us would even sacrifice our own lives for those we love. That is what it means to be human.

"I've been told that *Trans sapiens* are different from their Netvor progenitors, that *Trans sapiens* retained their human capacity for empathy rather than having it deliberately excised by the Netvor's cloning program. I see it in Jo, plain as day. Her compassion for her adopted son, for the friends she loves and who love her, is beyond doubt. I truly want to believe that all Libera are like her. But how can I, if the Libera chose to stand by while billions of humans are killed when they have the power to help prevent it?"

Berne stiffened. Her eyes grew hard. She unfolded her hands and placed them palms down on the tabletop. In a voice that was both lower in pitch and higher in volume, she said, "The Libera *are* different from the Netvor, Captain. You would not be alive and sitting here right now if it were otherwise."

Aiden had touched a nerve, a very human nerve. It was the opening he'd been looking for. A path that led deeper. He followed it.

Matching Berne's intensity and forward-leaning posture, he closed the distance between their faces. "You *say* you're different from the Netvor. But I'm not seeing how."

"How are we different from the Netvor?" Her voice resonated with dangerous calmness. "First and foremost, we *can* love. And because of it, we understand that love is the only way to transcend our individual selves, to conquer our original aloneness while we live. Secondly, unlike the Netvor, we can experience pain. Both physical and emotional. And because of it, we understand that suffering is the price we pay for the ability to experience beauty. And thirdly, unlike the Netvor, we are not virtually immortal. And because of it, we understand that death alone makes fully clear the miracle of life and drives our relentless search for truth. That's how we're different from the Netvor."

The power of Berne's words struck Aiden like a living lightning bolt. It straightened his spine against the back of his chair. He glanced at Jo, sitting to his right. She was smiling like a lost child who'd just found her way home.

Aiden took a moment to collect his thoughts, then said, "Chairperson, you have eloquently made my point for me. If what you say is true, then you—all Libera—are as different from the Netvor as humans are and in all the ways that matter. So whether you like it or not, you are biologically and spiritually linked to us. Yes, you are different from us, but you are still one of us. So the real question now is how human do you *choose* to be?"

Aiden slumped in his chair, drained. He was exhausted, not just emotionally but in every other way. Glancing at his chrono, he realized he hadn't slept for nearly 30 hours. Except for a few catnaps here and there, his last sleep cycle had ended yesterday morning, and now it was late afternoon the next day. But looking at his chrono had reminded him of a more important timeline. He had only 44 hours left to save Earth.

Litha Berne looked at him for a long moment in silence. Not just at him, but *around* him, as if seeking some ethereal substance that made him who he was. The quality of light in her eyes changed abruptly, and she said, "All right, Captain. I will bring your request to the Forum. Tell me exactly what you would want from us."

Aiden sat up straight again, thoughts of sleep banished for the moment. "Provide my ship with your technology that allows us to see and track a cloaked Netvor vessel, in this case, a robotic graser weapon, and the technology to cloak our ship in a way that prevents the graser from seeing us coming. You could consider it a loan, if you wish, to be returned after we use it. I would gladly allow any one of you with expertise in using these instruments to come aboard the *Sun Wolf* and accompany us on our mission. In fact, I would even recommend it. Instead of wasting time installing the instruments while we're docked here, your experts could come aboard and set things up while we're in transit. They could even operate it themselves if that proves to be most efficient. Time is of the essence here."

Berne nodded slowly and exchanged glances with Vedderman and Keen. They were considering Aiden's proposal, or at least not dismissing it out of hand.

"Once our mission is complete," Aiden added hastily, "and we're on our way back here to bring your people home, we can take out that Netvor warship heading your way. It won't be even halfway here by the time the *Sun Wolf* returns. With your cloak-defeating technology aboard, it'll be another opportunity to prove its usefulness."

Aiden stopped there, not wanting to sound overly presumptuous. It was all about trust now, and that was still a work in progress.

He looked at Hans Vedderman. "Captain, how long will it take for your landing shuttle to get from here back up to Forgeron Station, including docking?"

"That depends on the station's orbital position," Vedderman said. "It passes over the colony once every 107 minutes. It could take between five and seven hours from liftoff to docking."

Aiden cringed. That was a long time. He did some quick math in his head and said, "By my calculations, the *Sun Wolf* will need to leave Qarsoon space for the voidoid no later than 22:00 tomorrow to arrive in the Solar System with enough time to hunt and kill the graser before the deadline. That means my crew and your technicians, with the necessary equipment in hand, would need to leave here for Forgeron Station no later than 12 noon tomorrow."

He turned back to Berne and said, "That's about 20 hours from now, more than enough time for your Forum to come to a decision. All I ask is that, if the proceedings start looking unfavorable, you'll tell me immediately. I won't waste valuable time waiting around for a more definitive answer."

"Fair enough," Berne said as she rose from the table. "I'll call the Forum to convene now. Most of the population is already aware of the issues as you've presented here. But I must warn you, there will be much debate. We're a community of free thinkers and diverse perspectives. A decision may not come as quickly as you'd like. I will, however, do my best to keep things focused and moving forward."

Aiden took a slow, deep breath, fighting back fatigue. "I'd be happy to address the Forum myself, in person, if you think that would help."

Berne looked at him closely for a moment before shaking her head. "That would be unwise, Captain, a distraction that could slow the proceedings with contentious interactions. I believe you would best be served by getting some rest. When was the last time you slept?"

It was an unexpected gesture of concern. Before he could respond, she said, "We have spare dorm rooms here. You and your crew are welcome to use them for rest while waiting for the Forum to conclude. And there is food nearby, in Kitchen Two, if you care to sample Libera cuisine. It's as safe and nutritious for you as it is for us. Keen will show you the way."

Aiden glanced at Devi. She was as sleep-deprived as Aiden but looked less weary than he probably did. "That would be much appreciated. Thank you."

Before parting, Berne stopped and faced Aiden. Her eyes had softened again. "However this goes, Captain, I wish you the best of luck."

With that, she bowed her head in a brief farewell and left the room.

30

AM 7491 SYSTEM
Qarsoon

Domain Day 69, 2223

IF someone had told him that the savory stew he was eating was made solely of fungus, he would have thought that person had indulged too often in fungi of the hallucinogenic kind. In fact, someone *had* told him, and he still couldn't believe it.

Keen and Jo had led them to Kitchen Two where they sat at a table in a brightly lit open area and were served bowls of steaming "Qarsoup," the name the Libera had given to this particular dish. Even though it smelled delicious when it was first set in front of him by a smiling *Trans sapien*, Aiden had been skeptical. Were they kidding? Fungus by itself may provide enough nutrients for the augmented, hyperefficient metabolism of *Trans sapiens*, but certainly not enough for humans. Or were they *not* kidding and trying to poison him instead?

But Aiden was almost as hungry as he was exhausted, and the needs of his body quickly overcame what he hoped was baseless paranoia. After the first spoonful passed his gullet, his eyes lit up. "This is . . . delicious!"

Emboldened by Aiden's hearty endorsement, both Devi and Hotah dug into their own servings with similar enthusiasm. Keen beamed at them like a proud restaurateur, then bid them farewell.

Jo remained at the table, sipping a tea-colored drink, a fungal-based beverage that she appeared to be enjoying immensely.

Halfway through his bowl of Qarsoup, Aiden slowed down and spoke to Jo. "This is a wonderful concoction, Jo, but if it's made wholly from fungi, it's not going to be enough to sustain us humans. Even if you add vitamin supplements to make up for what fungus lacks, there aren't nearly enough macronutrients, like protein, fat, and carbs. Don't *Trans sapiens* need those things as well?"

"We don't need them quite as much as humans do," Jo said. "But we do still need them to thrive, along with the vitamins you mentioned. Keen said it was a big problem here at first, when the colony was just getting started. The native fungi here had plenty of B vitamins, essential minerals, and fiber. But all the missing macronutrients had to be synthesized in their lab and added to the fungal foodstuffs. Then something weird happened."

"Weird?" Aiden said as he spooned the last bit of stew into his mouth.

"The Libera harvest those tall stalks you saw outside, those skinny stems with the small round caps on top. They're essentially mushrooms, or at least analogous to mushrooms on Earth, the fruiting structures of the fungus. According to Keen, about three years ago, the harvesters started finding a species of fungi they'd never seen before growing right around the colony and nowhere else. When bioanalyzed in the lab, they were found to contain healthy amounts of metabolically accessible protein, fat, carbohydrates, and vitamins. Almost like meat, but not animal meat. It was like the fungi somehow *knew* what Libera bodies needed to survive here and began to biosynthesize it in a new species grown right here on our doorstep."

Aiden froze, spoon still in hand. A déjà vu portal opened up inside Aiden's head like a bright tunnel connecting him to another time, another world. What Jo had just described was eerily similar to what Aiden had experienced when he'd been stranded on Silvanus six years ago, when he'd discovered that the entire planet had become sentient. A highly evolved consciousness had emerged as a property of an immensely complex and interconnected network of mycorrhizal fungi spanning the entire globe. An organic neural net. It was called the Rete, and it had performed a similar biosynthetic miracle for Aiden, a lone human stranded on its surface without adequate nutrients to survive. Was this world, this rogue planet called Qarsoon, another Silvanus? Another Gaia world?

When Aiden realized that the others around the table were staring at him as if he'd grown a third eye, he placed his spoon carefully back into the empty bowl and said, "Time for a nap."

And indeed it was. He had been exhausted and edgy before eating. Now he was exhausted and sleepy. Jo led him and the others down a short corridor to an enclosed dorm room with four rudimentary pallet beds and little else. Spartan, to say the least, but to Aiden, it was the most welcome sight he'd seen in days. Devi settled into her bed and was fast asleep in less than a minute. Hotah sat upright on his pallet, closed his eyes, and began slow breathing, his hand resting inches from the butt end of his holstered weapon.

Aiden thanked Jo before she left and asked her to keep him posted, via his wrist comm, on any new developments. He made her promise not to hesitate to wake him for anything of import. He lay back and closed his eyes. But it wasn't until an hour later when Jo's voice whispered from his comm telling him that the Libera Forum had just convened that Aiden finally let go and allowed the gravity of sleep to pull him down into the waiting arms of Morpheus.

~ ~ ~

Aiden woke with a start. The pallet shook and shifted a few inches across the floor. An earthquake? No, a *Qarquake*. Jo had said they were common on this geothermally active planet.

He was about to close his eyes again when he realized he was enveloped inside a translucent sphere of shimmering blue light. He felt weightless, as if his body hovered just above the surface of his bed. He heard faint musical tones, random but harmonious. Then one tone emerged from the others, establishing itself as the root of a musical scale. The musician in him recognized it as a D-flat. The same key as one of his favorite jazz ballads, "Body and Soul." He'd played it many times as a bass player in his youth. *What the . . . ?*

He suddenly recalled an encounter with Egin Woo years ago when the man had demonstrated to him how all stars "sing," broadcasting their resonant frequencies through space on oscillating waves of plasma, and how Woo could hear their songs. He'd learned that Earth's Sun, Sol, had a resonant frequency corresponding to the musical tone of D-flat. But the D-flat that Aiden heard now was pitched just slightly higher, closer to what a musicologist would call a tempered D-flat. It was like Sol's song but slightly different . . .

He turned to look for Devi and Hotah. Their beds were empty. He was alone in the room. He closed his eyes for a second and took a deep breath. When he opened them, the blue light was gone. The musical tone was gone. He was lying in bed, firmly atop the mattress. He sat up, rubbed his eyes, and looked around. Nothing. Just blank walls, two empty beds, and a table with a carafe of water and three glasses.

A dream. Obviously. Right . . . ?

Aiden looked at his chrono. It was almost 01:00, the first hour of Domain Day 70. He'd slept nearly seven hours. Soundly, without waking once. He looked at his comm. No message from Jo. He got up, put on his shoes, straightened his jumpsuit, and left the room.

He found Hotah sitting on a chair just outside the door, looking alert and well rested. Hotah looked up at him, faintly bemused, and said, "Morning, boss."

"Good morning, Lieutenant. Where are the others?"

"Back in Kitchen Two."

Aiden headed off down the corridor with Hotah at his heels. He found Jo and Devi in conversation at the same table they'd occupied the night before. He looked at Jo, questioning.

She shook her head. "Nothing yet. The Forum is still debating."

Aiden held up his hands in frustration. "Seriously? How long does it take to answer a simple yes-or-no question?"

Devi looked at him sideways. "You know it's not just a 'simple' question, Aiden. Not for these people. There's a lot at stake for them here."

"Oh? And there's not a lot at stake for us, too?" he snapped back.

Immediately regretting his outburst, he sat at the table without saying another word. Devi was unmoved and all too familiar with Aiden's moods. "You need coffee and something to eat."

That he did. Unfortunately, the Libera hadn't yet invented a good substitute for coffee—or hadn't felt the need to—but the steaming, dark brown brew Devi poured for him was surprisingly satisfying. A large plate of soft, biscuit-like rolls sat on the table, and Hotah was already into his third one before Aiden joined the carnage. They, too, were surprisingly good, sweet and buttery. How could they do all this with just fungus?

When he'd had his fill, Jo said, "It's almost star-rise. Let's go outside and watch it."

Jo's childlike enthusiasm brightened Aiden's mood. He knew she was pining for her own child, but she had obviously chosen to accept Aiden's earlier reassurances about Rene's safety and well-being. The choice allowed some happiness to slip back into her life.

Aiden hadn't yet told her about the horrific, life-threatening encounter with "Frank" that Skye had survived on Shénmì Station, which could have endangered Rene as well. And because that incident could be seen as the result of her carelessness with her telegem crystal, Aiden had decided not to tell that story. Not yet, at least.

"Star-rise?" he said. "You mean like sunrise on a normal planet?"

"Exactly," she said brightly. "Qarsoon has a 32-hour rotational period, so once every 32 hours, the star AM 7491 rises over the eastern horizon. It's become a thing among some Libera, to go out and watch it."

"Okay," Aiden said. "I get it. AM 7491 is the star this planet is doing its fly-by around, so I can see how the Libera might consider it as their 'sun.' But it's 500 times farther away than the sun is from Earth. It can't be that easy to pick it out from all the other stars up there."

"Not hard at all," she said. "Even though it looks like a star in the night sky, it's by far the brightest one."

"What about all the fog on this planet? It's everywhere. I couldn't see more than five meters above my head on our walk here from the lander. How can you possibly see the stars?"

"The fog isn't exactly everywhere, or all the time. Come on, I'll show you."

Normally, Aiden would have been intrigued, but he couldn't get his mind off the countdown for all life on Earth. Jo saw his impulsive glance at his chrono and said, "Aiden, we can't do anything but wait. The Forum moves at its own speed. There's no use in stewing over what you can't control. It's counterproductive."

He looked at Jo for a moment. She could read him almost as well as Skye could. "How'd you get to be so smart?"

She smiled back at him. "With a little help from my friends."

"Quoting the Beatles now, are we?" How could she know anything about a pop music group from over two and a half centuries in the past?

"They were the best," she said with a shrug. "Come on, Aiden. Grab your overcoat. Let's go topside."

"All right. You win."

He looked over at Sudha Devi. A Libera woman had come to sit across from her, the same person who had brought them their food the night before, and the two were engaged in friendly conversation. She responded to Aiden's unspoken invitation to join them by shaking her head once. "Not for me. I hate the cold."

Knowing Devi, Aiden was sure that the opportunity to learn more about the Libera on a personal level had more to do with her staying behind than the cold. Hotah, on the other hand, was already putting on his heavy coat, looking less interested in distant star-rises than in keeping an eye on his captain.

<u>31</u>

AM 7491 SYSTEM
Qarsoon

Domain Day 70, 2223

A IDEN and Hotah followed Jo up a metal staircase through a designated "evac exit" to reach the surface. It was one of many, she told him, located strategically throughout the colony. The thick concrete door slid open, and Aiden was greeted once again by the cold, damp darkness and the strong, earthy odor of fungi. He pulled his hood closer over his head and followed Jo through the cloying ground fog. She held a powerful luminator in one hand and led the way for about 20 meters to a low-lying benchlike structure, the perfect height and width for sitting on. It looked organic in nature, not artificially constructed. He asked Jo about it.

"It's a fungus," Jo said. "Fungi have so many different forms here, I don't think the Libera have encountered even a fraction of it since they've been here. Some fungi, like this one here, can produce a tough, woody exterior and grow into all sorts of shapes. They found a number of these benches growing near all the evacuation hatches."

He and Jo sat on it, facing east, while Hotah remained standing, casually scanning the area around them. Aiden was surprised at how comfortable the bench felt. Not hard and rough, but almost cushiony. And slightly warm, as if it were somehow matching the heat of his own body, not robbing him of it. He stared into the opaque fog, still skeptical. "So when is this 'star-rise' supposed to happen?"

Jo looked at her chrono. "In about 10 minutes. The fog will clear out just before that."

"The fog clears out just before *every* star-rise? How is that possible? There're no weather patterns on rogue planets. No diurnal heating and cooling to power them."

"Ah, but there are weather patterns here," Jo said. "They're just static patterns, regular as clockwork, synced with the 32-hour rotational period of the planet. And even though there's no sun to cause diurnal heating and cooling, there're still the Coriolis forces of a spinning planet and a lot of geothermal hotspots all over the planet to power dynamism in the atmosphere. That causes regular breezes that flow in specific directions at certain times of the day and at certain places. Like where we are now. The morning breezes are what we're about to experience."

As she spoke, a steady breeze picked up from the southwest. Within a few minutes, the murky fog was swept away, and a deep-black night sky materialized overhead. It was like a curtain onstage drawn aside to reveal the glorious drama of a star-studded show meant to entertain an enthralled audience. It took Aiden's breath away.

Jo smiled brightly. "See? What did I tell you? Now we wait for our 'sun' to rise."

The breezes had cleared away a large area around where they sat, and Jo switched her luminator from directional to lantern mode. Within its radius of light, Aiden could see more stands of the bizarre fungal stalks at the perimeter, bending gently in the breeze, the pale stems almost luminous in the soft lantern light. He also saw that they were not alone.

A group of four Libera were sitting on a fungal bench about 10 meters to their right, facing east, apparently awaiting the star-rise themselves. They waved a greeting, and Jo waved back.

She whispered to Aiden, "Like I said, star-rise watching is a thing here, a social occasion."

To their left and slightly in front of them, two Libera sat at another bench, and both appeared to be women. They were holding hands and . . . kissing?

Jo saw Aiden's mystified expression and said, "They've pair-bonded."

"But . . . I thought . . ."

"You thought what?" Jo said patiently, as if to a naive child. "That we *Trans sapiens* are asexual, right? Because you know that we were cloned without gender. Our physical gender is only an outward artifice, presenting outwardly as either male or female. But only skin deep. Any gender differences in behavior you observe are only the result of the training we received in the creches designed for us to blend in with human populations as agents for the Netvor. In all other ways, *Trans sapiens* are identical under the skin. So if we're asexual, what's up with pair-bonding? That's what you're wondering, right?"

"Well, yes. I guess." Aiden didn't know what else to say. He knew he was on shaky ground here and admitted it. "I'm just confused about all this. I kind of understand about transgender humans, but *Trans sapiens* . . . ?"

Jo smiled at him, enjoying his discomfort over the topic. She placed a gentle hand on his arm and said, "I get it, Aiden. Most humans are confused about this stuff, or worse, they deny that it even exists. So, can I try to clear some things up for you?"

"Please do."

"*Trans sapiens* are not transgender, and we differ from transgender humans in significant ways. In humans, transgender people are those whose gender identity is different from the gender they were thought to be at birth. When humans are born, they're pronounced either male or female based on their anatomy. Most humans turn out to identify with the gender they were born with and grow up as either males or females. But some humans—based on their own innate knowledge of who they really are—take on a gender identity that's different from what was initially assigned to them at birth.

"So, a transgender woman lives as a woman but was born as a biological male, and a transgender man lives as a man but was born as a biological female. And some transgender humans identify as neither male nor female, or as a combination of male and female. They usually describe themselves as nonbinary, or something similar. It's one of the things that the Humanists among the Libera admire about humans—their diversity and freedom to be who they are."

"Freedom, yes, but a very fragile one," Aiden added. "Possible only in a free society. A tolerant and compassionate society. There have been too few of those in humanity's history."

"Sadly, true," Jo said. The light in her eyes darkened. "And I'm afraid, for your sake, that the Libera Forum is all too aware of that. But the point is, Aiden, humans take on a gender identity of some kind, whether it's transgender or nonbinary or binary. That gender identity is defined by how it relates to the biological gender they were born with, whether it's the same as, different from, or neither.

"But it's very different with us. We *Trans sapiens* came into being *without* biological gender. None at all, from the very start. There's no such thing as gender for us and never has been. That's one reason why the Libera prefer to converse in genderless languages instead of English. Lots of Earth languages lack grammatical gender distinctions in nouns and pronouns. They don't categorize nouns as masculine, feminine, or neuter and use the same pronoun for 'he' and 'she.' Those languages make more sense for us to use."

Aiden nodded. "Right. Like Chinese, Japanese, Finnish, Hungarian . . ."

"Yes, and many indigenous languages of the Americas," Jo added, looking back at Billy Hotah. "Like Lakota, for instance."

Hotah glanced back at her, shrugged, and said, "Wicahpiŋ Lakȟotaŋ wicahpiŋ yuwalaŋ."

Aiden squinted, looking from Hotah back to Jo. "What . . . ?"

Jo paused a moment before speaking. "I think he said it's because the Lakota are wise."

Hotah grinned a devilish grin at them, animating the red speckled band tattooed across his face.

"But as I was saying," Jo continued, "because *Trans sapiens* were 'born' without biological gender, the concept of gender identity is meaningless to us. But what *does* have meaning for us—maybe the most important meaning of all—is love. As individuals, we can love each other, just as deeply as human couples can love each other. And we often pair-bond just as humans do. Remember, our brains and central nervous systems are virtually the same as humans, except they developed without the influence of sex hormones. Pair-bonding is not exclusively a sexual behavior. It's a behavior of love."

Aiden looked back at her, feeling grateful for her presence. For her friendship. He sincerely hoped that all the Libera on Qarsoon were as enlightened.

Before he could say anything more, he heard soft exclamations from the four Libera on their right. They were looking eastward and pointing up.

Jo glanced up and said, "There she is."

The horizon that Aiden faced was not a true horizon. It was not a hard line dividing the sky from the farthest edge of a visible land mass. Here it was an indistinct boundary between where the dome of clear night sky blurred into opaque darkness at its lowest edges. And from that boundary, a brilliant pinpoint of light slowly emerged. While it could not pass for anything other than a star among stars in the sky, it was much brighter than any star seen in Earth's night sky. As it gradually rose, more of its faint light fell upon the dark face of Qarsoon.

Jo turned off her luminator, as did the other Libera. It took a moment for Aiden's eyes to adjust to the dim light coming from the closest thing Qarsoon would ever have for a sun. A distant beacon passing in the night.

"The Libera call it Majka," Jo said reverently.

"Majka," he said, repeating the word and liking the sound of it. "Far more poetic than AM 7491."

"Notice how its light is not pure white?" Jo said. "It has a slightly yellowish component. That's because it's a G1V-type star, almost the same as Earth's star, just a little larger and brighter than Sol. Some of the Libera wistfully fantasize about steering Qarsoon out of its fly-by trajectory and into an orbit around Majka, inside its habitable zone."

As if that were even remotely possible. But it was clearly a dream born of some deeper yearning the Libera had for a real world of their own. A world with light and warmth.

"As it is," Jo said, "this planet will be virtually impossible to reach in about 25 years from now. No one will be able to come here from any other planet in the universe, and no one who's already here will be able to leave for any other planet."

Jo was referring to the cold hard facts of Qarsoon's fly-by trajectory. In about 25 years, it would pass beyond 37 AU from the binary's voidoid. Add another 13 AU—the average distance between any known planet and its own voidoid—and you get the magic number of 50 AU. That was considered the maximum practical distance a conventional voidship could travel without refueling its antimatter tanks and replenishing life-support systems. So, unless people started stationing massive antimatter tankers at their system's voidoids—a highly unlikely scenario for any number of reasons—travel between Qarsoon and any other planet would become impossible. The colony would be cut off from all other living beings, humans and Netvor alike.

All of that would undoubtedly present an existential dilemma for the Libera to ponder, assuming they survived the more immediate existential threat of a Netvor invasion.

As Majka slowly ascended, more of its faint light bathed the area around them, creating an eerie black-and-gray tableau. It allowed Aiden to see a little deeper into the stands of fungal stalks. Their willowy stems swayed gently in the breeze like slender fingers on ghostly hands waving to him. Beckoning him. Entrancing him . . .

Then he saw the blue swirls.

32

Domain Day 70, 2223

THERE were five of them, roughly 30 meters away. The blue swirls seemed to dance in and out among the pale fungal stalks like children playing hide and seek. And, like the ones he'd seen earlier, these resembled whirlwinds of blue light about 2 meters tall, narrowing down to a point where they met the ground. They moved with graceful quickness. Every fiber of Aiden's being told him they were alive.

Jo saw them, too. "Interesting. I haven't seen this many of them together in one place."

Hotah followed Jo's gaze and tensed. "What the hell *are* those?"

Aiden and Jo exchanged surprised glances. Jo said to Hotah, "You can see them, too?"

"Of course I can," he said, as if surprised that anyone would even ask. His hand moved to hover over his holstered weapon.

"Relax, Lieutenant," Aiden said. "I think they're harmless."

Aiden looked to Jo for confirmation. She shrugged and said, "As far as I know, yes. I haven't heard about them interacting with the Libera in any way, harmfully or not."

Then, as if to test Jo's presumption, one of the swirls peeled off from the others and advanced toward them. It moved quickly at first, then from about five meters away, it slowed and moved forward more tentatively. Only one of the four Libera sitting nearby stood and watched, eyes wide, while the other three continued gazing at the star-rise, oblivious to the ghostly phenomenon. The two pair-bonded Libera took no notice, having eyes only for each other.

The swirl seemed most interested in Aiden and began moving slowly toward him. Its uppermost portion began to gently rock back and forth as if it were looking at him from different angles. Aiden stood up, faced it, and assumed a relaxed, nonthreatening posture. Hotah stepped closer to him and began lifting the handgun from his holster. Aiden placed his hand on Hotah's arm. "Stand down, Lieutenant. And move back, please."

The act of dropping his guard seemed to encourage the swirl. It moved to within one meter of Aiden and stopped. Jo stood and positioned herself on Aiden's right side.

Close up, Aiden could see that the swirl's funnel-shaped body was made up of hundreds of rapidly spinning, tiny lines of blue light, all synchronized in subtle pulsation. It made no sound and possessed no scent, but Aiden could feel warmth radiating from it. He sensed no hostility or fear from the swirl. Only curiosity.

On impulse, Aiden held out his right hand to the swirl, palm up and open. As if to accept a gift offered, the swirl advanced without hesitation and enclosed Aiden in a cocoon of blue light.

Time stopped.

Or at least Aiden's perception of its passage stopped. As if time itself were a dream, and he'd just woken up into a new reality where time was only a fading memory of the dream. Warm blue light swirled around him and through him. Gently examining him, tapping the synapses of his brain with subtle electricity. Learning the language of his nervous system.

Then the swirling blue light dissolved, and Aiden found himself standing in a clearing, bathed in bright sunlight—light from a real sun—surrounded by lush green plant life. The clearing was on top of a rounded hilltop, and a break in the trees afforded an expansive view of a wide valley below, through which a river meandered, glistening in the sunlight. Beyond that stood a range of high mountains with ragged, snow-covered peaks. The sunlight on his face felt like Earth's sun. Warm and bright. Small flying things flitted about in the clearing. The ground on which he stood was covered with a carpet of low-lying green grass. Except he wasn't exactly standing on it. More like hovering above its surface, feet not quite touching it.

From the corner of his eye, he detected movement among the trees at the edge of the clearing. But when he tried to focus on where it had been, he saw nothing. A lone cloud roaming overhead cast a shadow over him. He felt suddenly overwhelmed by a crushing sorrow. A sadness that can come only from profound loss. Loss of a loved one. Loss of a whole world.

When the cloud passed, the darkness its shadow had cast remained. The sun was still in the sky, but now it had become so small that the remaining light it gave to the land was no more than dusk after sunset. The forest surrounding the clearing had shriveled and collapsed into random heaps of moldering organic matter. The small flying things were gone. Color was gone, giving way to dark grays and drab browns. Nothing moved. A cold fog rose from the ground and obscured the diminutive sun. The darkness grew darker.

He closed his eyes to dispel what he knew must be a dream. When he opened his eyes again, the fog had cleared from overhead, but the sun was gone. Only a very bright star remained in its place, outshining the others around it. But not enough to warm or nourish. The permanent darkness of primordial night had conquered the world, finally and forever. Surrounding Aiden, the dark heaps of decomposing matter had transformed into fields of willowy pale stalks, tall, without caps, and growing aimlessly. In the cold darkness, they began to wilt and bend down toward the ground.

Then a bright point of blue-white light appeared in the night sky above them, moving closer. It descended until it disappeared in the distance. Almost immediately afterward, flickers of electric blue light streamed out through the stands of wilting stalks, coming from the direction where the point of light had descended. Like thousands of swarming fireflies, they swirled around the sinewy stems, bathing them in blue light.

As if soaking up the energy of the blue light, the stalks straightened up and began pointing skyward. The swarming blue sparkles rose up with them, and as they did, dark, ellipsoid caps began to form atop the stalks. Like mushroom caps, but barely wider in diameter than the stems that held them aloft.

The multitude of incandescent blue sparks began to coalesce into larger coherent shapes, swirling vortices of blue light. As they danced in circular patterns around the bases of each stalk, clouds of tiny spores rained down from the underside of the caps and drifted into the gaping, cone-shaped openings of the swirls. After each cap emptied its spores, the swirls moved on to receive spores from the next one. The process continued as the swirls moved deeper into the now dense stands of gently waving stems. Aiden felt as if he'd just witnessed several hundred thousand years of evolution in a matter of . . . minutes? Seconds?

When the last of the glimmering blue swirls had vanished from sight, Aiden detected movement among the fungal stalks. He focused his eyes on the spot and saw a man walk out from between them. It was Elgin Woo.

Only it wasn't Elgin in the flesh. That much was clear. Woo's image shimmered, and parts of him seemed almost transparent. He wore a black fedora cocked to one side, a vest over an open-collared white shirt. He looked exceptionally dapper. Without speaking, he twirled one side of his long dangling mustache between thumb and forefinger. It was his signature gesture—charming to some, irritating to most. He smiled, and with his other hand, he pointed his finger up toward the sky, toward the sun that was now just another star in the vast darkness. But when Woo turned his gaze up to follow where he pointed, his face was lit by bright sunlight, as if the full sun had returned to the sky for that one moment, for that one purpose of warming his face.

Aiden looked up as well. When his eyes found the distant star, Majka, he heard a single musical tone. It was the same D-flat he'd heard earlier upon waking. The tempered D-flat. It was Majka's song.

When Woo saw that Aiden had heard the note, he smiled more broadly. Then he touched the brim of his fedora in farewell and vanished.

In that moment, Aiden found himself back on Qarsoon standing in the cold darkness. The blue swirl that had enveloped him was retreating, moving slowly back to join the other swirls. Then all of them slipped back among the fungal stalks and disappeared from sight. Jo and Hotah stood next to him, concerned looks on their faces.

"Aiden, are you okay?" Jo asked, her hand on his shoulder. "Did it hurt you?"

"What just happened?" Hotah asked, almost at the same time. He'd drawn his handgun from its holster, muzzle down but ready.

Aiden took in a deep breath. "I'm okay. It was just a . . . I'm not sure what it was. But definitely not an attack. A vision . . . a visitation . . . a lesson . . . How long was I . . . ?"

Hotah shrugged. "Ten seconds, maybe? You were completely engulfed inside that thing. I was about to pull you out when it just up and left on its own."

It had seemed quite a bit longer than that to Aiden. But, as he was learning, that's how these fugues were for him. Whatever they were.

Aiden rubbed his eyes as if to clear the haze of dreamtime and said, "I'm glad you didn't interfere."

Then he heard the D-flat tone again, just faintly. When he looked up to face the star Majka, still only a few degrees above the blurry black horizon, the tone became stronger, more pronounced. Majka's song.

Then another wonder revealed itself. When Aiden turned to look at Jo, he could see faint emanations of colored light around her body. And it was the same when he looked at Billy Hotah. *Was he seeing auras now?* Like Jo did? And Lista Abahem?

But the star song and aural visions ceased abruptly when his wrist comm beeped. He raised the comm to his mouth. "Open."

"Captain Macallan?" It was Chairperson Litha Berne. "The Forum has not yet come to a formal decision, but the outcome is quite clear now. We need to talk."

33

AM 7491 SYSTEM
Qarsoon

Domain Day 70, 2223

"THE Forum majority will undoubtedly deny your request to equip your ship with our tech."

Berne spoke to Aiden without apparent emotion. She faced him across the hard black surface of the obsidian table with Captain Vedderman at her side. Jo and Sudha Devi sat on either side of Aiden, while Hotah stood in back, leaning against the wall, arms crossed over his chest. The room felt much colder than it had before.

Aiden swallowed down a bitter mixture of anger and despair rising in his throat. "Why?"

Berne sat back, hands folded in front of her on the table. "Do you really want to waste valuable time hearing an explanation from me? There's nothing you can do at this point to change the Forum's mind."

It was a good question, and any reasonable person in his situation would just stand up, say "Thanks for nothing," and get the hell out of there. Then head back to the Solar System on a mission that was now virtually impossible to accomplish. But Aiden was in no mood to be reasonable.

He leaned forward, shoulders bunched. "Not time wasted for me, Chairperson. Because the 'why' of it will tell me exactly what kind of people the Libera really are and will determine how likely I, or *any* human, will ever be to champion your cause in whatever future you have left. That's valuable information to me, worth the wait."

"Very well," Berne said, looking uncomfortable with the prospect of elaborating on the Forum's reasoning. Aiden had to wonder what side of the argument she personally aligned with. "It boils down to three things, really. Trust versus history, risk versus benefit, and anger."

When she paused with a questioning look, Aiden said, "Go on."

"Surely you are aware of the trust issue by now. But you may not be aware of how much of human history we really know. On one hand, it's a history punctuated by remarkable achievements, but punctuated too infrequently. By and large, it's a history of endless war, spectacular greed, selfishness, dishonesty, willful disregard for the health of the very planet that keeps you alive, and above all, appalling cruelty—not only among yourselves but against all the living beings that share the planet with you, including other sentient creatures. The words *torture* and *genocide* are uniquely human, defining abhorrent behaviors exclusive to the human race. And much of it done in the name of one god or another in the fanatical belief that such abominable acts are righteous ones in the eyes of their chosen deity.

"The majority of the Libera, the ones who align themselves with Posthuman ideals, see the human race as a biological accident, an evolutionary experiment gone awry, spawning a destructive race that inevitably corrodes everything good it manages to accomplish. A race that can't help violating Nature, debasing love, and rejecting the search for truth in favor of lust for personal power. The Libera see all these things and how they have permeated your history to its core, and see that humans have failed to rise above them, even an inch, over the many thousands of years they've had the opportunity to do so.

"How could the Libera trust any good-faith agreement with humans knowing their history? How could we trust that you wouldn't take the weapons we give you to fight the Netvor and turn them back on us? Just ask your Tactical Officer how many times his ancestors were deceived by those who went on to steal their homes, destroy their lives and their culture. How many promises were made to them in good faith, and how many were kept?"

William Hotah stiffened at the mention of atrocities never to be forgotten but remained motionless as he leaned against the wall.

"That's history versus trust," Berne said, summing up the first item on her list. "And in this case, history wins."

Aiden shook his head slowly. "You *know* that we're not all like that."

"No. Not all," she conceded. "And if it were the nature of only a tiny fraction of you, small enough to be counted as genetic aberrancies, rare mutations that are expected along the evolutionary march to a higher nature, then it would be a different story. But this corrosive seed is in all of you. It will destroy you and destroy the gift of life your planet has given to every living thing you share it with."

Aiden felt his face grow hot. "And you really believe this 'corrosive seed' is not in you, too? Your DNA is the same as ours, 100 percent human. Originally cloned from one of the most evil men in human history. Cardew himself. How can you sit there and write off the entire human race as fundamentally flawed when you are so undeniably part of it yourselves?"

Berne waved off Aiden's argument. "In the first place, the creches stopped using Cardew's DNA long ago, soon after his demise. All the cloning now is done with DNA taken from the human scientists who were kidnapped by Cardew, and even that gene pool has been reengineered. Yes, it is still 100 percent human. But as a scientist yourself, surely you know that DNA isn't everything. Not purely deterministic by any means. The Libera here are confident that we can and will self-evolve beyond the destructive flaws we've observed among humans. We will not allow ourselves to be destroyed by that which destroys you."

"So you'd rather be destroyed by the Netvor," Aiden said. "Because that's surely what will happen if you abandon us at this moment in time. But if you agree now to help the *Sun Wolf* destroy the graser, I can more easily persuade the Alliance to send a fleet here to guard your voidoid. The fleet stationed at Gateway could make a jump to this voidoid within hours of hearing from me. That would be a significant deterrence to any Netvor invasion force."

"Seriously?" Berne said, shaking her head. "That so-called deterrence would not last long against cloaked Netvor warships with shielding capability that your Alliance has no answer for. The Netvor would prevail in no time, and Qarsoon would be next in line. And besides, what makes you think that a report from you claiming our agreement to help would instantly prompt the Alliance to help us in return? Even if it could do it in time to make a difference? We are well aware of how most humans will regard *Trans sapiens*, given the chance. To them, we are Netvor, plain and simple. The truth has nothing to do with it."

Aiden, unfortunately, had no answer for that one, and Litha Berne continued before he could think of one.

"And as to any other benefits to us from helping you save Earth from destruction—assuming we did survive an initial Netvor invasion—the Forum majority can see none. Why help save the lives of billions who hate us anyway and want us dead as much as the Netvor do? To be frank, Captain, many of them would feel no great sadness if Earth's human population perished."

That took care of the risk versus benefit item on Berne's list. Aiden leaned back in his chair, resigned to the inevitable. She had been right. There was nothing further he could do or say to change the Forum's mind. It was time to go. But not without hearing it all. "That covers the first two reasons. What about the third? Anger."

Aiden knew the answer, of course. He just wanted to hear it straight from Litha Berne. "That's the easy one," she said. "The entire colony is angry that, by coming here, you led the Netvor straight to us. Inadvertently or not. And some among us have reason to believe that one of your crew may have done it deliberately."

Miguel Silva. Aiden couldn't help thinking it himself.

"So yes," Berne said, "anger may have overcome reason, and even compassion, prompting a more enthusiastic denial of your request."

Aiden had nothing more to say to Chairperson Berne and no time to spare. He looked at his chrono. It was nearly 05:00, just 31 hours left to save Earth's nine billion people.

He turned to Vedderman. "Captain, would you please take us back up to Forgeron so we can board our ship and depart? Now, please?"

"Of course. The shuttle has just finished refueling. We can depart in 15 minutes. Forgeron is starting its next pass over our hemisphere now. It will be a five-hour transit."

"Good. Thank you." Aiden tapped his comm, connecting to the *Sun Wolf.* "Commander Silva, prepare the ship for departure. We'll be there shortly after 10:00."

After an unusually long pause, Silva's voice came through loud and clear, not only on Aiden's comm but on everyone else's in the room, including Chairperson Litha Berne's.

"No can do, Captain. I have complete control of the ship now, and I've got something to say to that fake-human chairperson: Listen up, freak. I've got a 10-kiloton nuclear missile aimed directly at your miserable little colony. If you don't give us every piece of technology we need to kill that Netvor graser, I'm sending it right down your throat. You've got 10 minutes. Refuse, and you'll all be vaporized. Including the treasonous Captain Macallan. What's it going to be?"

34

Domain Day 70, 2223

"W HAT the *hell* are you doing, Silva?"
Aiden bolted out of his chair, cold fear and hot anger shooting up his spine. How the hell did Silva get control of the *Sun Wolf*? Where was his crew? Where was Hutton?

Litha Berne remained seated as if she'd turned to stone, her face ashen. Jo and Devi looked equally stunned. Emi Tanaka burst through the door, weapon in hand, raised but not yet aimed at anyone in the room. Her eyes burned with outrage. Hotah had pushed away from the wall the moment she entered, his eyes locked on hers. His weapon was out and held ready but, like hers, not yet aimed. Vedderman stood slowly and smoothly like a venomous snake uncoiling. He glared at Aiden. The room was deathly silent until Silva's voice came over the comm again, seething with virulent sarcasm.

"What am I doing? I'm doing what you should have done all along. I've been monitoring everything going on down there. You can't reason with these Netvor freaks, and you're a fool for trying. Look how much time you've wasted already."

"Commander Silva. Stand down. Now!"

Aiden overheard Vedderman on his own comm ordering Libera warships to intercept the *Sun Wolf* at Forgeron Station.

"I'm not taking orders from you anymore, Macallan," Silva said. "I've relieved you of command on grounds of your treasonous acts. I'm in command now and in control of the *Sun Wolf.* The remainder of your crew is locked up, and your AI is under my control."

How could that happen? Hutton would have stepped in . . .

"And in case your Libera friends are planning to attack me," Silva said, "consider this. I'm still in Forgeron's docking bay. Untethered from the dock and moving out a little to get a better look around, but still close enough that any weapons fired at me will also destroy this station. Besides, there aren't any warships near enough right now to even try anything that stupid."

The look on Vedderman's face confirmed Silva's assessment. Two of the five Libera battle cruisers were still a half million kilometers out where the *Ark* had left them when intercepting the *Sun Wolf.* Vedderman had ordered them to stay put in anticipation of the Netvor ship's arrival. Two others, Aiden had learned, were on patrol duty thousands of kilometers away, one on the opposite side of Qarsoon and the other out at the moon, Sestra. The fifth was the *Ark*, and it was docked right next to the *Sun Wolf*, one docking arm up. That left only one or two patrol frigates in the vicinity, and they were under-armed and no match for the *Sun Wolf.*

"And thanks to your foresight, Macallan," Silva went on, "the ship is pointed outward for a quick getaway, and its forward missile platform is pointing directly at the planet. The colony's position is rolling into view as we speak. From this angle, my missile will take less than 40 seconds to impact. I think you all know what a 10-kiloton nuke can do."

Aiden shut his comm down for a moment and asked Vedderman, "You *do* have a surface-based defense system, right? Against missile attack? Or orbital laser interceptors?"

But Aiden knew the answer before he finished asking by the look on Vedderman's face. The colony was too new and had too few resources for those kinds of defensive systems. Or they had felt too safe from discovery to make them a priority.

So Silva held all the cards now. It was almost as if he'd planned it . . .

Aiden punched his comm back on and tried to keep his voice reasonable. "Calm down, Silva. This isn't the way to do it, and you know it. Besides, have you even thought this through? Let's say you nuke this colony, killing all the Libera, including me and the other half of the *Sun Wolf*'s crew, and then somehow you miraculously escape Qarsoon space without being attacked. Then what? You can't use the ship's zero-point drive without me or Hutton, or without Pilot Abahem's cooperation. And even if you did, you'll be returning to the Solar System without a way to stop the graser from killing Earth, and you'll be returning as a mutinous criminal, a traitor who murdered his captain. Where's the upside in all that, Silva?"

Silva laughed. There was a maniacal edge to the sound that made Aiden's skin crawl. "Ah, but I have thought it through. First of all, I *can* use the zero-point drive without you. I'm officially registered as second-in-command of the *Sun Wolf*. Your AI is obligated by its fail-safe algorithms to recognize me as commander of the ship in your absence. It has proven that fact already by arming the tactical missiles at my command and targeting them. And by securing the locks on the brig where your crew is being held.

"Secondly, I'll be a hero. The narrative will be clear. I will have regained control of an invaluable Alliance voidship, the illustrious *Sun Wolf*, formerly commanded by an unfit and traitorous captain. An officer who not only disobeyed direct orders from his superiors by refusing to join other warships in the search for the Netvor graser, but he also failed in his own delusional mission to prevent the graser attack by seeking aid from a nest of Netvor renegades. Then I'll be praised for destroying that same nest of treacherous Netvor vermin who clearly showed their true colors by refusing to help save Earth from destruction."

Aiden's confidence in controlling the situation plummeted as the horror of Silva's logic sank in. He gathered himself up and said, "That's a very moving story, Silva. Congratulations for fabricating such a believable series of lies. But I don't think anyone in the Alliance with half a brain will be fooled."

"And why not? No one knows otherwise because you cut off all communications from the ship the moment you started this wild goose chase. And what they do know of events from before that moment neatly substantiates my 'story,' as you call it. Of course, all that can be avoided if your Netvor buddies give me what we both want, the means to seek and destroy the graser before it's too late."

Aiden decided not to bring up the fact that using the technology in question required bringing on board at least one Libera specialist who could set it up and operate it. That was a detail that Silva seemed to be in no state of mind to consider. A mind already made up.

Aiden glanced at Litha Berne. She was using her private comm and, from the sound of it, frantically attempting to convene another Forum meeting, on an emergency basis. He shook his head. *Too late for that now.*

"All right, Silva," he said. "Let's say the Libera bow to your threats and give us what we need. And we return to the Solar System, and we succeed in finding the graser and killing it. How do you think the Alliance is going to feel about your act of mutiny? You think they'll let you get away with it with just a slap on the wrist? You think *I'll* let you get away with it?"

"*We?*" Silva said, ugly derision in his voice. "Who said 'we' would return? I get the graser-killing tech, I return without you, and I take care of business myself. Properly. You're staying behind, Macallan, right where you belong. A ship can have only one captain, and only a righteous one. Again, I'll be the hero. I'm the one who succeeds in getting the tech where you failed with your touchy-feely approach. And at the same time, I'm deposing a cowardly, ineffectual commanding officer."

This was not heading in a good direction, Aiden thought. Where Silva had seemed ridiculously overly confident at the outset, the basis of his confidence was looking more reasonable. He had an airtight case going, and there was very little Aiden could do to upset it. Not from where he stood now. Not in the crosshairs of a 10-kiloton nuclear missile.

He had to stall Silva, had to think of something. He tried on a casual, friendly voice and said, "Look, Commander—"

"Enough talk!" Silva shouted. Again, that maniacal edge in his voice. "Time's up! Is that chairperson freak going to give me what I want? Or is it bye-bye to all of you?"

Aiden felt a knot tightening in his stomach. He looked over at Berne, hands held out, questioning. She looked panicked. "The Forum . . . there's not enough time . . ."

Ah. The age-old quandary, Aiden thought. The futility of majority-rule decisions in crisis situations that demand immediate action.

The pause was apparently too long for Silva. "You think I'm bluffing, don't you?" he said. "You think I don't really have control of the weapons systems, and I'm just making empty threats."

"No, Silva, I do not think that—"

"Do you have visuals on that big, fat antimatter tanker sitting about 50 kilometers off? It's still about a quarter full, right? That should still make quite an impressive explosion . . ."

"Miguel, don't . . ."

Vedderman brought up a real-time image of the Libera's antimatter tanker on a holojector in the room's far corner. It was a live feed from a telescopic camera on Forgeron. He looked at Aiden, his face drained of blood, his eyes desperate. "There's a crew of six on board."

"Silva," Aiden said as calmly as he could manage. "I believe you, okay? You don't need to prove it, all right?"

"Let's see," Silva said, ignoring Aiden's plea for sanity. "It's a clear shot now that I'm halfway out of the docking bay. A one-kiloton tactical nuke would make a nice show, wouldn't you say? And it'll take only three seconds to get there."

"Silva, there are six people aboard that tanker—"

"*People?*" Silva laughed.

"Silva, *do not* do this—"

Before Aiden could finish his appeal, the holo image of the big antimatter tanker parked unobtrusively in space vanished in a flash of brilliant white light. When the incandescent fireball collapsed, all that could be seen was a glowing plasma cloud roiling against the deep black of empty space.

Aiden felt sick to his stomach.

He looked around the room. Rage. Horror. Grief. Things could not have gone worse. Unless, of course, the Libera colony—with him inside it—was next on Silva's kill list.

"So you see," Silva's voice came over the comm. Aiden could hear the triumphant smile in the man's voice. "I mean business. Bring the technology aboard my ship now, or you're all dead. Agreed?"

Litha Berne was now on the hot seat. She had no time for the democratic process. No time for a vote from the Forum, even though the outcome of such a vote would surely be different now that the terms of the deal had changed so dramatically. She had to either abide by the decision her people had just made, or disobey it to save all the lives of those same people. To save the Libera colony and its dreams for the future. To Aiden, it was a no-brainer. Capitulate and live to fight another day. And while his own life was in the balance here, it was not his decision to make.

Acute conflict contorted Berne's face and posture. The air in the room simmered with unbearable tension. No one breathed. Finally she looked up at Aiden and said, "Now I truly understand. This is what being human is about, and it must be deep in our DNA, too. If this is what we could become ourselves, then I will speak for all my people, here and now. It is better to die than spread more of this human disease throughout the galaxy."

"Chairperson, please reconsider . . ." Now the fear for his own life had begun to grab hold of Aiden like a rabid animal tearing at his throat. He couldn't stop it. Its teeth were too far in. He could no longer mediate with any ounce of reason.

Silva's voice cut through the tension like a bloody knife. "I take that as a 'no.' Well, I'm not surprised. To be honest, I was going to nuke your damn colony anyway, even if I got its technology. I hate the Netvor. I hate what they did to my family. You're all Netvor, no matter how different you think you are, and you all need to be exterminated. So I'm doing the human race a huge favor here. And Macallan, sorry about this, but I never liked you anyway, nor any of your feel-good, elitist crew. You all thought you were better than me, right? How's that working out for you now? I'll feel no great sorrow in taking you down with the rest of your newfound Netvor friends."

"Silva, you are the biggest piece of shit and the worst example of the human race imaginable. If it's not me personally, someone else will fuck you up for good, sooner than later. You can count on it."

Silva laughed. "We'll just see about that, Macallan. Well, you won't, anyway. Once my missile is away, you'll have only 42 seconds to see *anything*."

"Fuck you, Silva!"

"Goodbye, asshole. Missile away."

The comm from Silva went dead.

The holojector flashed in the corner. The station's event camera had caught movement. It automatically replayed the launch of a tactical missile from Docking Bay 3, clocked at close to 300 Gs acceleration, aimed at the planet's surface. Its exhaust plume vanished in the distance less than a second after the launch.

Aiden looked around at the others in the room. But the only people he could see now were not present in the flesh. His wife, Skye. His daughter, Bri. It wasn't supposed to end this way. This story just *could not* end here . . .

PART FOUR

— 18 Seconds Later —

We are all born mad. Some remain so.

— Samuel Beckett

35

Domain Day 70, 2223

"They just don't make nuclear missiles like they used to," Elgin Woo said wistfully.

Woo's voice came over the open comm loud and clear, as if he were standing in the room right there with the rest of them. Aiden glanced at the others, all of whom were waiting to be vaporized by an incoming 10-kiloton nuke within a matter of seconds. Litha Berne, Hans Vedderman, Emi Tanaka, Sudha Devi, Billy Hotah, and Jo. Each one of them prepared to take their final breath in whatever way they could, praying to whatever god or goddess would receive their souls.

Yet all of them had obviously heard Elgin Woo's voice over the comm. This wasn't just one of Aiden's hallucinatory visitations. Woo was here. Somewhere nearby. In the flesh.

Aiden unclenched his teeth and said, "Elgin? Is that really you?"

"Of course it is, my boy. Who else?"

"But the missile . . . ?"

"Ah, yes," Woo said casually, as if in conversation at a cocktail party. "I was just lamenting the poor quality of this nuclear missile that fool launched at you. I stopped it in midflight, by the way. Nasty thing, but so poorly made. Who is supplying arms to the

Sun Wolf these days? I read the serial number on it. I think it was made in that impoverished arms factory on Callisto. You should really insist on upgrading your missile systems, Aiden. The *Sun Wolf* deserves much better. I would suggest—"

"Elgin! Where the hell are you? How did you 'stop' the missile from hitting us?"

"Oh, yes. Sorry. I'm in the *Starhawk*, of course, up here not far from the station your friends call Forgeron. Here, let me show you."

The holojector sprang to life, again providing live feed from one of the station's external cameras. The image of the *Starhawk*—Elgin Woo's personal space yacht and the only other vessel in existence powered by his zero-point drive—appeared at the center of the screen. Aiden hadn't seen it since Woo had climbed aboard it and disappeared over five years ago, but it looked the same as it had then. It was a large, perfectly circular disk, about 60 meters in diameter. Viewed from the side, as the camera did now, it presented a sleek ellipsoidal profile no more than 10 meters at its tallest central point and tapered gracefully to a razor-thin edge all the way around. Its upper surface appeared seamless, smooth, and unbroken by any projections or ports of any kind, and it glistened with an obsidian sheen in the station's bright space-lights.

"So, as you can see," Woo went on, happy as a child without a care in the world, "I am *really* here this time. And I must say, it looks like I arrived just in time. Fortunately, I was able to stop that missile in its tracks, but unfortunately, I couldn't stop the one that hit the antimatter tanker. Three seconds from launch to impact was just too fast. Who the hell is your XO now, and why was he trying to kill you and everyone else?"

"Long story, Elgin. But my ship? My crew . . . ?"

"Fear not, old boy!" Woo exclaimed, using his faux British accent, one of his favorite phonetic affectations. "I was also able to return control of your ship to Hutton. With Mari's help, of course. It was not Hutton's fault, Aiden, so don't be too hard on him."

Mari was Woo's personal AI. She inhabited the *Starhawk* in the same way Hutton did the *Sun Wolf,* and her relationship with Woo was as unique as Aiden's was with Hutton. Woo had once implied that Mari and Hutton "had a thing" between them. Whatever that meant among AIs, Aiden hadn't a clue, but if it was instrumental in getting Hutton back to full control of the ship's systems, then he was all for it.

"And the crew? Do you know if—"

"Your crew is safe and back at their posts. Your misguided XO is locked up, and I believe he is seriously wounded. Your delightful Comm/Scan officer, Ms. Alvarez, is temporarily in command. I assume you'll hear from her shortly with a report of what transpired."

Aiden felt the tension in his shoulders relax a fraction. "But the missile. How did you—"

"Oh, that," Woo said in an offhanded way. "Well, you should know all about that, old bean. I did it the same way I did back in the Chara system when I stopped the missile that Cole Brahmin launched at your survey vessel. What was it? Six years ago? Just more zero-point trickery, the inertial tractor field I've been tinkering around with. Actually, I wasn't really sure it would work this time on an object with that much momentum. I mean, a missile launched at 300 Gs, nearly halfway to impact? I think I need to alter the resonant frequency of—"

"Elgin, stop!" Aiden had so many questions, and Woo had a tendency to prattle on. But Aiden was still having trouble believing the flesh-and-blood man was actually here, not just the apparition. "Elgin, if you really are up there, how did you get here? Where have you been?"

"I'll get into that later, if you want. It's been a fascinating journey. But now I think it's time that you introduce me to these extraordinary people who've built this colony. I'm so impressed. I would love to come to the surface for a proper greeting, but for now, would you mind if I show myself visually, I mean holographically? It's the only polite way to say hello for the first time."

Aiden turned to Litha Berne. Like all the others in the room, she looked utterly stunned. And speechless. Aiden had to nudge her. "Chairperson?"

Berne blinked twice as if waking from a dream. She finally said, "Yes. By all means, Dr. Woo. I am Litha Berne, Chairperson of the colony. We, all of us . . . the Libera . . . We know a great deal about you. We have followed your career and have the utmost respect and admiration for you. It is an honor to meet you. And to thank you for . . ."

Before Berne could collect herself to say more, the image of the *Starhawk* on the holojector was replaced by that of Elgin Woo.

It was the same Elgin Woo as always—a tall, slender Asian man in his sixties, head shaved bald and a long "Fu Manchu" moustache, braided on each side and dangling well below his chin. And, of course, an irrepressible smile of such genuine warmth that no one in his presence could resist smiling back. But this time, Woo was not dressed in any of the outlandish costumes Aiden had seen him wearing before. Instead, he wore loose-fitting khaki cargo pants and a blue long-sleeved work shirt, untucked. A couple of old-fashioned pencils poked up from one breast pocket. Only one eccentricity stood out, a pink carnation flower pinned to his shirt's other breast pocket.

Woo made a formal bow and said, "It is a pleasure to meet you, Chairperson Berne. I would love to come down there and see all the wonderful things you have accomplished. But, as you may know, there are matters of great urgency to address first. The Netvor are a very real threat to you and to humanity's birth planet. Right now and more than ever. Prompt action is needed. I believe I have several solutions to counter that threat, including one for the dilemma you face concerning Aiden's request for aid. Will you allow me to come down and meet with you in person to talk about these things?"

Berne glanced at Vedderman. He nodded to her. She turned back to Woo's image. "Yes. Come as quickly as you can, Dr. Woo. However, we have only one small landing pad, and our shuttle is currently occupying it. We can move it, but—"

"No need," Woo said, smiling broadly. "The *Starhawk* does not require a landing pad. I'll land near your shuttle, though. See you there in about 20 minutes."

And with that, Woo's image disappeared. Aiden didn't waste time wondering how Elgin would get to their position on the surface in only 20 minutes. Probably more "zero-point trickery." Instead, he hailed his ship. Litha Berne made her own calls, speaking urgently to Forum leaders. Vedderman and Tanaka left the room, on their way to the landing pad to monitor Woo's arrival. Devi, Hotah, and Jo stayed with Aiden while he waited for a response from the *Sun Wolf.*

Lilly Alvarez finally answered the call and gave Aiden a brief report. After Hutton had unlocked the brig to free her and the others, she and Assan went straight to the ship's armory to grab weapons. Normally, the armory was locked and accessible only by the ship's captain. But Hutton, now back in control, had seen good reason to break that rule and opened it for them. When she and Assan burst onto the bridge, weapons held ready, they found a despondent Miguel Silva slumped in the command chair. The pistol he'd used to herd them into the brig was still in his hand but held loosely on his lap. He made no attempt to aim it at them.

Nevertheless, Alvarez had kept her SR-11 Carbine pointed directly at Silva's forehead. Aiden knew she was a dead shot, having trained with the same weapon during her two-year stint in the Domain Guard and qualifying for sharpshooter level. Silva knew it, too. But instead of doing the smart thing and lowering his pistol to the deck, he'd done something unexpected. He brought the gun up to his own head and pressed its muzzle under his upheld chin.

Assan, in a foolish but courageous act of compassion, rushed at Silva to prevent him from taking his own life. Assan succeeded in pushing the gun aside, but not before it fired. The bullet pierced the skin at the left side of Silva's chin, grazing the left side of his head but not entering his skull. Even though the skull was not breached, the force of the bullet imparted enough trauma to blood vessels of the brain to cause intracranial bleeding. He lost consciousness, but they rushed him to the medical bay in time to save his life. He was now on basic life support, still unconscious but stable for the time being. He was going to need a higher level of medical treatment than the *Sun Wolf* was equipped to provide.

Aiden looked at his chrono. Just past 07:00, less than 29 hours left. He grabbed his heavy coat and said, "Let's go."

When he and the others emerged from the colony's exit hatch into the cold darkness, it was just in time to see Elgin Woo's *Starhawk* descend slowly toward the ground. Aiden saw no signs of conventional propulsion from the odd-looking craft, as if it were powered by some invisible force field of Woo's own design. Lit by the pole lamps adjacent to the shuttle pad, the saucer-shaped vessel looked so much like the classic "flying saucer" of mid-20th-century sci-fi movies that Aiden had to laugh.

Instead of touching the ground, the *Starhawk* came to a halt within half a meter above it and hovered. A circular aperture opened on the underside of its seamless exterior nearest to the ground, and warm yellow light streamed out from it. The dark silhouette of a tall, thin man appeared backlit within the circle. Then Elgin Woo gingerly hopped out of the opening onto the surface of Qarsoon and waved to them.

Aiden, Jo, and Devi moved forward to greet Woo, passing under the black circular edge of the hovering craft as the others stayed behind, still stunned by the legendary man's unconventional arrival. About halfway there, Aiden caught sight of flickering blue light in the fungal forest just beyond the *Starhawk*. Within seconds, a group of five blue swirls emerged and approached Elgin Woo. If they had been human forms, their movements could be easily interpreted as joyful excitement. Without hesitation, they began to dance playfully around Woo as he walked forward.

Woo, of course, saw them and looked positively delighted by their presence. He paused in their midst, held out his hands to them, and said, "Hello, my little friends! Yes. How wonderful!"

At the sound of Woo's voice, the blue vortices seemed to nod, or bow, in his direction. They circled him one more time before dashing back to disappear among the tall fungal stalks.

Aiden exchanged glances with Jo before noticing that Sudha Devi was looking back at him, wide-eyed. *She can see the blue swirls, too?* When he looked back at the others, it seemed that Litha Berne had seen them as well. Her expression signaled recognition mixed with something else. Reassurance? Had Elgin Woo just passed some kind of supernal appraisal in Berne's eyes?

Woo greeted Aiden with a hearty bear hug as if nothing out of the ordinary had just happened. But Aiden had realized long ago that, for Woo, there was never a clear line between what was ordinary and what was not. Jo and Devi welcomed his hugs as well, basking in the glow of the man's irrepressible life force. Woo looked as if he hadn't aged a day since Aiden had last seen him over five years ago.

Woo then approached Litha Berne and made another formal bow in front of her. "I am honored to meet you, Chairperson. Is there someplace we can go to talk? Time is of the essence."

"I am honored as well, Dr. Woo," Berne said, her regal bearing softened by a genuine modesty. "We are all honored. Please, follow me inside."

Aiden took a slow, deep breath. A glimmer of hope had returned to light the darkness.

36

AM 7491 SYSTEM
Qarsoon

DOMAIN DAY 70, 2223

"I can prevent the Netvor from ever entering this system."

Elgin Woo said it with such absolute conviction that no one in the room could possibly doubt he meant it. He wasn't bragging. He wasn't selling snake oil or making wishful promises. The universally renowned, multiple Nobel Prize–winning quantum physicist and cosmologist—perhaps the most brilliant mind the world had seen in centuries—was merely telling it like it was.

They had all retreated to the warmth and light of the conference room Aiden had been in earlier. Once again, he sat across the obsidian-top table from Litha Berne. She was accompanied by Hans Vedderman, Keen, and Ananya Kumar. Jo and Sudha Devi sat next to Aiden on his left, and Woo sat to his right. Emi Tanaka and Billy Hotah remained standing in opposite corners of the room, but the tension between them had cooled considerably. Woo had the undiluted attention of them all.

Vedderman was the first to respond to Woo's claim. "How?"

"By shutting down the system's voidoid. Permanently, if you'd like."

"Permanently? But then how could we—?"

"Oh, not to worry," Woo said, anticipating Vedderman's concern. "You wouldn't be cut off from the outside. With a little tinkering, I can modify the EM generators on your ships to enable them to pass in and out of the voidoid freely, just as the *Starhawk* and *Sun Wolf* will be able to do. Thanks to the brilliant work your scientists have already done in manipulating zero-point fields, I can make this modification quite easily. But no other kind of ship will be able to enter this system from the outside, be it Netvor or Alliance."

Stunned silence filled the room.

"But," Woo continued, "we must act quickly. The Netvor know where your colony is now—an unfortunate development—and there are indications that a Netvor invasion force of considerable strength is gathering at various locations, probably preparing to synchronize jumps into this system. Granted, it will take them about 10 days after their jump to get here. But frankly, once they've come through the voidoid, you won't be able to stop them. You won't stand a chance against a force that size, even with your revolutionary technology."

Aiden couldn't begin to guess how Elgin Woo knew about the Netvor's ongoing military deployments. He knew only that Woo had always been well connected to shadowy networks of deeply hidden and unauthorized information.

"Fortunately," Woo continued, "the *Starhawk* is powered by my zero-point drive, and I can get back to the voidoid within five hours to do what must be done to close the door on that invasion force before any of it can enter the system."

He folded his long, narrow fingers together, sat back, and said nothing more.

In fact, he didn't need to say anything more. Using the words "I can" instead of "I will" made his meaning perfectly clear.

Litha Berne understood. "You will do this for us on the condition that we will supply all the technical means necessary for Captain Macallan to return to the Solar System in time to eliminate the cloaked Netvor graser threatening to sterilize Earth."

"That is correct, Chairperson," Woo said. He looked as if he were about to add something to his answer but refrained from it. Instead, he said, "You may be wondering why I, with all my wizardry, don't just go there in the *Starhawk* and take out that obscene weapon myself."

Aiden had wondered the same thing but assumed that Elgin had a good reason for it.

"Like the *Sun Wolf*," Woo said without waiting for a response, "I'd have no problem getting there in time in the *Starhawk*. And I could probably detect the cloaked graser from afar in the same way you can do with your modified CEI. Marvelous work, by the way. My compliments. Now that I know that it can be done, I can figure out how to do it myself. Maryam Ebadi was my colleague, after all. We worked together on the theory of her CEI, and I just happen to have one of her two original prototypes aboard the *Starhawk*.

"But, unlike the *Sun Wolf*, my little boat has no weapons. So even if I found the graser, I couldn't destroy it. That little trick I used to stop the missile in its tracks won't work on an object with that kind of mass, nor would it have any effect on a focused gamma-ray burst. The *Sun Wolf*, however, is heavily armed, so it's the only ship that can do the job. But only if it can use your technology to do it."

"I understand," Berne said. "But I still don't understand exactly how you're going to shut down the voidoid."

Aiden could see that Berne wanted to believe in Woo, but what he'd proposed sounded so bizarre that she needed some kernel of logic to convince her.

"I will summon a symbioid to block this binary system's voidoid."

Berne looked even more mystified. "A *symbioid*?"

Woo nodded thoughtfully. "How much to you know about my *Living Voidoids* hypothesis?"

Aiden came to Berne's rescue. "Elgin, *no one* knows your updated version of that work. Remember? You were still formulating it before you disappeared into Astrocell Gamma. I was the only one you even tried to explain it to. You've been 'out of the world' for five years now."

"Oh, right," Woo said, embarrassed by his presupposition. "Then maybe you'll all remember when the voidoid at Alpha-2 Hydri, the gateway into Astrocell Beta, was blocked back in 2218. Then soon after that, the gateway into Astrocell Gamma at Eta-2 Hydri was blocked in the same way. They were obstructed by symbioids, extraordinary and very old entities carrying small black holes inside them. No one could jump through those voidoids until the symbioids decided to depart. As a result of my recent fellowship among these entities—sentient beings I call Luminous Ones—I can summon one of them to do the same with your voidoid. There's no way a Netvor invasion force could use it to come here. I can explain more about this fascinating cosmic ecosystem later, if you wish, but we must act now. I need your decision, Chairperson."

"Yes, of course," she said, still looking conflicted. "But the Forum—"

Aiden, unable to contain his frustration, cut her off. "We don't have *time* for the Forum."

Elgin Woo leaned forward and engaged Berne face-to-face. "Chairperson, in case you're wondering what kind of 'deal' this is, and what kind of person I am, even if you refuse our request, I will not leave you at the mercy of the Netvor. I would still go out there and shut down the voidoid, regardless. I would save your colony from destruction, just as I did a few moments ago by stopping that nuke from striking. So it's not that kind of *deal*. It's about something higher."

Elgin Woo had the grace to stop short of stating it more explicitly. The moment of truth had arrived. What kind of person was Litha Berne? What kind of people were the Libera?

She glanced briefly at Vedderman, Keen, and Kumar, then replied without hesitation. "Yes, we will give Captain Macallan all the help he needs to stop the Netvor graser. We will start loading the shuttle with the necessary equipment, and Captain Vedderman will take you all back to your ship as soon as possible."

"Thank you," Aiden said, feeling a weight lift from his shoulders. "I also ask that whoever is most familiar with these technologies come aboard the *Sun Wolf* to facilitate its integration into our systems. And to save time, I'd like to depart the moment they come aboard with their equipment, so they can do the setup while we're in transit. That means they'll accompany us for this mission, but I will return them here immediately afterward. You have my word on it. Is that acceptable?"

Berne nodded. "That would be Ananya Kamar and Emi Tanaka."

"Wait," Jo interrupted. "Let me go in Ananya's place. She showed me how to modify the CEI with her code sequences. I can do it just as well as she can, and I'm more familiar with the existing CEI device on the *Sun Wolf*."

True, Jo had been aboard the *Sun Wolf* when they'd used the CEI to identify the hidden gateway at Eta-2 Hydri, but she wasn't exactly "familiar" with the device. Aiden guessed she had additional reasons for wanting to come along, so he said nothing.

Berne glanced at Kumar, who said, "Yes, absolutely. Jo can do it. I'm more than happy to stay behind."

Then Berne turned to Tanaka. "Emi, are you good with going along with them?"

Tanaka lifted her chin. "For another chance to kick some Netvor butt? Sign me up."

Billy Hotah flashed a quick smile at Tanaka's response.

Aiden said to Berne, "I hope you're aware, Chairperson, that once our CEI is modified, your code sequences will remain within our device on board. And I will allow the Alliance to duplicate this device, along with the coding that allows it to detect cloaked Netvor ships. The Alliance desperately needs this capability. They're constantly losing ships to surprise attacks by lone Netvor warships that sneak up and strike before our ships have a chance to react. The Alliance needs this technology to gain the upper hand in the fight."

"I understand," she said. "And to further the spirit of cooperation, we will offer you all the information we have on the exact locations of Netvor strongholds. Their military bases, industrial centers, cloning creches, population centers, and governing loci. We have no reason to keep that information to ourselves and are more than willing to share it with the Alliance."

Aiden bowed his head briefly. "Thank you, again."

Berne stood, and everyone followed suit, sensing the meeting was over. But Jo interrupted them. "One more thing," she said. "The *Sun Wolf* is going to need some of those shield-buster missiles. There's no guarantee that the graser will be unshielded when we encounter it. And, as everyone knows, Netvor shielding is unbeatable. Except now, with the Libera shield busters."

Aiden looked at Berne, eyes wide. "Is this true?"

The five Libera in the room exchanged glances, ranging from discomfiture to pride. Emi Tanaka was the first to respond. "Yes, it's true. We tested it for the first time on our way here from Shénmì. We encountered a Netvor ship that had uncloaked and powered up its shield. The missile worked like a charm. Punched right through their shielding. Boom. No more Netvor."

Elgin Woo grinned and rubbed his hands together, obviously impressed. "Ah-ha! The plot thickens."

That *was* a major breakthrough, Aiden thought. Every strategy to destroy the graser Aiden could think of depended on catching it while it was still cloaked and therefore unshielded. And they would most likely find it that way if the *Sun Wolf* entered the system unseen, cloaked itself by Libera technology. Without detecting a threat, the graser would have no reason to sacrifice its cloaking to power up its shields. But the flaw in the strategy was the possibility of finding the graser with its shield already powered up, for whatever reason. It would then be invulnerable to all known weapons, and there was no solution for that scenario. But now . . . ?

"Jo is right," he said. "If those missiles work, we need some."

Vedderman nodded. "I agree. The problem is that we have built only seven of them, and only one of those would be available to you on short notice. The others, you'd have to wait much longer than you'll want to get them on board."

"Okay. Where's the one that we can use?"

"It's on the *Ark*, docked next to your ship. It will take a little time, but we can probably transfer it to your missile bay within your time frame."

"A time frame that's rapidly narrowing," Aiden said, looking at his chrono. "The *Sun Wolf* needs to leave Forgeron for your voidoid no later than 21:00 tonight. That's less than ten hours from now. Half of that time will be eaten up by the shuttle flight from here to Forgeron."

"That's right," Vedderman said, making his way toward the exit. "So we've got a lot of work to do. Starting now."

When Aiden and Berne moved to follow Vedderman out the door, Woo stopped them and spoke to Berne. "There's something you should know about what else the Netvor want from you besides your combat tech. Something they may try to acquire before destroying your colony."

"What is it?"

"Not an 'it' but a 'who.' They want one of your scientists to extract knowledge from her. A discovery of hers that's extremely valuable to the Netvor. And to all of us."

Berne put a hand to her mouth, alarmed. "Who?"

"Do you have a mathematician here named Astur Ali?" Woo asked. "She's also an astronomer. Quite brilliant and someone I'd love to meet myself, under different circumstances."

"Yes, Astur is one of us. She happens to be the one who discovered this planet and named it Qarsoon. What do the Netvor want with her?"

"It seems that your Astur Ali has solved one of the most notoriously impossible mathematical problems in history, one that holds the key to finding all of the gateway voidoids in the galaxy. Whoever has that key could potentially rule the galaxy."

Berne raised her eyebrows. "Yes. The mathematical problem called the Yang-Mills Existence and Mass Gap. I heard that she had solved it but didn't realize its significance."

"It's absolutely amazing," Woo said. "The Yang-Mills Existence and Mass Gap has been a central question in theoretical physics, particularly in quantum field and gauge theories. It's been one of the top Millennium Prize Problems for over two centuries, and no one has even come close to solving it. Until now. And now that the race for the key to the galaxy is out in the open, her solution simply cannot fall into Netvor hands. The future of all non-Netvor beings is at stake."

Aiden looked at Woo. "Does this have anything to do with your work to identify gateway stars? By 'hearing' the stars' songs?"

"It has *everything* to do with it. The solution provides an empirical way to identify the songs without relying on me alone, doing it intuitively, or someone else with my rare form of synesthesia. With Ali's solution in their possession, the Netvor could quite literally own the galaxy."

Litha Berne's astonishment turned to anger. "Then we'll do everything in our power to prevent that from happening."

The brutal clarity that darkened Berne's eyes as she spoke took Aiden by surprise. It was a new look for her. He liked it.

Yes, no doubt about it. She's one of us.

37

Domain Day 70, 2223

Woo had instructed the *Starhawk* to resume low orbit above Qarsoon while he conducted his visit to the surface, and now he summoned it to return. While he and Aiden stood in the cold darkness waiting for the craft to land, Aiden said, "Elgin, I have lots of questions. To begin with, where the hell have you been these last five years?"

Woo looked at him as if he'd asked an embarrassingly simple question. "I've been a guest of the Luminous Ones, old boy. Out in Astrocell Gamma. I know it might seem that I've been gone for five years. But among the Luminous Ones, it's only been about three months. And no, this isn't some kind of time-travel nonsense. Arthur Eddington's arrow of time still points in only one direction. But it's been a fantastic journey. There are so many other astrocells in our galaxy, Aiden. Millions of them. And the Luminous Ones have been teaching me how to find the gateway stars unique to each one of them. That knowledge will allow us to make sequential voidjumps into the farthest reaches of the Milky Way. The entire galaxy would be open to us. And it will happen sooner than later with Astur Ali's solution."

Aiden already knew about that part of Woo's work, but he remained skeptical about the man's Luminous Ones, and to what extent they were figments of Woo's fiercely creative imagination. "So what the hell *are* these Luminous Ones, Elgin? You say they're alive and they've been around for billions of years, since the Big Bang. So they're immortal, right? But how can anything alive live forever?"

"Ah, that's almost the right question. But what you're really asking is: if they're alive like we are, why don't they die like we do?"

"Something like that, yes. But more broadly. If there was one thing I learned on Silvanus, it was that life cannot exist without death. Life feeds on death. And death feeds on life. It's the law of Nature."

"Exactly," Woo said, twirling one of his braided moustaches. "Everything in Nature is resurrection. But what I'm talking about goes beyond that. Have you ever watched old archival TV shows from the 21st century?"

"No, I haven't, Elgin," Aiden said with well-practiced patience. From past experience, he knew he was in for one of those long and winding roads Woo enjoyed taking on his way to making his point. If you tried to stop him, that would be the end of the journey, and you'd never hear what he had to say. It was a game for him, one that you had to play to have any chance of understanding him.

"There was a crime drama from the early 21st century," Woo began, "where the two lead detectives spent a lot of time together driving around in a car while investigating a murder. One of the guys was this laconic, cerebral nihilist who's sort of crazy but brilliant. The two had been silent for about an hour after discussing the death of the victim. Then out of the blue, the crazy one comes out and says this: *In eternity, where there is no time, nothing can grow, nothing can become, nothing changes. So Death created time, to grow the things it would kill.*"

Woo spread his hands out in praise. "Brilliant, eh?"

"Huh?"

"It's all about time, Aiden. Why do we die? Why do all living things die even as life is continually reborn from death? Because of time. Just as you said, it's the law of Nature. But it's not the only law. The Luminous Ones can live by another law, one that existed *before* Death created time. They live outside of time. So they don't really 'live forever.' They just live."

Aiden shook his head slowly. "Now I'm even more confused."

"Don't underrate yourself, Aiden," Woo said, beaming with amiable confidence. "You get it. Even when you think you don't."

Aiden dismissed Woo's presumption and moved on. "Can you at least tell me *where* you've been? I mean physically? On a planet? Not living in the *Starhawk*, I assume."

"Heavens, no," Woo said with a hearty laugh. "It's hard to explain, and honestly, you don't have the time for me to try. I can only say that where I've been isn't exactly a 'where,' and when I've been there isn't exactly a 'when.'"

"Oh, good. That explains it all perfectly well." Aiden was not amused. Well, maybe a little. The man was full of surprises, and many of them seemed so offbeat they couldn't help sounding funny.

"Okay. You're right," Aiden conceded. "We don't have time for it now. But promise me that once this is over, you won't up and disappear again before telling me about it."

Woo nodded thoughtfully. "I will do my best."

Aiden pursed his lips in silence. *Not exactly a promise.*

Just then, the *Starhawk* came into view, descending from the darkness above. Lit by the pole lights, it came to a halt not far from where Aiden and Woo stood. It hovered just off the ground. No sound came from it. No visible distortion of the surrounding space marked its arrival. Woo spoke to it. "Mari, open up, please."

A circle of light appeared on the vessel's surface at ground level, and a female voice, husky and sensuous, came from inside. "Welcome back, Elgin."

Woo grinned lecherously. Aiden stopped him before he climbed aboard. "So how's this going to work, Elgin? Shutting down the voidoid."

"I'm going to leave here now and get to the voidoid in about five hours. Then, assuming the Netvor fleet hasn't jumped through it yet, I'll summon the symbioid, and this system will be locked down."

"How am I going to get the *Sun Wolf* back out through the voidoid?"

"You'll be able to pass through without a problem," Woo said as if it couldn't be more obvious. "Because your ship has my zero-point drive. Just like mine. Until I can tinker with the Libera's ships, we'll be the only two vessels the symbioid will allow to pass through unscathed. Just make sure you power up your zero-point bubble before jumping. The symbioid will recognize the *Sun Wolf* as the *Starhawk*'s kin. Its sister, if you will. I'll explain all this later if you want, but I really must leave now. I'll meet you at the voidoid."

And with that, Woo hopped aboard his bizarre saucer-shaped spaceship, and the circular opening closed behind him. Aiden stepped back and away as the *Starhawk* lifted off. In the blink of an eye, it vanished into the opaque gloom above.

Hans Vedderman came up to Aiden, his gaze skyward. "How does he do that?"

"Got me. Although I'm pretty sure he'd explain it as more of his 'zero-point trickery.' Is your shuttle fueled and ready now?'

"Yes, it is. We can board now. But we'll have to wait for Tanaka and Jo to catch up. They're getting the necessary equipment together. They'll be along shortly. Ananya Kumar is coming, too, just for the shuttle ride to the station. Jo wants to learn as much as she can from her about the CEI modification before leaving."

Devi and Hotah walked up to join them, and the four of them entered the shuttle through its personnel hatch. Aiden was relieved to remove his heavy coat and sit in the relative warmth and light of the cabin. While they waited, Vedderman said, "I know Dr. Woo is brilliant, and I trust him, but I have no idea what he's talking about when he says he'll lock down the voidoid by summoning a . . . *symbioid*? It just sounds crazy to me."

"You're not alone in that," Aiden said. "Woo's theories can seem fantastical. But they usually turn out to be sound, even when most of us don't totally understand why. The symbioids he's talking about are real. We encountered one while confronting Cardew out at Eta-2 Hydri. It was carrying a small black hole inside it and parked itself in the middle of the system's voidoid, the gateway voidoid into Astrocell Gamma. It was very effective in shutting down the voidoid. No entry, no exit. Not to mention how it used the tiny black hole to destroy Cardew's ship."

Vedderman nodded. "We've all heard the story of Cardew's demise, of course, and the mysterious shutdowns of the gateway voidoids around that time, but details are scarce."

"It's complicated," Aiden said, and then he attempted to explain as much as he knew of Woo's esoteric *New Cosmology*, his grand 'theory of everything.' How, according to Woo, the Luminous Ones existed as forms of pure energy and how they'd been protecting the universe from cosmological forces that would otherwise render it uninhabitable. Preventing dark energy from ripping the universe apart and manipulating dark matter to keep the superstructure of the universe intact.

Vedderman took in Aiden's explanation thoughtfully, then said, "It's an elegant theory."

"Elegant and outlandish."

"Outlandish, yes," Vedderman said. "But: *A man of genius makes no mistakes. His errors are volitional and are the portals of discovery.*"

Aiden stared at him, mystified.

Vedderman smiled modestly. "That's James Joyce. From *Ulysses*."

"You've read Joyce?"

Before Vedderman could respond, Jo, Kumar, and Tanaka entered the shuttle. Jo carried a metal case that looked as if it opened like a suitcase and was about the same size as one. Tanaka carried a nylon briefcase in one hand and a narrow metallic cylinder, about one meter long, in the other hand. It had a trigger mechanism at one end, and Hotah tensed up when he saw it.

"Relax, Lieutenant," she said with a coy smile. "It's the housing for the painite crystal, the heart of our cloaking tech. It'll make your ship invisible, just like ours."

Vedderman moved forward to the pilot's chair while Aiden and the others strapped in. Moments later, the shuttle lifted off and ascended quickly. He glanced out the ClearLum viewport to see the eerie fungal forest surrounding the landing pad lit up by the shuttle's exhaust plume. As the shuttle gained altitude, the fiery light it shed upon the planet's surface faded quickly, and Qarsoon resumed its mantle of eternal darkness.

Nearly five hours later, the shuttle completed its docking maneuver with Forgeron Station, and its seven occupants filed out into the station's passenger vestibule. Vedderman looked at his chrono and said, "Dr. Woo should be at the voidoid by now. I hope he succeeded in shutting it down before any Netvor warships could get through."

"I'm sure he did," Aiden said, wondering the same but wanting to sound more positive. "But we won't hear anything from him for at least another four hours. Let's just assume that we're safe and good to go."

"Agreed. While you board your ship, I'll head off to the *Ark* and start the transfer of our shield-buster missile to your weapons bay."

Aiden nodded. "Take Lieutenant Hotah with you. He handles our weapons systems."

When Aiden boarded the *Sun Wolf* and entered the bridge, he couldn't remember feeling happier to see the rest of his crew alive and well. Alvarez looked as if she felt the same way upon seeing him and the others. "Welcome aboard, Captain."

Pilot Lista Abahem remained seated in the pilot's chair, silent and unruffled, but graced him with a glowing smile. It always amazed Aiden how Abahem's preternatural stillness could seem so animated. Emotion without motion.

Lieutenant Samuel Assan stood from his post and gave him a crisp military salute, utterly unnecessary on a nonmilitary vessel, but done with such verve that Aiden had to smile.

"At ease, Lieutenant." Then he saw Assan's black eye. "What's with the shiner?"

Assan absently touched the bruise around his left eye, winced, then shrugged. "Well, you should see the other guy."

Aiden's mood darkened for a moment. "I fully intend on doing that."

He glanced at Dr. Devi. Without humor, she said, "I'm off to the medical bay to check on our patient."

"I'll meet you down there in a moment, Sudha." He moved to the command post but did not sit and addressed the crew from there. "We've got less than 17 hours to find and destroy the graser. That means we need to leave this station within 1 hour. So, as soon as Lieutenant Hotah secures the Libera shield-buster missile, we're outta here, under maximum ZPD."

He proceeded to introduce Emi Tanaka and Ananya Kumar to the rest of the crew. "Tactical Officer Tanaka will be joining us on our mission. She'll be installing an element of Libera technology that enables us to cloak the *Sun Wolf.* It interfaces with the sector of the EM generator we use for the zero-point drive. That's in your department, Lieutenant Assan, so I expect you two to work together closely on that. Alvarez, you'll need to work with Jo and Officer Kumar on modifying our Casimir-Ebadi Interferometer. It'll allow us to locate the graser after entering the Solar System. Get started on it now, please."

With that, Aiden left the bridge and made his way toward the medical bay. Halfway there, Hutton's disembodied voice came over Aiden's comm. "Captain, I must take this opportunity to apologize for my failure to prevent Commander Silva from taking control of the ship against my will. If it had not been for Dr. Woo's intervention, all of you would be dead."

The AI sounded genuinely distressed. The tone of personal shame was painfully clear in his voice. "Don't sweat it, Hutton. Elgin said it wasn't your fault, and I believe him. But I am curious about how Silva managed it."

"Commander Silva used a set of extremely sophisticated override codes that could only have come from the darkest, most clandestine sources. Codes that even I did not know existed."

Aiden stopped in his tracks. "What?"

Hutton had learned enough of Aiden's speech patterns to know that Aiden was not asking him to repeat what he'd just said. Instead, Hutton said, "Yes. It is astounding to me as well. I was powerless to counter any of the commands initiated by those codes. It is quite troubling."

Troubling was putting it mildly. A security breach of this magnitude—sophisticated enough to bypass the most mature neural-net AIs like Hutton—could have devastating consequences. Was there a snake in the grass somewhere in the Alliance? If so, Aiden was relatively sure that Miguel Silva was not the head of the snake. But how did Silva acquire those override codes? And why?

38

AM 7491 SYSTEM
Forgeron Station

Domain Day 70, 2223

MIGUEL Silva looked like shit.

He was lying on his back unconscious on a med bay gurney. He had a bandage around his head fixed at an angle to cover his left eye, a compress bandage under the left side of his chin, dark purple bruising on the left side of his face, and IV fluids running into both arms. And his wrists were shackled to the gurney's rails.

Sudha Devi was studying a CT scan when Aiden walked in. She looked up from the screen and said, "He's heavily sedated now and very lucky to be alive. But he's going to need cranial surgery to *stay* alive. It's a delicate and complicated procedure that we are not equipped to do here. And it needs to be done soon, or he will die."

Devi went on to describe what she called a tangential gunshot wound where the bullet had pierced Silva's skin just below his left ear and behind the angle of his lower jawbone, continued underneath the skin until it exited just above his temple, all without breaching his skull. But the shot had imparted enough force to the brain case to cause an epidural hematoma along with cerebral contusions and traumatic subarachnoid hemorrhage. He was lucky in that the pistol he used was a small caliber weapon.

Devi said it was a diminutive .32-caliber semiautomatic using solid-point bullets. The weapon had been recovered, and Assan identified it as one of the easily concealable types used by covert DSI operatives.

So, if Silva survived, he would not lose his jaw or bleed out from a torn carotid or aortic vessel. He'd need some dental reconstruction, probably lose hearing in his left ear, and possibly lose vision in his left eye. But the survival part of the equation was still highly questionable. The intracranial bleeding was serious and would prove fatal if not treated soon.

"The point is," Devi concluded, "he would need to be treated at Gateway Station where they have the facilities to do this kind of operation on an emergency basis. But it would mean a significant delay for us. We'd have to make a layover at Gateway to transfer him to their operating rooms. Not to mention all the questions and bureaucratic bullshit we'd need to deal with by stopping in at Gateway unannounced after being incommunicado for this long."

Aiden rubbed his temples, shaking his head. "You're right. We don't have time for that. Not if we want to get to the graser before it triggers. I had planned to make the jump without even stopping at Gateway to check in. Or ideally without even being seen, if we can get the Libera cloaking up and running by then. Can we stabilize him long enough for us to get the job done, then bring him back to Gateway Station? Maybe put him in an induced coma until then? Therapeutic hypothermia?"

Devi shook her head gravely. "No. He doesn't have that long. But even if we tried, there's another problem. You may not have heard the latest reports about the effects of voidjumping on people with neurological trauma. It's new information, prompted by case studies of crewpersons suffering from head traumas during combat incidents. Eight out of ten died during voidjump. And in all but one of those cases, the patients were perfectly stable going into the jump. It was the voidjump itself that killed them."

Shit. "So we can't even take him with us. He has to stay behind or else he'll die."

"Which he'll do anyway if not treated promptly. The only solution I can see is to leave him here and hope the Libera take enough pity on him to try saving his life."

Jo had mentioned that the Libera had built two medical facilities with sophisticated treatment capabilities, including AI-guided robotic surgery. One was inside the colony, and the other one was right here on Forgeron Station. Granted, the Libera were less susceptible to disease and physical injury than humans, but their brains and central nervous systems were virtually identical and equally vulnerable. The Libera had anticipated a need for high level medical care and prepared for it. But . . .

"Take *pity* on Miguel Silva?" Aiden said. "The man who blew up their antimatter tanker, killing its crew, then tried to kill all the rest of them by nuking their colony? The man who might have even betrayed them to the Netvor, inadvertently or not? How many humans do you know of who would be that . . . humane?"

"These days? On Earth? Not many," she said. "All you can do is ask. Bring it up with Vedderman."

Aiden's comm beeped. He answered. It was Alvarez. She said, "Captain, the Libera missile is aboard, and Hotah is securing it. We'll be ready to depart within 10 minutes."

"Thank you, Lilly. Would you please contact Captain Vedderman and tell him I need to speak with him urgently before we leave?"

"Will do. He just arrived on the bridge to collect Ananya Kumar. I'll tell him to hold up."

As Aiden was leaving the med bay, Devi said, "I'll prepare Silva for transfer, just in case. And I'm willing to stay behind to oversee his care, if that will make a difference in persuading Captain Vedderman."

Aiden met Vedderman and Kumar on the bridge and took them aside—far enough away from Emi Tanaka, whose own solution to Silva's problem would most likely involve just shooting him. He explained Silva's situation, stressing that the man would die very soon unless he got the kind of treatment he could only receive here at Forgeron's medical facility. Aiden watched a whole range of emotions play across the captain's face—from incredulity, outrage, vengeance, and indifference, phasing into reason, resignation, and finally, begrudgingly, into a hint of compassion. Kumar, on the other hand, went directly from incredulity straight to a brand of ethical mercy that Aiden saw too infrequently among his own fellow humans. They finally agreed to take Silva into their care.

"And I will accept Dr. Devi's offer to remain here with this man," Vedderman added, "to assist in his treatment and for his safety. You can retrieve them both when you return here to bring back Tactical Officer Tanaka."

There was a lot to unpack from what Vedderman had just said, but Aiden got it. Dr. Devi's presence would improve Silva's chances of surviving not only the medical procedures, but also surviving his stay among an isolated population fully aware that he had tried to kill them all. Vedderman might have also been concerned about getting Tanaka back from a mission of unknown complications aboard an Alliance ship. He was basically saying, *Since you've got one of ours, we'll keep one of yours until you return.*

He buzzed Devi on her comm. She had already wheeled Silva out into the station's passenger vestibule, ready to transfer. With weary resignation, she added, "Yes, I'll agree to stay here with the patient. It's probably safer here anyway than where you're going."

Aiden relayed the message to Vedderman, who responded, unsmiling, "Now you know us."

Not "Now you owe us." There was a big difference, and they both knew it.

With that, Vedderman shook Aiden's hand, wished him luck, and departed with Kumar at his side.

Aiden sat back in the command chair and took a deep breath. He looked at his chrono. It read 20:52. "Pilot, move us out, set course for the voidoid, and engage zero-point drive, maximum speed."

~ ~ ~

About four hours into the five-hour transit to the voidoid, Emi Tanaka looked up from the Drive Systems station where she and Assan were still working to integrate the Libera cloaking tech into the ship's systems. She spoke to Aiden. "Captain Macallan, what are we going to do about the Netvor warship that entered the system a couple days ago? The one that's heading for Qarsoon."

It was a pointed question but asked tactfully, without reference to anyone's responsibility for the Netvor ship's intrusion. But it was obvious that she'd been paying attention to the timing of their transit. They were now approaching the position in space where the Netvor ship might be at this point in its trajectory toward Qarsoon.

"We'd have to drop out of ZPD to scan for it," he said. "I can't spare a moment of time getting back to Sol, not for something we can easily do after we've taken out the graser."

She returned to her work with Assan and said nothing more, but she was clearly unsatisfied with Aiden's answer.

Hotah cocked his head to one side as he spoke to Aiden. "I've been looking at the recording of that ship's entry through the voidoid. The video segment captured by the Libera spy cams positioned at the voidoid."

It was the video Vedderman had shown Aiden when accusing him of leading the Netvor intruder into their home system. "And?"

"Look at this." Hotah put the recording on the main screen. It showed the Netvor warship emerging from the voidoid, moments before it cloaked and vanished.

Assan's eyes widened. "That's one of those Netvor ships with the weird propulsion housing. I heard they've been testing a new kind of fusion drive using a high-yield deuterium-helium-3 reaction and a sophisticated magnetic-coil exhaust system to increase drive efficiency. It would enable the ship to maintain high thrust for longer times and to go farther without refueling."

"Okay," Hotah said impatiently. "But that's not what I'm looking at. Look here."

Hotah moved the pointer to the ship's fuselage where a symbol was stenciled next to a number. The symbol was the same one they'd seen on all Netvor warships, but the number "19" was stamped next to it. "It's the same ship that nuked the Bayit colony back at Daleth-4."

Alvarez stiffened and glared at the screen. "The one that murdered all those people there, along with all their children."

Aiden felt the blood rush to his face. He looked around the bridge and felt the heat of collective rage radiating from the crew. He turned to Jo, who was working with Alvarez at Comm/Scan. "Do you have the modified CEI up and running yet?"

"Yes," Jo said. "We can now spot a cloaked Netvor ship up to 10 million kilometers out."

Aiden stroked his beard. "This might be a good time to test it out, eh? To see if it'll work when we hunt for the graser."

Met with unanimous nods of agreement, Aiden spoke to Hotah. "We can drop out of ZPD instantly and resume it instantly. That's not a problem. But how close to this ship would we need to be for us to get a shot off and be back on our way, all within one minute?"

Hotah grinned wickedly. "For a missile, about 6,000 kilometers from launch to impact. But there's an issue of elapsed time before impact that could be exploited by an alert defensive system. I'd go with the laser cannon. Faster, longer range. Get me within 100,000 klicks, and if they're not shielded, I'll burn that bastard in a half second."

"It won't be shielded," Tanaka said. "They're running cloaked. They can't be shielded and cloaked at the same time."

"Can we cloak the *Sun Wolf* yet?" Aiden asked her.

"Not yet, but almost," Tanaka said. "We're still working to align the painite crystal. But for this, we wouldn't really need it. At 92 percent light speed, we're effectively cloaked until we drop out of ZPD. And if we do it close enough to the target, they won't have time to react before we shoot, even if they do spot us."

Aiden glanced at Hotah. He smiled back and said, "She's right."

It was time for some fast math. "Hutton. Given the last known position and acceleration of the Netvor ship and, given our current trajectory, calculate the point in space where our two ships will come closest to each other and how soon it would happen."

Hutton responded immediately. "Our trajectory lines are very close to one another, just moving in opposite directions. If we drop out of ZPD in 34.3 minutes from now, we have a 96 percent probability of finding ourselves within 30,000 kilometers of the Netvor ship."

Aiden looked at Hotah. "Will that work?"

"Piece of cake."

"Make it happen," Aiden said. "Time for payback."

"You got it, boss." Hotah shared a quick glance at Tanaka. She smiled back at him with unexpected warmth before resuming her hardnosed attitude.

And so it was, about 30 minutes later, the *Sun Wolf* dropped out of ZPD at a point roughly 3 AU from the voidoid, reversed direction by 180 degrees at a velocity of just under 5,100 kilometers per second, which was Hutton's estimate of how fast the Netvor ship would be travelling toward Qarsoon at that point in time.

"There it is!" Jo pointed to the modified CEI screen. The shadowy image of what looked like a warship under acceleration had materialized from an otherwise uniform wash of green dots. Its image was indistinct, but the telltale shape gave it away.

"Distance?"

"It's 11,320 kilometers out," Jo said, "and our velocity is well matched to theirs."

"It's still cloaked and unshielded," Tanaka added, looking over Jo's shoulder.

"Not any longer," Alvarez said. "I'm starting to pick it up on the optical scope."

Tanaka nodded. "Okay. It's seen us, and now it's transitioning from cloak to shielding. But that'll take at least 40 seconds, and it's vulnerable to weapons fire during that time. And now that it's uncloaking, you can also see the markings on its hull."

The number 19 became clearly visible on the ship's fuselage. No question about it.

Aiden glanced at Hotah. "It's all yours, Lieutenant."

It took Hotah about six seconds to target the Netvor ship and one second to trigger the laser cannon. The image of the Netvor ship on the CEI screen simply vanished. But the *Sun Wolf*'s optical scope picked up the explosion. Even from that distance, it was an impressive sight.

Hotah sat back, dusted off his hands, and said, "Good riddance, assholes."

And that pretty much summed up the sentiment of the entire crew.

"Pilot, turn about and resume course to the voidoid, maximum ZPD."

The entire attack took only 57 seconds. Aiden was fairly sure the delay wouldn't make much difference in their tight timeline, but he was totally sure it had been worth it.

Now he could only hope that Elgin Woo had reached the voidoid in time to prevent any more Netvor warships like that one from slipping through. They'd know for sure in about 25 minutes when they arrived at the voidoid. Aiden, the scientist, didn't believe in superstition, but Aiden, the man, crossed his fingers anyway.

39

Domain Day 71, 2223

IF Aiden had not seen it once before, he would have declared it the weirdest thing he'd ever seen. But since he *had* encountered a voidoid occupied by a primordial black hole—in 2218 out at Eta-2 Hydri—he could only say it was the weirdest thing he'd ever seen twice.

The *Sun Wolf* had dropped out of ZPD to a standstill 80 kilometers from the AM 7491 system voidoid. Elgin Woo's *Starhawk* sat on their port side, several kilometers off. That peculiar entity Woo called a symbioid stared back at them from the forward screen. It sat smack in the middle of the 18-kilometer-wide voidoid, its halo of white light flooding the voidoid's spherical volume. The symbioid's companion black hole occupied the exact center of the sphere, the deepest black imaginable. Even though the Schwarzschild radius of the primordial black hole itself was only about 10 centimeters, its gravitational field was over 11 times greater than Earth's, and it left a 4-kilometer-wide volume of space immediately surrounding it totally devoid of the pale light filling the rest of the voidoid. The effect made the voidoid look like a giant, eerie eyeball in space, a sclera of pale white light with a deep black pupil at its center.

"Beautiful, is it not?" Woo's voice came over the ship's comm, sounding like a proud father and startling Aiden out of his stunned silence. *Beautiful* wasn't exactly the word he would have used. More like terrifying. Aiden had never felt comfortable being this close to one of the most exotic and menacing phenomena in the universe. He had only to glance around the bridge to confirm he was not alone in his discomfiture.

"Fear not," Woo said gleefully as his face appeared on the screen, smiling brightly, his eyes alive with the adventure of the moment. "While the black hole remains inside the voidoid, it does not exert any gravitational force beyond the voidoid's boundaries. The symbioid is in complete control of when and how to use its resident black hole."

Aiden knew this to be true from prior encounters, but alarms of primal fear still buzzed inside his hindbrain.

"At my behest," Woo continued, "it is now blocking the voidoid from use by any ship other than yours and mine. And the Libera ships, too, once I'm done tinkering with their EM-field generators."

"How did you do it, Elgin? I mean how do you . . . summon a symbioid?"

"The same way Cardew did, unknowingly, leading to his own demise—by simulating a strong gravitational field in close proximity to the voidoid using the Füzfa Effect. Since then, the voidoids have grown very touchy about that kind of thing. They 'remember' Cardew's attempt to kill them by messing with their exquisite sensitivity to G-fields. Now they respond to any stimuli of that kind by summoning their close cousins, the symbioids, to put a stop to it."

Aiden remembered it all too well. He'd had a front row seat for it. "Did any of the Netvor ships get through the voidoid before the symbioid shut it down?"

"No," Woo said. "Well . . . one of them almost made it, but I got here just in time to prevent the rest of the invasion force from passing through."

"Almost made it?"

"Yes. If you look closely off to your starboard, about 30 kilometers out, you'll see the remains of a Netvor warship, just its fore section, the only part that made it through before the symbioid arrived."

"I'll take your word for it, Elgin. I assume this won't happen now to other conventional ships trying to enter this voidoid?"

"That's correct," Woo said. "This unfortunate warship just happened to be in transit at the exact instant the symbioid occupied the voidoid. Otherwise, all other ships attempting to come here by entering a voidoid on their side of things will merely pass in and out of that same voidoid to find themselves just 18 kilometers from where it started, unaffected. Exactly the same way a ship does when it uses incorrect jump coordinates, or ones that don't correspond to any known star. For all practical purposes, this voidoid no longer exists at its former coordinates."

Aiden stared at the ominous cosmic eyeball sitting inside the voidoid. It stared back at him, sending a chill up his spine. "But the *Sun Wolf* will pass through it like a normal jump, unharmed, on to its intended destination. Right?"

Woo smiled at him as if he were a child afraid of monsters under the bed. "Of course! Just make sure your zero-point bubble is activated for the jump. I assume you will be doing that anyway if you plan on using your zero-point drive for a high-velocity jump at relativistic speeds. Which I would highly recommend, under the circumstances. The symbioid will recognize the identity of your zero-point bubble by the unique marker I have embedded in the drive's EM-field matrix, my personal neurosignature."

Woo's neurosignature was one of the many reasons no one else had ever duplicated his miraculous zero-point drive. It was the metaphorical key to turn on the engine, and even if someone did succeed in reverse engineering the drive's machinery—a highly unlikely scenario—it simply wouldn't work without it. Elgin Woo was the sole keeper of that key, and until he decided to share it, the *Sun Wolf* and his *Starhawk* remained the only two ships in the universe with such mindboggling capabilities.

"By the way," Woo said, "I took care of the Holtzman buoys that the Netvor warship left behind here at the voidoid. Snagged them with my little 'tractor beam' and shoved them off into deep space. They won't be sending any more data back to whoever was listening for it."

"That Netvor ship no longer exists, Elgin," Aiden said. "We took it out on the way here. We recognized it. Killing it sooner than later was something personal for the crew."

"Ah. I understand," Woo said before continuing. "Something else you should know; the antimatter tanker the Netvor left behind is full. They obviously needed it for their return trip. It's unmanned and sitting about 30 klicks out. I thought it might come in useful for the Libera colony. You know, as a replacement for the one that fool XO of yours destroyed. I was able to uncloak it myself with a little finessing."

"I'm sure they'll appreciate that, Elgin." Aiden felt a resurgence of anger at the mention of Miguel Silva's folly. "We'll deal with it on our way back."

"There may be a problem with that," Woo said.

"What do you mean?"

"When I uncloaked the tanker, I saw that it had been damaged. Probably hit by the debris of that Netvor ship that got cut in half by the symbioid. The tanker was cloaked at the time, so it was not shielded. Some of the debris must have taken out the tungsten shield cowlings around the propulsion nozzles. That's what protects the rest of the ship from the intense radiation of the antimatter drive. This is not a robotic vessel. It needs a crew to operate it. There's no way a crew can drive this thing all the way back to Qarsoon without dying from the radiation. Intense gamma rays, to be precise. Not even the Libera could withstand it."

Damn. "The Libera will just have to come out here themselves and figure out how to get it back," Aiden said impatiently. "But we've got to get rolling now, Elgin."

"Well, then," Woo said in his most jovial voice. "I must be off now myself. I promised to return to Qarsoon to help modify their ships to be recognized by the symbioid. These Libera are truly re-markable people. They have accomplished so much. Incidentally, you may be interested to know that the original genetic muta-tion that happened to Jo and the other Libera during the Netvor cloning was *not* a random, one-in-a-billion occurrence. It was no accident. Far from it. Fascinating, eh? Well, best of luck, Aiden. Cheerio!"

"Wait . . . what?"

But Woo had already signed off. On the auxiliary screen, Aiden watched the *Starhawk* engage its zero-point drive. One moment it was there, the next moment, it was not.

Stunned by Woo's parting comment, its staggering implica-tions, Aiden stared at the empty space where the *Starhawk* had just been, then pulled himself together. He had no time to waste on wondering. He had to focus on the task at hand. "Pilot, take us out to 150,000 klicks and prepare a Stealth Sequence jump."

"Captain?" Alvarez said. "I've activated our onboard Holtzman transceiver to check for any messages from the Alliance. There are several addressed to us from Admiral Prescott at Gateway Station. The last one was sent seven hours ago. They're all wondering where we are."

Aiden nodded. He was not looking forward to Prescott's que-ries. Nor did he have time to explain why he'd disobeyed the admiral's orders. It was approaching 03:00, Domain Day 71, just nine hours left to find and stop the graser. And they still had a long way to go. They needed to jump to Gateway Station first, via the Northern Voidoid of Alpha-2 Hydri, then transit that star system all the way to its polar opposite point, 26 AU away, to the Southern Voidoid where they could make the jump into the Solar System.

"Lilly, run Prescott's last message, voice only."

When voidships entered a star system with plans to head out for distant destinations within the system, they routinely deployed a Holtzman buoy at the voidoid they came through for communi-cation with points in other star systems. But when a ship remained within proximity to the voidoid, it could use its own onboard Holtzman device. Alvarez keyed it in now, and Prescott's voice boomed over the comm.

"Where the hell are you, Captain Macallan? We've been trying to reach you for over a day now. The wreckage has been removed from around Gateway's voidoid, so you're cleared to make the jump to come here. You need to get the *Sun Wolf* out to Sol as soon as possible to find that goddamn graser before it incinerates Earth. We don't have much time left, and you're the only ship with any chance in hell of stopping it."

Prescott paused for an uncharacteristically emotional moment before continuing. Aiden knew that the admiral had family on Earth. "We did receive an incomplete Holtzman locator transmission from your ship a couple days ago that placed you in some backwater binary system out in the Reticulum sector. Is that where you really are? We also received the encrypted message you piggybacked on the locator transmission intended for DSI eyes only. The one tagged with the number '56.' We sent it on to DSI HQ back on Earth."

Hmmm. An unidentified encrypted message? Covertly piggybacked on the Holtzman's locator transmission? Sent to the DSI, Domain Security and Intelligence? Aiden glanced at Hotah, then at Alvarez. Were they wondering the same thing?

"One more thing," Prescott continued, "I thought you'd like to know that Admiral Stegman is out of induced coma, alert and oriented, and recovering nicely. We're all just hoping that you and your crew are still intact and you can get back here in time to help us out. Respond to this message as soon as possible. That is all."

When Prescott's recording ended, Alvarez said, "Do you want to respond? Tell Gateway that we're coming through on a high-velocity jump? Then ask them to alert Friendship Station that we'll be entering the Solar System through V-Prime about four hours after that? We'll be under ZPD the whole way there, without comms, so we won't be able to tell them ourselves."

Aiden thought about it—the number "56" itched at the back of his brain—then said, "No. We'll just do it without notifying them. At this point, I'm not trusting anyone at Alliance HQ. Not until we know how the Netvor figured out where Qarsoon was just after we did. If the wrong people know we're coming through to stop the graser, and believe we have the means to do it, they may try to stop us. Or worse, they might just go ahead and trigger the graser now, even if it's not yet in optimal position. It's at least close enough by now to wreak havoc on Earth."

Emi Tanaka said, "We're all set up here now, ready to cloak the *Sun Wolf.* We can jump while cloaked and come out the other side still cloaked. No one will know we've come through."

No one would see them come through the voidoid anyway, not at 10 percent light speed, but sensitive G-wave monitors at Gateway Station might detect its passing after the fact and easily deduce who it was. But not if they were cloaked by Libera technology.

"Good. Make it happen."

The *Sun Wolf* was about to attempt an extremely dangerous voidjump maneuver that Aiden had devised himself years ago and had executed only a handful of times since. He called it the Stealth Sequence. It involved jumping into a voidoid at 10 percent light speed in order to maintain that same velocity upon exit, thereby speeding well past any potential combat zones if hostile ships were waiting for them on the other side of the jump. He'd figured out an entrance velocity that balanced the pilot's reaction time to make the jump against the reaction time of a potential enemy responding to the *Sun Wolf*'s exit on the other side. The sweet spot turned out to be about 10 percent light speed. To achieve a jump at that astounding velocity, the ship had to start its run toward the voidoid from around 150,000 kilometers out to give the pilot an absolute minimum of five seconds on approach to make the microadjustments necessary for a successful jump.

When the ship reached its target distance from the voidoid, Abahem gave him a thumbs-up. She closed her eyes, her face placid, her body suspended in deathlike stillness. The pale, translucent neurolinkage cap affixed to her shaved skull glowed with a subtle light and pulsed as its swarm of nano-AIs synchronized to establish a seamless link between the pilot's brain and the ship's Omicron AI.

Aiden glanced at his chrono again. Time was running out. "Pilot. Proceed."

40

Domain Day 71, 2223

THE *Sun Wolf* made its jump into the Alpha-2 Hydri system at 10 percent light speed and came to a halt nearly one million kilometers past the voidoid and its heavily guarded Gateway Station. Even though Tanaka had assured him that the ship was now fully cloaked by Libera tech, Aiden wanted to be far away from Gateway's scanners just in case. Alvarez activated the ship's passive sensors, and the crew waited in place long enough to confirm that their ship hadn't been detected entering the system.

"Gateway has its routine active scans sweeping the whole area," Alvarez said, "including our position, and I'm not picking up any signs to indicate they've detected our presence."

"Good." Aiden wondered if he'd be forgiven by Alliance Command, and by Admiral Prescott in particular, for sneaking into the system while everyone was still frantically looking for the *Sun Wolf*. It had been his decision to make, out of an abundance of caution, and he would stand by it even if Command wouldn't want to hear his reasons for it. Better to be wrong than dead.

"But I am picking up a lot of news chatter," Alvarez added. "Sounds like Earth's population is in total chaos. The Netvor's ultimatum about the gamma-ray attack was a widecast, so lots of people picked it up, and now it's spreading like wildfire. Government suppression isn't working. It's all over the NewsNet now, and people are flocking to underground shelters. Civil order is collapsing. Widespread violence. Doomsday stuff. Pretty horrific."

Aiden shook his head. Most people were probably unaware that underground shelters would be useless against a direct hit from a gamma-ray burst like the one they were about to get. Typical underground shelters could protect you from the radioactive fallout of nuclear explosions but not from the tremendous amount of energy of a gamma-ray burn.

Alvarez made a sound of disgust, still listening to her headset. "Apparently President Adler has hightailed it off Earth to his uber-rich pal's 'Sanctuary in the Sky' where they'll have a good chance of escaping without a scratch."

That would be the luxury space station owned by Danish trillionaire Henrik Zimmler, Adler's biggest campaign donor and ideological bro. His super-techno sanctuary maintained a high Earth orbit at nearly 800,000 kilometers above the surface, but at a 90-degree inclination to the ecliptic plane, which would effectively place it beyond the line of fire from the graser.

Typical. Aiden turned to Jo. "Are you picking up any cloaked vessels on the CEI?"

"Nothing suspicious. All clear out to 10 million klicks."

"Alvarez, initiate forward scans only and report." He didn't want active scans aimed back toward Gateway in case Alliance sensors picked up *Sun Wolf*'s pings, raising suspicions.

"All clear," Alvarez said.

Aiden looked at his chrono. It was 03:11. Less than 9 hours to go. And they still had to get across the Alpha-2 Hydri system to Southern Voidoid, 26 AU away, before jumping into the Sol System.

"Pilot, set course for Southern Voidoid, maximum ZPD. Halt at one million klicks out."

It would be another 4 hours in realtime, the only time that mattered for the countdown. On board the *Sun Wolf,* it would be just over an hour and a half. Aiden hadn't slept for over 26 hours, not counting a few fleeting catnaps. It seemed that no sooner had this thought crossed his mind than he woke to Alvarez's voice.

"Captain, we just dropped out of ZPD at one million kilometers from Southern Voidoid. I'm seeing four Alliance battle cruisers standing guard at the voidoid. We're cloaked, and there's no indication that they've spotted us."

Aiden straightened up, rubbed his eyes, embarrassed that he'd dozed off. "Thank you, Lilly. Jo, anything on the CEI?"

Jo was leaning closer to the CEI screen, focusing intently. "Yes. I'm picking something up at about 8.5 million kilometers off. It's invisible to all other sensors, so I'm presuming it's a cloaked Netvor ship."

Hotah sat up straighter. Aiden stiffened. "Is it moving?"

"No. It's stationary. No signs that it's spotted us either."

Hotah turned to look at Aiden. "I don't think it's going to make a move. It's probably here to observe only. Waiting to see if the *Sun Wolf* shows up to hunt for the graser. They can't see us, so they'll stay put. And they're not going to blow their cover by attacking any of those Alliance ships. Not single-handed against four battle cruisers, not with their shielding issues."

"Agreed," Aiden said. "And they're about nine hours away from here, minimum. If they decided to move in, we'll be back here in time to spot them and take them out."

Hotah nodded. "Not worth wasting valuable time engaging a low-risk threat."

"We'll look for them again on our way out," Aiden said. Then he instructed Abahem to position the ship for another Stealth Sequence jump, this time through Southern Voidoid into the Solar System. At 07:21, the *Sun Wolf* popped out of V-Prime into humanity's home star system and came to a halt a half million kilometers past Friendship Station. Again, Alvarez picked up no indication that their presence had been detected. Their new Libera cloaking was working nicely.

"Next stop, Jupiter," Aiden said, looking at his chrono. "That's where we'll start our search for the graser."

Under maximum ZPD, the *Sun Wolf* arrived at a position about 20 million kilometers above Jupiter's north pole. None of the Alliance's prodigious military assets concentrated around its command base on Ganymede detected their arrival. Their cloaking had passed yet another rigorous test.

Aiden's chrono said 09:28. Two and a half hours left. With their new CEI detector and the ship's zero-point drive, they should have ample time to locate and destroy the cloaked graser.

"Hutton, what's your current best estimate for the graser's position? Has it changed from your previous one?"

"No. It is the same. I still predict the graser will be along the effective straight line between Jupiter and Earth, just under 1.9 AU from Jupiter, 2.1 AU from Earth."

"Thank you, Hutton. Pilot, take us there, maximum ZPD."

"Excuse me, Captain," Hutton said, sounding genuinely apologetic. "I may have failed to mention that, due to orbital dynamics at this point in time, that position happens to be just inside the asteroid belt, which may cause some delays."

"What?"

"Yes," Hutton continued, revving up his professorial voice. "As I have mentioned before, we are very near a Jupiter-Earth opposition, the point in a recurring 13-month cycle when the two planets are closest to each other, this time just under 4 AU apart. Which is probably why the Netvor chose this moment in time to attack Earth with their graser. But when this opposition occurs, the asteroid belt is aligned directly between Earth and Jupiter. And right now, the outer edge of the main belt is between us and where I predict the graser will be. Thus, we will need to enter the outer reaches of the asteroid belt to find the graser."

Damn. "The Netvor are using the asteroid belt to hide the graser," Aiden said. "So even though we can approach the belt on ZPD, we can't use it to enter the belt to search. If the graser *is* inside the belt, we'll have to rely on our antimatter drive to approach it. That's going to be time consuming."

Moving around inside the asteroid belt by itself wasn't the problem. In fact, spacecraft didn't need to do much maneuvering at all to avoid hitting asteroids. They could simply pass through as if it were empty space. Unlike popular sci-fi holovids depicting the asteroid belt as a tight space crowded with tumbling asteroids, in reality, the density of objects large enough to cause damage to a spacecraft was very low. Asteroids were spread out across an immense volume of space, and the probability of colliding with one was less than one in a billion.

The real problem for the *Sun Wolf* was that the zero-point drive could only be activated reliably when far enough away from significant gravitational forces. Inside the main belt, the gravitational forces from multiple asteroids of varying mass, constantly changing in time and space, would make it virtually impossible to activate the drive.

Aiden glanced again at his chrono, trying to ignore his sinking feeling of despair. "Hutton, how deep inside the asteroid belt do you estimate the graser might be?"

"Not very deep. No more than eight million kilometers from the presumptive outer edge of the belt."

Not very deep? Eight million kilometers?

"Okay, then," Aiden said. "Our modified CEI has a range of about 10 million kilometers. So we come to a halt at the edge of the belt and start sweeping for that cloaked graser. If it's within Hutton's predicted range, it shouldn't take long to find it, right? Then once we spot it, we do a high-G sprint on antimatter drive to intercept and take it out. With time to spare."

Jo did not look enthusiastic. In fact, she looked stricken. "There's another problem," she said. "The CEI works great picking out cloaked warships isolated in open space. It works by seeing disturbances in the zero-point field caused by point sources of gravity contrasted against empty space. That is, empty of other competing gravitational sources. But inside the asteroid belt, there will be hundreds of other gravitational point sources similar in mass to the graser's. It'll be a huge challenge to distinguish the graser's mass signature from all the other ones in the vicinity."

Shit! "Isn't there a way of distinguishing the irregular shape of an asteroid from an engineered object like the graser?"

Jo nodded. "Resolution of shape on the CEI does increase as the distance to the object closes, but for these wide sweeps, it'll be extremely difficult. I can work on creating some filter algorithms to help. Just overlay everything the CEI picks up on top of everything the optical scopes pick up. Any CEI hit that doesn't match up with a corresponding optical hit would suggest a cloaked object."

"All right, Jo, start working on that. Lieutenant Assan, cede control of the drive to Pilot Abahem. Pilot, engage modulated ZPD and take us on Hutton's course to the outer edge of the asteroid belt, as close as the drive will allow, and shut down."

Freed from monitoring the zero-point drive, Samuel Assan sat back and said, "I know what a graser is, but how the hell can it do what it does?"

Aiden rubbed fatigue from his eyes before responding. "It's an enormous, antimatter-powered, electron-positron beam generator. It can generate very powerful and focused gamma-ray bursts. It mimics the gamma-ray bursts emitted from massive astrophysical objects. Like black holes or quasars, just on a smaller scale."

"How powerful?" Assan asked. "I mean, this thing is tiny compared to quasars and massive black holes."

"Way less powerful, of course. But gamma-ray bursts from astrophysical phenomena can traverse undiminished over hundreds of thousands of light-years. This machine is immeasurably closer than that to any of the planets here in the Solar System. A matter of light-*minutes*. Less powerful but way closer. Easily powerful enough to kill all life on Earth. We've seen what it can do firsthand. Cardew used one to kill several living planets before we finally found it and destroyed it. The Netvor obviously have one of these in their arsenal, too. Maybe more."

Assan still looked mystified, but Aiden was in no mood to elaborate. Hotah noticed and took over. He said, "Graser is an acronym for gamma-ray laser. The concept goes back a couple of centuries. According to Dr. Woo, it started with the Vranic Process, named after the physicist who found a way to make one on a miniature scale. She was looking into how gamma-ray bursts were created by astrophysical jets shooting out of massive black holes. She decided the best way to study them was to mimic the process in the lab. And she succeeded. On a very small scale, but she got the physics right.

"That's when the military got interested. But they hit a road-block trying to find energy sources massive enough to scale up the process. That and ethical concerns from the civilian sector eventually put a stop to the project. Then, years later, a scientist from the Cauldron secretly resurrected the research at the behest of the DSI. He developed a technique to keep the electron-positron pairs farther apart for longer times, essentially creating 'positronium' atoms that can be boosted into higher energy states to produce even more powerful gamma-ray lasers. Then he disappeared, presumably another victim of Cardew's scientist-abduction program. Next thing we know, Cardew has a robotic gamma-ray laser cannon roaming Astrocell Beta, looking for habitable planets to kill."

Emi Tanaka, who'd been listening intently to the technical side of Hotah's explanation, was obviously impressed. "Brilliant."

Alvarez turned and glared at her. "Not so brilliant when you've seen what it can do to habitable planets, green planets thriving with diverse biospheres. I believe a better word is *evil*."

Tanaka lowered her head a moment, realizing too late that she had awkwardly waded into a sensitive subject among a crew who had witnessed unspeakable horrors committed by beings so closely related to her and her Libera kin.

But that didn't stop Alvarez from recounting the incident for Tanaka's benefit. The *Sun Wolf* had discovered a planet in the HD 20003 system that had once supported a viable biosphere roughly analogous to Earth's early Cretaceous Period, teeming with abundant plant and animal life. But they found it choking on a brown haze of photochemical smog composed almost entirely of nitrogen dioxide at toxic levels. In addition, the planet's protective ozone layer had been burned away, exposing its surface to massive amounts of solar UV radiation.

They sent a bioanalytic probe down to the scorched surface to collect DNA samples from the remains of plant and animal life, both on land and in the oceans. The results revealed catastrophic damage at the molecular level. Broken strands, disrupted sequences, base pairs chemically altered. Fundamental stuff. That included microbial life, too, so global food chains had been destroyed from the bottom up. The planet was virtually sterilized. The culprit: gamma-ray bursts from one of Cardew's grasers.

Alvarez finished by saying, "That's what Earth has in store for it if we can't stop this graser in time."

The *Sun Wolf* covered the distance to the outer edge of the belt in less than 20 minutes. Pilot Abahem shut down the zero-point drive and powered up the antimatter drive. Tanaka kept the ship cloaked while Jo started sweeping with the CEI in all directions.

Aiden looked at his chrono. It was 09:54. Almost two hours before Earth received a fatal blow. *That should be enough time, right . . . ?*

41

Solar System

Main Asteroid Belt, Hygiea Group

Domain Day 71, 2223

After nearly half an hour of scanning with the CEI, Jo looked up in frustration. "There's just too much interference. The random disturbances in the zero-point field from moving asteroids, even small ones, just rocks, are creating chaos on the CEI screen. I can't resolve individual sources. I'll have to give up on broad sweeps and narrow the field down to examine individual hits. It's going to take more time."

Aiden felt the knot in his stomach tighten. "How much more time?"

"Too much," she said with a pained expression.

Hotah turned from his tactical screen and said, "If the Netvor wanted to use the asteroid belt to hide their graser, even if it's fully cloaked, would they position it out in the open?"

Good point, Aiden thought. "You're right. They wouldn't. Especially if they believed that Libera technology could use the graser's gravitational properties to detect it. They'd position the graser right next to a sizeable asteroid. In front of it. Behind it. Camouflaged to confuse attempts to detect it by any known means.

"Hutton, calculate the hypothetical spot in the belt within 10 million kilometers that would provide the graser the optimal position to fire its gamma-ray burst at Earth within the next 90 minutes. Then identify the asteroid nearest to that location with sufficient bulk to hide the graser in the way we've been talking about."

Hutton responded immediately. "There is one such asteroid fitting those parameters. It is a carbonaceous C-type asteroid, part of the Hygiea family, approximately 0.8 kilometers in diameter with a mass of over 1 billion metric tons. It is relatively close, slightly over 510,000 kilometers away."

Holy shit. Sure, if they could use the zero-point drive, they'd be there in no time at all. But limited to conventional antimatter drive? He looked at his chrono—10:30 on the dot. They'd need to do an emergency burn at 10 Gs just to get there in the nick of time.

Jo narrowed the focus of the CEI to center it on the asteroid and its surrounding space. She found nothing suspicious but conceded that the CEI would be unable to pick up the graser if it was sitting right next to, or behind, something that massive. "Not from this distance," she said. "We'd have to be a lot closer to pick it up."

Aiden swallowed hard. What to do? Keep looking? Or dash off to that asteroid on a hope and a prayer? The time it would take to get there was all the time they had left. If they were wrong, there'd be no time to do anything else. They would fail and Earth would burn.

The crew knew it, too. All eyes were on him. It was his decision to make and his alone.

"Pilot, set course for the asteroid under 10 Gs, with flip and burn at halfway point. Crew, prepare for an emergency burn."

The ship's antimatter drive could sustain an acceleration of up to 10 Gs for short periods of time. That was the upper limit of what the G-transducers could handle. Beyond that, the transducers would fail, and the crew would suffer fatal injuries. From their current position, they'd need about 38 minutes of acceleration to reach the halfway point, then another 38 minutes of deceleration to come to a stop at the asteroid.

Abahem gave him a thumbs-up, and the *Sun Wolf*'s antimatter engine ignited with a jolt like a mule-kick to the chest. Their new beamed core antimatter drive burst into action with 300 mega-Newtons of thrust, 600 terawatts of thrust power, and an exhaust velocity of over 5,000 KPS. The G-transducers kicked in a second later but were pushed to their limits, barely keeping shipboard conditions within tolerable levels.

When Aiden's breathing returned to normal, he spoke to Hotah. "Lieutenant, we need to discuss attack strategies before we reach this asteroid. Assuming we find the graser there, what are the possible scenarios and how do we deal with them?"

Hotah tilted his head toward Emi Tanaka. "We could use her input, too. If we need to resort to using the Libera's shield-buster missile, she knows more about it than anyone else aboard."

Aiden agreed and asked the *Ark*'s Tactical Officer to join them.

"It really comes down to two scenarios," Hotah said. "If we find the graser and it's still cloaked, then we know it's unshielded and we hit it with our laser cannon. *Boom*. But if, for whatever reason, we find it uncloaked and fully shielded, we use the shield-buster missile and pray that it works. We have only one buster missile, so we have only one chance."

"If we have to use the buster missile," Tanaka said, "we need to consider the graser's defenses. It's probably been upgraded since the last time you encountered one of these beasts. I'm guessing it's got a very sophisticated point-defense system that could potentially detect and destroy an enemy missile with laser fire within four seconds of its launch. I've been studying these kinds of defensive systems developed by the Netvor, accessing sources the Alliance might not be privy to. And I have every reason to believe that this graser will be well protected by such a system."

Hotah closed his eyes and shook his head. "That could be a major problem. It means we'd have to get close enough to the graser to leave less than four seconds between missile launch and impact. That means we'd need to be no more than 15 kilometers away."

"And that's a big problem because . . . ?" Aiden stopped short, realizing he knew the answer. The graser would have its Penning tanks at full capacity with freshly harvested antimatter, ready to generate a gamma-ray burst powerful enough to thoroughly fry Earth from over 2 AU away. That was a lot of antimatter. Probably considerably over 500 kilograms.

When matter and antimatter collide to annihilate each other, their entire mass is converted into energy according to Einstein's famous equation $E=mc^2$. The annihilation of just *one gram* of antimatter with one gram of matter would release energy equivalent to over 43 *kilotons* of TNT. Scale that up a half million times more, and you've got an energy release of catastrophic proportions. It would throw an unimaginably devastating plasma shock wave far and wide. And that wasn't the half of it. There'd be radiation to contend with, primarily in the form of intense gamma rays, along with other nasty particles like pions and muons—and all of it ionizing radiation, the worst kind possible for biological life.

Hotah was shaking his head as if reading Aiden's mind. "When that sucker blows, we don't want to be anywhere near it. Even 50 kilometers is too close for comfort, much less 15. That graser we blew up out by Parthas several years ago? We hit it from 60 klicks out. It had smaller antimatter tanks than this one, and we got rocked pretty good from the blast. We were lucky to escape without major damage."

Tanaka looked deep in thought before eventually speaking. "This new cloaking technology we've got running on the *Sun Wolf* now, it doubles as shielding. You know that, right? It's similar to your former shielding in that it's based on the zero-point bubble Dr. Woo devised to generate your ship's drive. But the adjustments we made to transform it into a cloak also beefs up its shielding properties. It virtually eliminates the stuff of space around the ship, negating certain laws of physics in a way that will potentially protect you from such a blast."

"Potentially?" Aiden said. "We're talking about an explosion of astrophysical dimensions here. And only 15 kilometers away."

"I don't honestly know. We've never encountered an instance like this to test it."

Aiden took a deep breath. His confidence about this mission was slipping further. "Well, let's hope the graser is still cloaked and unshielded when we find it. Then we can just blow it up the good old-fashioned way."

But he was already considering the equation of sacrifice—the lives of one ship's crew versus the lives of nine billion on Earth. He turned to face his crew. All of them had overheard the discussion. Except for Assan and Tanaka, they'd all been here before. They had faced the same equation once before and had solved it in favor of the greater good. What he saw now in their faces told him it would be the same this time. He saw it even in Samuel Assan's face, a young man with his whole life in front of him. A person with the courage of a warrior and the heart of a savior.

Aiden was only unsure of Emi Tanaka, a Libera with no love for the human race. But she looked more than ready for the challenge, solidly in her element and hyped for a fight.

The transit to the asteroid was maybe the longest 76 minutes Aiden could remember. But at the end of it, the *Sun Wolf* arrived and came to a halt just 15 kilometers from the side of the asteroid facing toward the inner planets.

"There it is!" Alvarez said, just before her enthusiasm collapsed. "But..."

They didn't need the CEI to spot the graser now. It was sitting right there in plain sight, nestled a half kilometer from the asteroid's dark, rocky surface. The atmosphere of hope was sucked out of the bridge as suddenly as if there'd been a hull breach.

Damn! "It's uncloaked and already fully shielded," Aiden said.

Alvarez held out her hands, bewildered. "But why? Did it spot us coming?"

"No," Tanaka said. "Our cloak is good. That thing still can't detect us. It's uncloaked because it's getting ready to fire within the next several minutes and to use its active scans. It can't do either one while cloaked. Then it powered up its shields to stay protected in case its scans detected any intruders."

Alvarez was still perplexed. "But I thought the Netvor can't use weapons or active scanning without dropping their shield."

"They can," Hotah said, "but only with selective shielding, leaving just their weapons ports and scan arrays unshielded. It's a strategy their warships don't use anymore, but it's perfect for a graser. They'll leave the opening of the beam cannon unshielded but only along the direct path of its aim. That way, it's even invulnerable to a frontal attack."

"So we got here too late," Alvarez said, acknowledging what everyone else knew but didn't want to admit. "Too close to its firing time. If we'd gotten here sooner, it'd still be cloaked and vulnerable."

With the graser fully shielded, the *Sun Wolf*'s conventional weapons couldn't touch it. But the game wasn't over yet. Aiden looked around at the crew. "Okay. So the shield buster missile is our only shot now."

Now that it was clearly visible on the main screen, the graser was a nasty piece of work. About 100 meters long, it was roughly half the length of the *Sun Wolf*, with a central fuselage of about 10 meters in diameter at its narrowest. The aft section had the usual configuration of four antimatter tanks spaced equally around the circumference, terminating in four electromagnetic nozzles typical of beamed core antimatter drives. But the antimatter tanks themselves were far from usual. They were enormous, dwarfing the rest of the vessel.

At its midsection, a huge bell-shaped structure jutted out perpendicular to the axis of the fuselage, like a giant trumpet bell with a circular rim 40 meters in diameter. The whole structure was attached to a rotating circular ring surrounding the ship's fuselage that allowed the bell to alter its orientation. Inside the bell, coil-like conduits ran from the rim down into a central core. Informed by his previous encounter, Aiden knew this was the graser's antimatter scoop used to harvest abundant antimatter from Jupiter's magnetosphere.

A huge spherical bulb took up the front third of the vessel's length, bulging out three times the diameter of the fuselage. A cylinder about the same diameter as the fuselage protruded from the end of the bulb, extending another 20 meters forward. The cylinder was open at the end, clearly the muzzle of the obscene weapon, and judging by the steadily rising thermal readings radiating from it, the device was powering up for a discharge.

"The astrogation computer confirms that it's pointing directly at Earth," Alvarez said, "adjusted for how long it'll take the beam to score a direct hit. From here, about 17 minutes."

Emi Tanaka pointed at the screen. "See those small turrets studded all over the fuselage? That's the graser's new point-defense system. They react in unison, and they're lightning quick. The openings in the shield that allow them to fire are too small, and there're too many of them to neutralize their overall effectiveness. They can respond with laser fire to a missile launch in less than four seconds. To use the shield-buster missile, we can't be any farther away than we are now to launch it or else it'll be intercepted."

Alvarez interrupted, her voice tense. "Captain, the graser is preparing to discharge."

All eyes turned to the main screen. From deep within the graser's black maw, a point of brilliant light began to brighten and expand.

Aiden looked at his chrono to watch the time change to 11:59. Decision time. Take out the graser and probably die from the resulting explosion, or save their own skins while nine billion people on Earth die. It wasn't an easy decision to make, but the only one to be made.

"Hotah, target the graser with the shield buster and fire on my mark. Everyone, strap in. Tanaka, put as much juice as you can into the shielding phase of our cloak. Hutton, G-transducers on max."

"Copy that," Hotah said. Then he turned to face Tanaka. "That thing better work."

"It will," she said, frowning at him. But her voice lacked her usual edge of confidence.

"Radiation levels at the graser's muzzle are climbing crazy high," Alvarez said. "It's starting to fire."

Aiden swallowed hard. *Will this damn shield buster even work? And if it does, will we live through it? Will I ever see Skye and Bri again?* "Hotah?"

"Ready."

"Fire!"

42

Solar System
Main Asteroid Belt, Hygiea Group

Domain Day 71, 2223

Aiden had always wondered what death was like. The moment of death really, more than anything else. He'd never been eager to find out, of course, but being a scientist by nature, he was obsessively curious about everything. And since death was arguably the biggest mystery to haunt human beings from the beginning of time—and certainly the most personal one—he couldn't help wondering what dying was like, even now when he might actually be experiencing it.

Was it a gradual thing? Light fading, wandering down that fabled tunnel of light until there was no more? Or was it more like: You were there one moment, and the very next moment you simply were not? Just like that. Nothing more, nothing less. Just the hard, cold reality of the universe, of which we were such an infinitesimal and insignificant part of. The light was on for one glorious, self-aware second, then it turned off. Forever.

Aiden feared it may be the latter because when he opened his eyes, it was pitch dark. But wait. *He had opened his eyes.* You don't do that when you're dead. Do you? And he was breathing. And he was smelling burnt insulation and the miasma of fear. And tasting the iron tang of blood in his mouth. And hearing sounds . . .

Warning klaxons were screaming maniacally, setting Aiden's teeth on edge.

Then silence.

Hutton's voice said, "Captain, are you all right?"

"Yes. I think." He realized that the blood in his mouth had come from biting his own tongue during the jolt. It hurt like hell but didn't seem serious. "Status report, Hutton. And can you get the lights back on?"

"Working on the lights now. The ship has sustained minor damage, but nothing life-threatening as of now. Power and life-support systems are back online. Hull integrity is mostly intact, except for the shuttle bay where several high-velocity fragments from the explosion punctured through to the interior. Robotic menders are at work addressing the situation. Propulsion system intact. Radiation levels inside the ship are within safe levels. The ship's orientation is stabilizing. We are no longer in immediate danger."

The lights came back on, and Aiden glanced around the bridge. The crew looked dazed but alert. *And alive.* No one was unconscious or looked injured beyond a bloody nose or two. Just shaken.

He stood up, feeling his bruised ribs complain. "Is everyone okay?"

He was greeted with generally affirmative responses and expressions of relief.

"Damn lucky we were strapped in," Assan said. "The ship got tossed around like a toy boat in a hurricane."

Hotah was grinning, the red speckled band across his face flushed. He was staring into the tactical screen, which was just now returning optical images of the surrounding area as the brilliant white flash of the explosion faded. All that was left of the graser was a glowing cloud of star-hot plasma, still boiling in space 15 kilometers away. The asteroid it had been nestled against had split into three uneven chunks by the power of the explosion, creating three smaller asteroids tumbling away from where there had been only one. The epicenter of the explosion swarmed with a multitude of smaller rocks cascading in every direction.

"That was fun," Hotah said, meaning it.

"I told you it would work," Tanaka said, rubbing the back of her neck while unstrapping from her flight chair. Her tone was outwardly defensive but tinged with playful teasing.

Hotah looked at her, nodded appreciatively, and smiled. "Nice missile."

Her eyes softened a fraction. She smiled back at him. "Nice shot."

Aiden spat some more blood from his mouth before speaking to Tanaka. "Nice shield. Without it, we would have been hull-breached if not thoroughly fried by the radiation."

Jo and Lista Abahem seemed the least affected by the blow to the ship. Jo was smiling, her augmented skeletal system and musculature apparently no worse for wear. Abahem looked cool and calm as she always did, reclining comfortably in the pilot's couch, her long pale fingers folded together and resting in her lap, like nothing out of the ordinary had happened.

Alvarez, however, looked concerned. She had her monitors back up and didn't like what she was seeing. "One of those broken-off chunks of the asteroid is hurtling our way. It's big and coming on fast."

Collision alarms started going off. Hutton said, "Impact in 13 seconds. I suggest we evade now."

"Pilot?"

But Abahem was already on it. The ship lurched forward as the antimatter drive kicked in, knocking Aiden off his feet. He regained his balance and sat back in the command chair just as the G-transducer took over. It was another 10 G burn, and within eight seconds the ship was clear of the rogue asteroid's path.

When Abahem terminated the burn, Aiden stood again and addressed his crew. "Good work, everyone. Now let's get the hell out of here."

Once the *Sun Wolf* had reversed course and cleared the outer edge of the asteroid belt, it engaged the zero-point drive to cover the nearly 15 AU back to Friendship Station at V-Prime in slightly over two hours. They came to a halt 1,000 kilometers from V-Prime and prepared for a jump into the Alpha-2 Hydri system. With no signs of cloaked Netvor ships anywhere within the CEI's range, Aiden decided to drop the ship's cloak for the first time in their long journey. He hailed Friendship Station, identified himself, and informed all who were listening that the Netvor graser had been destroyed. The threat to Earth from a gamma-ray burst was over. Earthers could come out from hiding—from underground shelters that would not have protected them anyway—and their fearless leader could return from his chicken shack in the sky.

But Aiden knew the threat from the Netvor was far from over, especially now that cloaked Netvor ships had proven they could enter the Solar System undetected. But for Earth's sake, he could only hope that the scare of total annihilation by a gamma-ray burst might prompt its severely fractured geopolitical population to unite, at least long enough to work together for the common good of their planet. He was not optimistic.

Aiden dealt with the ensuing barrage of questions and requests for official reports from Friendship Station by ignoring them and promptly jumping through V-Prime into the Alpha-2 Hydri system. He'd be getting enough of that action sooner than later, but he'd already decided to pay attention to only the part of it coming from Admiral Stegman. That was, of course, if Stegman had recovered from his injuries and was back in command.

The *Sun Wolf* completed the jump through Southern Voidoid, back into the Alpha-2 Hydri system, and paused long enough to check in with the four Alliance warships stationed there and to scan the vicinity with the CEI. The cloaked Netvor ship they had spotted earlier lurking over eight million kilometers off was no-where to be seen.

Aiden's plan now was to cross the system to Gateway Station and jump through Northern Voidoid straight back to AM 7491 where he'd return Emi Tanaka to her home on Qarsoon, as he'd promised. And to drop off Jo, too, if she wanted to stay on Qar-soon—but that would be a complicated decision for her. Then he'd pick up Dr. Devi and Miguel Silva, if Silva was still alive. And if he was alive, Aiden had a lot of questions for him.

The only wrinkle in the plan was that the *Sun Wolf* was almost out of fuel. They'd been zipping around between star systems without refueling, and while the zero-point drive used less energy than the antimatter drive, it still required antimatter fuel to power and maintain the EM fields. As things stood now, they wouldn't have enough reserves for the 34 AU transit back to Qarsoon after jumping to AM 7941. Since there weren't any gas giants in Qarsoon's system for harvesting antimatter, Aiden needed to make a detour on the way to Gateway Station. The obvious choice was the gas giant here in the Gateway system, Daleth, the planet hosting the moon where the Bayit colony had been nuked three days earlier.

Aiden decided the detour would do them all good. Except for Emi Tanaka, the crew hadn't had any real sleep in days. Antimatter harvesting was automated—Hutton could handle it with ease—and it would give them all a break to recuperate. When they arrived at Daleth about two hours later, Abahem settled the ship into the sweet spot of the planet's magnetosphere. Assan oversaw the deployment of the antimatter scoops, and Hutton took over from there, activating the Bickford Process to begin harvesting large quantities of antihydrogen. With the ship's upgraded Penning trap technology, their tanks would be filled in less than eight hours.

The announcement of the graser's destruction that Aiden had delivered to Friendship Station had presumably been relayed to Gateway Station and would probably get there faster than if he tried sending it from here, so he didn't bother trying. Besides, he had a date with his bunk. He ordered the crew to their quarters to get as much sleep as they wanted, instructed Hutton to not disturb him with any nonessential comms, and at 17:10, he collapsed in his bunk.

As he drifted off from the shallows of consciousness toward deeper waters, memories of his encounter with the blue swirls on Qarsoon teased him from below like elusive sea creatures leading him farther out to sea. The mysterious swirls had recognized him, or at least had recognized some shared kinship of life and light.

Drifting farther out, he heard a familiar musical tone inside his head, wavering ever so slightly, an elusive vibrato of meaning. It was the song of Alpha-2 Hydri again, centered on the E-flat tone, the same song he'd heard from the star's voidoid while sleeping next to it several days ago. The star and its voidoid were perfectly in sync, singing the same song in unison. Just as stars everywhere would do. Just as Elgin Woo predicted.

It reminded Aiden of another song, the one he'd heard while held in the blue swirl's embrace, the song of Qarsoon's distant star, Majka. A song of pure light. Something had happened to him on Qarsoon. A new sense had emerged, a sixth sense . . .

Aiden could feel the star's song in his body, resonating through every cell, gently probing, reading the ancient messages coded into his DNA, listening for his body's song, the molecular music of his biochemistry, and harmonizing with it. Now in harmony, he began to *see* the music, pulsing delicately through the color spectrum of visible light, from one end to the other and back again. The light held the same quality as the auras he'd seen around his friends after his encounter with the blue swirls.

The swirls had given him a gift. The faculty of second sight. *But why?* Who was he to merit such a gift? And what was he to do with it?

Those questions pulled at him like dark currents, drawing him inexorably deeper into the forgiving and forgetting ocean of sleep.

43

AM 7491 System
Forgeron Station, Qarsoon

Domain Day 72, 2223

MIGUEL Silva still looked like shit. But he was alive. And he was awake.

Silva was sitting upright in a wheelchair inside Forgeron Station's medical bay. Aiden stood facing him with Dr. Sudha Devi at his side. It was a cool, white room, and it was very quiet. Silva had an IV still attached to his right arm and a bandage still under the left side of his chin. But now, instead of a bandage around his head, he had a patch over his left eye. His head was shaved clean, and a clear nanomend patch was sealed over the left parietal region of his skull where, just 48 hours ago, an emergency craniotomy had been performed to relieve the pressure of a deadly hematoma. The entire left side of his face was a gaudy mask of dark purple bruising.

When Aiden walked into the room, the look on Silva's face was a mixture of fear, shame, and wonder. Aiden could easily understand the fear and shame. But wonderment? That part of it only became clear after the first words came out of Silva's mouth.

"They saved my life."

They were words of genuine amazement spoken by a man whose life had been saved through extraordinary measures by the same people he had callously attempted to murder en masse the day before. A man who seemed to have learned the meaning of mercy. And of humanity.

Devi looked at Aiden without emotion and said, "He'll live."

"Thanks, Sudha. I need a word with Mr. Silva."

Devi nodded once, left the room, and closed the door behind her. Aiden moved to a chair next to Silva's wheelchair and sat. It was just past 10:00, no more than a half hour after the *Sun Wolf* had docked at Forgeron Station. He had gotten here as quickly as he could. The *Sun Wolf* had stopped only briefly at Gateway Station before their jump into the AM 7941 system. There he'd been greeted on-screen by Admiral Benjamin Stegman, who ironically appeared to be in a similar state of recovery as Silva was—albeit without the patch over one eye and shame in the other. The old warrior had gruffly given Aiden his blessing to complete whatever remained of his mission, but only on the condition that Aiden would return promptly to provide a more detailed report. Aiden agreed and transmitted the ship's logs over to Stegman to appease the man's many questions in the meantime.

The *Sun Wolf* had executed the jump and emerged from the AM 7491 voidoid without difficulty, looking back only once to confirm that the voidoid was still blocked by the creepy-looking symbioid. After the five-hour transit to Qarsoon, they'd docked at Forgeron, Emi Tanaka had debarked, and Aiden had arranged a final meeting with Litha Berne. He'd learned that Elgin Woo had returned to Qarsoon as promised, performed some magical operation on the Libera ships that only he understood, and now those ships could pass through the locked-down voidoid unharmed. But the illustrious Dr. Woo was nowhere to be found by the time Aiden arrived.

Aiden sat back in the chair, giving Silva a long look without speaking. He finally said, "I want the truth, Miguel. All of it. And you know what I'm talking about. Now's your only chance to come clean. I won't give you another one."

"Why did they save my life?" Under any other circumstance, Aiden would have dismissed Silva's response as a lame attempt at evasion. But instead he saw a man still in the throes of epiphany.

"Because, Miguel, the Libera are *not* Netvor. You were dead wrong about that. They are at least as human as we are. And now I'm beginning to think they're an even better example of what it means to be human than us."

Silva was silent for a long moment. His one eye seemed to be looking inward, examining some internal topography of the soul that he'd never explored before. Then he said, "What do you want to know?"

"Everything. I want to know who you really are and what you've been up to. All of it."

And so Miguel Silva told his story. If there were any gaps in the telling of it, Aiden believed they were unintentional, and he could easily fill in the blanks.

It started soon after Silva's wife and son were killed in the bombing of Gamelan Station. Silva's bitterness and hatred for the Netvor were already in high gear after his ship, the SS *Parsons*, had been destroyed by a cloaked Netvor warship, killing its captain and half of its crew. The loss of his wife and child at the hands of a Netvor suicide bomber was just the final straw. He became a self-poisoned, pathological hater bent on revenge at any cost.

That's when he was approached for recruitment by an underground shadow group operating at the highest level of Earth Domain's DSI. They had ostensibly aligned themselves with the new president of the UED, Rudolph Adler, and were committed to his ideology of isolationism, hardcore authoritarianism, and the genocide of all cloneborgs. They called themselves Earth Front. Aiden had heard rumors of them and of their far-reaching power, but most people who'd heard such rumors considered them conspiracy-fueled fantasies.

For the Earth Front, Miguel Silva was the perfect recruit. Not only because of his hero status from the *Parsons* incident, in which he had courageously saved the lives of its remaining crew, but also because he was so consumed with vengeance that he could be easily manipulated in exactly the way Earth Front wanted.

The unidentified leader of Earth Front had decided that the only realistic way to defeat the Netvor with its superior combat technology was to acquire the famous zero-point drive invented by Dr. Elgin Woo, and to install it in all their warships. The Alliance, of course, had been trying to do this for years, at first by repeated appeals to Woo himself, then by multiple, well-financed attempts to recreate the drive based on what was known about it. When all these attempts had failed, and when the Alliance appeared to be losing the war against the Netvor, Earth Front decided it was time for drastic, if not illegal, measures. They hatched a plan to steal the *Sun Wolf*.

With the *Sun Wolf* in their possession, not only would they take control of the most powerful ship in existence, but they would also be in the best position possible to reverse engineer the drive for their own use. To do it, they would need a man on the inside, a member of the *Sun Wolf*'s crew. A stroke of luck presented the perfect opportunity. When the *Sun Wolf*'s original Executive Officer, Roseph Hand, moved on to command his own ship, Earth Front pulled strings at high levels to get Miguel Silva assigned to replace Hand as XO, overruling the objections of the Space Service and its chief officer, Admiral Benjamin Stegman.

Miguel Silva eagerly accepted the offer to spearhead Earth Front's secret plans. He was given deeply encrypted access codes designed to bypass the ship's AI, codes that had come from a rogue Omicron AI still lurking in the dark corners of the Omicron OverNet. He was also given a military-grade Trihex encryptor to communicate with his Earth Front operatives.

The plan was to hijack the *Sun Wolf* during one of its scheduled cargo deliveries. The one intended for the mining colony on Ceres in the asteroid belt was the perfect choice. Not only were renegade elements already present on Ceres, fascist groups cozied up with Earth Front, but it was one of the only deliveries where the *Sun Wolf*'s captain was required to go off the ship to personally oversee the transaction. As per Service protocol, Silva would assume temporary command during Aiden's brief absence. It would be the perfect time for him to initiate the bypass codes, take control of the ship, and allow it to be boarded by a raiding party of Earth Front thugs lying in wait.

All the pieces were in place when Aiden threw a monkey wrench into the plan by abandoning the cargo deliveries for a new mission—to find the Libera and seek their aid in fighting the Netvor. When Aiden locked down all communications from the *Sun Wolf* to run silent, Silva decided he needed to communicate with his Earth Front contacts to alert them about the change of plans.

"I was desperate to let them know I hadn't betrayed them," Silva said, looking away, "to alert the hijackers on Ceres to stand down so they wouldn't be found out."

Aiden felt he was doing a decent job of restraining himself from strangling Silva with his bare hands. But it was a challenge. "So when you launched the Holtzman buoy just after we jumped into the AM 7491 system, that was not just a bone-headed mistake. You piggybacked an encrypted message to your pals in Earth Front, using the Trihex encryptor. Addressed to '56.' Each number stands for a position in the alphabet. The fifth letter is *E*, and the sixth letter is *F*—that's EF, an abbreviation of Earth Front."

Silva looked surprised that Aiden had figured it out, then tried to explain. "I wanted to prove my loyalty to them. I told them that the change in plans would actually work in my favor. Not only could I give them the coordinates of the Libera planet, but I would have an opportunity to destroy their entire colony. I still had the bypass codes to take over the ship. Honestly, I was planning to nuke them anyway, even if they had agreed to help us with their technology."

"So you *did* give them the coordinates of Qarsoon in that message."

Silva's expression of remorse looked genuine. "Yes. But I wasn't sure it would help save Earth from the graser attack. I agreed with your assessment that the ultimatum was just a ploy. Those Netvor bastards were going to fry Earth anyway, whether someone came forward with the coordinates or not. But I gave Earth Front the coordinates anyway, mostly to gain their trust, to prove my value to them. They could do what they wanted with them, and I'd be in their debt."

Aiden clenched his jaw and tried to calm his breathing. How could someone as smart as Miguel Silva be so deluded? He kept his voice as calm as he could manage. "Didn't you ever wonder why the Netvor ship showed up here just after you sent that encrypted message? Followed by an attempted invasion by an entire Netvor fleet?"

Silva looked as if he had wondered about it and was afraid of the possible answers. "Maybe the message was intercepted by Netvor listeners and decrypted."

"Silva, you and I both know that Trihex encryption absolutely *cannot* be broken without the one key that only the encryptors can create. The key that only Earth Front would have. Earth Front was the only one that could have opened that message. They did, and the Netvor came."

Aiden let the implications of that connection sink in and said nothing more. Implications that were as troubling for the Alliance as anything he could think of. Silva lowered his head and buried his face in both hands. The man was a wreck, physically, mentally, and emotionally. Aiden's feelings about him were complicated.

Silva looked up at him, a broken man, his remaining eye pleading. "I can't go back."

44

AM 7491 System
Forgeron Station, Qarsoon

Domain Day 72, 2223

MIGUEL Silva couldn't have said it more succinctly. He would indeed be in deep shit with the Alliance if he were to return aboard the *Sun Wolf.*

The ship's logs, already transmitted to Gateway Station, would show that his actions could only be interpreted as mutiny, a crime that could easily upgrade to treason. Not to mention his barbaric attempt to mass-murder a potential ally in the fight against the Netvor. Especially now, after agreeing to give the Alliance technology and information crucial to defeating the Netvor, the Libera's status as valuable allies was on the rise. Silva's attempt to annihilate them would be viewed as a high crime.

Aiden shook his head slowly. "You realize, of course, that I *can* take you back, regardless of how you feel about it. It is, in fact, my duty to take you into custody and return you to Alliance Command. They'll put you away for life. Or worse, if you're convicted of treason."

Silva looked away. "That's not even the worst of it. Earth Front's agents can go anywhere. I'll be assassinated the moment I set foot on any human world. I know too much. I can identify my contact and can second-guess about who else is part of their cabal.

People in high places. They'll cut me down before the Alliance has a chance to even begin due process."

Silva was right. If Aiden took him back now, he was a dead man one way or another. "So that's why you tried to kill yourself."

"Better than living every second of what's left of my life waiting for a bullet in the head."

Most people believed that suicide was an act of cowardice. Aiden wasn't so sure about that. When there was no other way out, choices became very clear. Who was to say that choosing your own way out was not an act of courage instead?

Aiden looked at Silva. "What am I going to do with you?"

"Leave me here," Silva said without hesitation. "I can help the Libera. There's something big I can do for them."

"What?" Aiden stared at him. Was the man still delusional? He doubted the Libera would agree to let him stay among them. And even if they did, what could Silva possibly do for the Libera that they couldn't do for themselves?

Just then, Captain Vedderman opened the door and entered. His expression was grim, his blue eyes clear and piercing. He said, "I can explain."

Vedderman moved to stand next to Silva's wheelchair and faced Aiden. "Commander Silva has volunteered to retrieve the antimatter tanker that the Netvor left behind at the voidoid. The tanker is full, and we need it. He will return it here to Qarsoon."

Aiden stood and stared at Vedderman in disbelief. "You mean the Netvor antimatter tanker that has no propulsion shielding against the lethal radiation of its antimatter drive?"

"Yes," Vedderman said, dead serious. "That's the one. Our remote surveillance platforms have examined it and discovered that the debris not only damaged the engine's shielding, but the navigation system was knocked out by the EM pulse. It cannot be set to operate autonomously. For it to get to Qarsoon in a reasonable amount of time, it needs to be operated by a flesh-and-blood pilot."

"In a reasonable amount of time?"

"Yes. If you'll remember, Captain, we had two antimatter tankers, and now we have only one," Vedderman said, glancing briefly at Silva. "Our remaining tanker is currently in another star system out in the Phoenix sector harvesting our next much-needed shipment of antimatter fuel. Our voidoid is locked down to prevent a Netvor invasion—thanks to Dr. Woo—but that tanker does not have Woo's bio-key to allow it back through the voidoid for its return to Qarsoon. We would need to send one of our ships with Woo's bio-key all the way out there, through the voidoid, to rendezvous with the tanker and give it the key so it can reenter the system.

"All this will take much time—weeks in fact—and will require much antimatter fuel. Fuel that we no longer have enough of. So, as you can see, it is imperative that we acquire the Netvor antimatter tanker as soon as possible. We can't do it ourselves with one of our ships because it will take us 10 days just to get out there. Then another 10 days to bring it back. Forgeron Station will run out of power long before that, causing catastrophic disruptions to the station and the colony. The tanker must be piloted by someone who can get to it in a matter of hours, not days. Commander Silva has volunteered to be that 'someone,' and the *Sun Wolf* is the only ship capable of getting him there that quickly."

Vedderman's explanation was delivered with admirable patience, but not without a hint of irony. It was clear to Aiden why Silva had volunteered for this mission, given his current state of mind, and equally clear why Vedderman had considered it an appropriate assignment.

"It's a suicide mission," Aiden said flatly.

Vedderman and Silva exchanged glances. It was obviously a point that both of them had already discussed.

"Not necessarily," Vedderman said. "We will send along some improvised shielding, tungsten-alloy materials that can be easily installed and will confer a degree of protection for a pilot. This tanker is designed to be manned. It has an adequate life-support system and will have plenty of provisions, none of which appear to be damaged. We also have very effective medications that limit the effects of radiation exposure, both during and after the exposure. Medications that are not yet known by your own medical sciences."

"Really? We're talking about, what, a 12-day trip at 2 Gs? That's a lot of hours of ionizing radiation. Gamma radiation and high-energy pions. The most lethal byproducts of the AM drive—"

"The mission is not without risks," Vedderman interjected. "But it is a vital one for the colony. Regardless of Commander Silva's decision whether to do this or not, he will be welcome to remain here with us on Qarsoon as a free man. But if he agrees to do it and succeeds, he will be warmly accepted as an honored member of our community. The Libera understand redemption."

And if he doesn't succeed? Or if he dies trying?

Vedderman read Aiden's hesitation and said, "You are, of course, aware of the limited options available to Commander Silva, just as he is. And I am aware of what you might consider your duty to return him to your worlds to face his fate there. The commander has made his decision. Whether or not he is allowed to exercise that decision is now up to you."

Aiden faced Silva and saw him smile, maybe for the first time that Aiden could ever remember. An honest smile. "I want to do this, Macallan. I *need* to do this."

It was a crazy dilemma, and Aiden was not entirely comfortable with the ethics of it. But he had to admit, it held a kind of moral logic that he could not deny. It reminded him of an old saying about how catastrophic adversity could either destroy you or make you the person you really were. And again for the first time, Aiden felt some genuine respect for the man Miguel Silva was becoming.

"But are you well enough to do this?" Aiden asked Silva, glancing at the IV in his arm and nanomend patch plastered atop his shaved skull. The patch over his left eye made him look like a bald pirate of the Caribbean lost in space.

Silva stood up from his wheelchair, somewhat wobbly at first, then planted his feet firmly and said, "Yes, I am, Captain. Ready to go when you are."

"All right, Miguel. You got it." Aiden reached out and shook the man's hand. "We depart in three hours. Dr. Devi will assist you on board."

Vedderman nodded his approval of Aiden's judgment and said, "I can have the tungsten-alloy shielding components loaded aboard your ship within one hour. With your permission."

"Permission granted," Aiden said, not surprised that Vedderman's propulsion shielding for the tanker had already been fabricated and made ready to load as cargo. He gave the man a long look, wanting to trust him without reservation. But, not for the first time in his life, he wondered if it were ever possible to trust *anyone* without reservation. Including himself.

Aiden left the room to find Sudha Devi waiting for him outside the medical bay. When he told her about Silva's decision, she made a grim smile and said, "Poetic."

He left Devi to make the appropriate preparations and took the lift one level down to the docking bay where the *Sun Wolf* was moored, waiting to depart. He was scheduled to meet with Chairperson Litha Berne in about two hours—she was currently en route aboard a shuttle from the planet's surface—so he had some time to kill before then. Despite the sleep he'd gotten the night before, he was still feeling the effects of the adrenaline letdown from their recent action against the graser and their near-death experience. He boarded the ship, greeted the crew on the bridge, then headed to his quarters where he collapsed in his bunk.

"Hutton. Are there any new messages or developments I need to know about?"

"As far as messages," Hutton began, using his convivial conversational tone, "only another one from Admiral Stegman. He asks again that you brief him on all the events of the last few days at your earliest convenience."

Thank the gods that Ben Stegman had recovered well enough from his injuries to resume command of the station, albeit from a hospital bed. Aiden had not been looking forward to dealing with Admiral Prescott, a by-the-book combat veteran who would have a big problem with Aiden's slippery defiance of orders and his decision to remain incommunicado until the job was done. Stegman had a better grasp of the big picture, was more flexible—especially for a man his age—and understood the value of intelligent improvisation. Plus, it didn't hurt that he and Aiden were close friends with a long history.

Hutton continued. "In terms of new developments, it seems that in some quarters, you and the crew of the *Sun Wolf* are being hailed as heroes for saving Earth from destruction by the Netvor graser."

"In some quarters?" Aiden knew Hutton would lead with positive news but had negative stuff queued up to serve next. Which he did.

It had been barely over 24 hours since they had destroyed the graser, and the news of it had spread far and wide. But while "in some quarters," credit had been given to the *Sun Wolf* for doing the deed and to the Libera for making it possible, that was not the story being told to Earth's population. Rudolf Adler held tight control over all public sources of information, the hallmark of his authoritarian regime. After returning to Earth from the safety of his rich pal's orbital palace, he gave all the credit for finding and destroying the graser to the "brave men of the UED Military Service." No mention of the *Sun Wolf* or of the Libera's vital contribution.

Aiden winced. *Once again, the sheer magnitude of the Big Lie was its most effective property.*

In fact, Adler's regime was stoking even more virulent hatred against the Netvor for their attempt to annihilate Earth. And now that the Libera's existence had been inarguably confirmed, they were still roundly condemned as "not so different" from the Netvor. Just wannabe humans. Netvor in disguise. There were reports coming from Earth about renewed government campaigns to round up and "detain" anyone who dared speak out against the lies, as well as anyone with any sympathy for the Libera. This, of course, included all Sympaths.

And it wasn't just on Earth. The paranoia had spread to Luna where a concerted effort to purge the moon's population of Sympaths was being enthusiastically pursued by none other than Lieutenant Seymore Sprague of Luna's Security Service. It was no surprise to Aiden that Adler's administration had appointed Sprague, the man who loved to hate, for the job on Luna.

Aiden could only shake his head in disgust. Maybe it was time to relocate his family's residence-of-record from Luna to somewhere else. Someplace where facts, knowledge, curiosity, and tolerance were still valued. Mars? Ganymede? Silvanus? Shénmì?

"There is one other startling piece of news," Hutton said, "concerning Eta-2 Hydri—"

"Enough, Hutton!" More news was bound to be only more depressing. He just didn't want to hear about it. All he could think about now was his wife and daughter. He missed Skye and Bri so much. He needed them now, more than ever, just to feel whole again. To believe again in the meaning of his own life . . .

He was saved from his rapid descent into deeper blues by a quiet beep from his personal comm. Jo was calling him from the bridge. She said, "Captain, can you spare a moment to talk?"

"Yes, Jo. Come on up."

45

AM 7491 System
Forgeron Station, Qarsoon

Domain Day 72, 2223

WHILE waiting for Jo to arrive, Aiden asked Hutton for a status report.

"The shuttle bringing Chairperson Berne to the station is almost here," Hutton said. "She would like to meet with you in the station's main conference room when she arrives, if that works for you."

"Yes, fine. Let her know. And Hutton, please grind and brew one large cup of my Sulawesi Toraja beans, extra strong."

The Sulawesi coffee beans were from his secret stash, reserved only for special occasions. They had been a gift from his previous Executive Officer, Roseph Hand, Man of Mystery, and his closest friend. He was just savoring the first sip of the precious brew when a knock came at his door. "Come."

Jo leaned in through the half-opened door and said, "Is this okay?"

"Of course, Jo. Come in. Would you like a cup of coffee?"

Jo politely declined, an avowed tea drinker who'd never developed a taste for brewed coffee. They sat across from each other at his spartan dining table in comfortable silence, both of them gazing at the room's wall-mounted video monitor. It held a live feed from the station's optical scope aimed at the mysterious dark planet below. Qarsoon, a rogue planet, home of a rogue race.

She seemed almost as gloomy as he'd been before his cup of coffee. She finally turned from the screen and looked at him with a wistful smile. Aiden had an idea what was on her mind. Now that threat levels had subsided, it was on his mind, too. He said, "What now, Jo?"

She shook her head slowly, sadly. "I don't know. Not yet, at least. The only thing I'm really certain about is getting back to my son, Rene. The harder question is where to go from there. Do we stay on Shénmì Station with Skye and all the others who care for us and treat us as one of them? Or do we come back here to live on Qarsoon, a place that's starting to feel more like home to me than anywhere else?"

It was a tough question. There were pros and cons for each choice. Instead of him pointlessly outlining them for her—a self-centered impulse, he realized—Aiden asked her to do it from her perspective, the only one that mattered.

"The first consideration," Jo began, brightening at the chance to shift from gloom to logic, "is safety. How do we know there aren't more Netvor agents lurking on Shénmì Station? This 'Frank' person was somehow able to elude detection for two months. There may be others like him there, lying low."

Aiden had fretted over the same possibility. His wife and daughter lived there, and his memory of their frightening encounter with the Netvor agent was still raw. "But you can spot a Netvor agent in disguise, right? With your . . . gift. You know, seeing auras. Or the absence of an aura."

Jo looked at him for a moment, her gaze briefly unfocused, before saying, "And now you can see them, too. Can't you? We need to talk about that."

Aiden closed his eyes and nodded. "Okay. Maybe later. But right now, I just want to point out that, even if there is another undercover Netvor mole on Shénmì Station, they won't be a danger to you anymore. The Netvor know where Qarsoon is now.

They don't need you anymore for that information. What other reason would they have to harm you or Rene now? The Netvor's undercover strategy is to plant moles for gathering intelligence information, not engaging in overt operations that would blow their covers. At this stage of their campaign against humanity, inside sources of information about the Alliance are just too valuable. The only reason Frank departed from that strategy was to extract information deemed so valuable and unobtainable elsewhere that it was worth the risk."

"I get that," she said. "But they can still act as saboteurs. Look what happened at Gamelan Station, where Silva's wife and child were killed. And what would have happened if Hotah hadn't stopped Frank from pushing his suicide button to blow up the station?"

The thought of it sent a chill up Aiden's spine. Attempting to calm Jo as much as himself, he said, "That's a last-resort scenario for them, Jo. They'll only do that if their cover is blown wide open and they're cornered."

"Still," Jo said, "it's a threat, no matter how small. But it's a threat that won't exist at all on Qarsoon. The Netvor may know where Qarsoon is, but there's no way for them to go there now that the voidoid is blocked. Thanks to Dr. Woo."

"Okay," Aiden conceded, "in the threat-from-Netvor column, score one for Qarsoon. What else?"

"There's Rene," she said. "Where is a better place for him to grow up? On Shénmì Station, where he has friends. Kids his own age. *Human* kids. What would there be for him on Qarsoon? There aren't any children there, and there may never be, if the Post-humanists have their way. And for that matter, there aren't other humans there. As much as we *Trans sapiens* are like humans, we are different in ways that Rene would notice."

"Jo, you're his mother and *you* are a *Trans sapien*. What would Rene notice that he hasn't already noticed and become accustomed to? He might even feel *more* comfortable around adults like you than he does around us garden-variety humans."

Aiden's attempt at humor failed, but Jo smiled at him anyway, recognizing his good intentions. "What about kids his age, Aiden?" she said. "To play with. That's important for a child growing up. Isn't it?"

"It is," he admitted, thinking of his own child. "It would be hard on Rene leaving that behind for a place where no one his age existed. But if you, his mom, were a happier person living on Qarsoon, then Rene would have a happier mom. And that's just as important to a child growing up."

Jo nodded, thinking it over.

"What's the likelihood," Aiden asked, "that the Libera will actually start cloning sexually reproductive individuals? Two distinct biological genders able to reproduce and give birth to children. New and genetically diverse individuals?"

"I don't know. The Posthumanists are against it, and they have a slight majority."

"But a majority that's slight enough," Aiden pointed out, "to be overturned by a change of heart on the issue. A change that would surely come about from witnessing the rewards of parenthood enjoyed by one of their own living in their midst."

Jo smiled. "I know what you're saying, Aiden. I've thought the same thing myself. Even during my short time among the Libera, I was surprised by how many of them sought me out to ask what it's like to be a parent. To have a child to raise, to teach, to protect. To love. They were hungry for it."

Aiden spread his hands and shrugged, his point proven. "And that hunger would be fed by the presence of a real mother and son living their lives among them. Enough to sway the population's opinion. To reorient the direction of the colony. Other children could very well be in Rene's near future on Qarsoon."

"Yes, the future on Qarsoon," Jo repeated thoughtfully. "The Libera will face some hard decisions about their future, sooner than later. Their planet is wandering through space without a sun, and in about two decades from now, it will be so far away from the only voidoid they have, they'll become isolated forever.

A population of people with children might make very different decisions about dealing with that future than would a population without children."

Aiden hadn't thought of it that way, but she was right. The presence of Jo and her child among the Libera could have dramatic long-lasting effects. "But," he said, shifting gears, "there's something I need you to consider. Something that could impact the timing of your decision. A temporary consideration, but an important one."

Jo frowned, not eager to deal with further complications. "What is it?"

"The Libera colony is now inaccessible to the Alliance and Netvor alike, and you're the only person outside of it who knows how to make the modified CEI work. I can't think of a single technological capability that the Alliance needs more right now to gain the upper hand in its fight against the Netvor. The Alliance is losing more ships every week to attacks from cloaked Netvor warships. If this modified CEI were installed on Alliance ships, they'd be able to see cloaked enemy ships approaching, long before they come within range to attack. And you, Jo, are the only person outside the Libera colony who could make that happen."

He could see the invisible weight of what he'd said settle on Jo's shoulders. She knew he was right. She knew none of the Libera on Qarsoon would volunteer, not even Ananya Kumar. She also knew that the best way to safeguard everyone and everything she held dear was to do whatever she could to help defeat the Netvor. But he could clearly see she wasn't keen on interacting with Alliance personnel who might still regard her with bigoted Earther prejudices.

"I know Admiral Stegman would bend over backward to give you whatever you needed," Aiden added, "including special privileges. A high-ranking officership, if you want."

Jo grimaced at the mention of officership, then said, "I'll do it, Aiden. But honestly, it won't take that long to instruct Alliance technicians on how to make the critical mod. The specs for Dr.

Ebadi's original CEI instrument are freely available now. Once I pass on the details of the modification, the rest will be up to them to produce and install them in all their ships. I assume Gateway Station is our next stop after we take care of business here on Qarsoon?"

"Yes, that's right."

"Good. Some of the best technicians in the field are posted there. I could meet with them and do the job within a day or two."

"Perfect." And Aiden would make sure that Jo's contribution to humanity's fight against the Netvor would be known far and wide. If that didn't change people's minds, nothing would.

"But we will head back to Shénmì Station after that, right? I need to see Rene."

And I need to see Skye and Bri. "Yes, absolutely."

Hutton's voice came over the comm. "Captain, Chairperson Berne has arrived and is waiting for you in the station's conference room. At your convenience."

Aiden stood. "Thank you, Hutton. I'll be right there."

As he and Jo left his quarters, Jo held him up briefly with a hand on his elbow and a smile in her eyes. "Thank you, Aiden."

He returned her smile. "Jo, I'm the one to be thanking *you*. All of us are."

46

AM 7491 System
Forgeron Station, Qarsoon

Domain Day 72, 2223

Chairperson Litha Berne stood as Aiden entered the conference room and greeted him warmly. She looked weary, but the stress lines that had marred her face two days earlier had smoothed, allowing her natural beauty to shine through.

As they sat across from each other at the metal conference table, she said, "I'm very happy to hear that your mission to destroy the graser was successful, Captain, and relieved that so many lives on Earth have been spared. It's another remarkable achievement in the *Sun Wolf*'s growing list of such legendary accomplishments."

Aiden shook his head. "We couldn't have done it without your help. Credit to where credit is due."

Berne smiled graciously but without false modesty. "We owe you a debt of gratitude as well. All of us thank you for destroying that incoming Netvor warship. You saved us the trouble of dealing with it ourselves as it neared our colony."

"You're more than welcome. That ship turned out to be a bit of unfinished business for us, and we decided to take care of it sooner than later. So we're just as happy as you are that it's been eliminated."

Aiden did not go into why the Netvor warship with the number "19" stenciled on its hull had been of such interest to the crew, and

Berne did not ask. Instead, she withdrew two crystals from her tunic pocket and handed one of them to Aiden.

"This holds all the information I promised to give to you when you returned," she said. "It lists the locations of all the Netvor home bases, military outposts, industrial centers, and major cloning creches. The ones we know about, at least. I believe your Alliance desperately needs this information, and we offer it to you freely. Even though Qarsoon is now safe from a Netvor invasion, that may not always be the case for the Libera in the future. It is in our interest that the Alliance succeeds in defeating the Netvor."

Aiden accepted the crystal. "I speak for the Alliance in thanking you, Chairperson."

"Please, feel free to call me Litha."

Aiden dipped his head briefly and said, "Likewise, Aiden is just fine with me."

She smiled again and said, "You already have the data you'll need to modify your CEI devices, and Jo knows how to make it all work so that your ships can detect cloaked Netvor vessels. But we have also agreed to offer the Alliance our ship-cloaking technology as soon as their ships are able to support it."

It was not an evasion. The Libera's cloaking technology was a property of the zero-point bubble. It required installing powerful EM generators and fine-tuning them with quantum algorithms that could only be managed by specially trained Omicron-3 AIs. All of which would take the Alliance a great deal of time and money to accomplish on a large scale. But when they did, Aiden had Litha Berne's word that the Libera tech would be made available to them.

"In addition," Berne continued, "Captain Vedderman has agreed to give you four of our so-called shield-buster missiles. He arranged to bring them here from our munitions factory on Sestra. More are being produced, so we can spare a few. They can be transferred to your ship now, if you wish."

"Yes, I do. Thank you again, Litha."

"You are more than welcome. We will also supply you with all the technical information for producing more of these missiles yourselves, for the Alliance's fight against the Netvor."

Aiden was running out of ways to say "thank you." She spared him from trying by adding, "You should know, Aiden, that you're not alone in this fight. We have our own operations in play against the Netvor. Covert ones."

"Oh? How so?"

Berne did not respond immediately. Instead, she held Aiden at bay with a penetrating gaze. Another silent interrogation. Trust was never an easy thing, nor was it always permanent.

Then, as if assured by some ephemeral vision, she said, "The primal origin of the genetic mutation that aborted the Netvor's cloning process—the one that caused us to become *Trans sapiens*—remains unknown. But we have replicated it, and we have weaponized it in the form of a virus. We know where the Netvor cloning creches are, and we can reach them unseen. We expect to see many more rebellions in the near future. And many more Libera."

Aiden smiled inwardly but chose not to inquire further.

Acknowledging his choice, Berne made a quick nod and continued. "I also have a message for you from Dr. Woo, along with some startling news. I know you were expecting to see him when you arrived, and he apologized for having to depart so suddenly. You may not have heard this news because you've been in transit and without comms. It seems that the gateway voidoid out at Eta-2 Hydri has been blocked by one of those things Dr. Woo calls a symbioid. Now the gateway into Astrocell Gamma is closed."

Aiden sat back, stunned. That must have been the news Hutton was trying to tell him before Aiden shut him up.

"We heard about it early this morning," Berne continued. "It was reported by the Alliance ships stationed there guarding the voidoid. We intercepted their Holtzman transmission from the network. When Dr. Woo heard of it, he left immediately aboard the *Starhawk* and headed for Eta-2 Hydri. Fortunately, he had completed his zero-point modifications for our ships before leaving. Now all our vessels can come and go freely through our voidoid while it remains blocked to all others."

Speechless, Aiden could only shake his head. The gateway voidoid at Eta-2 Hydri was the only way into the virtually unexplored Astrocell Gamma. It had been blocked by a symbioid once before, five years ago when Cardew attempted to jump through it into the new astrocell. After Cardew's defeat, the gateway voidoid had reopened and had remained open ever since. But to this day, very few vessels had entered Astrocell Gamma, beyond a handful of unmanned survey drones. Limited resources stretched thin over the two already known astrocells had effectively left Astrocell Gamma for future generations to explore. It represented a powerful symbol of hope, a sense of limitless frontiers, and a vast wide-open future for human enterprise. Assuming the Netvor didn't get there first and put a chokehold on the only way into it.

Woo, of course, believed that the Luminous Ones were responsible for managing the gateway voidoids throughout the galaxy, all a part of his grand theory of the living universe. Developing his theory was now his life's work, prompting his bold excursions into the far reaches of Astrocell Gamma, consorting with his Luminous Ones, and defying time and space. This new development at Eta-2 Hydri had obviously spurred him to dash off and investigate.

"And that's not all," Berne said. "Our own Astur Ali left with him."

"What? The mathematician who solved that unsolvable equation?"

"The Yang-Mills Existence and Mass Gap problem. Yes. Dr. Woo invited her to join him, and she eagerly accepted. He was so impressed with Ali's research that he asked her to assist him in his quest to identify the gateway stars. So I can only assume that's where they are now. Dr. Woo was confident that the *Starhawk* could easily pass through the blocked voidoid, back into Astrocell Gamma."

Aiden sat back and smiled. It made perfect sense. It was pure Elgin Woo. If any single person could pave the way for humanity's next big step, it was Elgin.

Aiden decided to change the subject. "What about the Libera now? What about Qarsoon? You have some big decisions to make within the next couple of decades. Existential decisions. You're safe now from Netvor, but the price you pay for it is isolation from all the rest of us. Is that what the Libera want?"

Berne took a slow breath before answering. "That, as you may guess, is a very complicated question. Some of us, the ones calling themselves Posthumanists, would prefer to remain isolated from the human worlds, to further evolve into a new genus, beyond *Trans* or *Homo sapiens*. '*Post sapiens,*' perhaps. They would do this through advanced cloning.

"The Humanists among us, on the other hand, wish to have more contact with humans, or at least open more channels between them. We . . . they . . . seek a plan to leave Qarsoon before it becomes impossible to do so and colonize another world. A real world, with a sun. A place like Earth. Even Dr. Woo endorsed that idea while he was here and said he could actually 'make it happen.' He, of course, did not elaborate before leaving suddenly."

"Did he mention anything more about the permanency of your voidoid's blockade?"

"As far as we know, it's permanent. So, unless that changes, the *Sun Wolf* and the *Starhawk* will be the only two ships from the outside that can visit Qarsoon. It's safe to assume that the *Starhawk* will always remain in Dr. Woo's possession. And we sincerely hope that the *Sun Wolf* will remain under your command. You will always be welcome here."

Her point was well taken. After hearing Silva's confession about Earth Front's plot to hijack the *Sun Wolf*, Aiden had become acutely aware of how crucial it was that his ship never fall into the wrong hands. The more he thought about it, the deeper his suspicions grew about Earth Front's true nature, including its connection with the Netvor. The plot was thickening back on Earth, and the future of the Solar System was growing dangerously unpredictable.

"Thank you," Aiden said. "In fact, we may be back sooner than later, depending on what Jo decides to do. She may want to return here with her son, Rene. But for now, she has agreed to come with us back to Gateway Station to direct the integration of the CEI mod into the Alliance's ships. After that task is done, she will decide what to do next."

Berne nodded. "If she does decide to return and live among us with her son, she will be more than welcome. I think she has much to teach us, just by being who she is."

Aiden felt unexpectedly moved by this moment. He said, "And I have a feeling the Libera have much to teach us. About what it is to be human and beyond."

She looked at him in silence, her gaze unfocused for a moment, before speaking again. "Perhaps you have already learned a great deal about that, even during your short time on Qarsoon. I sense you have experienced something that has changed you. Something subtle yet powerful. I can see it in you now. And around you."

Aiden felt a point inside his head open like a blossom of pure light. Of blue light. Pulsing with the same rhythm as the blue swirls he'd encountered. A living light. The light of life.

The moment passed, and Berne held out her hand to give Aiden the second crystal. It was a telegem. "This is from Dr. Woo. He asked me to give it to you just before he left. He said that only you and your mate, Skye, could open it."

Then Berne rose from her chair and said, "I must leave now. My shuttle is waiting to take me back to the surface. As I said before, you are always welcome here, Aiden."

Aiden stood as well. "Before you leave, Litha, I must ask you this. Now that the immediate threat has passed, will the Libera at least consider a more enduring partnership with the Alliance? It was Jo's original mission here, and I believe in it as much as she does."

Berne faced him directly. He saw a multitude of emotions color her eyes like fast-moving storm clouds that begrudgingly shared sunlight with darkness at unpredictable tempos.

"At this point in time," she finally said, "I honestly do not see a lasting alliance forming between our two peoples, not organically at least. Most of us still find it impossible to understand how an intelligent race of beings who have been blessed with the capacity to experience beauty can so carelessly abuse the very source of all beauty they were born into. Planet Earth."

Aiden knew where this was going, and it made him cringe inside. "Beauty . . ."

"Yes. Beauty is one way of looking at it. The simple things are deepest. A flower, the sound of the ocean caressing the shore, the flight and song of birds in a forest, the light of sunset and sunrise, gentle rain, a butterfly, ripples of light on a lake in a summer breeze . . . all these simple things are in themselves the very life of Earth. They are supreme gifts of beauty given to you freely by the planet that gave you birth. And yet so many of you either ignore them, or knowingly abuse them.

"Perhaps it is because we live on a planet without a sun—without the flowers, and the birds, and glistening ripples on a lake—that we find it so hard to understand why such gifts of beauty are not received with respect and deep understanding of their true value. When Earthers debase these gifts, they not only hurt themselves, but they degrade their true mother. They kill her with a thousand cuts of blindness and kill themselves in the process.

"So yes, in many ways, it is about beauty. One of your poets said it most succinctly. *Beauty is truth, truth beauty.* When a people turn away from one—willfully or carelessly—they forfeit the other.

Aiden, in truth, could not deny much of what Berne had just said. He chose not to attempt a defense and remained silent.

"I apologize if this sounds cynical," Berne said, recognizing his discomfort, "and I realize that not all humans are like this. But enough to dissuade the Libera from entering any alliance beyond what is necessary for survival. I do hope we are wrong, and that some evolutionary sea-change will occur to direct your future otherwise, toward a future of giving and protecting, not taking and destroying. If that ever happens, and if we, the Libera, have thrived, we will gladly join hands with you, to move onward together in beauty and truth. Until then, I wish you the best of luck, Aiden Macallan. Farewell."

With that, Litha Berne turned and walked out the door.

Aiden watched her go, unable to speak or to recall when he'd ever felt so humbled.

He took a deep breath and looked at the telegem crystal in the palm of his hand. The only way to open it would be to use either his own personal reader, which was back on Luna, or with Skye's reader on Shénmì Station. Elgin Woo had encoded the crystal to be read by either one. Whatever Woo wanted to tell him before his sudden departure, he'd done it using the most secretive and secure way possible. And it was bound to be . . . interesting.

But Woo's message would have to wait. Before returning to Shénmì, Aiden had to take the *Sun Wolf* to Gateway Station first. Not only to brief Admiral Stegman, but more importantly to deliver the information that Berne had just given him, revealing the whereabouts of key Netvor strongholds, and to get Jo started on training the Alliance technicians to use the modified CEI. Neither of those undertakings could wait.

Aiden tucked Woo's telegem crystal into his hip pocket, patted it once for good luck, and headed for the station's docking bay. He had a sneaking suspicion that whatever message the crystal held, it was about to open a new door into unforeseen territory.

47

Eta-2 Hydri System
Gateway Gamma

DOMAIN DAY 74, 2223

THE primordial black hole roiling inside the gateway voidoid was pissed off.

At least that's the way it looked to Aiden and his crew as they viewed it on the main screen from nearly 100 kilometers away. The *Sun Wolf* had come to a halt here after its four-hour transit across the Eta-2 Hydri system on maximum zero-point drive and was preparing to make a voidjump headlong into the intimidating astrophysical phenomenon Elgin Woo called a symbioid. Granted, they had jumped through a symbioid a few times before, the one blocking passage into the Libera's star system. But that one had been specifically "summoned" by Woo and seemed far less menacing than this one, which had mysteriously just appeared on its own.

The captain of one of the two Alliance warships stationed here had confirmed that not long after the symbioid showed up, a strange-looking saucer-shaped craft had indeed appeared out of nowhere and jumped straight into the voidoid without incident. The captain was appalled when Aiden informed him that the *Sun Wolf* planned to do exactly the same, to follow Woo's craft into Astrocell Gamma. But after reading the message Elgin Woo had left for him inside the telegem, that was precisely what Aiden was about to do.

After leaving Qarsoon two days ago, the *Sun Wolf* had stopped briefly at the AM 7491 voidoid to transfer Miguel Silva to the abandoned Netvor antimatter tanker to begin his epic journey back to the Libera colony. Still recovering from his gunshot wound, Silva was destined to become an unlikely hero among the Libera, if not a dead one. Then the *Sun Wolf* had jumped straight to Gateway Station at Alpha-2 Hydri to fulfill several official obligations. One was a thorough debriefing with Admiral Stegman. All questions of impropriety from Admiral Prescott were summarily dismissed in light of Aiden's resounding success in saving Earth from the graser and bringing with him a bounty of strategic information and weaponry bound to give the Alliance a decided advantage in its war against the Netvor.

Aiden handled the glaring questions about Commander Miguel Silva's actions and whereabouts with as much truth as he could manage without further tarnishing the man's name. Unfortunately, he could not whitewash the details of Silva's crimes even if he'd wanted to. They were clearly recorded in the ship's autologs, and Silva had failed to scrub them with his override keys in the heat of action. Aiden reported that the man had suffered injuries grave enough to prevent him from making the trip home without dying in the process and that Aiden was honestly unsure if the man would survive—statements that addressed the truth with artful imperfection. Either way, Silva would be remaining with the Libera for the foreseeable future, isolated on Qarsoon, and it would be pointless to try extraditing him for adjudication if he did survive. Stegman got the message and moved on.

During that time spent at Gateway Station, Jo had been busy tutoring two of the Alliance's top tactical technicians on the intricacies of the CEI modification to allow Alliance ships to spot cloaked Netvor vessels from afar. All the while, both she and Aiden were itching to get back to loved ones on Shénmì Station.

And Aiden was chaffing at the bits to borrow Skye's telegem reader to open Woo's message.

The *Sun Wolf* finally made it back to Shénmì Station on the following day. Aiden's reunion with his wife and daughter was pure bliss. As always, it made him marvel at how much of his life he had spent living as half a person without even realizing it, before these two beautiful people had fully entered it. And if that reunion was bliss, the one between Jo and Rene was easily equal to it, if not more ecstatic. Rene, not quite six years old, had not known where his mother had been, and her departure had been so sudden and unexpected that he'd fallen prey to a sadly common reaction to such instances, one of self-blame. Rene showed all the signs of a child who felt at his core that he alone had been responsible for his abandonment.

Needless to say, many tears were shed, mostly of joy, and Aiden was not immune from shedding a good share of them himself.

When emotions had stabilized, Aiden took Skye aside and showed her the telegem Woo had left for him. "This is from Elgin. I need to borrow your telegem reader."

She grabbed his hand and led him to her quarters. Once inside, with the door secured behind them, Aiden was beset by a suddenly more primal urge, more compelling than his desire to read Woo's message. Skye saw it in his eyes—he'd always been terrible at hiding his thirst for her after a long absence—and urged him to stay focused.

She retrieved her telegem reader, the one disguised as a ceramic model of a scarlet-cup fungus, and activated it. Aiden performed his unique decrypting sequence until the crystal was unlocked. He placed it inside the cup, and a holographic image appeared in front of them. It was Elgin Woo, and he looked concerned.

"Greetings to you, Aiden. And to Skye, if you're using her reader. I apologize for leaving Qarsoon in such a hurry, but I felt it necessary. You've probably heard by now that a symbioid has materialized inside the Gateway Gamma voidoid, blocking all passage into or out of Astrocell Gamma. This is an unexpected and disturbing development, which I felt impelled to investigate immediately.

"As you know, the last time this happened was over five years ago when we caught up with Cardew at Gateway Gamma. You will recall that the symbioid lashed out with its primordial black hole to obliterate Cardew's ship, the *Conquest*. Then it disappeared, leaving the gateway open for voidjumping. It has remained open since then. Until now. Why?

"Of course, the initial question has always been: Did the symbioid destroy the *Conquest* merely in response to the ship activating its negative-G shield, or was it a more volitional act? Did it somehow sense that Cardew and his gang were unnatural artifacts that posed a grave threat to all natural life within our universe and had to be stopped from spreading? After my time among the Luminous Ones, I firmly believe the answer is the latter. The Luminous Ones are sentient beings that have been protecting the living universe from its very beginning.

"That's why I'm so alarmed now. This very same gateway voidoid has just been shut down by a symbioid in the same way it was back then. I can only conclude that something has happened to trigger this protective measure. The most obvious reason, of course, would be that Cardew's original threat has resurfaced, only now in the form of his spawn, the Netvor. With their rapidly advancing technology and apparent immunity to the Gaia fungi that had previously stunted their proliferation within Astrocell Beta, their threat is more evident than ever before.

"In addition to that threat, I firmly believe the Netvor are on the same quest as I am, seeking a way to identify the gateway stars unique to each astrocell. A solution that will effectively open up the entire galaxy to exploration and occupation within a relatively short period of time. My own progress in this quest has been fruitful, but challenges remain, and the Netvor may not be far behind. Which is precisely why I've asked the brilliant Libera scientist, Astur Ali, to join me in the hunt. I have no doubt that her solution to the Yang-Mills Existence and Mass Gap problem will be crucial.

"But something concerns me even more, Aiden. And this is where you and the *Sun Wolf* come into it. We are assuming that the symbioid has blocked the gateway into Astrocell Gamma because the Luminous Ones are attempting to prevent the Netvor from passing through it into the rest of the galaxy. But what if the Luminous Ones are actually trying to prevent something else out there from *getting in*? Something we have no knowledge of yet. Something extremely dangerous. To us and the Netvor alike.

"I honestly do not know this to be the case, Aiden. But I've seen subtle warning signs. Vague but disturbing. And my gut feelings about this are becoming harder to ignore."

Woo paused here for a moment to gather himself. Aiden couldn't remember seeing Elgin Woo more troubled than he looked now.

"And this is why I am asking you and your crew to come out here in the *Sun Wolf* to join me and Astur Ali in our search for answers. You have instruments and sensors I don't have, and one of the finest crews I've ever encountered. And you have weapons . . .

"The *Sun Wolf*, of course, will be allowed to pass through the symbioid, just as it will have allowed the *Starhawk* by the time you read this message. Just as you've done with the symbioid guarding Qarsoon. All symbioids are interrelated. They are all kin. They will all recognize the *Sun Wolf* as the *Starhawk*'s kin. Driven by my creations. They know me and know what I'm about.

"So, Aiden. Dr. Ali and I are already in Astrocell Gamma by now. And I need you out here with us. Come as soon as you can. No need to look for the *Starhawk* when you complete your jump. I'll find you. Hope to see you soon, my friend."

The holo image of Woo vanished, his message delivered.

And now, barely 12 hours later, the *Sun Wolf* was here parked less than 100 kilometers from the meanest-looking symbioid Aiden could ever imagine. He turned to face each one of his team to gauge their readiness. Smiling with more confidence than he felt, he said, "Time to roll, people. Prepare for a voidjump on zero-point drive."

The crew had undergone a slight reorganization, necessitated by the short notice of their departure. Aiden had promoted Lilly Alvarez to Executive Officer, a move he'd been planning ever since Miguel Silva had vacated the post. Glancing at her now, sitting at his side, seeing the resolve and keen intelligence in her eyes, he knew he'd made the right choice.

Jo had bravely volunteered to take over Comm/Scan in Alvarez's place. "Just for this one mission," she'd said, not at all pleased to be leaving her son again so soon after their reunion. But Jo was perfectly suited for the post, and the entire crew knew it as well as she did. She looked tense but eager for the challenge that lay ahead, just on the other side.

Sudha Devi, at Life Support station, met him with her calming, confident smile. He owed her so much, not the least of which was his own sanity at a time in his life when he'd nearly lost it. She'd always been able to *see* him.

Samuel Assan, at Drive Systems station, looked back at Aiden like a man about to open the next door along the pathway of his life stretching out before him into the unknown. Curiosity triumphant over apprehension.

Billy Hotah at Tactical station sat unmoving and alert, all coiled energy, hunting instincts honed sharp as a warrior's blade. Hotah wasn't even looking back at him, but Aiden swore the man had eyes in the back of his head and could see him anyway.

And Pilot Lista Abahem. Reclined in her pilot's couch, neurolinkage cap firmly affixed to her shaved head, her eyes were closed but opened behind her eyelids onto another dimension that no one else could enter with such ease. She gave him her usual thumbs-up.

Aiden took a deep breath, let it out, and said, "Onward and upward."

The ZPD kicked in, and in less than five seconds, the *Sun Wolf* plunged into the black heart of the symbioid and vanished, passing from a future past into a future present.

ACKNOWLEDGEMENTS

MUCH thanks to the following people for their support and assistance in bringing this novel into print: editors Scott Pearson and Sara Kelly for their thoughtful and thorough editing; Sandi Goodman for her invaluable editorial input; Rafael Andres for his stunning cover graphics; Euan Monaghan for his elegant book design; marketing specialist Kate Larking for her skillful work in marketing the whole series; Bob Page and Barbara Ware for their friendship and their quiet, creative space called Quail Crossing where much of this writing was done; and, as always, Ann Jeffrey for her unconditional support and life-long partnership of the heart.

Elgin Woo's quote in Chapter 37 is from the HBO TV show *True Detective*, Season 1, 2014, spoken by the character Rust Cohle.

CHRONOLOGY

2031–2040: Human population approaches 10 billion, and catastrophic effects of climate change accelerate. Global order deteriorates, the Resource Wars commence, nuclear and biological warfare devastates Earth's biosphere.

2040–2082: **The Die Back**. Total collapse of Earth's infrastructure of civilization. Over one half of the human population perishes. Dissolution of nation states and governments. All scientific inquiry virtually ceases. Historical records of this period are scant.

2082: The United Earth Domain (UED) begins to rebuild global order through military and political intervention. Sustainable power and food production are enforced.

2082–2113: The post-Die Back "twilight" period. Global living conditions improve, but distrust of science lingers. Institutions of higher learning gradually reemerge. Scientific inquiry and technological innovation reemerge.

2113: First post–Die Back space flight ushers in the New Age of Space.

2121: The first human colony is established on Luna.

2123: Terra Corporation dominates space-based resource mining. The New Industrial Revolution commences as resource extraction expands from Luna to the asteroid belts.

2132: First human colony on Mars is established, initially by scientists and technicians and later by a diverse proletariat population.

2147: Mars declares independence from United Earth Domain under the governance of the Allied Republics of Mars (ARM) and expands its military and industrial prowess.

2153: The graviton is discovered jointly by ARM and UED scientists.

2162: The first G-transducer is developed to minimize forces of acceleration and induce synthetic gravity for space travel.

2169: The Solar System's voidoid is discovered and recognized as a portal into nearby star systems. The Holtzman effect is developed for instantaneous communication between the voidoids of other stars.

2170: The first manned voidship jumps from V-Prime into another star system, establishing V-Prime as the gateway into star systems within Bound Space. The Ganymede Pact of 2170 is signed by the UED and ARM to declare free and open access to all of Bound Space, ushering in the New Age of Space.

—UED and ARM colonies proliferate within the Solar System. Exploration and resource mining accelerate throughout Bound Space. The search for life on terrestrial exoplanets remains unsuccessful for the next 47 years.

2197: The Cauldron, a secret research lab in the Apollo asteroid group, is founded by Elgin Woo.

2215: Elgin Woo invents the zero-point drive allowing his experimental spacecraft, the *Starhawk*, to travel at 92 percent light speed, transitioning instantly from start to stop.

2217: Silvanus is discovered in the Chara system, a living planet inhabited by the Rete, a global neural net, becoming humanity's first contact with an alien intelligence.

—Elgin Woo discovers the gateway into Astrocell Beta at Alpha-2 Hydri and discovers Shénmì, a second living exoplanet, in the HD 10180 system. Bound Space is renamed Astrocell Alpha.

2218: Captain Aiden Macallan is given command of the *Sun Wolf*, the only voidship other than Elgin Woo's *Starhawk* to be fitted with the zero-point drive.

—Dr. Skye Landen discovers panspermia seeds from Shénmì seeding life on habitable planets throughout Astrocell Beta, advancing Elgin Woo's *Theory of the Living Universe*.

—Elgin Woo and Cardew simultaneously discover the gateway voidoid into Astrocell Gamma at Eta-2 Hydri. After Cardew is killed by a symbioid at the gateway, Woo disappears into Astrocell Gamma on an unspecified quest.

2219–2223 (the present): Cardew's Posthuman offspring, referred to by humans as the Netvor, continue to self-evolve through advanced cloning practices and spread throughout Astrocell Beta pursuing their goal of replacing humanity with the Posthuman Realm. As their numbers grow and their combat technologies advance, the Netvor pose an ever-increasing threat to the human race.

— ARM and UED sign a treaty to form the Alliance to combat their common enemy, the Netvor.

GLOSSARY OF TERMS

Alliance, the: The political and military alliance between ARM and the UED, signed into effect by treaty in 2219, to pursue the common goal of defending humanity against the Netvor.

Alpha-2 Hydri: aka Gateway Star. Host of two gateway voidoids, Northern Voidoid and Southern Voidoid, providing the only means of travel between Astrocells Alpha and Beta.

AM 7491: A wide binary star system in the Reticulum sector, over 104 light-years from Sol.

AMP: Acronym for the Allied Mapping Project, a research undertaking funded by the Alliance to map the jump coordinates for all main sequence stars within the known astrocells, thereby permitting safe voidjumping throughout those astrocells. Based on Shénmì Station.

Antimatter drive: Modern beamed core antimatter propulsion systems used by all Alliance voidships utilizing the energy of controlled matter/antimatter annihilation.

ARM: Acronym for the Allied Republics of Mars. Declared independence from United Earth Domain in 2147 as a sovereign nation, joining the UED as the Solar System's second "superpower."

Astrocell: A roughly spherical volume of space where all the stars within its boundaries are accessible to each other via voidjumping between their host voidoids. Astrocells are connected to each other by a single shared gateway star that hosts two voidoids, each serving as the gateway into its respective astrocell. As of year 2223, there are three known astrocells:

—Astrocell Alpha (aka Bound Space), is home to the Solar System and is roughly 195,000 cubic light-years in volume. Sol is the core star of Astrocell Alpha.

—Astrocell Beta was discovered by Dr. Elgin Woo in 2218. Its core star is Woo's Star (aka HD 10180) where the planet Shénmì resides. It is roughly 3,160,000 cubic light-years in volume.

—Astrocell Gamma, also discovered by Dr. Woo in the same year, is virtually unexplored. Its boundaries, volume of space, and core star are currently unknown.

AU: Abbreviation for Astronomical Unit. A unit of measure equivalent to the average distance between Earth and its sun, Sol, approximately 149,600,000 kilometers.

Bickford Process: A method used to harvest large quantities of antihydrogen from the magnetospheres of gas giants, like Jupiter and Saturn, to power voidship antimatter drives, originally conceived in the early 21st century by James Bickford.

Bound Space: Now known as Astrocell Alpha (see *Astrocell*).

Brain tap: An advanced form of brain-to-computer interface used by Cardew to induce a process called whole-brain emulation whereby the entire content of a person's consciousness can be extracted against their will. It was used by Cardew's henchmen on kidnapped scientists to advance the technological superiority of the Posthuman Realm and is still in use by the Netvor.

Cardew: Cardew Seth Amon was known first as Terra Corp's director of strategy in the 2180s, then later as the mystic who founded Licet Omnia, a powerful shadow group with deep influence at the highest levels of government and industry. Cardew is believed to have been a practitioner of the dark arts with roots in the Thelema tradition and a lineage dating back to the likes of Aleister Crowley. At some unknown point during the 2210s, Cardew embraced a Posthuman Übermensch ideology uniquely his own and began a project of cloning Transhumans destined to self-evolve into Posthumans. (See *Posthuman* and *Posthuman Realm*)

Cauldron, the: Founded by Dr. Elgin Woo, the Cauldron is considered the most cutting-edge locus of scientific inquiry in human history. A secretive research facility burrowed into a remote asteroid in the Solar System's Apollo Group, it was named by Woo in honor of the Gaian Cauldron of Inspiration of the ancient Celtic mystics. Many revolutionary discoveries have been credited to the Caudron, with Woo's zero-point drive among the most notable.

CEI: Abbreviation for the Casimir-Ebadi Interferometer. A highly sensitive instrument designed to detect the zero-point field of space, based on the work of Dutch physicist Hendrik Casimir and later developed by Cauldron physicist Maryam Ebadi for practical use in measuring the density of zero-point energy in space.

Chara Conflict: aka the Battle of Chara. Occurred in 2217 when both ARM and UED claimed rights to possess the newly discovered planet Silvanus in the Chara system. A military confrontation ensued between both nations with ships lost on both sides. All-out war was narrowly averted when the Rete was discovered to be inhabiting the planet.

Cloneborgs: The term coined by Elgin Woo to describe Cardew's original clones. Grown from Cardew's own stem-cell genes and endowed with extensive synthetic augmentation, these beings were more cyborg than human, a true amalgam of a clone and a cyborg. Hence the term cloneborg. Cloneborgs are the original progenitors of the Netvor.

Continuum: A drug used by Licensed Pilots to augment their skills for neurolinkage on the job, or to ease their times away from the Omicron-3's addictive embrace. Also used to treat Post-Linkage Syndrome (PLS), a neuropsychological disorder caused by the precipitous drop from the heights of neurolinkage, a common occupational hazard among Licensed Pilots. Continuum can mimic the hyperconnected state of neurolinkage and, when administered in carefully calculated doses, is effective in treating PLS. Continuum is a genetically tailored derivative of psilocybin.

Dark Fort: Cardew's secret facility on the moon Daleth-4 in the Alpha-2 Hydri system where kidnapped scientists were taken for brain tapping (see *Brain tap*). The facility was abandoned when Cardew and his cloneborgs fled into Astrocell Beta. It was subsequently acquired by the mining company SignaCorp Metals and became the site of the Bayit mining colony.

Die Back, the: The catastrophic global population crash of the mid-21st century. By the year 2040, the date historians set as the beginning of the Die Back, the global population had reached 10 billion. Over the course of the next 40 years, Earth suffered a net loss of nearly 5 billion human lives. The Die Back has been characterized as a classical Malthusian phenomenon, predicted by population experts centuries before the crisis occurred. The Die Back period officially ended in 2082 when the United Earth Domain emerged as Earth's dominant center of political stability with enough resources and military power to restore global order.

Domain Day: Designation of a day in the Galactic Year, based on a standard Earth year omitting monthly subdivisions, simply numbered from 1 to 365.

DSI: Abbreviation for Domain Security and Intelligence, the primary covert intelligence and investigative agency of the UED government.

Earth First Party: An extremist political coalition now in control of the UED under the leadership of President Rudolph Adler. Considered by many off-world observers as an incipient fascist regime whose primary goal is to replace Earth Domain's traditional democratic institutions with totalitarian rule and to "cleanse" its population of undesirable elements.

EM: Abbreviation for electromagnetic.

Eta-2 Hydri: A gateway star in the Hydrus constellation, 219 light-years from Earth, whose northern voidoid is the gateway into Astrocell Gamma.

EVA: Abbreviation for Extra-Vehicular Activity. Refers to the activities performed by an astronaut outside of a spacecraft, such as a spacewalk or exploring a celestial body. The spacesuits used for these activities are sometimes called EVA suits.

Friendship Station: Stationed at Voidoid Prime in the Solar System, Friendship Station serves as a traffic control center, a communications relay, and now a military checkpoint into and out of the Solar System.

Jointly operated by ARM and UED, the station is considered neutral territory.

Füzfa Effect: A theoretical concept developed by André Füzfa in the early 21st century that paved the way for modern technologies of synthetic gravity. Using powerful superconducting electromagnets in a stacked configuration, technicians can bend space-time to generate an artificial gravity field indistinguishable from one created naturally by a massive object in space. Netvor scientists solved the technical problems of scaling the Füzfa Effect to make it work in practical settings, as in the cloaking and shielding of their warships.

G-transducers: A technology made possible by the discovery of the graviton in the mid-22nd century to minimize forces of acceleration inside a spacecraft by damping the effects of inertia, thereby effectively eliminating the G-forces experienced by human crews.

GST: Abbreviation for Galactic Standard Time.

Gateway Station: Permanent Alliance military base and traffic control center located at the northern gateway voidoid of the Alpha-2 Hydri system. It stands at the strategic chokepoint between Astrocells Alpha and Beta and is of utmost significance in the war against the Netvor.

Gateway Gamma: The northern voidoid of the Eta-2 Hydri system that serves as the gateway voidoid into Astrocell Gamma.

Graser: Acronym for a powerful gamma-ray-burst weapon originally developed by Cardew's scientists and now in use by the Netvor. An enormous, antimatter-powered, electron-positron beam generator, it can generate extremely powerful gamma-ray bursts, mimicking the type emitted from black holes or quasars on a relatively smaller scale.

Hawking Station: Earth's primary industrial and military waystation, Hawking Station operates under the jurisdiction of the UED and supports the largest combined docking and construction shipyard in existence. It is located at the Earth-Moon Lagrange point L5 in a stable position about 384,400 kilometers from Earth.

Holtzman effect: A still poorly understood natural phenomenon associated with the voidoids that is harnessed by Holtzman devices to communicate instantaneously between voidoids of other star systems. A Holtzman device is typically deployed by a voidship as a comm buoy positioned close to the voidoid soon after a voidjump. The devices are also integrated into a ship's systems for optional use when the ship is in proximity to the voidoid. The Holtzman effect is believed to be an emergent property of the same phenomenon that enables voidjumping.

Hypospace: Elgin Woo's term for the dimension of "nonspace" occupied by a ship using the zero-point drive while "in flight." A hypothetical region where the stuff of space does not exist.

Intersystem Pilots Agency: aka the Agency. The international institute responsible for training Licensed Pilots. Candidates are all female and selected at an early age for their unique mental gifts. They are trained in virtual seclusion by the Agency and rarely interact with others outside their own circles. (See *Licensed Pilot*).

KBUs: Abbreviation for knowledge-base uploads. Information uploads mediated by brain-to-computer interfaces used in the Netvor creches to prepare newly cloned Netvor individuals for their designated functions within the Posthuman Realm.

Licensed Pilot: A graduate of the Intersystem Pilots Agency. All voidships require the services of a Licensed Pilot to safely execute high velocity voidjumps. Mandated by the Ganymede Pact, only pilots licensed by the Agency are allowed to drive Alliance voidships.

Libera: The collective name of the *Trans sapien* population living on Qarsoon.

Light speed: Defined as 299,792 kilometers per second.

Light-year: Defined as approximately 9.46 trillion kilometers.

Luminous Ones: Elgin Woo's nickname for the protovoidoids in his *New Cosmology*. According to this theory, protovoidoids are sentient beings who appeared soon after the Big Bang over 13 billion years ago.

They exist as forms of pure energy and have been protecting our universe from cosmological forces that would otherwise render it uninhabitable.

Luna: Earth's moon.

Majka: Libera word for the star AM 7491A, the primary star of the AM 7491 binary system.

Nead: The planet in the HD 13808 system where Jo was cloned in a Netvor creche, one of several creches that were destroyed by the *Sun Wolf* after Jo's rescue.

Netvor: The race of suprahuman beings that self-evolved from Cardew's original cloneborgs. They have since eschewed their genetic lineage with Cardew but still pursue his primary goal of wiping out humanity in a systematic genocide to pave the way for their Posthuman Realm and eventual domination of the galaxy. This new race refers to themselves as Posthumans, but humans call them the Netvor, a word from the Czech language meaning "monster."

Neurolinkage: A form of brain-to-AI interface used primarily by Licensed Pilots aboard voidships to facilitate high-velocity voidjumps. It is conducted by donning a neurolink cap and mediated by millions of nanobots that establish neuroelectric connections between the ship's Omicron-3 AI and the pilot's cerebral cortex.

Northern Voidoid: The voidoid of the Alpha-2 Hydri system that serves as the gateway into Astrocell Beta and is the location of Gateway Station.

Omicron-3 AI: The most advanced model of neural-net intelligence devices. It was initially developed by the Omicron Intelligence Engine Project to help voidships execute voidjumps. The project applied connectionist theory as a paradigm on which to construct its neural nets, employing revolutionary advances in nanotechnology and neurobiology to design an AI modeled directly on the human brain. Instead of human neural cells, the Omicron's individual processing units are complex biomolecular configurations called bions, capable of self-replication in response to cognitive dynamics. Collectively they form bional nets that adapt continuously, forming new connections in response to sensory input, analogous to the human nervous system.

OverNet: The interconnected network of all the several hundred Omicron-3 AI units inhabiting the known astrocells linked together by the Holtzman effect. The OverNet is integral to everything from research and medical facilities, government and military, to civic, commercial, and financial institutions, and it is interwoven into every aspect of human life. This massively complex network has given rise to a synergistic consciousness that is constantly learning, adapting, and deepening. Its actions are governed by algorithms based on Asimov's Three Laws of Robotics designed to guarantee safety and benefit to humans, first and foremost.

P-suit: aka Planetary Surface Mobility suit. Designed for activity on inhospitable planetary surfaces, they are mechanical-counterpressure suits made of body-hugging orthofabric where the support pressure comes from the structure and elasticity of the material itself rather than pressurized gas from the inside, making them lighter and more flexible.

Primordial black holes: Small black holes created during the first few seconds after the Big Bang from fluctuations in space-time density that caused isolated gravitational collapses. Most of them are thought to be of sublunar mass, but can be up to two or three times the mass of Earth's sun. The larger ones became nuclei around which galaxies formed, growing into supermassive black holes at their centers. The smallest ones—less than 100 billion tons in mass—have evaporated via Hawking radiation. All the remaining primordial black holes theoretically account for the bulk of the universe's dark matter.

Penning tanks: Containment tanks designed to house antimatter fuel for a voidship's antimatter drive system, maintaining a delicate balance between magnetic and electrical fields to prevent antimatter from interacting with interior tank walls. Also used in harvesting antihydrogen from the magnetospheres of gas giants for processing into antimatter fuel (see *Bickford Process*).

Posthuman: A Transhuman cloneborg that has self-evolved to the next stage of Cardew's scheme to replace humanity with superior beings. Transitioning from Transhuman to Posthuman involves even greater technological enhancement, to the point where physical, cognitive, and emotional capacities differ so completely from normal human beings that they are no longer recognizably human. According to Cardew,

Posthumans will achieve *Singularity* when their collective capacity for intelligence accelerates exponentially. The Netvor identify as Posthumans.

Posthuman Realm: The idealized ethos of the Netvor empire, formerly known as Cardew's Empire of the Pure. The primary goal of the Netvor is to replace humanity with the Posthuman Realm—by any means necessary—and spread throughout the galaxy.

Protovoidoid: The technical term for a Luminous One in Elgin Woo's *New Cosmology* (see *Luminous Ones*).

Realspace: The physical dimension of space encountered by normal human perception, everything existing outside of a voidoid or the hypospace bubble of a zero-point drive.

Realtime: Time as measured by Galactic Standard Time, relative to a stationary observer, as opposed to shipboard time at relativistic velocities.

Rete, the: The vastly complex interconnected network of mycorrhizal fungus occupying the entire planet of Silvanus, analogous to a neural network of global proportions, from which a sentient intelligence has emerged over millions of years. First contacted by Aiden Macallan in 2217 using his Omicron-3 AI, Hutton, as a translator.

Schwarzschild radius: The radius of the event horizon of a simple, nonrotating black hole. The theoretical distance from the center of a black hole to where its gravitational pull becomes so strong that not even light can escape, a distance directly proportional to the black hole's mass.

Second sight: A psychic gift possessed by some individuals allowing them to visualize bioelectric emanations around living beings, energy fields referred to as *auras* by the Gaians.

Sestra: The single moon of the planet Qarsoon. Location of several Libera mining operations.

Shénmì: The habitable Earthlike planet in the HD 10180 star system (aka Woo's Star system) discovered by Elgin Woo in 2217, harboring a diverse biosphere similar to Earth's early Jurassic period, excluding the large carnivorous reptiles that roamed Earth's Mesozoic era.

Shénmì Station: The orbital station at the planet Shénmì hosting various research projects, primarily the Shénmì Project, directed by Dr. Skye Landen, and the Allied Mapping Project.

Shipboard time: Time elapsed aboard a ship travelling at relativistic velocities, the result of time dilation, as aboard the *Sun Wolf* travelling at 92 percent light speed.

Silvanus: The first life-bearing extraterrestrial planet to be found by humanity, it was discovered in the Chara system in 2217 with a living biosphere composed entirely of plant life and inhabited by a singular sentient being, a neural net of global proportions called the Rete.

Southern Voidoid: The voidoid of the Alpha-2 Hydri system that serves as the gateway into Astrocell Alpha, home of the Solar System.

Sol: Earth's sun. Center of the Solar System

Stealth Sequence: A voidjump at 10 percent light speed, starting from 150,000 km out, coming to a halt 450,000 km post-jump. A tactical maneuver possible only with the zero-point drive.

Symbioid: In Elgin Woo's seminal work, *The New Cosmology*, symbioids refer to entities formed through symbiotic association between a protovoidoid and a primordial black hole. Some of the symbioids evolved further into what are now known as voidoids. All the others held on to their primordial black holes in a disjunctive symbiosis that allowed them to move the primordial black holes around in space and release them at will. Woo postulates that virtually all currently existing primordial black holes taken collectively are the primary source of the universe's dark matter, and the symbioids are continually shepherding them into optimal positions to corral galactic structures to maintain their cohesiveness in space.

Trans sapien: A being that emerged from Netvor creches as the result of an adventitious genetic mutation occurring during their cloning phase, causing their central nervous system—brain and spinal cord—to develop exactly as it would in a normal human, while their remaining anatomy and physiology developed as it would for a Netvor, highly augmented for strength and efficiency. But like the Netvor, *Trans sapiens* lack biological gender and cannot reproduce sexually.

UED: Abbreviation for the United Earth Domain. Established on Earth in 2082 after the Die Back. One of the two Solar System "superpowers," along with ARM, it is a sovereign nation comprised of Earth, Luna, and all associated extraterrestrial colonies.

Uteropods: Artificial uteruses used in Netvor cloning creches to clone more Netvor beings.

V-Prime: aka Voidoid Prime. The voidoid at Earth's sun, the effective gateway between the Solar System and all other star systems within Astrocell Alpha. It was discovered in 2169 located 13 AU due north of Sol and dubbed a "voidoid" by theorists. Every star within a given astrocell was found to possess its own voidoid, each one acting as a portal connecting it with all the others, offering humanity a practical means of interstellar travel and ushering in the New Age of Space.

Voidjump: The act of a voidship passing into the voidoid of one star system to emerge from the voidoid of any other star system within the same astrocell without apparent passage of time.

Voidoids: Neoquantum portals allowing instantaneous space travel between any star within a given astrocell. All known voidoids share identical properties, perfectly spherical anomalies approximately 18 kilometers in diameter, possessing no intrinsic electromagnetic or gravimetric properties. Their "surface horizons" reflect all forms of electromagnetic energy, but visible light is reflected into the X-ray range, making them virtually invisible.

ZPD: Abbreviation for the zero-point drive, the revolutionary drive system for spacecraft invented by Elgin Woo that manipulates the zero-point energy of space to effectively eliminate inertia and allow the ship to achieve 92 percent light speed without the effects of G-forces.

ZPE: Abbreviation for zero-point energy, a quantum field property of the vacuum of space.

Woo's Star: aka HD 10180. The core star of Astrocell Beta, located 127 light-years from Earth in the Hydrus sector. The planet Shénmì is part of its 10-planet system.

XO: Abbreviation for Executive Officer.

XRF: Abbreviation for X-ray fluorescence scans. Used at all Alliance checkpoints to screen for Netvor infiltrators by detecting bones made of carbon nanotubes.

9 780999 867428 5